SEEKING SILVERIO

Also by Paco Sevilla

*Paco de Lucía: A New Tradition
for the Flamenco Guitar*

*Queen of the Gypsies:
The Life and Legend of Carmen Amaya*

*Flamenco Dance:
Secrets of the Professionals*

*Paco Sevilla's Guide to
Studying Flamenco in Sevilla*

Ritmos Flamencos (CD)

SEEKING SILVERIO
THE BIRTH OF FLAMENCO

PACO SEVILLA

SEVILLA PRESS   SAN DIEGO, CALIFORNIA

SEEKING SILVERIO:
THE BIRTH OF FLAMENCO

Published by:
Sevilla Press
P.O. Box 40331
San Diego, CA 92164
www.flamencobooks.com

ISBN: 978-0-9646374-4-3
Copyright © 2007 by Paco Sevilla.
All Rights Reserved

Cover Design by:
Sarah Soto Photographics
www.sarahsoto.com

Printed in the USA by:
Morris Publishing
3212 East Highway 30
Kearney NE 68847
800-650-7888

Acknowledgements

This book might never have happened if it had not been for the *cantaora* Marysol Fuentes, who encouraged me and helped me with research more than twenty years ago, when I was beginning the work. It was she who somehow pursuaded a Spanish flamencologist to present me with a copy of Javier Molina's memoires—the inspiration for this book. Throughout the years she has remained a reliable resource, helping me with tricky translations and subtle nuances. Her proofreading of the final version gave me some confidence in going forward with publishing (any remaining errors are my responsibility, not hers).

If it hadn't been for the constant encouragement by my old friend Mimette Wishart, who has been instrumental in the writing of all of my books, I might not have had the confidence to keep writing these many years. Her suggestions have always been valuable.

I have to thank Peter Stanley for his insightful reading of the manuscript. Since he is not a flamenco person, his comments and positive feedback were especially meaningful.

Another source of encouragement has been my friend Dr. Bob Mallon, an avid and intelligent reader who has been a big fan of my writing and has given me inspiration in times of doubt.

I am indebted to Carl White, who has experience in professional editing, for his careful reading of the finished manuscript. He, too, made me feel more confident in going ahead with publishing.

Finally, I would like to thank Sarah Soto for her work on the cover and flamenco dancer Julia Daria for allowing me to use the photo on the back cover, taken during a performance in 2007.

Table of Contents

Introduction
Prologue
Chapter One — Chacón 1
  Early life of Antonio Chacón; gypsy blacksmiths and *martinetes*; Juan Torre and the birth of Manuel Torre.
Chapter Two — Javier 19
  Chacón apprentices in the *tonelería*; Silverio's return to Sevilla; Javier Molina; fiesta in Molina home; Julián Arcas and Paco el Barbero.
Chapter Three — Breva 37
  Juan Breva; Paco de Lucena; *malagueñas*.
Chapter Four — Fosforito 53
  Fosforito in Jerez; Enrique el Melizo; *seguiriyas* of Joaquín La Cherna, El Marrurro, *El Señor* Manuel Molina.
Chapter Five — Los Artistas 67
  Travels through Andalucía; *rondeñas*; meeting El Morrongo.
Chapter Six — The Gypsies 95
  The gypsy family Los Morrongo; *serranas*.
Chapter Seven — La Feria 116
  The fair in Villamartín; El Puli; Los Morrongo; the fight with El Quico.
Chapter Eight — El Café de Silverio 130
  Arrival in Sevilla; a night in the Café de Silverio.
Chapter Nine — Salvaoriyo 142
  Travel through western Andalucía to Zafra and the *feria*; *tangos extremeños*; Huelva with Salvaoriyo: *cantes* of Silverio, *seguiriyas*, biographies of El Fillo and El Nitri, Paco la Luz; Isla Cristina, *serranas*, *livianas*, *seguiriyas* of María Borrico; return home.
Chapter Ten — María 177
  The flamenco cafés of Jerez; Chacón's romance.
Chapter Eleven — El Canario 192
  Chacón in Sevilla: Café de Silverio and Café del Burrero; Miguel Macaca, La Serrana, El Chato de Jerez, Maestro Pérez, Antonio el Pintor and Lamparilla, Juana and Fernanda Antúnez, La Bocanegra, Concha Peñaranda, El Loco Mateo; life and death of El Canario; Chacón composes his first *malagueña*.

Chapter Twelve — El Mellizo 212
   Fiesta with El Mellizo, Hermosilla, and Joaquín La Cherna; *malagueñas* of El Mellizo.

Chapter Thirteen — Patiño 222
   Chacón in Cádiz for the Verbena; José Patiño; *malagueñas*; Silverio's return from America and early performances in the 1860s; guitarists of Cádiz.

Chapter Fourteen — Curro Dulce 235
   Gypsy families of Cádiz; Paquiro Ortega, José el Águila, Curro Dulce, Gordo Ortega; fiesta in the *taberna*: *soleá de Cádiz, seguiriyas, alegrías* and *cantiñas*; *cante* of Curro Dulce; Juan Fernández and *la caña*.

Chapter Fifteen — Juan Junquera 257
   El Mellizo, Fosforito and the "academy" of *malagueñas*; Chacón and Juan Junquera.

Chapter Sixteen — Silverio 271
   Café Filarmónico with Patiño; Fiesta for María Borrico in San Fernando, Silverio *por seguiriya*; coach ride to Cádiz with Silverio and Patiño, Silverio's biography, encounter with El Morrongo.

Chapter Seventeen — Sevilla 288
   Chacón's debut in the Café de Silverio: Paco de Lucena, La Parrala (*soleá* and *seguiriya*), Paco el Sevillano, Romero el Tito, *romeras* and *caracoles*, Salud Rodríguez; Fosforito in Café del Burrero; Demófilo and his writings; Ramón el Ollero and the *soleá de Triana*, Mercedes la Serneta, Caganchos and Pelaos; Juan el Perote, El Canario Chico.

Chapter Eighteen — The Pope of the Cante 330
   Chacón in Málaga: Café Siete Revueltas and Café de Chinitas; La Trini, Juan Breva; Café del Burrero: Concha la Peñaranda, *cartageneras*, África Vázquez, *granaínas*, Pepa de Oro, *milonga*, Paco el Sevillano, El Mochuelo; competition with Ramón el Ollero; Jerez with Javier; death of Silverio.

Epilogue 353
Appendix A: A Historical Novel? 355
Appendix B: Fact or Fiction? 361
Selected References 387
Glossary 393

Introduction

I was inspired to write a history of early flamenco by my curiosity about several of flamenco's legendary, almost mythological, historical figures. Information about these larger-than-life personalities, whose reputations resulted as much from their eccentricities and personal charisma as from their artistic merit, proved to be sparse and scattered. In the years I spent ferreting out fragments of fact and fiction, I became aware of the immense amount of existing flamenco knowledge that would never be widely available to the English-speaking aficionado, both because of inaccessibility and the language barrier. I set as my goal the writing of a readable history built around the lives of these legendary giants.

I chose to write in the form of a historical novel, hoping to produce a work that could be read and enjoyed by a wide audience, while creating a coherent overview of flamenco's richest period of development. You can refer to Appendix A for an explanation of my approach to separating fact and fiction, reasons for including a great deal of Spanish language, and other such technical matters. It is especially important to read this appendix if you are bothered by the inconsistent and unusual Spanish spellings employed in the text. Appendix B gives chapter-by-chapter notes detailing the factual elements and my sources.

This book is more than a novel and a history. It also serves as a kind of textbook of early flamenco. Styles and forms of song, dance, and guitar playing are discussed in detail, including information that has not appeared previously in print. It is a study of the fascinating flamenco *copla*, each song verse connected to its creator and placed in historical context. Along with the most complete to-date biographies of flamenco's legendary figures, many lesser-known, yet equally colorful, historical personalities make their appearance. Early gypsy life is treated in depth, as is the philosophy of flamenco, placed against a background of life in Spain as it was in period of 1878-1889.

I chose the subtitle, *The Birth of Flamenco*, because the story takes place during the period in which flamenco as we know it was being created from its many disparate elements. The word *flamenco* first appeared in print in 1853, but it didn't come into widespread usage until the 1870s, and even then the terms *cante* (or *baile* or *toque*) *andaluz* and *cante gitano* predominated.

During the 1960s through the 1980s most flamenco aficionados were familiar with the many styles of *cante*, the various *soleares*, *siguiriyas*, the many styles of *malagueñas* (of Chacón, Fosforito, El Canario, La Trini, El Mellizo, etc.), and other *cantes*—because that was the focus of recordings. When I began this book, those were the aficionados I intended to write for. Times have changed: today we don't often hear those songs. Commercial recordings today consist primarily of *bulerías* and *tangos*, or singers' original variations of some other *cantes*. But I think all aficionados will enjoy learning about the roots of the art that they love, and will find a new respect for its complexities.

Dedicated aficionados will be familiar with the names of many of the artists described here, but probably know little about them. Likewise, they will be familiar with many of the locations I describe in detail for their enjoyment. The casual reader will be at a disadvantage, but should be able to skim difficult sections and still enjoy the story.

If you are unfamiliar with flamenco song, it wouldn't be a bad idea to listen to an example of a *siguiriya* and a *malagueña* just to give you an idea of the singing that forms the core of this book. You might find it difficult to understand the passion evoked by the singing of these songs. Given today's environment, with its almost constant barrage of background music, easy access to recordings, radio, and live music performance, it is almost impossible for us to imagine what music would have meant to those living in 1800s Andalucía. People made music for themselves, in their homes and in their fiestas and celebrations, but the rare opportunity to listen to professional musicians and singers must have been something marvelous and moving.

Prologue

Spanish music represents the culmination of centuries of cultural blending. Invasions and colonizations by Phoenicians, Greeks, and Romans brought to the Iberian Peninsula the roots of its musical tradition. Over that base, the Moorish occupation of almost eight hundred years laid down a veneer of elaboration and refinement that matured in remote and isolated villages into a rich variety of festive folk songs and dances accompanied by primitive orchestras of string and percussion instruments.

In the late 1400s, as the last Moors were being driven from southern Spain, the peninsula was invaded once more. Practically unnoticed, groups of small swarthy people began to enter Spain, ending a centuries-long migration that had begun in India. Thought at first to have come from Egypt, the newcomers were called gypsies or *gitanos* (corruptions of "Egyptian"), although they called themselves *rom* or *zincalé*. The new land suited the *gitanos* and they stayed, especially in the southernmost province of Andalucía.

After more than seven hundred years of Moorish domination, there was little tolerance in Spain for religious or cultural differences. Moors and Jews who did not convert to Christianity were forced to go into hiding or risk banishment. The *gitanos,* with their unfamiliar customs and appearance, suffered a persecution that would become increasingly severe over the following three hundred years and last well into the present century. Royal decrees forbade the *gitanos* to travel, to work at traditional trades, or even to speak their Sanskrit-based language. Yet, under the constant threat of imprisonment, beating, banishment, mutilation, and even death, many *gitanos* managed to continue their nomadic lifestyle and maintain their customs, including a musical tradition that was private, personal, and almost ritualistic. Songs and dances rooted in an Eastern heritage became an expression of suffering and a release from the fears and hardships of daily existence.

The mid-1800s saw the emergence of the *café cantante*. These cafés, which exploded in popularity in Andalucía and eventually all of Spain, formally presented the music of the *gitano* to the Spanish public alongside traditional Andalucían folk music. For the first time, gypsy and non-gypsy artists appeared together on stage. The result was a new breed of professional gypsy artist and the introduction of new elements into his music. In the crucible of the *café cantante* the amalgamation of the rustic folk music of the Spanish peasant and the almost liturgical musical ritual of the Spanish gypsy forged a new and powerful art form that transcended mere folk music and came to be called FLAMENCO.

*"Los pueblos que más cantan
son los que más sufren."*

"The peoples who sing the most
are those who suffer most."

—Guillermo Núñez de Prado
(*Cantaores Andaluces*, 1904)

Chacón

Jerez de la Frontera, Spain, 1878 [1]

A blast of chilly December air gripped the boy and he clutched his worn jacket tighter about him. At his back he could still feel the heat of the forge, and it was with reluctance that he started out across the plaza. Only the realization that he had stayed much longer than he had intended and the fear of his father's anger had prompted him to leave the cozy warmth of the blacksmith shop. The heat of the forge, so unbearable in summer, had been welcome on that cool winter afternoon, and Antoñito had gladly stayed to help his friend Joselito work the bellows that kept the coals glowing in the stone hearth.

A piercing yelp of agony startled the boy before he had taken more than a dozen steps. Turning, he saw nothing at first. But no sooner had a second howl rung out, accompanied by cheer and jeers, than a young gypsy ragamuffin rounded a corner into the plaza gleefully dragging behind him a sorry spectacle of an animal. Through the dust Antoñito made out the form of a writhing dog being yanked along the ground by rope tied to its deformed and obviously broken leg. The animal's cries of pain and terror were accompanied by the shrill laughter and delighted shrieks of a horde of gypsy urchins who threw stones and kicked mercilessly at the pitiful creature.

From a doorway across the plaza an old woman dressed in black looked on impassively through deeply wrinkled slits that served for eyes. Two men glanced up momentarily, laughed harshly, and returned

---

[1] Jerez: Pronounced *heh-RETH* or *heh-RE*; the English mispronunciation of this word gave us "sherry." The population of Jerez in 1878 was about 40,000.

to their conversation. The cruel play would continue until the children tired of the game.

A pang of envy surged through Antoñito. He longed to join in the fun, a reminder of the freedom he had lost as he had grown older. His father seemed to demand more of him each day. Antoñito knew it was a time of struggle for everyone in San Miguel—hunger, sickness, and death in the neighborhood were daily subjects of conversation in his father's *zapatería* [shoe shop]. Large numbers of ragged children slept in the streets of Jerez, begging or stealing food to survive, and the young shoemaker's apprentice had heard that many had wandered into the city from the countryside after being abandoned by their parents. Drought and greedy landowners often drove desperate tenant farmers to abandon farms and children in the middle of the night.

Saddened by what he saw around him, Antoñito escaped into dreams of the day when he would be a great singer, leaving poverty and the drudgery of the workshop behind. From his gypsy friends he heard stories of *cantaores* [flamenco singers] who led exciting lives, who were admired and earned great sums of money. It seldom occurred to the boy that he was different from his friends, that he was not gypsy and might be at a disadvantage in the *cante* [flamenco song].

Antoñito was unlikely to be mistaken for a gypsy. The stocky nine-year-old stood out among his dark-skinned friends. A softly rounded face, prominent forehead, and deep-set dark eyes gave the impression of intelligence. What appeared as sadness in the down-turned corners of his small, thin-lipped mouth only reflected a serious demeanor and a tendency to dream. The boy lived in an inner world much of the time, preoccupied with the music in his head, the melodies and poetry of the *cante*.[2]

Antoñito's pale skin testified to the dreariness of his daily schedule. He spent mornings in school under the stern tutelage of *Don* Francisco Posse Segacira. After the heavy afternoon meal and the siesta, he labored with his father in the *zapatería* making shoes or, more often, tough boots for field workers. The boy and his father spent long hours seated at the low *banquilla*, its many compartments holding the various knives,

---

[2] *Cante* is flamenco song. Other kinds of songs are *canciones*. A Spanish singer is a *cantante*, but a flamenco singer is a *cantaor*—the Andalusian pronunciation of *cantador*. *Cantes* are not specific songs, but rather strictly defined song forms within which a singer is free to improvise and select from a wide variety of verses (*coplas* or *letras*).

awls, pliers, and burnishers, as well as different sizes of tacks, threads, and polishes. Under the *banquilla* a ceramic bowl held water for wetting the leather, while the *brasero*, a flat metal pan filled with glowing charcoal embers, provided warmth on chilly winter days. The walls were hung with leather, wooden lasts of various sizes, and partially completed shoes.

Young Antonio didn't have the strength needed to wield the huge shears used to cut calf leather for shoe uppers, but with the sharp edge of a *chaveta* blade, he could trace around the patterns and mark the leather for cutting. Along with the lighter stitching, his job involved the preparation of waxes and polishes. He knew how to maintain the proper consistency of the *cerote* used to wax hemp sewing cord, altering the proportions of resin and beeswax according to the weather.

While the boy worked, pounding thick sole leather with a heavy stone to soften it or burnishing the edges of a finished sole and heel with the *pata de cabra*, a stick of polished oak shaped like a goat's foot, music sounded constantly in his head. Forbidden to sing by his father, he sang to himself, silently memorizing and practicing the songs he had heard in the neighborhood. Rubbing in the dandy he had prepared earlier from resin, water, and coal tar dyes, Antoñito brought a dull luster to a new boot. But his eyes did not see the budding shine; his mind was filled with death:

Una noche e trueno	One stormy night
yo pensé morí,	I thought I was going to die,
cuando tenía una	when I discovered a black
[*sombra negra*]	[shadow]
encima e mí.	hanging over me.

These enigmatic words, not completely understood by the young apprentice, took the form of the *seguiriya*,[3] the most powerful lament of the gypsies. This brutal and violent chant-like *cante*, highly favored by the gypsies of Jerez, was likely to be heard wherever men gathered.

Although Antoñito had neither the vocal qualities nor the power required to sing this most difficult of *cantes*, he found himself gripped

---

[3]The word *seguiriya* was most likely derived from *seguidilla*, an unrelated popular Spanish song form; the modern spelling is *siguiriya*. The rhythm alternates measures of 3/4 and 6/8, which is expressed as three fast beats followed by two longer beats. The verse is characterized by the long third line.

by its intensity. Even at his young age he knew that this particular version had been created by his idol, the great Silverio Franconetti, a *gachó* [non-gypsy] of Italian ancestry who sang like a *gitano* [gypsy]. Silverio was the most celebrated *cantaor* of the time and the only *gachó* to be accepted by most gypsies. Antoñito had never heard him sing, but dreamed of the day he could travel to Sevilla to see the great man in his café.

"María, where is Antoñito? He should have been back long ago." The gruff voice of Antonio Chacón Rodríguez bellowed from where he sat at the cluttered workbench of his tiny shop.

"I don't know! Probably playing in the plaza." The plump woman straightened up from sweeping the cobblestones of the white patio, welcoming a pause to rest her back. She brushed a strand of gray-flecked brown hair back from her forehead and spoke soothingly. "You know how easily he is distracted."

"I sent him to the blacksmith to pick up the *rascastaca* I need to finish these shoes. He should have returned long ago!" The shoemaker shook his head in frustration. "Why do I send him to the blacksmith? They only encourage his crazy notion of learning to sing like a *gitano*."

The woman replied meekly, "He's only a child, and you know how he is with the *cante*. He forgets everything else when he…"

"He won't forget what I am going to do to him when he comes home. *Cante!* The only singing he'll do will be to cry for mercy. No son of mine is going to become a *cantaor*, an *artista!*" The shoemaker spat out these last words. "The *cante* is for drunks and *gitanos*, not for the son of a decent family. If I had known that he would choose to disgrace us, I never would have adopted him."

María García Sánchez de Chacón had heard all of this before. Her husband enjoyed song and dance as much as did any of their neighbors in the Barrio San Miguel—music was part of daily life and singing came as naturally as speaking to the people of Jerez de la Frontera. But it was one thing to sing and dance in a wedding or baptism celebration and quite another to consider becoming a professional flamenco singer, a *cantaor*. *Cantaores* were usually gypsies and led difficult, even miserable lives, always dependent upon the whims of the *señoritos* [wealthy gentlemen] who hired them. They passed their nights in endless drunken orgies, often earning only enough for a meal and more wine. Everyone knew of gypsy women who seldom saw their husbands and, even less often, any of their earnings. To provide for their many children, these gypsy mothers resorted to working long hours in the fields or begging in the streets.

Antonio Chacón momentarily forgot his rage when a chorus of loud voices burst in upon him from the street. A shrill cry cut through peals of laughter. *"Premita Undebé...* may God allow a bad fever to enter your body, and may all yours become undertakers!"

There could be no mistaking the strident harangue of a gypsy woman. The *zapatero* [shoemaker] rushed from his workbench to find a small crowd gathered in the dusty street in front of the two-story communal patio the Chacóns shared with several other families. At the center of the group of neighbors, he recognized one of his customers being vilified by a gypsy woman.

"May a wicked witch give you the evil eye..." screamed the woman.

The shoemaker interrupted, yelling out, "Rafael, what's going on?"

Stopping mid-sentence, the *gitana* turned toward the *zapatero*. Probably much younger than she appeared, her skin had been coarsened and darkened to a deep coppery chocolate by life under the harsh Andalusian sun. On her left hip she held an infant clad in filthy rags, mucous dripping and crusting under its nose. Sizing up the man in front of her with a darting glance, the woman spoke in a voice suddenly soft and entreating. "And you, *señó*, would you allow me to tell your fortune?"

Before the *zapatero* could respond, Rafael interrupted, his eyes twinkling with mischief, "Go ahead Antonio, let this creature tell your fortune!"

Clearly, the crowd had been having fun at the *gitana's* expense. Caught up in the mood, the *zapatero* replied to the woman, "If you're wrong, by my health, I'll give you a smack with my strap!"

Instantly the *gitana* reverted to her former self. "Go smack your wife...who most certainly has a dirty apron!"

Angered, the *zapatero* retorted, "Get out of here, away from my doorstep before you foul it, *cochina* [pig]!"

"That goes for you...I'm not the dirty one, you simpleton. You look like a tanned pigskin in those clothes!"

"Your clothes are filthy..."

A voluminous skirt covered the *gitana* to the ankles. Over it, a grease-stained apron of coarse cloth draped her from the waist. A faded and filthy black shawl, its fringe tattered and tangled, covered her shoulders and wrapped across her bosom to tie in the back. But, while her clothing was shabby and dusty, there was nothing humble in her demeanor. Sparks flew from her intense black eyes as she spat, "May God give you three years of itchy mange!"

The *zapatero* laughed, changing tactics. "Let's talk! Come here and have a seat...in the dirt!" He laughed out loud, then added before the *gitana* could interrupt, "Do you want to come work for me in exchange for meals, and let me keep everything you earn?"

"You can keep such a good proposition for your sisters...boring cockroach!"

"Did you really think I wanted you?"

"Cursed be everything you eat, stingy...didn't I say no, anyway?" She turned to an old man whose broad grin revealed a single yellow tooth. "How about you, handsome, do you want to know your future? *Anda!*"

At last, undaunted but tiring of the affair, the woman moved slowly away, mumbling to herself. At some distance, she turned to fling back one last trifle: "God willing, may a fighting bull find you in open country...with no more shelter than the shadow of a star!"

As the people slowly dispersed and vanished into doorways, their entertainment over, the *zapatero* led the way to his shop. "Come in Rafael, come in!"

"What nerve that *gitana* had!" Rafael chuckled as the shoemaker cleared a place for him on a cluttered bench. "Antonio, can you repair these shoes for me again?"

"*Hombre* [Man], not again! I can only do so much...I'm not a magician. There isn't much left to repair."

"I know, but what can I do? As you well know, times are hard...I can't afford new ones."

"I understand, we're all suffering. It wouldn't take much for us to be in the street with that *gitana*."

The other nodded, then grinned. "That reminds me of *La Tía* Boleca, a *gitana* who lives over by me on the Plaza de las Angustias. She and her daughter are very poor...poorer than bad luck, *sabe?* [you know?] I heard that, once, when the daughter met her mother in the street carrying a broom and a jar of oil, the little girl asked, '*Pero...mare mía* [mother dear], are we moving?'"

The *zapatero* laughed, then said, "Let's see what we can do with these shoes."

Rafael grunted his appreciation. As he watched the shoemaker's strong hands attack the torn shoe with a knife he asked, "How's your boy...still dreaming of becoming a *cantaor?*"

"Yes, the same as always. It wasn't so bad when he was younger...I thought he'd grow out of it. But it's still the same. I've forbidden him to sing around the house, but..."

"*Hombre*, there's no way to keep him from the *cante* here in San Miguel."

The *zapatero* knew that his friend spoke the truth. The Barrio de San Miguel was, as his son would describe it years later, the Mecca of gypsy song. Less than one block from the Chacón home at Calle Sol, Number 60, the dusty Plaza Orellana teemed with gypsy blacksmith shops. Throughout the day the *fraguas*[4] [forges] resounded with the songs of the blacksmiths, accompanied by the incessant rhythm of hammers beating metal into shape on heavy anvils.

In the heat of late afternoons, the plaza often rang with the staccato pulse of gypsy *palmas* [handclapping] ricocheting off sun-baked white walls. Above the crisp and complex beating of many hands, shrill voices of gypsy children rose and fell in the melodic cadence of the *tango gitano*. Shouts of encouragement punctuated the song: "*Ole!...Ole Manué!...Así Manoli! Toma, que toma!...*" Bronze-skinned children, their bare feet raising dust from the hard-packed earth of the street, pounded out the rhythms of their race as they took time out from playing games of hide and seek, leapfrog, and diabolo. Tiny faces contorted in imitation of adult expression. Tensed fingers and hands fluttered like butterflies at the ends of arms that moved in gracefully curved arabesques. Young gypsies—and they were very young, their older brothers and sisters already hard at work with their parents—copied what they saw in family gatherings. Gypsies believed that their babies were born dancing, that they absorbed the music even before birth. The *gitano* felt that his art was in the blood and could not be learned by the *gachó*.

Each evening, workers from the wineries gathered in taverns to ease their weary bodies with wine and song. Here, as well as in frequent and festive wedding and baptism celebrations, the *gitanos* sought release from poverty and the dreary routine of daily life in

---

[4] *fragua:* blacksmith shop; the *fragua* is, strictly speaking, the forge or furnace, but gypsies commonly referred to the shop as the *fragua*.

their outpourings of song and dance.

Living in that gypsy environment, it was almost impossible for even a young *gachó* to grow up without feeling the pull of the music and absorbing its insistent and primitive rhythms.

As the sounds of the tortured dog faded from the Plaza Orellana, Antoñito hurried homeward, shivering from the cold and the anticipation of his father's anger. He had not meant to stay so long in the *fragua*. But the blacksmith, knowing well the boy's love of the *cante*, had gestured with his head toward where his son worked at maintaining a flow of air through the bellows and said that it would be a few minutes before he finished shaping the piece of hot metal that glowed in his hands. Antoñito had been only too glad to join his friend, to help with work in the warmth of the forge, all the while hoping that his wait would be rewarded with more than just the tool his father had ordered.

José Cruz, a black-skinned gypsy whose wiry body had sinews as hard as the iron he worked, grunted occasionally to the boys, commanding them to force just enough air into the coals to give the precise heat he needed. Each forging operation required a different temperature, which the blacksmith measured by the color of the heated metal. José Cruz was one of the most respected smiths in the barrio and his customers included many wineries and local craftsmen. He was one of few metalworkers, even among the gypsies, who dominated all phases of his craft. Many others were no more than *machacadores*, wielding heavy hammers under direction of the smith, or understood well only certain phases of forging. But José was an artist, a master alchemist working with the four primordial elements—fire in the forge, air from the bellows, iron from the earth, and water used in the tempering process. He understood the complex behavior of wrought iron and worked it with the same gypsy genius that inspired the cape work of a torero or the spine-chilling lament of the *cantaor*.

Antoñito had relieved Joselito of one of the two rough wooden levers that worked the bellows. Under the hypnotic influence of the moving levers and the breathing of the huge bellows, he soon found himself absorbed in the magical aura of the *fragua*. A smoky haze filled the small, earthen-floored room with the orange glow of reflected fire. The sweaty bodies of the blacksmith and his older son glistened in the firelight, while the steady whoosh of the bellows, the hiss of molten metal striking water, and the clang of hammers on iron combined to conjure up the mysterious, otherworldly atmosphere of the *fragua*.

Antoñito watched José Cruz pull a heavy iron rod from the fire, its tip glowing white-hot in the dim light, and strike it once with his hammer to send scale flying in a shower of sparks. As he laid the end of the bar across the flat table of a massive anvil, he grunted in a deep hoarse voice. *"Niño, el currandó!"* [Boy, the hammer!]

Without further words, the blacksmith tapped the metal with his hammer and the young *machacador* followed immediately with a blow from a much heavier sledgehammer. The smaller hammer guided the larger in a series of precisely timed strikes.

The iron had begun to assume its new shape when, suddenly, a throaty cry of anguish rent the thick air. At first it was just an *"Ay...ayeee..."* as the smith tuned his voice. Then, in a harsh and nasal tone, the *cante* of the *fragua*, the *martinete* [from *martillo*: hammer], resounded through the small smithy:

Yo toíto me lo encontraba hecho	I would find everything set for me:
el lavaíto y el planchaíto,	the tempering basin and iron plate,
y la fragüita encendía,	and the forge glowing,
y el martillo preparaíto.	and the hammer ready.

To the rhythmic ring of metal on metal, José Cruz poured forth the anguish of his race in his tortured melody, expressing centuries of hardship and persecution:

Nadie diga que es locura,	Don't anyone tell me that insanity
lo que yo estoy aparentando,	is what I am experiencing,
qué la locura se cura	for insanity can be cured,
y yo vivo agonizando.	while I live in agony.

The singing held Antoñito transfixed, his errand forgotten. He deeply felt the music of this rough *cante*. It never occurred to him to question why he, a *gachó*, should be so moved. Although he did not always understand the meaning expressed by the words, the music of the songs held no secrets for him. He had memorized the verses and knew by heart the melodies he had heard so many times. In spite of their familiarity, the *cantes* never failed to enthrall him, for they were never done exactly the same and the emotion was always new.

José Cruz paused in his singing and turned to reheat the bar of iron. No sooner had he bent to the glowing coals than a lusty cry burst out of the darkness behind him. Antoñito, as startled as the others, turned to see a tall, slender man with immense bushy sideburns standing in the shadows just inside the doorway, his face twisted with the emotion of his song:

Desgrasiaíto él que come	Unfortunate is he who accepts
el pan de la mano ajena,	bread from a stranger's hand,
siempre mirando a la cara	always studying the face
si la pone mala o buena.	to see if there is favor or disfavor.

The last notes of *cante* were still echoing off the walls when the newcomer broke into a grin and said, "*Buenas tardes* José, how's it going?"

"*Viva la mare que te parió*, Juan!" ["Long live the mother who gave you birth, Juan!"[5]] José Cruz shook his head, as if in disbelief. "I have never heard that *martinete*. What a *cante!*"

"I learned it from a *gitano* who worked with me in Algeciras. He said it came from Juan Pelao of Triana."

"*Ozú!* [Jesus!] Not even Silverio could sing it better."

"*Claro!* The *cante* is ours, it's in our blood and no *gachó* can feel it the way we do."

Antoñito only half-heard the conversation. The haunting melody had burned itself into his memory and he was struggling to remember the words—words that held little meaning for him. But the mention of Silverio caught his attention and he thought to himself, *someday I will sing these cantes as well as any* gitano!

The blacksmith warmly gripped his friend's hand as he asked, "What are you doing here? Why aren't you working?"

"*Hombre!* There is no work at the moment. And I have just had a new son..."

"*Vaya*, Juan, congratulations!"

"The baptism will be tomorrow...you'll be there, won't you?"

"Of course! But why wait, let's go have a drink right now!"

As José Cruz dropped what he was doing and the two men prepared to leave, Antoñito remembered his errand and timidly asked, "Excuse

---

[5]Part of the impact and humor of this common Andalusian saying stems from the fact that *parir* (to give birth) in normally only used for animals.

me *Señor* Cruz, the tool my father ordered?"

The gypsy turned to the boy, "*Ay, niño*, I forgot. Here you are." He picked up the hooked iron tool from the bench. "Tell your father I will come to see him about those shoes he promised me."

Antoñito followed the men out into the plaza, reluctantly leaving behind the warmth of the *fragua*. The man named Juan towered over the blacksmith. Around the barrio he was known as *Torre* due to his extraordinary height. At over six feet, he was the tallest gypsy Antoñito had ever seen. Torre, a fieldworker and sometimes *matarife* in the slaughterhouse, had a reputation as a singer that extended well beyond the barrio San Miguel.

With one hand Antoñito attempted to pull his threadworn jacket tightly about him, while in the other he clutched the heavy wire *rascastaca*. His father had needed the tool to finish a pair of shoes and would be furious at the delay. Although the boy knew he should hurry, his feet held him back. No amount of haste would save him from severe punishment.

At the far end of the plaza, near the entrance to Calle Sol, the blacksmith and his tall friend ducked into a small doorway. The entrance stood out in the dim twilight and beckoned to Antoñito. Even at a distance he was assailed by familiar odors—the musty smell of the white earthen floor, packed hard and darkened over the years by the tread of *alpargata*-clad feet[6], the acrid odor of black tobacco, the salty tang of dried *bacalao* cod, and the strong mixture of cheap wine and workmen's bodies. The boy knew well the sparse furnishings, little more than a few rickety chairs, one table, and the fly-specked pictures of the bullfighters Lagartijo and Frascuelo behind the worn bar. It was the local *taberna* [tavern] and, inside, workers from the barrio and nearby wineries were already gathering faithfully for the evening ritual.

This had always been a magical place for Antoñito. He had spent many hours seated on the ground at the threshold, magnetized by the scene within. When the *taberna* was full, something happened that for a long time had been beyond the boy's understanding. The men, wearing threadbare jackets over white shirts with frayed cuffs and collars, sagging pants, and dusty *alpargatas*, limited themselves at first to staring into the glasses of cheap red wine or *manzanilla*[7] they held under their noses and uttering occasional monosyllabic grunts between gulps of

---

[6]*alpargata*: a rope-soled slipper worn by the poor.

drink. It appeared that the purpose of the gathering was to pass the hours as cheaply and painlessly as possible.

But, evening after evening, the miracle happened. Suddenly, when least expected, came the rap of rough, hardened knuckles on the wooden bar. To the boy, the sound of hard flesh against wood was a music that quickened his breath and made his heart pound. He knew what would follow, although he did not fully grasp the importance of this call to an ancient ritual.

The men began to awaken from their stupor. They looked around furtively. Some drew themselves erect, like bullfighters, giving strength and dignity to their weary bodies. Others stretched their arms out to grasp the bar and fixed their gaze on the whitish earth beneath their *alpargatas*. They waited, seemingly in communion, for the inevitable. Then it happened. At first a barely audible voice moaned as it searched for its tone. Moments later a modulated wail pierced the air. *A palo seco*[8] the *cante* made its appearance.

Caminito de presidio	On the road to prison
hicimos una pará;	we made a stop;
a los jeres dieron agua;	they gave water to the soldiers;
a los gitanos…ná!	to the gypsies…nothing!

The gypsy had broken the ice with the song of his trade, a song of racial pain and suffering—the *martinete*. That first burst of song transformed the room. Within the walls of the *taberna* the lament of the *cantaor* reverberated in perfect harmony with the *"Ole!…Arsa!…Ea!"* of the others. A warm communal language flooded the room, with the *cante* as its cornerstone. It was expressed in gestures and postures, in whispers, shouts, and exclamations, in knocks and taps on wood or the hard clay floor. Another man continued:

Al que mendiga, lo encierran,	He who begs is locked up,
y meten preso al ladrón;	and they imprison him who steals
él que no pide ni roba	he who neither begs nor steals
muere de hambre en un rincón.	dies of hunger in a corner.

---

[7]*manzanilla*: dry, golden, sherry-like wine made in the coastal area around Sanlúcar de Barrameda; cheaper and lower in alcohol content than sherry, it was often favored by the poor.

[8]*a palo seco*: a capella; without instrumental accompaniment; means literally, "to the accompaniment of a dry stick."

Uno decía que mueran;	One judge was saying they [should die;]
otro anaqueraba, "Por qué?	another was asking "Why?"
"Que dañito habrán cometío	"What harm has been done
los probes de los calé?"	by these poor gypsies?"

Something old and vital vibrated under the nose of the young spectator and, unconsciously, he drank deeply from it. Over time, the strange ceremony became etched in his mind and heart and, slowly, he began to decipher the code. It was an apprenticeship during which he absorbed knowledge of *ecos, melismas, quejíos, sones,* and *compases*—the rhythms and vocal qualities that are required by the *cante.* He came to know the geography of the *cante* and its many styles and ended up knowing the great *cantaores*—the Mellizos, the Fillos, the Silverios—as if he had met them in person. He could recite the genealogy of generations of gypsies and families of singers. He drank from the fountain of gypsy lore until it became part of him. Yet, at his young age, he could not fully grasp the essential truth that lay at the core of the nightly ritual. He could not yet comprehend the value of the catharsis that the men experienced in their communion, the purifying effect of the *cante* and companionship that enabled them to return to their impoverished existences and face another day of exhausting labor.

Reluctantly, Antoñito turned from the warm invitation of the *taberna* doorway. On this night he could not stay to await the magic of the *cante.* He braced himself against the chill and plunged into the shadows of Calle Sol, singing softly to himself the *martinete* of Juan Torre. In the dim light, the gypsy's words still rang in his head and he thought: *A* gachó *can sing the* cante. *Silverio can do it and one day I will too. If* gitanos *are born with it in their blood, then why can't a* gitano *like Ignacio sing a note? Why do so many of them sing so badly?*

Calle Sol was deserted, unlike in warmer weather when it would be filled with laughter, gossip, and the cries of street vendors. From the doorways, however, came the sounds of families. Children shrieked at play in the shelter of the patios, while their parents stayed near the cooking fires or huddled around the *mesa camilla*—a round table draped with cloth to enclose the warmth that emanated from glowing coals in the flat, pan-shaped *brasero.*

Antoñito turned into the doorway of Number 60. No sooner had he entered the patio than he was assailed by his father's voice bellowing from the small room that served as his workshop.

"Antonio!" In the flickering light of an oil lamp, Antoñito could not clearly discern the expression on his father's face as he handed over the new tool. But he winced when he saw the elder Chacon pick up his *tirapié*, a heavy leather strap with its ends stitched together to form a continuous loop. Antoñito had felt its cruel bite on many occasions, and he tensed in preparation for the inevitable.

To the boy's surprise, his father remained silently at his bench and looped the *tirapié* under his foot and over his thigh. Placing an almost-completed shoe under the strap, the shoemaker held it tightly in place on his leg by downward pressure on the other end of the loop. Then, with the sharpened, blade-like hook that made up one end of the *rascastaca*, he began to scrape inside the shoe, trimming off the protruding ends of small cane pegs that had temporarily held the layers of the sole in place on the last until they could be stitched together.

The anticipated beating would have been easier for Antoñito to bear than the grim silence. His father's reaction was something new and he began to fidget nervously. At last, when the boy felt he could endure it no longer, his father spoke.

"Antonio, I have tried everything with you. I have tried to be patient. I have beaten you. Your mother has pleaded with you. Yet you continue to disobey me." There was something in the voice that Antoñito had never heard before—an air of resignation.

"You are never going to be a successful *zapatero*...just as you will never do anything but disgrace yourself and your family if you follow the path of the *cante*."

The shoemaker paused. He reached for another shoe, and then looked up at his son. The boy's downcast eyes did not meet his father's gaze.

"I have decided to find other work for you, work that will make a man of you and someday provide for you and your family. Perhaps you will listen to others, since it is clear that you will not listen to your own father..."

"But, Papá..."

"There will be no further discussion! Tomorrow I will ask around and try to find something. When I do, you will no longer go to school, where you are wasting your time and our money. *Don* Francisco tells me that you pay little attention to your lessons. It is time you worked like a man. Now go! Leave me to finish these shoes!"

Later, in bed, Antoñito lay awake for a long time. He would have preferred the familiar beating to the disturbing change in his father's attitude. There had been little conversation at dinner and Antoñito had barely tasted the rich *potaje* of garbanzos, cabbage, and squash flavored with green peppers and pieces of spicy chorizo sausage. It was true that Antoñito did not enjoy working with shoes and that school did not interest him. He had learned to read and write, but school represented to him only another form of punishment. *Don* Francisco, an ill-tempered master, instilled fear in his students to keep them pinned to their hard benches in a more or less orderly manner. Antoñito escaped from the dark, dreary schoolroom in his daydreams. He often envisioned himself singing and on more than one occasion, unaware that his *cante* had not confined itself to his dream world, he had been snapped out of his reveries by a stinging blow on the knuckles and the delighted laughter of his classmates.

No, he wouldn't miss school. But he had mixed feelings about leaving his father's shop. He would be freed from the tedious work, and he felt proud to think that he would be going to work like a man. But what would he do? He couldn't imagine laboring long hours in the fields as some of his friends did. It would be fun to work with a blacksmith, but his father would never permit that—blacksmithing was for *gitanos*. And the blacksmiths preferred to keep their trade within their own families. Besides, he would never be permitted to work where there was *cante. Cante!...how did Juan Torre's* martinete go? As the words *"desgraciaíto él que come el pan..."* came to him, Antoñito drifted off to sleep.

The following evening, after a solemn day of working under his father's supervision, Antoñito hastily ate his evening meal and slipped out of the house. He met Joselito in the Plaza Orellana and the two boys made their way through the darkness to Calle Alamos a short distance away. They felt their way along the deeply rutted street, guided by the light and noise coming from the doorway of Number 22 at the end of the block. Long before reaching that doorway they could distinguish laughter and shouts of encouragement amid the crackle of rhythmic *palmas.*

On entering, the boys were momentarily dazzled by the intense commotion of the fiesta. The patio, a small one with a central courtyard, served several gypsy families whose whitewashed dwellings formed its irregular walls. Low doorways, cave-like and arranged seemingly without plan, overflowed with a steady stream of bustling human bodies. Antoñito and Joselito shoved their way through the crowd of revelers. There was no hint of the evening chill in that teeming mass of human warmth and excitement. Antoñito felt completely at ease among the gypsies. As a child of the barrio and friend of Joselito and other gypsy children, his presence was accepted without reservation.

Breaking through to the center of activity, the boys found a heavy woman moving gracefully to the beat of dozens of pairs of hands and the rough voices of *gitanos* who had been drinking steadily since the baptism ceremony earlier in the day. The *gitana*, with white carnations arranged in her thick black hair and an immense fringed shawl draped about her shoulders, presented a haughty figure in the flickering light of the oil lamps. Cries of *"Arsa!"* and *"Ole!"* accompanied the graceful arabesques of her hands and upraised arms. Laughter burst out at a particularly suggestive undulation of her ample hips.

Antoñito beat his hands and mouthed the words of the songs when he knew them, or listened carefully when he didn't. A young girl replaced the woman, dancing with an innocence that only accentuated the sensuousness of her movements. Suddenly, an apparition in black, a gnarled old woman, approached a figure who towered above the others and offered him the bundle she held in her arms. "Look Juan, *mira qué peaso de niño has bautizao hoy!"* [look at what a fine specimen of a son you have baptized today!]

In the dim light, Juan Torre was an imposing figure, his dark good looks highlighted by a strong, regally arched nose and massive bushy black sideburns that curved down to the corners of his mouth. A white shirt with full, bloused sleeves and a vest with a heavy gold watch chain dangling from the pocket radiated gypsy elegance. As Torre turned toward the old woman, the blanket fell away revealing a naked infant. The child, reacting to the chill of the night air, let out a lusty cry that brought the dancing to a halt. Someone yelled, *"Viva Manuel,* the son of Juan Soto Montero!" Another voice chimed in, "Look how well he sings already!"

Torre took the screaming child in his hard hands and held it high, his face broken by a broad grin. A woman's shrill voice cried out, "Look, the child is already a *torre* [tower] like his father!" Laughter filled the patio at this reference to the baby's prominently displayed male endowments. The father beamed, his face flushed with wine and pride. He passed his son back to the fondling hands of the women amid bawdy cries of praise and peals of laughter: "What a man you're going to be Manué!" *"Qué susto!"* [It's scary to think about!] "He will father a tribe!" "Women beware!"

Turning from the commotion created by the baby, Torre spotted Antoñito among several children. Like many gypsies in the barrio, he admired the boy's *afición*, his love of the *cante*. But he had to chuckle at Antoñito's seriousness in attempting to imitate the *cante gitano*. Now he called out, mischief evident in his voice, *"Mira*, it's the son of the shoemaker! *Toñico,* come here!"

As Antoñito approached hesitantly, the tall gypsy knelt to the boy's level while barking at the restless mob, *"Callarse!"* [Quiet everyone!] And then, bringing his face close to Antoñito, so close that the boy could not escape the heavy odor of wine and black tobacco, he said, *"Chiquillo*, now you will sing for us!"

Torre smiled with satisfaction when Antoñito nodded in acquiescence. The gypsy's deep voice boomed out over the gathering with feigned seriousness, *"Callarse, que va a cantar el chumajarró!"* The humor of this request for quiet was heightened by Torre's use of the gypsy word for shoemaker.

Antoñito, fearless in his youthful innocence, threw himself into the first thing that came to mind—the *cante* that had echoed in his head constantly since hearing it the day before in the *fragua*: *"Desgraciaíto él que come..."*

Scarcely had he completed that first *tercio*[9] when Torre let out an *"Ozú!"* and sat back on his heels. Open-mouthed, he allowed the boy to continue, the childish voice breaking in difficult passages and the little face contorting from the effort.

Torre interrupted the final tones of the *cante*, a smile on his face, *"Niño*, that is my *cante*...where did you learn it?"

The forceful tone of gypsy intimidated Antoñito and he answered timidly, his head lowered. "I heard you sing it yesterday in the *fragua*."

"Caray! You learned that from hearing it only one time?" Torre paused a moment in thought. *"Pues,* look here, if you are going to sing it you must sing it correctly. It begins like this, higher..." And he

---

[9]*tercio*: a complete phrase of singing, which may or may not coincide with one line of verse; one word can be stretched to fill a *tercio*, or two lines of verse can be combined in a single *tercio*.

demonstrated by singing the first *tercio*. Then he said, "Now, you!"

Antoñito imitated the line. Torre shook his head. The boy made several more attempts before the gypsy nodded, "That's it, you've got it! Now, the rest of the *letra* [verse] goes like this, '...*siempre mirando a la cara, si la pone mala o buena*.' Sing it with me!"

The two of them sang the *cante* again, together. When they had finished, Torre sat back and grinned proudly. He stood up and bellowed over the growing din—most of the gypsies had by this time lost interest in the little boy—"Cherna!" He looked around. "Where is Joaquín?"

Others repeated the cry and, a moment later, Joaquín la Cherna stuck his head out of a doorway. "Ea, Juan?"

Torre looked over at his brother-in-law and said, "Joaquín, come here! Listen to what this boy has learned...what I have taught him!"

The tall gypsy beamed proudly as Antoñito repeated the *cante*. When the boy had finished, La Cherna, looking incredulous, said, "That's your *cante*, Juan...and he's not even *gitano!* I hope that my new nephew, Manué, can sing that well when he's the same age!"

The harsh cry of a gypsy *seguiriya* burst into the night behind them, and in a moment Antoñito was forgotten by the gypsies. But the boy felt a warm glow inside and a deep satisfaction from the approval his singing had received from two of the most revered *cantaores* in the Barrio San Miguel. He stayed to listen to the singing as long as he dared, and then slipped away into the dark. He knew that the fiesta would continue on through the next day and into the following night.

Javier

It was not until the following spring that Antonio began to work as a *peón* [laborer] in the Tonelería Regife, a barrel-works that supplied casks to local wineries. Each morning, the nine-year-old boy strolled down cobblestoned Calle Sol toward the center of Jerez, his stomach warmed by hot coffee and fresh bread spread with spiced lard. In spite of its narrowness, Calle Sol appeared as sunny as its name, with bright light reflecting off the whitewashed one and two-story homes on either side. Green awnings over the windows and potted plants on the balconies created a splash of color against the white backdrop. At that early hour, the street was alive with activity, filled with black-clad women making their way to the market amid a ceaseless hum of chatter and laughter.

The deep clank of a tin bell announced the arrival of the *burrero*. Burro's milk, traditionally a panacea for colds, was considered by some to be a cure-all, and sickly children were subjected to endless glasses of the rich, strong-flavored drink. The *burrero* delivered milk directly from his donkey's udders. Other donkeys were laden with heavy loads—immense soft baskets suspended on either side of their backs and piled high with everything from fresh-baked bread and produce to crockery cookware and cooking charcoal. The animals moved at a sprightly pace in response to lusty commands and the stinging flicks of a flexible switch, their hooves clicking sharply on the polished cobblestones. Or they stood patiently, heads hung in resignation, while rustic vendors intoned inviting *pregones*. A grizzled vendor sang out in a rough but melodious voice:

Meloooones de la Isla,	Melons from La Isla,
a prueba y a calá!	to be tried and tested!

So confident was he of the quality of his melons that he cut a generous slice for his customer. If it proved not to be sweet, he did not sell it, but brought another from the donkey's back to be tasted.

The seller of sweet rolls approached the doorways of the patios and cried out:

Al bollero, al bollero;	Come to the bun man;
bollos de aceite, empiñonaos,	sweet rolls, with pine nuts,
bollitos de leche...	milk rolls...

As Antoñito approached the huge central market, the symphony of the streets built in a crescendo of voices, braying donkeys, and vendors' cries from dozens of booths inside the market. Stout countrywomen wearing black head kerchiefs and capacious aprons carried baskets of green vegetables or live snails and clusters of wild birds, fluttering chickens tied and hung by their legs, or rabbits strung up by the ears. Antoñito's mouth watered at the *churrera's* invitation to try her "*calentitos*" [*churros*: fried pastry]. Once, he stopped to watch a peasant farmer struggling with a squirming, squealing piglet under his arm while calling out, "A live piglet for sale!" On another occasion, he laughed at the antics of a ragged derelict who had stationed himself in front of a store to sing the praise of the merchandise sold inside. When the desperate owner paid him to be on his way, he moved on—only to repeat the process further down the street.

Antoñito continued past the market, down Calle Unión and across Calle Veracruz, into the Plaza Romero Martínez. This was not the shortest route to the barrel-works, but the boy reveled in the sights and sounds of the marketplace and, more importantly, it took him past *the café*.

Café Vera Cruz occupied part of an old and stately building that overlooked the plaza. Antoñito had never been inside, but he knew that the owner of this café was Juan Junquera, a prominent businessman and a *cantaor* whose *seguiriyas* were admired and sung by the gypsies of San Miguel. The boy could only imagine what it must be like behind the thick stone walls and heavy wooden doors when, each night, the finest singers, dancers, and guitarists of Jerez appeared onstage to perform. He felt a sense of reverence for the café, and he envisioned himself there, among men who sang like gods and beautiful women who danced like angels, singing to an audience of admiring aficionados.

Lost in the world of *cante*, the young boy's morning walk always went too quickly. Far too soon, he found himself on Calle Clavel, in front of the Tonelería Regife. The fragrant odor of newly worked oak and the pungent smoke from the blacksmith's fire invariably snapped him out of his reveries.

As a *peón*, Antoñito was set to tedious and laborious tasks. He carried wood to the workers and helped to unload and stack the newly arrived rough-hewn American oak—it would have to be dried for more than a year before it would be ready for final shaping by the *toneleros*. The young apprentice was amazed by the way the craftsmen shaped the staves with double-handled drawknives and beveled the edges so perfectly that they fit together to form leak-proof wine barrels. When the boy first saw the bulging muscles in the arms and backs of the *toneleros* as they hammered hot iron hoops down over casks that stood almost as tall as they, he knew that he would never be suited to a life of barrel-making.

During his first weeks in the *tonelería*, Antoñito tried to concentrate on the work. But the hours were long and soon he began to grow weary of the dull and tiresome tasks. His only relief was to help the gypsy *herreros* who did all of the necessary blacksmithing—forging countless iron hoops and maintaining the wide variety of knives, adzes, shavers, planers, and hammers used by the *toneleros*. As often as possible he sought some pretext to be near the forge, where he might be rewarded by the rough *cante* of the *herreros*. Those moments were usually cut short by the appearance of the foreman, who kept an alert eye on his new apprentice.

Antoñito began to seek every opportunity to avoid work. He tarried when sent on errands and often slipped away to hide between the stacks of barrels or among the piles of drying staves. There, he would sing quietly to himself and drift off into a private world of *cante*. It was always a shock to be abruptly shaken from his daydreams by the bellowing of the foreman: "Antonio, what are you doing? I told you to bring more charcoal for the forge!"

Again and again he was warned, but he persisted in his apathy and escaped from his assigned tasks at every opportunity. One evening, shortly after his tenth birthday,[1] Antoñito arrived home to find his father waiting for him with heavy brows gathered in a stern frown. "*Don Eduardo* tells me again that you are not putting much effort into your work. He feels that it's a waste of your time...and his...for you to continue at the *tonelería*. He says that you have no interest and will never become a good apprentice. I have tried to find a career for you that would give you a better life than that of a *zapatero*, and you have rewarded me by shaming our family. You will no longer go to the *tonelería*, but will help me here, where I can see to it that you do not continue with this crazy obsession for the *cante!*"

"But, Papá, I want to sing, why can't I..."

"You're not a *gitano*, that's why. You will never be able to sing the way they do... they have it in their blood!"

"But what about Silverio?"

"Silverio, Silverio! That's all I ever hear...Silverio! You are not Silverio. You will never be Silverio. There is only one Silverio...other *cantaores* starve and bring shame upon themselves and their families."

"But..."

"No more! That's settled and I won't discuss it further."

During the following year, Antoñito worked as well as he was able with his father, the strain between them continuing to grow. When the Chacón family moved to the Plaza Orellana, where the *cante gitano* was a constant presence, the boy became even more distracted and harder to control. On the occasions when he could slip away from the *zapatería,* Antoñito sought out the old men and begged them to tell him about the great *cantaores.* He bothered them as they sat in open doorways taking sun on chilly afternoons, and nestled at their feet in the dirt to bask in tales of musical intrigue. The grizzled old gypsies invariably illustrated their stories with fragments of *cante*, and Antoñito's quick mind absorbed all it heard. The adventures of Silverio especially enthralled him and he never tired of hearing them over and over. His favorite had been told to him by his uncle, *Tío* Juan García. *Tío* Juan, the elder brother of Antoñito's mother, felt a special affection for his nephew and shared the boy's enthusiasm for the *cante.*

---

[1]Born May 16, 1869.

Antoñito went often to the *casa de vecinos* [house of neighbors] at Number 11 on Calle Cazón to visit his uncle. A small entryway opened into a square patio bordered by marble columns supporting a rickety second-story walkway. In the small rooms opening onto the patio on both levels lived a dozen families in forced intimacy, sharing kitchen and washing facilities in the central courtyard. *Tío* Juan occupied a room in one corner of the patio, but spent much of his time observing life from an *esparto* grass chair in the entryway. There, Antoñito would sing for him or ask for stories. The first time the boy had mentioned Silverio, the old man had jerked himself erect and wheezed, "Silverio! Now there's a *cantaor!* I first heard him in Jerez long before you were born, when he had just returned from across the pond...from America.[2] *Niño* [Child], listen and I'll tell you what happened when Silverio first came back to Sevilla.

"He had been gone for so long that people had forgotten him...they thought he was dead. One night, a well-dressed and bearded *señorito*...they thought he had come from the Indies...appeared in the Venta Laureano[3]...on Calle San Jacinto, there in the gypsy barrio, in Triana. The *gitanos* at the bar, hunger growling in their stomachs, took in the wealthy gentleman's manners, his well-tailored clothes, his gold watch chain, and the diamonds on his fingers. When the gentleman ordered a round of drinks for everyone, the *gitanos* said to themselves, '*Ozú!* What have we here?' And quicker than a rooster crows, a guitar appeared and the stranger found himself at the center of a fiesta. *Venga cante, venga vino*, more *cante*, more wine...throughout the night!"

"But what about Silverio, *Tito*?" blurted Antoñito impatiently.

The old man responded by hoisting himself up from his chair with a grunt and shuffling unsteadily toward the charcoal stoves at the back of the patio. When he had returned and settled once again into his chair, puffing on the relit stub of a cigarette, he asked, "Where was I, *niño?*"

"The *gitanos* sang all night..."

"Ah, yes! It was almost daylight. The *gitanos* were tired and wanted to leave, but they hadn't been paid. Imagine how their spirits sank when the Indian *gachó* said, 'Now it's my turn. Play *por seguiriyas!*'

---

[2]It is generally accepted that Silverio returned to Spain in 1864, after an eight-year stay in South America.

[3]A *venta* is a rustic tavern usually located on the outskirts of town.

"*Hombre!* It was bad enough that he wanted to sing, but...*por seguiriyas?*[4] The *gitanos* cursed under their breaths, or elbowed each other in the ribs in anticipation of the joke to come. All while making a show of encouraging the *señorito*, hoping that he would be generous in the end. Then that awesome voice burst forth, *ronca, aguardientosa, muy cantaora* [hoarse, coarsened by drink, very suited to the *cante*], and the room fell silent. *Qué barbaridá!* [It was outrageous!] Fatigue vanished as the *gitanos* hung on every word, the power and expression of the man's song bringing tears to their eyes."

Tío Juan attempted to imitate the *cante* as it had been sung that night, but in his feeble and broken voice it came out more as recitation than song:

Nochesita oscura	On a dark night
pensé yo morí,	I thought I was going to die,
porque yo ví a la mare	because I saw my dear mother
[*e mi arma*]	
juntito a mí.	standing beside me.

The old man let a moment pass in silent suspense before continuing. "Listen well, boy, because no sooner had the echo of the *cante* begun to fade than a raspy voice cried out, 'Stop!'"

"The guitarist stopped as the *señorito* looked up to see who had spoken. It was an old gypsy dancer, one of those who had been most reluctant to listen to the stranger. All eyes were on her as she spoke, 'It cannot be! There is only one person who can sing that *seguiriya*...'

" 'Who is that,' said the stranger, smiling.

" '...that person is you, *Señor* Silverio!' "

Antoñito laughed and clapped his hands with delight as his uncle continued. "Imagine the excitement, *Jozú!* The *gitanos* no longer thought about payment or sleep. The fiesta began anew and continued into the morning. Word spread like dust through the barrio of Triana, through the *fraguas* on Monte Pirolo and Calle Cava Nueva.[5] The cream of Sevilla's gypsy artists...Los Cagancho, Los Pelao, all the best...gathered in the *venta* to listen to Silverio. The great *cantaor*

---

[4]The *por* means "to play in the musical form of *seguiriyas*." There is no specific song called *seguiriyas*, only an assortment of verses and styles selected or improvised at the moment by the singer.

[5]Today: Calle Rosario Vega and Calle Pagés del Corro.

sang everything, perhaps better than he would ever again—*seguiriyas*, the *martinetes* of the blacksmiths, *serranas*, and even *la caña*...nobody could sing *la caña* like Silverio. What a fiesta! It lasted three days and was never forgotten by those who were there."

Tío Juan drifted off in thought for a moment and then added, "By the following year Silverio was known all over Andalucía. I'll never forget when he filled the Teatro Principal here three nights in a row, long before you were born...back in '65. Imagine, a *cantaor* performing on the same stage as the symphony orchestra...*qué barbaridá!* And he sang the pure *cante*, not the popular *canciones* they sing today. He sang *por cañas, polos, serranas,* and *seguiriyas*, all the old *cantes*. *Hombre!* No one has ever equaled him; no one has ever taken the *cante* to such heights. He is the greatest *cantaor* of all times...although many *gitanos* won't admit it. The great *Señor* Manuel Molina, as great a *cantaor* as we have here in Jerez, is said to have told a group of gypsies who refused to listen to Silverio sing...because he is *gachó*, 'He who does not go to listen to that man should be ashamed of himself. You must go to hear him sing!'"

The turning point in young Chacón's life came the following spring, shortly after his eleventh birthday. The wedding celebration was into its third day. Antoñito had stopped by whenever he could find a free moment, but as he rounded the corner of the entryway on the third evening, an unexpected sound brought on a flush of excitement. There could be no mistaking the distinct musical thrum of a guitar coming from the patio. In his entire life Antoñito had heard the *cante* accompanied by guitar only a handful of times. The *cante* of San Miguel was almost always done *a palo seco*, without guitar, stark in the simplicity of its accompaniment by muted handclapping, knuckles on a tabletop, or the thump of a walking stick. Even the dance seldom enjoyed the accompaniment of more than *cante* and hard, dry *palmas*. The guitar was a luxury that few gypsies of the barrio could afford, and the technique to play it was not likely to be found among laborers and blacksmiths.

The patio was packed—word of the guitar had spread quickly—and Antoñito had to force his way through the revelers. The warm, humid air hung heavy with the smell of wine and some of the men, those who were into their second or third night, were a bit unsteady on their feet. Among the many familiar faces of his neighbors, he spotted Juan Torre and Joaquín la Cherna. When the boy finally succeeded in breaking through the wall of clapping and yelling bodies, he found an old wrinkled *gitana* moving to a lively *tango* rhythm. Bent forward at the waist with her buttocks protruding and swaying, the old woman flapped her bent elbows like wings and jerked her head in birdlike movements. The clapping and yelling grew louder as the crowd egged on this dancing hen in heat.

Suddenly an elderly man, eighty if he was a day, stepped out from the crowd, his face contorted in a toothless grin. Like the woman, he flapped his wings, strutted and posed, all while gyrating and thrusting his pelvis in a suggestive manner. He pursued the hen until at last he caught her from behind. The old *gitana* cackled and backed into the rooster, grinding her buttocks against him. The old man continued to thrust and flap his wings, all while shuffling his feet to the driving rhythm of the *tango gitano*. Drink-reddened faces roared with laughter and yelled encouragement. The men cried, *"Dale, qué dale!"* [Give it to her!] The women shouted, *"Toma, qué toma!"* [Take it, take it!] Until at last, their act completed, the rooster strutted off, leaving the satisfied hen to dance off on her own.

Antoñito took in the scene in an instant, and then just as quickly forgot it when his eyes fell upon the *tocaor*. The guitarist appeared to be about Antoñito's age. His face revealed his youth, although there was nothing youthful in his manner of dress, his confident bearing, nor the force of his attack on the guitar. Slender fingers blurred as they beat out rhythm on the six strings. Antoñito was mesmerized, enthralled by the way the *cante* took on a new dimension with the support of the guitar. As he watched and listened for over an hour, he tried to imagine what it would be like to sing with such accompaniment. At a lull in the music, he impulsively approached the young *tocaor* [guitarist].

"*Hola!* I am Antonio Chacón...I'm going to be a *cantaor.*"

The guitarist turned his head to look at the boy before him. His lively, penetrating black eyes took in the knee-length pants and worn shirt, a far cry from his own dress jacket and smartly striped trousers. Yet, if Antoñito had been less in awe, he might have noticed the repair in the other's jacket sleeve, the frayed cuffs, and the shiny worn spots where the guitar rubbed at the chest and thigh.

"So, Antonio Chacón, you're going to be a *cantaor*, eh! Perhaps the next Silverio?" The guitarist spoke as if to a child, a smile playing about his lips. He was about to turn away when a deep voice burst out from behind him.

"Javier, I see you have met Antonio, the shoemaker's son." It was Joaquín la Cherna. "Antonio, sing for us! Javier, *tócale*, accompany the shoemaker!"

The guitarist raised an eyebrow as if to say, "Me, play for that?" And then, shrugging his shoulders, he lifted his instrument into playing position.

La Cherna continued, "Sing Antoñico! Show those from Santiago how even the children of San Miguel can sing!" Clapping his hands loudly, he roared at the noisy crowd, "*Callarse!*"

Without waiting for the guitar, Antoñito threw himself into a verse *por soleá*:[6]

Tan solamente por tí,	Just because of you,
las horas del sueño pierdo;	I lose hours of sleep;
yo camelaba morí!	I wish I could die!

The guitarist's expression gradually changed from disdain to surprise and then relaxed into a smile. *"Bien!"* he said when Antoñito had finished, "That is the *soleá* of Enrique el Mellizo, and not badly done."

Antoñito began to sing again, but the other stopped him by putting a hand on his forearm and saying, "Wait! *Donde templas por soleá?*" [Where is your pitch for the *soleá?*]

Antoñito looked confused.

"On which fret do you sing? What are your tones?" continued the guitarist.

Antoñito had no idea that "fret" referred to the metal crossbars on the fingerboard of the guitar, nor that he sang in any particular tone. He grew more puzzled as the guitarist ran his fingers up and down the bass strings, testing different tones, and then clamped a small piece of wood across the strings by twisting a peg to tighten a cord wrapped around the guitar neck.

"I believe this is where you were singing. You must tell the *tocaor*,

---

[6]*soleá*: also used in the plural form, *soleares*. Although in its infancy at this time, the *soleá* would become one of the primary forms of the *cante gitano*. Derived from the word *"soledad"* [loneliness], which describes its melancholy mood, the music is in cycles of twelve beats, accented on beats 3,6,8,10,12.

'*Pónmela en el cuatro, por medio*'[7] [Put the *cejilla*[8] at the fourth fret, in A]."

Antoñito had just had his first lesson in singing with guitar accompaniment. When Javier began to play, the youngster launched into his song without hesitation. Verse after verse poured forth with little pause between them. The singer swelled with joy as the sound of the guitar filled out his voice, giving him added strength and inspiration. Around him the noise subsided, and those who knew the *cante* encouraged him with quiet utterances of *"Bien dicho, niño...Eso é...Cómo canta er chavá ese!"* ["Well said, boy...That's the way to do it...How that boy can sing!"]

When, at last, the young *cantaor* had exhausted his repertoire, the guitarist rested the guitar in his lap and sat back. "*Muy bien*, Antonio. You don't know how to sing with the guitar...you come in at the wrong times and your singing doesn't always fit with the music. But you seem to feel the rhythm at times and your tones are accurate. With a little practice you would do much better. I have to leave now, to go to work, but we could get together sometime to practice if you'd like."

"I'd love to sing with you some more," responded Antoñito, still somewhat in a daze from the thrill of singing. "Where do you work?"

The young *tocaor* sat up straight and his chest swelled as he replied, "I'm a guitarist in the Café Vera Cruz of Juan Junquera!"

Antoñito's jaw dropped. He found it hard to believe that this boy, seemingly not much older than himself, mingled with the god-like *cantaores* of his fantasies in that great café that he had seen only from the outside. He could only utter, "Café Vera Cruz! How old are you?"

The other stood and raised himself to his full height. "I'm twelve years old. I have to go now." He took a step, then turned back and added, " My name is Javier Molina. I live on Calle Merced in Santiago." And then he was gone.

---

[7]*por medio*: in the chords of A-Major or minor. Knowing neither music nor chord names, *cantaores* referred to the common chord positions based on how the chord appeared to them: *por medio* [in the middle] was A-Major or minor; *por arriba* [above] was E-Major or minor; *por abajo* [below] was D-Major or minor. In time, these terms became established.

[8]*cejilla*: a device clamped across the guitar strings, effectively shortening the neck of the guitar and raising the pitch.

A week passed before Antoñito was able to make the long walk to the opposite side of Jerez and the Barrio Santiago. He had visited the barrio only a few times previously, with his father, but he knew that the gypsies of Santiago were renowned for their *cante* and *baile*, and many of them had become well-known artists. The *casa de vecinos* of Santiago, in the area around Calle Nueva and Calle de la Sangre,[9] was often an extensive labyrinth of whitewashed passageways, dotted with irregularly placed doorways and splashed with the intense colors of potted plants and clothing hung to dry.

Inquiries led Antoñito to the Molina home in a small two-story patio on Calle Merced, not far from Plaza Santiago. The sound of a guitar guided him past a throng of curious children to an upstairs doorway. He peered timidly into a dimly lit room, his eyes requiring a moment to recover from the intense glare of the afternoon sun. A gaunt-faced woman turned toward him, wiping her hands on a frayed apron. Her voice sounded tired.

"*Sí, chiquillo?*"

Antoñito replied timidly, "Is this the home of Javier Molina?"

"Yes it is. Come in, come in!" The woman called out, "Javié!" She smiled, "*Niño*, I don't know you...where are you from?"

"I'm Antonio Chacón, from San Miguel."

"Ah, San Miguel...JAVIÉ, there's a young man here to see you."

Javier came into the room, guitar in hand, and welcomed Antoñito warmly. With his dark skin and jet-black hair, the boy might easily have been gypsy, but, like Chacón, his family was *gachó*, living in close proximity to gypsy families. In Jerez, gypsies and non-gypsies mingled and mixed so freely that it was often difficult to tell one from the other. Javier introduced his mother and shooed away several younger brothers and sisters who had gathered, giggling, in the doorway. *Señora* Cundi de Molina served the boys coffee while they chattered excitedly. It wasn't long before they were interrupted by the appearance of a sleepy-faced youth from the back room.

"Is this the would-be *cantaor* you told us about, Javié?"

"Yes, this Antonio Chacón, from San Miguel. Antonio, this is my oldest brother...his name is Antonio, too."

The older boy smiled broadly and said, "Can you sing *para bailar,*

---

[9]Calle de la Sangre means "Street of Blood" and is the unofficial local name for Calle Taxdirt.

tocayo?" ["Can you sing for the dance, you with the same name as mine?"]

Antoñito was puzzled by the question. His friends often danced to his singing. "Of course," he replied.

The other continued his inquiry. "Do you sing *por alegrías?*"

The *alegrías*, a lighthearted *cante* that had recently become popular in Cádiz and neighboring port towns, was not heard as frequently among the gypsies of Jerez as their preferred *soleares* and *siguiriyas*. Antoñito, attracted to the darker sounds, had only a superficial knowledge of that festive *cante*. But he did not admit this deficiency to the Molinas, assuming that he could get by with what he knew. Naively, he replied, "I sing everything!"

Javier had been idly coaxing melodies from his guitar, a worn instrument, stained by sweat and covered with dents, scratches, and cracks. He asked Antoñito to sing the *soleares* they had done together in the fiesta, but this time he stopped the singer's attempt to interrupt his guitar introduction.

"No, Antonio! You must wait until the guitar has finished its song. Listen to how it will call you to sing!"

The guitarist began again. Antoñito listened attentively to the strong, thumb-driven melodies that seemed to pour forth effortlessly, and for the first time he became aware of their beauty. Strong chords brought the music to rest, and Javier looked up and nodded his head for the *cante* to begin. Antoñito understood—it seemed so simple when it was explained, and he was surprised that it had not been obvious to him before. His lessons had begun.

From time to time Javier had to stop the singer in order to point out that he was rushing the rhythm of his singing, thereby losing his place within the *compás*. Over and over the guitarist stressed the importance of singing in *compás*, that is, with proper rhythm and correctly placed accents. He also encouraged Antoñito to place his phrases so that the guitar could accompany them with the best result. At first the boy did not see the value of these restrictions, but when he did as Javier asked, he could hear and feel the difference. The harmonious beauty of voice and guitar working together became evident.

The balcony leading to the Molina home gradually filled with neighbors who welcomed the opportunity to set aside chores and enjoy a moment of festivity. They kept up a constant chorus of "*Oles*" and other shrill exclamations of encouragement. Whenever Javier stopped to correct Antoñito, heads nodded and coarse voices cried out, "*Así é*...You're right, Javié...Listen well, *chavá*...Javié knows!" The neighbors who shared the *casa* had little knowledge of the technicalities of the *cante*, but they respected the art of young Molina. Antoñito, in his enthusiasm and thirst for knowledge, was oblivious to their comments.

Later, *tangos* went much better, with their bright and more obvious rhythm:

Vale más millones	You're worth more millions
que los clavelitos graná	than the scarlet carnations
que asoman por los balcones.	that adorn the balconies.
El vecino del tercero	The neighbor on the third floor
a mí me mira con seriedad,	looks at me very seriously,
porque dice que yo tengo	because he says that I have become
con la vecina, amistad.	too friendly with his wife.

The patio came alive with the crisp beating of *palmas* and the joyous shouts of the neighbors. Cries went up for the older Molina boy to dance: *"A bailar, Antonio...Venga baile!"*

Easily persuaded, the young *bailaor* [flamenco dancer] stepped to the center of the room and began to mark time to the lively rhythm. The din of cries and shouts grew louder. The boy combined the *gracia* and spontaneity of the barrio, where practically everyone danced in some fashion, with the professionalism of one who took dancing seriously and depended upon it for his livelihood. Holding his arms raised to shoulder height and snapping his fingers sharply, he beat out strong rhythms with his feet on the rough tile floor. One moment he had the neighbors "oohing" and "ahing" with his virtuosity and, the next, roaring with laughter at his humorous *gracia* [clever wit, humor, style].

When the *tango* had finally exhausted itself, after children and their full-figured mothers had sung and danced, Antonio Molina said to his brother, "Javié, play for me *por alegrías!*"

Javier changed the position of the *cejilla* on the neck of the guitar. Not knowing Antoñito's tones for this *cante*, and not wishing to interrupt the fiesta to go through the laborious process of working with the singer to find the best key for his voice, he picked a tone that was most commonly used by other singers he worked with. The *tocaor's* slender hands beat out a strong rhythm on the strings.

Antoñito felt the two brothers eyeing him expectantly. He was struggling to recall a verse for the *alegrías*, when the dancer said, *"A templarse!"* The singer didn't know how to do the *temple*, the singer's warm-up, for the *alegrías*, so he improvised something to try to find his voice. The tones of the guitar were not comfortable for him and he struggled to sing on pitch. When he launched into a verse, he could tell that neither Javier nor his brother were pleased by what he sang. They yelled at him to sing at one point and not to sing at another. Finally the dance ground to a halt, having survived only due to the strong playing by Javier. The neighbors cheered wildly, oblivious to the conflicts taking place.

"Antonio, you haven't the slightest idea of how to sing the *alegrías*," reprimanded the *bailaor*, "not the slightest idea of the *compás*, of when to sing, of how to carry the dance with the rhythm of your voice, or of how to do the *palmas*. Javié, show him how it's done!"

They did the dance again, with Javier playing and singing in a voice that was thin, but carried the dancer with its *compás* and correct structure. Antoñito felt humiliated, but, at the same time, enthusiastic about learning.

The fiesta ended only when it neared time for Javier and his brother to leave for work. The Molina family depended upon the small income of the two young artists. The neighbors wandered off to feed their families, while Antoñito, in spite of his protests, shared in the Molina's evening meal of hearty garbanzo beans and potatoes flavored by a few meager bits of spicy *chorizo* sausage. He had stayed in Santiago much longer than he had intended and, after accompanying the two brothers to the Café Vera Cruz, he made his way through the darkened streets to face the wrath of his father.

Later, in bed, he lay awake for hours, unable to sleep with the thrumming of the guitar pounding in his head and a dizzying array of new ideas and *cantes* spinning through his mind.

In the months that followed, Antoñito became a frequent visitor to Barrio Santiago. He and the Molina brothers were soon inseparable, sharing close friendship and an overwhelming enthusiasm for their music. Antoñito worked less and less with his father, their relationship becoming ever more strained. As he put it to his father, *"Los zapatos me están grandes!"* [The shoes are too big for me (don't suit me!)]

The young *zapatero* changed his apprenticeship from shoemaking to that of the *cante*. As the months passed, he gradually mastered the secrets to singing with the guitar. He learned where the *cejilla* should be placed on the instrument in order to get the most from his voice and how to phrase properly within the *compás* in order to take full advantage of the guitar. Before he could accompany the dance with his singing, he had to master the *compás*, to be able to provide rhythm to the dancer even if a guitar were not present. Equally important, he had to learn to place his verses correctly within the dance, to watch for subtle signals that would tell him when to sing. He sought out those who could teach him the *alegrías*, and with the help of Javier and Antonio he mastered its infectious rhythm. The three aspiring artists were soon well in tune with each other.

The Barrio Santiago became a second home to Antoñito. The gypsies of the barrio were field workers, spending most of the year weeding and cultivating wheat, barley, beans, and grapes on the huge *cortijos*. They set out for the fields before daybreak and labored at the backbreaking work until dusk.

In the evenings, exhausted women gathered in the patios to smoke and drink wine. They shared gossip, told jokes, and occasionally burst into what the men referred to as "*cantesitos*" [little songs]. Weary bodies could not resist rising to mark out a few steps of *baile* and, more often than not, the suggestive undulations of ample hips brought forth peals of shrill and raucous laughter.

The men headed immediately for the many *tabernas*. The more tired they were, the sooner the wine brought out the *cante*. And the drunker they became, the more each man felt the need to express himself in song—every man became a *cantaor*. In spite of moments of artistic inspiration, more often than not the gatherings degenerated into drunken silliness. Eventually the men drifted home for a few hours of sleep before going off to the fields for another day.

Many evenings Antoñito and the Molinas wandered from *taberna* to *taberna*, stopping to listen wherever they found a fiesta that held promise of good *cante*. Seldom did Javier carry his instrument with him, for few of the gypsies knew how to sing with guitar, preferring to accompany themselves by rapping out *compás* with their knuckles on the bar. It was in Santiago, in the *tabernas* and patios, that Antoñito first saw the gypsies sing and dance an up-tempo version of the *soleá* that they called *bulerías*. It was a wild untamed dance, full of humor and *gracia*. But the *cante por bulerías* held little appeal for Antoñito, who preferred the somber majesty of the original *soleares* to the rowdy and noisy shouting that accompanied the raucous dance *por bulerías*.

Late one afternoon, Antoñito lazed on the stairway of the Molina patio, idly watching flies circle overhead and listening to Javier practice. The guitarist, an avid student of his instrument, practiced four to six hours each day in addition to performing at night. The music he played at that moment was unlike anything Antoñito had heard before. Impressed by its lyrical beauty, the singer asked, "What is that music, Javié?"

Javier looked up. "It's a mazurka, from the music of the opera *Lucrecia Borgia*. It was arranged for guitar by Julián Arcas. My teacher, Paco el Barbero,[10] showed it to me."

"It's beautiful! But who is Julián Arcas?"

"You haven't heard of Julián Arcas? *Hombre!* He is the greatest guitarist who ever lived. *Vamo*, he is old now, but everybody plays his music. Listen to this one...it's a *bolero* from the *zarzuela 'El diamante de la corona'* [*'The Crown Diamond'*]."[11]

Javier plunged into a bright, lively music that had his left hand dancing over the fingerboard. Several times he faltered and struggled with complex passages, muttering apologetically, "*Ozú!* That's a tough one!"

When he had finished, he explained, "That one is very difficult. I never heard Arcas play, but Paco attended many of his concerts and says that he could make the guitar speak and cry. He played a guitar called *La Leona* [The Lioness], made for him by Antonio Torres in Sevilla. They say that guitar could almost speak by itself. If only I had a guitar like that..." The guitarist's voice faded wistfully.

Antoñito asked, "But did he play our music, *el toque andaluz?*"

"Of course! He played everything. Listen!"

Javier took up the guitar again, raising it almost vertically from its resting place in his lap. The musical variations that came from the strings were lyrical, not greatly different from the operatic themes he had just played. When he had finished, he said, "Those are *falsetas*

---

[10]Francisco Sánchez Cantero: died in 1910.

[11]*zarzuela*: light opera, similar to the modern musical and very popular in Spain at that time.

[flamenco melodies] from the *soleá* of Arcas. When you hear a *tocaor* play solo, you will often hear him say, 'This is the *seguiriya* of Arcas' or 'That was the *granaína* of Arcas.' Almost all of the *falsetas* we play have the mark of Arcas on them."

"What a phenomenon he must have been! Is your teacher as good as Arcas was?"

"Paco? He's better...and he plays *más flamenco* [in a more flamenco manner]. Remember, Paco learned from the great Maestro Patiño in Cádiz. He is faster and stronger than Patiño, he knows all of the music of Arcas, and he accompanies all of the *cantes* and *bailes*. You should hear him when he accompanies Joaquín La Cherna as I have heard him in the Vera Cruz."

Having heard La Cherna sing on several occasions, Antoñito could easily imagine that to hear him with such guitar accompaniment would be inconceivably wondrous. He asked, "Where is El Barbero now?"

"I think he's in Sevilla. He's been playing there a lot, in the Café de Silverio. He always told me he wants to open a *colmao* [flamenco tavern] there and retire from performing."

"The Café de Silverio! I can't wait to go there to listen to Silverio and learn his *cantes*." After a moment's thought, Antoñito added, "Javié, do you know of anyone who sings well the *cantes* of Silverio?"

"I have heard that there is a *gachó* from here, from Jerez, who knows all of Silverio's *cantes*. His name is Salvaoriyo and he was a good friend and favorite student of the maestro. I think he was even in charge of directing the *cuadro* [performers] in Silverio's café. They say he's a great *cantaor*. I don't know where he is now, but he could probably teach you everything you want to know."

"Salvaoriyo...I have to remember that name."

The following year, Juan Junquera closed the Café Vera Cruz and Javier found himself out of work. He became more dependent upon what he could earn from giving guitar lessons, something he had done since he was ten years old, and from hiring out for private fiestas. But, more than ever, he and his brother spent time with Antonio Chacón. Antoñito wanted nothing but to sing, Javier to play the guitar, and Antonio Molina to dance. Rare was the engagement party or baptism celebration that didn't count on the presence of the three boys. It was on just such an occasion that Antoñito, twelve years old, was paid to sing for the first time.

At close to one o'clock in the morning the three boys were preparing to leave a baptism fiesta when the father of the newly baptized child offered to pay them if they would stay longer. The Molinas looked pleadingly at Antoñito. They could not afford to turn down the opportunity, and without their friend's *cante* they could not work. Antoñito knew he should go home, but he rationalized, *If my parents see that I can earn money with my singing, they will certainly give in and accept my desire to be a* cantaor.

Shortly before four in the morning, Antoñito pocketed his share of the money that had been slipped to the older Molina boy. The six *reales* [one and a half *pesetas*[12]] felt like a fortune to him, swelling his pocket with small coins and his chest with pride. He knew it would be impossible to slip through the patio gate and into his home without disturbing anyone, but he hoped his father, who normally slept deeply, would not awaken. Unfortunately, it was his father who welcomed him, roused in anger from a fitful and agitated sleep. Neither the announcement of his earnings nor his pleas were able to save Antoñito from the bite of the *tirapié*.

That beating had an unexpected effect upon the Chacón family. The sting of the strap crystallized young Antonio's resolve. Exhilarated by the six *reales* he had earned, he felt little of the remorse that normally accompanied such punishment. The money and his indifference to the beating made it clear to the boy that nothing could stop him from pursuing the *cante*.

The elder Chacón spent a restless night, his son's last words ringing in his ears: "I'm as out of place here in the *zapatería* as a guitar at a burial," the boy had said, repeating Antonio Molina's words. When the father arose in the morning he realized that, with the snap of the *tirapié*, something had snapped inside him and he could not continue the futile attempts to discipline his son. They never spoke of it, but more and more Antoñito fulfilled his obligations in the *zapatería* during the day and did as he wished at night.

---

[12]*real*: 25 *céntimos*. 100 *céntimos* equaled one *peseta*. The modern *peseta* is approximately equivalent to a USA penny, but in 1880 it was used more like the modern dollar (to get a better feeling for its actual purchasing power in dollars, multiply *pesetas* by ten). Therefore, the *real* was equivalent to a quarter.

Breva

A rainy evening early in 1881, and an excited Javier greeted Chacón in the doorway of the Molina home.

"Antonio, look at this!"

"What is it?"

"Juan Breva and Paco de Lucena are going to be in the Café del Conde!"

And without saying another word, Javier handed the singer a folded newspaper and pointed to an announcement that read:

> The Café del Conde will present, in an extraordinary function, *el gran cantador*[1] *de malagueñas*, Antonio Ortega Escalona "Juan Breva" and *el maestro lucentino de guitarra*, Francisco Díaz "El Niño de Lucena."

"Juan Breva...here!" Antonio was almost speechless. "I can't believe it. He's supposed to be the best singer from Málaga..."

"Isn't he the one who sings the new *malagueñas?*"[2] The interruption came from the other Molina, who had just appeared in the patio.

"That's him," responded Chacón. "But Javié, who is Paco de Lucena?"

"*Hombre*, El Niño Lucena is said to play the guitar *a las mil maravillas* [like a thousand miracles]. El Barbero told me that he went

---

[1] *cantador*: the correct spelling of *cantaor*.

[2] *malagueña*: a *fandango* from the province of Málaga. Each area of Andalucía developed its own variation of the *fandango*, one of the older folk musics in Spain, dating back to the Moorish occupation.

all the way to Málaga just to listen to the Lucentino,[3] who, he says, is making a lot of noise among guitarists. I really want to hear him play."

Chacón, all excitement by this point, blurted out, "We have to go. Where can we get the money?"

"What are you talking about?" It was the older Molina. Pointing at the newspaper, he explained, "See what it says here, under the announcement of the large *cuadro* of dancers...admission is *por el consumo*...we can afford a few drinks!"

El Café del Conde occupied a large, sober stone building on the Plaza del Arenal in the commercial heart of Jerez. Antonio Molina, followed by his brother and Chacón, passed through the imposing doors and found the café filled to capacity. They squeezed through a crush of men gathered along the side walls and found a place to stand at one end of the bar. Tables in the center of the smoky, noisy room were all occupied—primarily by men. The only women present were some of the dancers who had just come down from the stage, draped in immense embroidered shawls and still perspiring from their exertions.

It was still early and the *cuadro* had just completed its first performance. Two chairs sat empty at the center of the small stage set into one wall. The room quieted somewhat in anticipation as a small, wiry man strode onstage carrying a guitar. He dressed impeccably in tight striped pants that flared out over his boots, and an embroidered short jacket with velvet lapels, open in front to reveal a white ruffled shirt buttoned to the neck. There was an air of confidence, perhaps arrogance, in his erect posture and the manner in which he sat and raised his instrument into playing position. A second man followed and took the other seat.

In contrast with the guitarist, Juan Breva appeared unpretentious and humble. Middle-aged and heavy in body, he dressed well but simply, in a dark gray suit with vest, white shirt and tie. Even from the back of the room the boys felt the warmth of the smile Breva directed at his audience as he settled into his chair. He seemed relaxed, his large hands resting easily on his thighs as he looked over at El Niño de Lucena, who was adjusting the tuning of his guitar. The plinking of the strings rang out clearly in the hazy room, for the clamorous din had subsided in anticipation.

---

[3]*Lucentino*: from Lucena, a small town about forty miles south of Córdoba.

At the rear of the salon, Javier followed every move of the guitarist, mumbling a steady stream of comments into Chacón's ear: "Look how well he dresses! What a guitar...it must be very expensive...look, the sides are made of a dark wood! *Qué gorpeaó má raro!* [What an unusual *golpeador!*[4]] I have never seen one made of such dark wood."

Javier gripped Chacón's arm at the first passage of music. *"Ozú,* Antonio, how does he do that?" A thin, sweet melody, sustained like that of a mandolin, floated through the thick air, while it seemed that an invisible second guitar accompanied with simultaneous bass notes.

As the music continued, it became clear even to Chacón that it was unlike anything he had ever heard. Javier and the other guitarists of Jerez depended upon strong thumbs to play powerful driving melodies on the bass strings. Javier was unique among local guitarists in playing solo pieces and extending the range of his music into the higher registers by using his fingers to pluck the strings. But even Javier played nothing like that which poured forth from the stage of the Café del Conde on that memorable night—cascades of crystalline notes, delicate melodies, and lightening-quick scales.

Javier let out an astonished *"Ole!"* at the first rapid-fire burst of notes in a descending scale. His cry was lost amid shouts from around the room and a scattering of applause. It was unheard of for an accompanist to receive such attention. "I have never heard the *punteado*[5] played at that speed," commented Javier.

All eyes shifted away from the guitarist at the first sound of Breva's voice. It took no more than the *ay* of the singer's *temple* for Chacón to realize that he was witnessing something extraordinary. The warm-up was rich with warmth and feeling. Breva had chosen to open with the *petenera*, a popular song that had been much in vogue for several years and had only recently been converted into a flamenco *cante* worthy of respect.[6] However, it was still not a *cante* likely to appeal to the aficio-

---

[4]*golpeador*: a protective plate of hardwood (today: plastic) glued to the face of the guitar below the strings.

[5]*punteado*: *picado*, the forceful plucking of scales and melodies with alternating middle and index fingers.

[6]It is now generally accepted that the flamenco *petenera* was created about 1880 by the *cantaor* El Medina (José Rodríguez Concepción) who, although born in Jerez, spent most of his life between Sevilla and Madrid. However, there had been songs called *peteneras* in existence since at least the early 1800s.

nados of Jerez, who nourished their souls on the earthy and rough *cantes gitanos*.

Yet, even the gypsies were moved by the majesty Breva gave to the *petenera*, and his voice alone was sufficient to bring forth a steady stream of cries of approval and encouragement. The unpretentious *cantaor* gave forth a sweet, warm sound, lacking the gravelly, broken quality of gypsy voices, yet rich and strong in the low notes and powerful in the highs. The audience responded with enthusiastic applause when Breva had finished. But when the amiable *cantaor* announced in a quiet voice that his next *cante* would be *por soleá* and dedicated to the aficionados of Jerez, who "know the *cante* well," the room erupted in thunderous approval.

Juan Breva's *soleá* was more melodious than the styles commonly heard in Jerez:

Lo que intento, logro;	That which I attempt, I achieve:
yo no me quejo a mi estrella.	I do not complain about my luck.
Qué yo no he intentaíto cosita	I have never attempted anything
que no me salgo con ella.	at which I have not succeeded.
Si no fuera por mi hermano	If it weren't for my brother,
me hubiera muerto de jambre.	I would have died of hunger.
Nunca le falte a mi hermano	May my brother never lack
cachito de pan que darme.	a piece of bread to give me.

Chacón leaned toward his friend and whispered, "What is that *soleá*, where is it from?"

Javier responded, "It sounds a little like *cantes* from Sevilla[7], but I have never heard anything quite like it."

The other Molina added, "It's very much in *compás*, very danceable..."

"It *is* well done," interrupted Javier, "for a *gachó* from Málaga... but then we can't expect him to sing like a gypsy of Jerez!"

Although Chacón loved the *cante gitano*, with its unabashed emotion and rough, direct delivery, he found qualities in Breva's voice that gripped and touched him profoundly. And he became aware of something new, of the possibility of having complete mastery over one's

---

[7] What we would call today the *soleá apolá* of Triana.

voice and the *cante*. How different was this man's singing from the way workers in the taverns blurted out their coarse, drunken sentiments.

Chacón's thoughts were cut short by the renewed sound of Breva's voice. The *cantes* that followed brought the crowded room to a state of pandemonium, for the *cantaor* had begun to sing the songs of his homeland, the *fandangos* of Málaga. Many *cantaores* were beginning to sing a new type of *malagueña*, a rhythmless, ad-libbed *cante* that gave free reign to the emotional message of the *cantaor* and reduced the guitar to a minimal role of supplying occasional supporting tones. Juan Breva had unwittingly been one of those responsible for the evolution of the new *malagueña*. Although he remained rooted in the traditional dance forms, he had extended the *tercios* and augmented them melodically until they became something new and very personal.

The guitar beat out a persistent *dum-diddy, dum-diddy, dum-dum*, interspersed with occasional rapid scale passages that had Javier agape. Then, in a high, almost nasal voice, reflecting the Arabic heritage of these *fandangos* and the strident manner in which they were sung by peasants in their village fiestas, Breva opened himself completely, exposing the poetry of his soul. His words no longer spoke of the fiesta, but revealed his darkest fears and sorrows:

Ni la fuente más risueña,	Neither the most bubbling fountain,
ni el canario más sonoro,	nor the most harmonious canary,
ni la tótula en su breña,	nor the turtledove in the bush,
cantarán como yo lloro	could sing like I sing
gotas de sangre por ella.[8]	tears of blood for her.

The audience again roared its approval and then quickly silenced as the *cantaor* changed from this terse *corta* style to one *más larga*, longer and more difficult:

---

[8] All *fandangos* have six lines or *tercios* of song, but only five (or even four) lines of poetry. The difference is made up by beginning with the second line, which often sets the theme, and then starting over from the first line and continuing through the verse. A four-line verse might require the repeat of the second line again, at the end.

Tienes tan malas entrañas	You are so evil inside
que gozas en mi agonía,	that you enjoy my suffering,
pero el día llegará	but the day will come
que, llorando noche y día,	when, crying night and day,
me has de venir a buscar.[9]	you will have to come looking for me.

When Breva had finished, after close to half an hour of *malagueñas*, it seemed that the storm of applause and shouts would never subside. Many in the room had to wipe tears from their eyes. Chacón felt overwhelmed, swept away by the beauty and intensity of the songs, as well as the skill of the artist. Normally, he tried to memorize melodies when listening to singers, but this music was so unfamiliar that he could do little but experience its full emotional impact.

The *cantaor* stood on stage and raised his hands for quiet. When, at last, the noise had subsided, Breva addressed the audience. "*Gracias!* You are very kind. Now, my *compañero*, the great maestro of the guitar that is Francisco Díaz, 'El Niño de Lucena,' will play for you some *solos de guitarra.*"

With that, Breva bowed once more and departed from the stage to renewed applause, leaving behind the seated Paco de Lucena tuning his guitar. The crowd grew noisy with clinking glasses, shuffling chairs, and discussion of the merits of Breva's *cante*. Few in the room considered the guitar by itself to be worthy of attention. El Niño finished tuning, but did not play. He sat in silence, waiting. Some in the crowd noticed and began to yell for quiet or made loud shushing sounds.

Javier said suddenly, "Look, there are some chairs! Let's go...I want to be able to hear!"

The three boys dashed to an empty table near the stage just as the guitarist announced to the room, now largely quieted by curiosity, "*Señores*, I have the pleasure of playing for you original music *por tangos*, *farrucas*, and *alegrías por rosas.*"

El Niño de Lucena began to play, and such was the novelty of the music that the audience remained quiet and attentive. Javier's eyes never left the agile fingers, and an almost steady stream of utterances flowed from his lips: "*Ozú!...Ole!...Qué barbaridad!... Imposible!...Es un Diablo!* [He must be the Devil!]"

---

[9]Many words that do not appear to rhyme would actually do so when sung. In Andalusian dialect, consonants such as *d, s,* and *r* are silent or barely audible. Thus, *llegará* and *buscar* (*buscá*) would rhyme in this verse.

At the end of the *alegrías* called *rosas*, Javier turned to his companions and said, "You probably don't realize what this man has done. This *alegrías* he has played *por arriba* [E-major] is something new. It has beautiful new melodies, new techniques, and uses tones that are different from our *alegrías por medio* [in A-major]. I have to learn from this man!"

Before the others could comment, all attention returned to the stage, where Juan Breva had reappeared carrying a guitar. The astonished crowd buzzed with curiosity as the *cantaor* sat and placed the guitar on his lap.

"*Señores*," he said in a voice that was quiet yet audible in the farthest corner of the salon, "I wish to finish with the *cantes* of *mi tierra* [my land],[10] which is Vélez-Málaga,[11] because I am *Veleño*. These *fandangos* were taught to me by my mother, may she rest in peace, when I rode on the burro with her to the countryside to collect *brevas* [figs]. *Señores*, the *verdiales*[12] *de Vélez*."

With that, Breva lifted the guitar into playing position, his large, heavy hands dwarfing the instrument, and began again the droning, persistent roll of the *malagueña*. El de Lucena joined him and, with the support of the second guitar, demonstrated a new level of virtuosity in music that sparkled with lightening-quick scales and astounded his audience. Then, once more, the voice of Juan Breva filled the room:

En La Cala hay una fiesta;	In La Cala there is a fiesta;
mi madre me va a llevar,	my mother is going to take me,
y como iré tan compuesta,	and, since I will look so good,
me sacarán a bailar	they will all ask me to dance
con mi par de castañuelas.	with my pair of castanets.

---

[10]*mi tierra*: my land; can have many meanings for a Spaniard: An Andalusian outside of Spain might be referring to his country; within Spain, he could mean Andalucía; in Andalucía, he would mean his hometown.

[11]Vélez-Málaga is a small town about twenty miles east and slightly inland from Málaga.

[12]*verdiales*: All of Juan Breva's *malagueñas* would, today, be called *verdiales* (from "green" and referring to green olives called *verdiales* that are grown near Málaga) or *verdiales pa escuchar* (for listening to, rather than dancing), or *bandolás*—a word that is rejected by some. These contrast with the more primitive *verdiales* intended for dancing, with a more rigid structure and performed by groups called *pandas* to the accompaniment of orchestras of violins, guitars, mandolin-like *bandurrias*, tambourines, castanets and a variety of primitive country instruments.

These *malagueñas*, the *verdiales de Vélez*, differed considerably from those Breva had sung earlier, being lighter in mood and less elaborate. Clearly, they were sung as his mother had sung them, from a young girl's perspective. Yet Breva made them his own, and the audience, touched by the tribute to his mother, clamored for more. The singer gave them *coplas* of his own, his soaring melodies and the combined strength of the two guitars creating an effect that kept the audience spellbound.

When, at last, the two performers rose to their feet amid thunderous applause, many in the room stood and begged for more. Breva apologized, explaining that they would be performing again later in the evening and would be happy to comply with requests at that time.

The two men were mobbed when they appeared at the bar. The *cuadro* was returning to the stage as Chacón asked his friends, "Do you think we can meet them?"

"I hope so," replied Javier. "I *must* speak with El Lucena. But we couldn't even get close now, with so many others around them."

The boys sat smoking and sipping *manzanilla*, biding their time and watching for an opening. Javier entertained the other two with a story he had heard from his teacher:

"El Barbero told me that the first time El Niño visited Sevilla, to work as a soloist in Silverio's café, the other guitarists were jealous and began to spread the word that the Lucentino didn't know how to accompany, that he couldn't play in *compás*.

"Well, when El de Lucena became aware of the rumors, he came out on stage earlier than usual one night and announced, 'I am going to play a little with the *cuadro*, *pa hacer pulsación* [to warm up my hands].' He then accompanied all of the dances and stunned the other guitarists with his playing...very intricate, very much in *compás*, and *bien acoplao*, very precise in the accompaniment."

"*Qué barbaridá! Qué fenómeno!* [Outrageous! What a phenomenon!] It was Antonio Molina, who had been wondering how the guitarist would be with the dance. His brother's story had impressed him. Suddenly he sat up in his chair and said abruptly, "Look, there's Juan Junquera with Breva. Let's ask him to introduce us!"

Indeed, it was Molina's former employer in an animated conversation with the *cantaor*. The three boys made their way across the room and stood patiently, their eyes on Breva. Close up, the man seemed even more modest than he had appeared on stage, although his small-town bearing was tempered with the manners of a gentleman. He listened intently to Junquera, a pleasant smile on his round face.

When Junquera finally noticed the boys, he perceived their intent immediately and gestured for them to come closer.

"Juan, I'd like to present two young men who worked for me before I had to close my café over on Vera Cruz. Javier Molina is a fine guitarist and his brother Antonio is one of our best *bailaores*. Javier, I'm sorry I don't recall the name of your friend."

"*Señor* Breva, this is Antonio Chacón, an excellent *cantaor*."

Breva smiled as he took Antonio's outstretched hand. "Antonio, my pleasure. I must hear you sing before I leave."

"*Señor* Breva," Antonio blurted out with youthful exuberance, "I have never heard anyone sing like you. Where did you learn all of those beautiful *letras*?"

"I can only sing what is in my heart, *muchacho* [young man], so I must speak of that which I have lived and suffered. I would not feel comfortable wearing somebody else's sentiments."

Awed, Chacón could only blurt, "What genius!"

Juan Breva waved aside the flattery with a thick hand. Javier took advantage of the awkward moment to interject, "*Señor* Breva, I would really like to meet your guitarist."

The *cantaor* turned his head toward where El Niño de Lucena stood with his back to them, leaning on the bar in conversation.

"*Oye*, Paco!"

The other looked around, "Eh?"

"*Ven p'acá!* [Come here!] There is a young guitarist who would like to meet you."

El Lucena said something to his companion and came to Breva's side. He appeared even younger than he had on stage, perhaps in his early twenties.[13] He had an unusual face. Although not unattractive, his thin Romanesque nose projected without a break from a sloping forehead, giving him a somewhat rodent-like profile. Large luminous protruding eyes had a softening effect, producing the sensitive appearance of an artist.

Upon being presented to Javier and the others, the guitarist offered a slender hand and, in a thin, nasal voice, said, "Pleased to meet you."

Before anyone could respond, he sucked deeply on his cigarette,

---

[13] born 1859.

said, "It's been a pleasure," and turned back to the bar and his interrupted conversation.

Breva shrugged his shoulders in resignation. "That's the way he is. But he's a phenomenal guitarist." Then, almost as an apology, and in a conspiratorial tone, the *cantaor* asked Javier, "Have you heard what he did to El Águila in the Café de Bernardo in Málaga?"

Javier shook his head.

Breva glanced over his shoulder at the guitarist, leaned slightly toward the boys, and in a lowered voice began his story:

"*Pues*, listen well, because this has *gracia*.[14] Paco, known as El Lentejo at that time, came to Málaga from Lucena to learn to play flamenco. He knew how to play the guitar, but he had never accompanied the *cante* or *baile*. In fact, he had once been embarrassed to find that he couldn't accompany a *cantaor* and *bailaor* who came to Lucena to perform in the local *casino* [men's club]. So he came to Málaga, where he found work as a barber's assistant, a trade he had learned in Lucena. The barber was *Don* Salvador Ruiz, a great friend of artists and bullfighters. *Don* Salvador is also a good friend of mine, you know...he told me this story himself."

Breva paused to savor his drink and then continued: "*Pues*, when *Don* Salvador saw the great *afición* and talent of the boy, he began to take him around to all of the *cafés cantantes*. Paco, nicknamed 'El Niño de Lucena' by the barber, watched and listened carefully. Later, in his room, he practiced what he had learned and quickly improved his execution and knowledge. At the same time, he didn't stop composing solos...solos that were models of *compás* and filled with strange notes.

"*En fin*, at that time there were no fewer than eleven *cafés cantantes* in Málaga. One afternoon, Salvador went to the Café de Bernardo to give the owner a shave. *Don* Bernardo happened to mention how unfortunate it was that he would have to cancel the performances that evening due to illness of the guitarist, one Francisco Reina...better known as Paco el Águila.

"Salvador quickly offered, 'I have a young apprentice in my shop who plays a great deal and very cleanly. What I don't know is whether he would be useful in playing for such good artists as you have in your *cuadro*.'

---

[14]*gracia*: literally "grace," but is widely used to mean humor, wit, personality.

" 'Well,' replied Bernardo, 'considering that you say he plays well, see if he can come early, before time to work, to rehearse. If he does well in rehearsal, the job is his.'

"Of course El Niño was thrilled. But he missed the rehearsal, arriving just before time to go on stage, as if everything had been arranged. The artists asked him, 'Have you played for a *cuadro* before?'

"The cocky youngster, with the nerve that he had, replied, 'Me? Never! But you will see how well it comes out."

"And so it was. They sang and danced, and it came out a complete success, with *compás* and harmony. *Total, qué*...Paco continued to fill in for El Águila and, when the latter returned, El Niño played as second guitarist for the *cuadro* and played solos between shows. But El Niño did not understand that the second guitarist should not attempt to outshine the first. So he played *falseta* after *falseta*, and naturally the public reacted enthusiastically, with ovations and cries of *'Valiente, niño!'*

"Night after night El Águila smoldered with anger and resentment. Finally, unable to endure it any longer, he thought of a trick that would put the youngster in his place. One night, when he went out to play alone with the singer, he pulled a glove from his pocket, placed it on his left hand, and proceeded to accompany the *cante*. When the audience saw the gloved hand fretting the strings, they applauded wildly. But El de Lucena hardly seemed to notice. When it came his turn to go *alante*[15] to play solo, he sat down and very deliberately removed one shoe and sock."

Breva deliberately paused and took his time to light a cigarette. The boys couldn't be bothered with drinks or smokes—they were practically holding their breaths in suspense. At last the *cantaor* continued.

"Placing the sock on his left hand, El de Lucena then played a complicated solo that drove the audience into a delirious frenzy. After that, El Águila had no recourse but to accept the merit of the young guitarist."

Breva finished by saying, "So that is the way of this phenomenon. I am fortunate to have him playing for me...he has been very busy

---

[15]*alante*: a deformation of *por delante*, "in front." In this case it means to go to the front of the stage to perform solo, in contrast with *atrás* or *por detrás*, at the back of the stage to accompany the dancers. Most *cantaores* seek the prestige of singing *alante*, as soloists, and some refuse to ever sing *atrás*. Also seen as *p'alante* and *p'atrás*.

giving solo guitar concerts these last few years."

The *cuadro* had finished and it was time for Breva's second performance. The boys stayed until the early hours of the morning, enthralled by all that they saw and heard. They didn't attempt to impose further upon Breva or Lucena that night. The two artists were to be in Jerez for a week, so there would be ample opportunity to attempt to speak with them.

Each evening, the three aspiring artists went early to the Café del Conde, hoping to catch Juan Breva before he went on stage. On several occasions, they had an opportunity to speak with the *cantaor*. Breva was always considerate and gave freely of his time. He spoke with the boys about *cante* and told them of his humble childhood. His artistic name had been inherited from his grandfather, although as a youth he too had sold *brevas* by singing his *pregón* in the streets of Vélez and Málaga:

Brevas de los montes	Figs from the mountains
de Vélez-Málaga	of Vélez-Málaga
son las más dulces;	are the sweetest;
las doy pa'probarlas.	I'll give you some to taste.

Chacón basked in the great man's presence. Javier, being more interested in the elusive Paco de Lucena, was thrilled one afternoon to spot the guitarist seated by himself at an outdoor café. Timidly, he approached and asked apologetically, "*Señor* Lucena…"

El de Lucena raised his head with a questioning look. After a moment, his dark eyes softened in recognition. "Ah, the guitarist! Have a seat. What do you drink?"

Slipping into an esparto-grass chair, the boy replied, "*Manzanilla*."

Lucena snapped his fingers. "Waiter, bring the *muchacho* a cognac!"

Javier seldom drank anything but cheap wine or *manzanilla*. He mumbled, "*Gracias,* maestro!"

"*Nada, hombre!* So you play, eh?" A hint of distain revealed itself in the thin voice of the *tocaor*. "Which *toques?*" [flamenco guitar styles]

Javier, recovering somewhat from his feeling of intimidation and seemingly oblivious to sarcasm in Lucena's question, sat up straight and replied, "All of the *toques* of Jerez, and solos such as the mazurka from *Lucrecia Borgia* and the bolero from *El Diamante de la Corona…*"

Lucena looked up from his glass with a raised eyebrow. He had not expected to find a young guitarist who knew much more than how to pound out rhythmic accompaniment. "*Chiquillo!* Those are things of Arcas. Where did you learn such music?"

"My teacher, Paco el Barbero..."

"El Barbero? Don't tell me! That man is a monster on the guitar."

Lucena's opinion of the young man before him had changed considerably. Although he remained somewhat aloof, the two of them fell into warm conversation. At one point Javier asked, "Maestro, what is the technique you used to begin the *petenera*?"

"Oh, you mean *el trino*...the tremolo, as it is called by *los músicos*.[16] I am the first to use it in the *toque flamenco*."

"How did you learn it?"

"*Pues*, listen, it was like this. When I was a child I worked in the fields with my family. In order to earn more money, I was apprenticed to a barber. I chose to work for Maestro Espinoza because he knew how to play the guitar. He taught me everything he knew and soon I had exhausted his repertoire. But then, one of his clients, El Marquez de Campo de Aras, who was a marvel at playing the guitar from music notation, learned that I played and invited me to his home. He was pleased by what I played for him and asked me, 'Would you like me to teach you?'

" 'Of course,' I told him, 'but there is one problem.'

" 'What is that?'

" 'You play only by notes, *en fino* [classical music], and I don't like anything but flamenco.'

" '*Hombre*,' he said to me, 'the little bit of flamenco that I play is very difficult, but if you like it, I will teach it to you.'

"Then he took up the guitar and began to play. I watched, amazed by so much complexity, and by exercises that were strange and unknown to me."

"*Total que*...eventually I learned all that the marquis could teach me, all of his flamenco and many of his other techniques...scales, tremolo, and various arpeggios with two and three fingers. That same marquis gave me my first good guitar, the one I took with me when I went to Málaga to learn how to accompany the *cante* and *baile*."

---

[16]*Los músicos* refers to musicians who play from written notation (today we would say "classical guitarists"). Flamenco guitarists were very suspicious of anyone who could read music, and many felt that, if you could read music, you could not play flamenco.

Javier had been listening with intense interest. Now, as El Lucena sipped on his drink, the boy asked, "Maestro, would you show me how the tremolo is done?"

El Lucena paused a moment. His confidence was such that, unlike many guitarists who were secretive about their music, he felt no need to hide anything. Nobody would ever perform as he did.

"Come to the café early tonight, when I am warming up, and I'll show you. But, I need to remind you of something, *muchacho*. It's fine to learn all these fancy techniques and solos, but never forget that the *compás* [rhythm] is the soul of flamenco. Without *compás* there is no magic...and without magic, there is no art. It is the same with singing. The *cantaor* who doesn't understand the *compás* might sing well, but he can't sing the *cante*. He is like the man who writes well, but doesn't really know how to write because there are so many errors in his spelling and handwriting. There are *cantaores* who have a beautiful voice, but they don't reach your heart because they don't know the *compás*...how to measure the *cante*. And there are others who have hardly any voice, but they use it in a measured way and you have to say, *'Eso e güeno!'* [That's really good!] There are *cantaores* who sing what they know, and *cantaores* who know what they sing.

"So, always remember, *muchacho*...the guitar and the *cante* must always follow the same path, with the same *compás*, because, if not, it's like a fight between two cats rather than *cante flamenco*."

"I understand, maestro. Don't worry about me...I may play solos, but I have dedicated myself to accompanying the *cante* and *baile*."

"*Bien!* Come tonight and I will see what I can show you."

As the two guitarists rose and parted to go their separate ways, El de Lucena called after Javier, "Muchacho!"

"Yes, maestro," said the youth, turning back.

"One more thing. Never forget...a guitar is like a woman. You have to know how to *pegarle el palo* [lay the wood to her] when she deserves it, show her who's the boss...but then you also have to remember to say, *'Qué guapa eres!'* [How beautiful you are!]"

Javier could hardly wait for the evening and arrived at the Café del Conde well before Paco de Lucena. He flushed with pride when El de Lucena acknowledged him upon entering the café, but waited until the guitarist was well into his warm-up before disturbing him.

"Maestro, the guitar sounds beautiful! Who made it?"

"*Ah, muchacho!* You like it? This was made for me by Antonio de Torres,[17] in Almería. It is the best guitar I have ever owned."

"What is that dark wood? I have never seen anything like it."

"The body is made of *palosanto*, or as some call it, *palobrazil*, because it comes from Brazil. Torres uses it only on his best guitars.[18] Not only is the rosewood very beautiful, but I feel it gives more sound than the cypress you are accustomed to seeing."

"It looks like it has been damaged...I see some cracks on the side, and it appears that the top has been repaired."

"You are observant, *muchacho*." El de Lucena lowered his voice. "I'm going to tell you one of my secrets. When I get a new guitar, the first thing I do is to smash it against a table. A guitar always sounds better after it has been repaired."

Javier didn't know what to think about this revelation, but it seemed a good moment to try for another secret. "Maestro, the tremolo?"

True to his word, El de Lucena showed Javier how the tremolo was accomplished by sounding a bass string with the thumb, followed by the plucking of a treble string with the ring, middle, and index fingers in succession.[19] When done rapidly the effect was of a sustained treble note accompanied by melody in the bass. Javier also learned that El de Lucena had invented several ways to play arpeggios with three fingers rather than the customary two, and that his *picado* owed its speed to the practicing of scales he had learned from the marquis.

---

[17] Antonio de Torres (1817-1892) is considered to have been instrumental in creating the modern guitar through his innovations in size, shape, and bracing.

[18] At this time no distinction was made between woods to be used in the *guitarra de tablado* (flamenco guitar) and the *guitarra de musica fina* (classical guitar). It was instead a matter of economics: Cheaper guitars, the type likely to be owned by flamencos, were made of common Spanish cypress, which the builder could cut for himself, and featured wooden tuning pegs (like a violin). Guitars made of more exotic woods, such as rosewood or maple, and employing mechanical tuners, were of necessity more expensive. It is likely that the preference for the dry, percussive sound associated with flamenco guitar developed later, as a consequence of the customary use of the cypress guitar, rather than the wood being chosen originally to get that sound. This concept is well documented by José L. Romanillos in his excellent book, *Antonio de Torres: Guitar Maker*.

[19] This is the standard three-finger tremolo used by classical guitarists. It would be another 25 years before the great Ramón Montoya would invent the modern four-finger flamenco tremolo.

Javier was ecstatic. In the weeks after Paco de Lucena departed from Jerez, the young guitarist practiced diligently all he had learned, and soon had invented many new melodies to add to his growing repertoire.

Chacón never sang for Juan Breva, but meeting the great man and listening to him sing left a profound impression on the aspiring *cantaor*. Not only had he discovered that there were other ways to sing than those he had grown up with, but he found a man who lived the kind of life he had imagined for himself—*and the man was not a gypsy!*

Fosforito

Several months after Juan Breva's departure from Jerez de la Frontera, as the baking heat of summer settled over the city, a young singer arrived from Cádiz to make his debut. At age fourteen, Francisco Lema was a tall, gangly youth with a winning smile. His height and slender build had earned him the nickname "Matchstick," and so it was as "Fosforito" that he had been brought by Juan Junquera to join the *cuadro* in his new café, El Palenque.

El Palenque—so named for the cockfights held there on Sunday afternoons—had become a favorite haunt of Chacón, Javier, and Antonio. There, they listened to the best singers of Jerez, to Joaquín la Cherna, Diego el Marrurro, or to El Loco Mateo and his sister, La Loca. They delighted in the *baile* of the many superb dancers who had learned their art in the gypsy barrios of Jerez. Among their favorites were La Chorrúa, a devastatingly sultry beauty, and the diminutive and dynamic María la Macarrona from the Barrio Santiago. Most of the women specialized in the *baile por soleá*, and none did it better than Juana Peña. But it was another Juana who had caught the attention of Antonio Molina. Antonio had become enamored of Juana Antúnez, a sultry young gypsy dancer whose maturity belied her twelve years of age. His attempts to speak with the girl alone were constantly frustrated by the ever-watchful eye of her older sister, Fernanda, a blond beauty and a popular performer, if not as gifted as the younger girl.

Juan Junquera felt sympathetic toward the boys and allowed them to stand at the back of the café when they had no money to spend. That is where they were the night Fosforito first appeared on stage. The young Jerezanos were drawn to the *cantaor* immediately. The maturity of his singing impressed them, and when they spoke with him they were won over by the warmth of his personality. Jovial and easygoing, Fosforito leapt at any opportunity for a joke or prank—except when it came to the *cante*, which he took very seriously. Although the same age as Chacón, he towered over all three of his new friends. At first meeting, Antonio Molina had looked up at him and exclaimed, "*Ozú*, you're longer than a day without food!"

The four boys became inseparable during Fosforito's six weeks in Jerez, wandering the streets by day and spending nights in El Palenque.

Fosforito's preferred *cante* was the *malagueña*—a *malagueña* very different from that sung by Juan Breva. High in the mountains northwest of the city of Málaga, in the little village of Álora, the festive *verdiales* had taken a different path. The thin mountain air and the slow village life had created a more somber and majestic form of these *fandangos*. When men of Álora, men such as Juan el Perote and El Canario, took their *malagueñas* to the cafés of Málaga, the *cantes* created a furor and were soon on everyone's lips. As they gained in popularity, the songs evolved into an ad-libbed expression that gradually freed itself from the restraints of rhythm. More and more, as the melodies became increasingly elaborate, the guitar was relegated to a minor role, supplying occasional supporting tones and short melodies between *tercios*.

The *malagueñas* that reached Cádiz bore little resemblance to the original *verdiales*. They also had little in common with the *cante gitano*. Where gypsy songs—the *seguiriya*, *soleá*, and *martinete*—communicated through direct brutal confrontation with deep emotions, in often monotonous chants broken by cries, shouts, and sobs, the new *malagueña* of the *gachó* transmitted its message through more literate verses, beautiful melodies, ornamented flourishes in the Arabic tradition, and the use of a modulated voice that more often than not lacked the gypsy *rajo*.

Fosforito excelled in the new *malagueña*, his clear, controlled voice well suited to the flowing melodies and sentimental lyrics. Chacón loved to listen to him sing. As with the *cante* of Juan Breva, he found that Fosforito's *malagueñas* stirred him in a different way than did his beloved *cante gitano*. He didn't give it much conscious thought, but it seemed to be the technique, the control of the voice, and the emphasis on melody that appealed to him. He found that these songs adapted easily to his voice and he didn't have to strain to sing them as he did with the gypsy styles.

One hot, dusty afternoon found the boys lounging about the Molina patio, Chacón and Fosforito avidly discussing the *cante* and illustrating their points to the accompaniment of Javier's guitar. Antonio Molina lay back on the cool tiles, smoking cigarettes and tossing out the occasional comment.

"I'm more bored than an oyster...let's go down to the plaza!" The *bailaor*, tired of the endless discussions, often suggested forays to the Plaza de Santiago to tease girls, or dared Chacón and his younger brother to accompany him to the local brothels.

The other three ignored him.

"You really learned from El Mellizo?" Chacon asked of Fosforito, envy apparent in his voice.

"Yes, right in his house, which is not far from mine in the Barrio de Santa María. Every day I used to go to learn from him before he went out in the evenings. He was very strict with me and helped me to perfect myself, to learn the secrets of the *cante*."

Fosforito spoke intensely of his mentor, drops of sweat gathering in his furrowed brow and running down the length of his narrow, pointed nose. "He taught me to give shadings to my voice, to have strength in the high notes and control in the middle range, to dominate my throat. He showed me how to produce *ayes* that, as he says, 'will give shivers like knife stabs,' and how to tear the guts out of the *coplas* and bring the music to life."

"What luck you have had!" Chacón was impressed. "Do you think he is as great as Silverio?"

"Enrique is the greatest there is..."

"But Silverio sings everything and, besides, he has created his own *seguiriyas* and..."

"Look, Antonio, Enrique not only knows all of the *cantes*, but he sings them better than those who specialize in only one or two. He is a genius. He doesn't know music, in fact he can't even read or write, but he has created new *soleares*, *seguiriyas*, *malagueñas*, and many more."

Stymied in the defense of his idol, Chacón changed track. "Silverio is very rich. Does El Mellizo earn a lot of money?"

"*Hombre, que va! Es un gitano mu raro.* [Are you kidding? He is a very eccentric gypsy]. With all that he knows, and as crazy as he is about the *cante*, he doesn't even try to make a living by singing. He is a *matarife* [slaughterman] in the public slaughterhouse of Cádiz. Do you know what he does after a day of work in the slaughterhouse? Instead of going home, he buys a paper of fried fish and goes to the church to listen to the *cantes* of the priests as they say Mass. He listens and listens, and then, walking home later, he hums what he has heard and puts it into his flamenco."

"*Ozú, que raro!*" [Jesus, how strange!]

"Is he very religious?" Intrigued, Javier had stopped playing to listen.

"I don't really know," replied Fosforito.

"I can tell you about gypsies and religion," interrupted Antonio with a smirk on his face. He had been lounging in the background, seemingly not listening. "This *gitano*, a bit tipsy, is passing by a church and sees a woman seated at a table in the entrance. On the table, a tray containing a few coins. He goes up to her and asks, '*Oigozté* [*Oiga usted*: Excuse me], can one know the purpose of that money?'

"The woman answers, 'It has been given to save blessed souls from Purgatory.'

"The *gitano* holds up a *peseta* and says, 'Tell me, is this enough to get my family out of there?'

"The woman says, 'If you do this act of charity, I assure you that all the souls of your relatives will cease to suffer and will go straight to Heaven.'

"The *gitano* tosses the coin into the tray, saying, '*Pos*, there you are!' And he continues down the street. But a few minutes later he returns and asks, 'Does it take long for the souls to get out of Purgatory?'

"The woman answers, 'No *señor*. The moment you made your offering the souls of your relatives were on their way to Heaven. God's mercy is infinite.'

"Hearing that, the *gitano* retrieves his coin from the tray and, putting it into his pocket, says, '*Pos*, I did enough in getting them out...now they would be fools to go back!' "

Antonio laughed loudest at his own joke.

"I don't know how religious El Mellizo is," said Fosforito, all seriousness once more, "but he does sing about God in his *cantes*. There is a *seguiriya* that goes:

*Ay, pare mío, Jesú
de Santa María,
que estos pesares que
    [mi cuerpo terela[1]]
sean alegrías!*

Ay, My Father, Jesus
of Saint Mary,
let these sorrows that
    [weigh my body down]
become joys!

"And he sings this *soleá*:

*En mis cortas oraciones,
anaquero con Undebé
en ver lo poco que somos,
los probes de los calé.*[2]

In my brief prayers,
I speak with God,
on seeing how insignificant we are,
we poor gypsies.

"Here's one more, *por malagueña*:

*Hincaíta de rodillas,
a mi Dios me encomendé.
Qué remedio buscaría
pa olvidar yo tu querer?
Y me dijo que no había."*

Down on my knees,
I turned myself over to my God.
What cure could I look for
in order to forget your love?
And He told me there was none."

"*Qué bonito, hombre*," exclaimed Chacón. "Enrique el Mellizo must be a genius!"

"You can hear the music of the Mass in it...*Qué barbaridad!*" It was Javier, intrigued by tone he hadn't heard before. Sing it again Francisco, *a ver si lo cojo yo!*" [to see if I can catch onto the accompaniment!]

The boys passed the remainder of the afternoon repeating El Mellizo's *malagueña*. Shadows had cloaked the patio and brought relief from the heat by the time Javier had worked out a satisfactory accompaniment and Chacón had committed the song to memory.

Early one evening, Chacón and the Molinas wandered into El Palenque to find Fosforito relaxing in preparation for his night's work. Outside, the balmy air carried a trace of jasmine from neighboring patios, but the atmosphere inside the café was heavy and noxious, reeking of

---

[1]*terelar*: gypsy word for *tener*, to have.
[2]Gypsy words: *anaquerar*, to speak; *Undebé*, God; *los calé*, gypsies.

tobacco, sherry, and fried squid. No sooner had they ordered drinks than Chacón began hammering his friend for more information about the mysterious El Mellizo.

"Francisco, you say El Mellizo won't sing for money?"

"*Hombre, que va!* [That's not true!] He sings in fiestas and he has worked in the cafés, but he only sings when he feels like it. He works in the slaughterhouse and sometimes he goes with the matador Manuel Hermosilla as *puntillero*,[3] so he doesn't have to sing. Besides, *es mu raro* [he's very eccentric]. He will be with his friends, very agreeable, even funny, when all of a sudden, in an instant, he changes. He becomes very sad and distracted, like a madman, and he doesn't want to know anything or talk to anybody. He just goes off alone…"

"Where does he go?"

"Who knows?" He disappears for days, and then reappears as if nothing had happened, smiling and recognizing everyone. They say he goes out on the *murallas*[4] [seawalls] and sings to the sea. He even sings about it in one of his *seguiriyas*:

Me asomé a la muralla	I went up on the seawall
y me respondió el viento:	and the wind answered me:
'Pa que suspira y por qué [pasas pena]	'Why do you sigh and why do you [suffer]
si no hay remedio?'	if there is no hope of a solution?'

"When he's like that, all the money in the world can't get him to sing for you. He'd rather go alone to sing to the water…or go down to the Capuchinos asylum to sing to the poor *locos*."

Fosforito saw that he had a captive audience. Chacón and Javier were wide-eyed, as if listening to a ghost story. The young *Gaditano*[5] couldn't resist milking his subject further.

"Enrique Ortega told me that one night when El Mellizo was singing on the seawall near the governor's house, a *sereno* [night watch-

---

[3]*puntillero*: bullfighter's assistant, the one who administers the coup de grace by severing the bull's spinal chord with a small knife.

[4]*murallas*: The ancient seawalls of Cádiz. The city sits at the tip of a peninsula, like an island connected to the mainland by a narrow strand. On three sides, wide seawalls drop far down to the sea below.

[5]*Gaditano*: a person from Cádiz. It derives from the Phoenician and Roman names for the city: *Gadir, Gades*.

man] approached him and said, 'Listen here, don't you know you can't sing at this hour?' El Mellizo was about to be arrested and taken away when the governor appeared on his balcony and yelled out, 'Listen here, *sereno!* Please do me the favor of allowing him to continue!' Can you imagine! The guard departed and the drunken Enrique continued singing."

"*Un monstruo!*" was all Chacón could say. "The man is a giant!" The boy's head spun with visions of the world of *cante* that must surround El Mellizo in Cádiz.

"Enrique has only one flaw," continued Fosforito.

The other three looked at the Gaditano in surprise.

"He's one of the ugliest men you will ever see...uglier than a tortoise. I heard that once he was in the back room of a tavern with friends having coffee. There were signs in that tavern saying 'Singing Prohibited.' But Enrique was in the mood to sing, so he sang. The tavern owner burst into the room, and when he saw who was there, he said, '*Ojú*, I thought there was an angel singing in here, and now I find it's the devil!' "

Fosforito's stay came to an end far too soon for his new friends. After more than a month in Jerez, he was contracted to sing in Puerto de Santa María. At first the Jerezanos found their days empty without the easygoing companionship of the young Gaditano, but they soon fell back into the nightly routine of making the rounds of *tabernas*, cafés, and fiestas.

In the fall of that year, 1883, Juan Junquera reopened the Café Vera Cruz. Antonio Molina returned to dance and Javier was hired to play second guitar to Luis Vargas "Juanero," son-in-law of Junquera and a mediocre guitarist at best. With both Molinas working, fourteen-year-old Chacón was at a loss. It meant the end of nights spent going patio to patio and *taberna* to *taberna* with his companions in search of fiesta, or sitting for hours in the taverns and cafés in the hope of being hired.

The Molinas appealed to Junquera, asking him to hire Chacón also. But Junquera was not interested. Chacón was young and inexperienced. There were so many others who were much better. The brothers persisted, pleading and giving the young *cantaor* such high recommendations that, in the end, Junquera relented and agreed to try him for a few days. Chacón was given a minor role in the *cuadro*, primarily singing for the dance of Antonio Molina. But he was uncomfortable on stage. He wore ill-fitting borrowed clothes, and he found that his voice did not have the power needed to be heard clearly over the dancers, two guitars, and the noise of the crowd. In attempting to be heard, he often shouted, causing him to sing off-pitch.

At the end of a week, Junquera took the boy aside, gave him six *reales*, and said with brutal gypsy frankness, "*No sirves, nene* [You won't do, child], it's not working out. Just being from Jerez is not enough to please the public."

No sirves, nene! Chacón's face burned with humiliation, and those words reverberated in his mind for days. He vowed that one day Junquera would beg to hire him and he would refuse to work for the man. For the moment, all he could do was to continue to sing in baptisms and fiestas, although, more and more, he found that his thin, childish voice betrayed him. The vocal qualities that had been appealing in a ten-year-old were no longer an asset to an aspiring professional. And to make matters worse, his voice often cracked or wandered off pitch at inappropriate moments, as if it could not decide whether it belonged to a child or an adult.

Most evenings, Chacón wandered the Plaza Orellana, stopping at the *fraguas*, *tabernas*, and anywhere that men gathered for a few moments of drink and song. Not infrequently, he ended up in the patio on Calle Alamo. He had been warmly welcomed by the Torre family ever since the time he sang at the baptism of the newborn Manuel, now a husky four-year-old.[6]

To reach the Torre patio, the youth had to pick his way carefully up a rutted street that served as a toilet for the gypsy families. From a distance he could hear the sporadic crowing of the fighting roosters kept by Juan Torre in makeshift cages. On entering the doorway, he would expel his held breath and was usually relieved to find that only a hint of the stale, pungent odor of the street had followed him inside. In the tiny communal courtyard he was likely to find young Manuel sprawled naked amid the greyhound dogs owned by Torre's neighbor, El Marrurro. The sleek hunting dogs would leap to their feet, growling menacingly until they recognized the newcomer, and then greet him with wagging tails.

---

[6]Manuel Torre would grow up to become one of flamenco's greatest figures, renowned as much for his eccentric ways as his great *cante*.

Most of the Torre family worked in the fields surrounding Jerez, including Juani and Juan, who were older than Chacón, and Gabriela, a dark-skinned younger girl with jet-black hair who tended to giggle when the aspiring *cantaor* came to visit. Torre's wife, Tomasa Loreto, like her brother Joaquín la Cherna, was fair-skinned with brown hair. Her appearance and her family name suggested that she was more *cuchuchí* [*gachó-gitano* mix] than pure gypsy. In the barrios of San Miguel and Santiago it was not uncommon to find mixed marriages. In almost all cases the non-gypsy, whether husband or wife, adopted the ways of the gypsies and soon became completely integrated into their lifestyle. So it was with Tomasa, who felt pride in her gypsy heritage and never considered herself to be other than *gitana de pura cepa* [of pure gypsy stock].

Chacón loved to listen to Tomasa sing soothing *nanas* to lull her youngest son, Manuel Luis, to sleep. The songs reminded him of when, as a child, he used to try to stay awake to listen to his mother's lullabies, although he never made it through an entire verse. . The *nanas* sung by Tomasa were more like the *cante gitano*, more haunting than those of Mama Chacón:

Mi niñito va a ser bueno	My baby is going to be good
porque se quiere dormir,	because he wants to go to sleep;
tiene un ojito cerrado	he has one little eye closed
y el otro no lo puede abrir.	and he can't open the other.
Duérmete, niño chiquito;	Go to sleep, little boy;
mira, que viene la mora,	look, here comes the Moor,
preguntando puerta en puerta:	going door to door, asking:
"Cuál el el niño que llora?"	"Which is the child that is crying?"

Juan "El Torre" found it hard to resist the enthusiasm of the young *gachó*. "Toñico," he would say, "have you heard this one?" And then he would launch into song *por seguiriya* or *martinete*. When he had finished, a story was sure to follow, telling the boy where he had learned the *cante*, or who had created it.

On one occasion, Torre found Antoñito playing in the dust with his son Manuel—the little gypsy always greeted the young *cantaor* joyfully, running up to hug his leg and begging him to sing. "Toñico," grunted El Torre, in that unmistakable deep voice, "listen to this!" And, seating himself in a rickety chair, he sang an immense *seguiriya*:

Dices que duermes sola;	You say you sleep alone;
mientes como hay Dios,	you lie, as sure as there is a God,
porque de noche, en el	because at night, in your thoughts,
[*pensamiento,*]	
dormimos los dos.	we sleep together.

This single verse expanded into a magnificent song through repeated words and phrases, the stretching of single words into intricate melodies, and the insertion of prolonged "*ayes.*" The result was a majestic and spiritual *cante*.

"Do you know whose *cante* that is?" asked Torre when he had finished.

"Isn't it the *seguiriya* of *El Señor* Manuel Molina?" replied Chacón.

"*Sí, muchacho*, it is indeed the *cante* of the great *Señor* Curro Molina, as we called him."

"He's dead, isn't he?"

"Yes, he died a few years ago, may he rest in peace. The poor man could no longer sing, and people who saw him wandering the streets didn't realize that he had once been a great artist. I knew him when he was '*un señor*,' very dignified and serious, with a power in his voice that was beyond the imagination. Listen to this." And Torre sang the verse that began, "*M'asomé a la muralla...*" It was the very *letra* that Fosforito had attributed to El Mellizo, only sung with more power and mastery.

"My friend Fosforito told me that El Mellizo used to sing that one on the wall in Cádiz..."

"*Sí, sí, chiquiyo!*" El *Señor* Curro Molina and El Mellizo were very good friends. Molina created that *letra* when he was sick, when he was losing his hearing. That's why he sang '...the wind said to me: Why do you sigh and complain of your suffering when there is no cure?' *El probe* [the poor man[7]] went deaf from the power of his own voice."

With great interest, Chacón absorbed all he heard. But he was not the only one enthralled by the *cante* and the stories. Little Manuel stood at his side, unmoving except to fidget with his genitals and occa-

---

[7]*probe*: *pobre*; poor

sionally scratch his unruly jet-black hair. The youngster showed a fascination with the *cante* far beyond that of his brothers and sisters, his dirt-streaked face a picture of intense concentration as he watched and listened.

The tiny patio of Juan Torre became a veritable school of *seguiriyas* for young Chacón. In addition to El Torre, he was exposed to two of the great *seguiriyeros* of the time. Joaquín la Cherna frequently visited his sister, and Diego el Marrurro shared two tiny rooms in the Torre patio with his wife and children. Marrurro's doorway, just inside the entryway to the right, was so low that Torre had to bend almost double to enter. Diego, a short man in his thirties, was the most successful professional *cantaor* of San Miguel, although he was not gypsy. His singing had taken him to the theaters and cafés of Sevilla, as well as those of Jerez. Chacón had heard him often in the Vera Cruz.

It was because of El Marrurro that Chacón had begun to carry a *varita de estilo*, a singer's style stick. While Chacón made due with a slender tree branch, El Marrurro's *vara* had been carefully carved and polished. Like most professional *cantaores*, Diego was seldom without this instrument, this *bastón de mando del cante* [staff to command the *cante*]. When he sang he held it lightly about one-third of the way down and tapped out the rhythm of his song.[8]

El Marrurro had a unique manner of singing the *seguiriyas*. In contrast with the prolonged and majestic wail of *El Señor* Manuel Molina, the *cante* of El Marrurro was shorter and released its anguish in two *ayes* that choked off the song as the *cantaor* fought with his emotions and then burst forth in an overflow of grief to continue the melody of the *tercio*. They were not notes that sobbed, but sobs that sang. His verse went:

Por los siete dolores	Through the seven pains
que mi Dios pasó,	that My Lord suffered,
los ha pasaíto la mare de	also went the mother of my soul,
[*mi arma,*]	
de mi corazón	the mother of my heart.

---

[8]The custom of using a staff to mark the *cante* probably originated with nomadic gypsies who carried the *vara* both as a walking stick and as a highly specialized instrument for use in the buying and selling of livestock. A *vara* is a unit of measurement equal to 83.59 centimeters, or a little less than a yard. Two *varas* was a standard used in measuring the height of a horse at the shoulders.

But when El Marrurro sang, it came out as a profound, pain-filled *cante*:

> A...y, por los siete, ayii, ayii, dolores
> que mi Dios pasó
> por los siete, ayii, ayii, dolores
> que mi Dios pasó
> los ha pasaíto la mare de mi arma,
> de mi corazón,
> los ha pasaíto la mare de mi arma,
> de mi corazón.

Joaquín La Cherna, a field worker like his brother-in-law, had a more primitive and direct way of intoning the *seguiriyas*. His broken, untrained voice cut right to the heart of his emotions in a plaintive *seguiriya* that expressed its pain as if from a bleeding wound:

Día grande, mare,	It was a great day, mother,
el que la encontré;	that on which I found her;
lo he señalao a punta é navaja	with the point of a knife I
sobre la pared.	carved it on the wall.

Once, when La Cherna had sung a *seguiriya* that Chacón did not recognize, the boy asked, "What was that *cante*, *tío* [uncle; said out of respect for an elder]? It was very different from what you usually sing."

"That *cante*...that *cante* is of Paco la Luz. Paco is from my barrio, from Santiago. We used to sing together often, but now he spends most of his time in Sevilla where his daughter is becoming famous singing his *cante*. That is why you haven't heard him. But everyone sings the *seguiriyas* of Paco la Luz in my barrio. The one who really knew those *cantes* was Sarvaoriyo..."

"Sarvaoriyo!" blurted Chacón in surprise. "Javié told me that this Sarvaoriyo knows the *cantes* of Silverio like nobody else."

"Yes, that's him. He was the best disciple of both Silverio and Paco la Luz. He was extraordinary, that *gachó*. Like Silverio, he was not *gitano*, but he could sing the *cantes gitanos* very well...*sí, mu bien, con la voz afillá y tó* [yes, very well, with a rough gypsy voice and all]. But he retired from the *cante* very young and left Jerez. I don't know where he went."

Disappointment showed clearly on Chacón's face. For a moment he had thought he might learn where to look for the elusive Salvaoriyo.

Winter came and went in Jerez. The cold biting winds and rains gave way to the fragrant blossoming of the spring of 1884. Fosforito returned to sing in the Café Vera Cruz for three weeks. His performances in Puerto de Santa María and other towns of the province of Cádiz had matured him considerably, both in his singing and in his stage presence. The return to Jerez cemented his friendship with Chacón and the Molinas.

The stifling heat of summer descended upon the city, at times baking the inhabitants until their skin cracked in the dry air, or suffocating them in a blanket of humidity. In August all but the most essential work ceased. Café Vera Cruz closed for the month.

Chacón and the Molinas found themselves, as they often did, lying about the Molina patio on Calle Merced, seeking what little coolness they could find in the clay tiles. Chacón's ears perked up when Antonio Molina suggested in a distracted manner, "We should do something different, something to help us make a name for ourselves. Maybe go somewhere else..."

Chacón sat upright. "*Hombre*, you're right! We're not getting anywhere here in Jerez." Of course, Chacón was having the least success in Jerez.

"Where would we go?" Javier's skepticism was evident. "We have no reputation...who would hire us?"

Undaunted, his brother continued with increasing enthusiasm. "We could go to a small town, like Arcos, where there are no cafés or artists. There, we would be noticed—it's better to be the head of a rat than the tail of a lion! We go to the *casino* or *taberna* and offer to give a concert. If nobody will pay us, we pass a hat after the performance. It couldn't fail!"

"Why should we stop at Arcos?" added Chacón with growing enthusiasm. "From there we could go on to the next *pueblo* and do the same thing."

"But...what about the Vera Cruz?" muttered Javier. "We could lose our jobs."

"*Qué pesao eres, hermano!*" [What a pain you are, brother!] replied Antonio. "Junquera pays us almost nothing. We can earn a lot more this way...and become known at the same time."

"And how will we travel? What will we do for money? *Estamos mas tiesos que un ajo!* [We're tighter than a garlic; we're broke!]."

"*Hombre!* We can walk to Arcos in one day. And if we have to sleep outside, the weather is warm. Then, as we earn money, we can live better."

"Maybe..."

"*Ole! Vamos por la nación!*" Chacón jumped to his feet. "We're going to travel the nation!"

Los Artistas

Early September, 1884

In the distance the heavy bells of the Colegiata Church sounded their ponderous tones for the eighth time. Eight o'clock and already the merciless Andalusian sun beat down with white brilliance upon cobbled streets. Jerezanos hurried about their morning tasks, anxious to return to the soothing shelter of shaded patios. Above the acrid scent of animals and scorched dry earth the air hung heavy with the pervasive aroma of *mosto*, the newly barreled juice of grapes already fermenting and evaporating through porous oak casks to envelope the city in a heady cloud of intoxicating vapor. The breathing of the wine enlivened the people and alleviated somewhat the stifling effects of the heat.

"It's a shame to miss the *vendimia*," said Javier wistfully, referring to the grape harvest.

"And the fiesta," added Antonio Molina, stopping in the street to shift a tattered cloth travel bag from one shoulder to the other, where it joined a dangling *bota* wineskin. "I hate to miss the fiesta...so many beautiful women in the streets."

Chacón adjusted his wide straw hat as he waited for Antonio to catch up. "And the *cante*. The fiesta of the *vendimia* is the best time for *cante*..."

"Don't forget work," interrupted Javier. "It's also the best time of the year for us artists. We should have waited until after the *vendimia* to leave. We could have made a lot of money and then..."

"And then we never would have gone!" Chacón waved his crudely carved *vara* to emphasize his words. "The Vera Cruz would have opened again, you two would have gone back to work, and I would have been left with nothing. Besides, we are going to make a lot of money this way. Just wait and see!"

Chacón and the Molina brothers were heading eastward out of Jerez. Earlier, Chacón had slipped out of his home undetected to join his friends in front of the Café Vera Cruz—the point of origin of the road to Arcos de la Frontera.

"*Tocayo*, did you really leave without telling your parents anything?" Antonio Molina still found it hard to believe what his friend had told them.

"It's true. Can you imagine what my father would have done if he knew? The only way I can hope to convince him that I know what I am doing is to become successful in the *cante*. But I did leave a message with the neighbors."

At almost every step the trio had been hailed by a barrage of good-natured greetings from neighbors and friends: "Where are you headed, *muchachos*? Have your parents kicked you out?"

To which the adventurers replied in high spirits, "We are going to see the country. We're going to be famous!"

"May luck be with you, *muchachos…vayan con Dios!*"

The youths were not likely to escape attention with their raggle-taggle appearance. Antonio Molina, now a strapping eighteen-year-old, sported a flat-rimmed hat tilted at a rakish angle and wore a vest over his blousy white shirt. Chacón, at fifteen, looked anything but elegant in a fieldworker's straw hat and carrying a bundle of clothes slung over his shoulder. Like his companions, he traveled in rope-soled *alpargata* slippers. Javier, who carried the much-repaired boots of the three in order to preserve them for performing, had freed his hands for this task by strapping his guitar case to his back. The guitarist wore a very wide-brimmed sombrero *calañés* of heavy black felt. The hat, with its pointed conical crown and tightly rolled circular brim adorned by two fuzzy black pompons, drew a comment from Antonio.

"Brother, we have to get you a new hat as soon as possible. That *calañés* is too old-fashioned. You look like a gypsy from the back country."

"Your hat may be the latest style, but I look more like an artist, and where we're going everyone wears the *calañés*. Besides, this hat belonged to our father and will bring us luck."

Conversation came to a halt when the boys realized they had reached the outskirts of the city. The reality of their adventure struck them. The cobblestone streets had come to an end, replaced by a hard-packed earthen roadway. Across the railroad tracks, endless rows of vivid green grapevines stretched in gently rolling waves to the horizon. Here and there, small farms—thatched huts surrounded by fences of prickly-pear cactus— interrupted the fields of green. In the distance glared the shimmering white of warehouse-like bodegas, where wine was being processed and stored.

The harvest had been underway since daybreak and workers bent under the blazing sun to collect the heavy clusters of glistening amber grapes. Mules fitted with special harnesses carried grapes in huge baskets, four to a side, toward the bodegas. The boys, in high spirits, saluted the workers in passing:

"Buenos días nos dé Dios!" [May God give us a good morning!]

"Buenos días," came the reply. *"Que les vaya bien!"* [May all go well for you!]

Traffic on the dusty highway thinned as the morning wore on. In their excitement the young travelers did not yet feel the effects of the intense heat. An occasional donkey passed by, heavily laden, with a stolid peasant farmer seated on top of the cargo. Long-eared mules bore heavy burdens of straw or wood toward Jerez.

Far behind the trio, the Colegiata faintly sounded nine o'clock. Ahead, a landscape of blinding whiteness that had the boys squinting. The low green vines still ran in parallel lines as far as the eye could see, but between the rows the soil was no longer the reddish-brown clay that gave great yields of *palomino* grapes. In its place was the most prized soil in Andalucía, the *albariza*, a snow-white chalk with a texture like soap, seemingly incapable of sustaining life. The *albariza* formed a marble-hard crust when it dried out, retaining deep moisture throughout the scorching summer. Although this soil yielded less fruit than did the red *barro*, the resulting grapes produced the finest *jerez* wine. It was these *tierras albarizas* that made Jerez de la Frontera unique in the production of sherry.

Already feeling the heat, Antonio Molina came to a stop and slipped the wineskin from his shoulder. "My throat is drier than the eye of a one-eyed man!" he said as he took a drink and then passed the *bota* to the others.

"Look, there's a bodega up ahead," said Javier, "maybe we can get some water."

The boys turned off the road and headed for a large white building. Among the workers spreading grapes to dry on eight-foot circular esparto-grass mats Chacón spotted an unmistakable figure.

"Torre, is that you?"

A dark gypsy face turned and broke into a grin at the sight of Chacón and his friends. "*Chumajaró*, what are you doing out here?"

"*A la aventura!* We're going to tour the country...to try our luck as artists."

"*Ozú*...just like true *gitanos!* With that hat you look like you should be working here with me."

"Javié gave it to me...it was his father's."

"Where is your father working now, Javié?"

"He's over with Domecq...they made him a field boss."

"Who else is working out here?" asked Chacón.

"Juan and Juani are out in the harvest" El Torre stopped to wipe the sweat from his face. "What heat! It is too hot for work...or even to be traveling."

"It *is* hot. Is that good for the grapes?

"Of course. With this heat the *palominos* will dry out in eight or ten hours."

Like most Jerezanos, Chacón and the Molinas were intimately acquainted with the complex process of making sherry. Not without reason did people say, "*El jerezano nace ya viñador*—the people of Jerez are born vintners." The boys knew that the golden palomino grapes needed to be baked in the sun for a number of hours to concentrate the juice, while other varieties used for blending, such as the *pedro ximénez*, might be dried for days or weeks, to a raisin-like texture.

Two more grape-laden mules arrived and El Torre waved them toward an empty mat. Then, indicating a large clay jug, he said to the boys, "There's the water...I have to help here. *Chumajaró*, don't forget the *seguiriya* of *El Señor* Curro Molina that I taught you, the one that goes, '*Dices que duermes sola.*' With a *cante* like that you can't fail. Good luck to you...*que os vaya bien!*"

By mid-day, the boys had covered half the distance to Arcos. The landscape had become more varied, small farms, orchards, and herds of livestock breaking up the vineyards. The exhausted travelers stopped for lunch in a grove of olive trees. Chacón spoke for all of them when he said, "I'm as tired as a *pisador!*" The youths found it easy, in that moment, to empathize with the *pisadores*, the workers who trod the grapes in large wooden bins from midnight until noon, walking a greater distance each night than Chacón and his companions would travel in an entire day. Chacón's father had made many pairs of the nail-studded boots worn by the men to crush the grapes but leave the seeds intact.

The aroma of warm cheese and spicy chorizo sausage emanating from Chacón's pack had tantalized the boys for several miles. Now they ate with great relish, breaking off hunks of hard-crusted bread and washing the food down with wine from Antonio's *bota*. The food made them drowsy and they lay back in the sparse shade of a gnarled olive tree.

"Smoke?" Antonio spoke as he withdrew the pouch of tobacco that had cost him too much of the little money he had saved, and he began to roll a cigarette. He tore off a piece of cigarette paper—he had splurged on the best, from Alcoy, Valencia—added a bit of tobacco, rolled it, moistened the edge to seal it, and bent over the ends. As he bit off one end, he passed the makings on to his brother. They had to share their meager resources. Javier had spent his money on spare guitar strings. The fragile strings, made from sheep intestine, were undependable, breaking often under the stress of heat and perspiring fingers. New ones would be hard to find in small towns and villages. Chacón had even less money than the Molinas, but he made up for it with enthusiasm.

"What luck!" said the singer as he finished lighting his cigarette from the smoldering piece of rope Antonio had lit with a flint and steel. "This is the life! We're free, and we have everything we need...except for money. But we will change that in Arcos, and then we can..."

"That is, *if* we find work," interrupted Javier, still skeptical.

"We'll find work, and when we do," said the older Molina, "I know what I am going to do with the money. *Tocayo*, when are you going to go with a woman?"

It was Antonio's favorite way of teasing Chacón, who, at fifteen, had not yet attempted his first sexual experience. When he got no response, the dancer continued in the same vein.

"*Tocayo*, do you know the nine things a woman must have if she is to be beautiful?"

Chacón shrugged.

"You're hopeless! Do I have to teach you everything? A woman must have nine things. There are three of black...her hair, her eyes, and her lashes. Then there must be three of red...her lips and cheeks, and the palms of her hands. And lastly, she must have three things of white...her teeth, her bosom, and the whites of her eyes."

"That's silly!" said Chacón in answer. "And what if she is blond with blue eyes?"

Thinking of Juana Antúnez, Antonio replied, "A blond is worthless. A dark-skinned *morena* wastes enough salt in a minute to last a blond an entire week."[1]

"If you can't think about anything but women, you'll never be an artist," came Chacón's retort. "By the time we return to Jerez, I want to be somebody, to be known. I don't want to spend my life working for nothing and end up as my father predicts—poor and a disgrace to my family. The *cante* is an art and I want to be an artist. I'm going to sing *p'alante* [in front], not in the *cuadro*..."

"*Hombre*, you can't decide those things," interrupted Javier. "In this life an artist doesn't choose, he takes what work he can get."

"Not me!" replied the other. "I won't live that way...drunk, dirty, and sick all the time. Silverio and El Mellizo live well from the *cante*, and I will too."

"But those men are giants...and even *they* don't depend upon the *cante*. Silverio has his café, and El Mellizo works in the slaughterhouse. And here in Jerez, El Torre and La Cherna work in the fields. Nobody lives from the *cante*. Junquera has his cafés, and half of the guitarists are barbers..."

"And Juan Breva?"

"Breva is an exception. There is only one Juan Breva."

"And there is only one Antonio Chacón. You'll see."

The Molinas made faces and threw up their hands. The older brother spoke as he rose to his feet. "Well, maestro, does Your Honor think he can accompany us the rest of the way to Arcos...or will you wait for your coach?"

Well rested, the adventurers resumed their journey with renewed vigor. Ahead lay the foothills of the Serranía de Ronda, the dominant mountain range of southern Andalucía. The long walk was relieved for several miles when a farmer returning from Jerez offered the boys a

---

[1] In the province of Cádiz (including Jerez) salt is equivalent to spice and wit. A person having these qualities is said to have *salero* (literally "saltshaker").

ride in his donkey-drawn cart. But all too soon the donkey turned off onto a narrow track and the young travelers had to leave the relative comfort of the bone-jarring wagon and continue on foot. As they walked, they chatted about their hopes and plans, about *cante* and *baile*. Chacón fell silent, listening to the Molinas as they fervently debated whether to begin future performances with *cante* or with *baile*, and whether to include guitar solos. He felt a pang of doubt, recalling his debut in the Vera Cruz. In an attempt to bolster his confidence, he silently evaluated his repertoire.

The core of his *cante* lay in the *cantes gitanos* of Jerez. He could sing a great variety of the *martinetes* he had learned in the *fraguas*. He felt confident in his knowledge of *seguiriyas*, especially in the styles of La Cherna, El Marrurro, El Señor Manuel Molina, and scattering of others, including some *cantes* of Silverio and Juan Junquera. His *soleares* were those of El Loco Mateo and other *cantaores* of Jerez, as well as some verses from Cádiz—those of El Mellizo, taught to him by Fosforito. *Por alegrías*, he sang the minimum needed to accompany the dance of Antonio Molina. If he were called upon to sing *por fiesta*, he had a large repertoire of bright and lively *tangos*. And finally, since meeting Fosforito he had begun to cultivate the new *malagueña*, depending largely upon *letras* he had learned from the Gaditano.

At the thought of Fosforito, Chacón felt a pang of envy. The Gaditano had been fortunate to have Enrique el Mellizo as his teacher. The maestro's guidance had enabled him to become a professional at such a young age. He had been earning twenty-five *reales* [6.25 *pesetas*] a night in Jerez. Chacón thought to himself: *If only I could go to Cádiz to be with El Mellizo, or learn from Silverio in Sevilla...or even Silverio's disciple, Sarvaoriyo...*

Suddenly, a distant rumbling shook the boy from his reveries. He looked up to see an immense cloud of dust approaching. Seconds later a chaotic apparition came over a rise, moving at great speed. In single file, six sweat-frothed mules, blowing hard, strained against their tasseled harnesses to pull a wildly careening coach. A young man sat astride the lead mule from where he could attempt to control the charging animals.

"*El omnibus*, watch out!" yelled Antonio as the boys leapt to the side of the road. Behind the string of animals came two more mules, hitched in tandem directly to the vehicle and responsible for steering it under guidance of the *mayoral* in his high seat. The coachman wore a yellow silk scarf tied about his head under a high-peaked, loaf-shaped *calañés* and, in spite of the heat, a black linen jacket adorned with ornamental buttons, a green sash, and green plush-velvet breeches tied at the knees with cords and tassels. The large double-decker *omnibus* carried four passengers seated on top amid luggage and freight, and a dozen more inside.

Antonio Molina marveled at the spectacle. "Look at the *zagal!*" he shouted over the din of pounding hooves, cursing men, and the clattering rigging of the coach. He pointed to a young boy who had leapt from the vehicle to run alongside the mules, prodding them and clubbing them mercilessly to the accompaniment of curses directed at their ancestors. Antonio laughed. "*Dale, dale zagal, que no hay razón como la del bastón!*" [Give it to him, give it to him *zagal*; there's no reasoning as effective as that of the club!]

The huge rear wheels rolled by and the lurching behemoth sped away. When the dust had settled slightly, Chacón said, "Let's get to Arcos...I want to earn enough money to travel like that!"

The sun sat low in the sky when at last the boys, on leaden legs, crossed a stone bridge over the sluggish Guadelete River. Arcos de la Frontera perched above them on a precipitous crag overlooking the river valley. From where the town sat like a gleaming white jewel, perpendicular cliffs dropped off sharply to the river below.

Javier dropped his bundle of boots to the road and leaned the guitar case against his hip. "Let's rest here before we climb that hill."

"Good idea...I'm exhausted," agreed Chacón.

Antonio Molina removed his hat and wiped the sweat from his forehead with the back of his hand. "We should change clothes too. Let's go down by the bridge...*vamos!*"

They placed their belongings on the bank of the river under the bridge, removed their *alpargatas*, and soaked their blistered feet in the tepid water.

"*Ozú*, what a relief!" sighed Antonio. "*Tengo lo pié ma muerto que tu puñatera alma!*" [My feet are deader than your damned soul!]

After snacking on the last of their food, the youths changed into their dress clothes, futilely attempting to smooth out the wrinkles with their hands, and squeezed swollen feet into their boots. Slinging jackets over one shoulder and hoisting their bundles, they began the ascent up the steep winding road to Arcos.

The town was still out of sight above them when the boys halted in front of a large whitewashed building set into the side of the mountain. Long shadows of evening already obscured the outline of the Posada de las Cuevas [Inn of the Caves].

"I'm tired," groaned Javier. It's too late to be looking for work now. Let's get some rest and do it tomorrow."

The others readily agreed and the three young travelers passed through a large arched doorway into a covered courtyard that appeared to serve as stable, kitchen and sleeping quarters. The back wall was carved out of the solid rock of the mountain, while immense arched columns supported the ceiling of the huge room. Straw covered the stone floor and, already, muleteers and other travelers had staked out space for sleeping among the mules and donkeys. The air was thick with the stench of men and animals. Smoke drifted from a cavernous sooty fireplace in one corner, where the stout figure of a woman bent over an assortment of pots and frying pans.

A voice spoke from behind the boys. "*Buenas tardes, señores!* How can I help you?"

The youths turned to see a short, balding man limping toward them. Javier was first to speak. "We need lodging for the night...there are three of us."

"I have a room with two comfortable beds, and one of you can share with another guest."

"How much will that cost us?" asked Javier.

"Eight *reales* each..."

"Does that include a meal?" asked Chacón.

"We are not permitted to serve meals here...but, if you wish to take care of *el ruido de la casa*, perhaps something could be arranged..."

"The noise in the house?"

The innkeeper seemed reluctant to explain, but finally offered, "Well...the guests bring considerable noise and dust into our humble home..."

Javier grasped the man's intent. "And how much will it cost for your trouble?" He was interested in the bottom line.

"Ah...I think two *reales* each would do it."

Javier looked at his companions. "That's ten *reales* each...we can't afford that!"

"Of course, you can sleep here on the floor for four *reales*," added the innkeeper, "but, as you can see, it is quite crowded and not as comfortable."

Hungry, exhausted, and grimy with dust, the boys yielded to the temptation of a good night's rest. They were shown to a room simply furnished with a chair, a table and two low beds—straw-filled mattresses set on a meshwork of rope strung across a wooden frame. Coarse but clean blankets lay folded at the foot of each bed. If the travelers had not been so fatigued, they might have noticed that the walls were stained with bloody reminders of nocturnal battles with the "horses of Satan," tick-like bedbugs that emerged from cracks in the walls at night to feed on the blood of their sleeping victims. While the Molinas placed their belongings on the beds, Chacón was led to a second room.

The boys ate around the fireplace, where many of the travelers had done their own cooking. They attacked the stew of rice, red peppers, and dried, salted cod as if they hadn't eaten in a week. Accompanied by bread, the meal was simple but satisfying. After dinner, a wineskin made the rounds of the room, amid stories and jokes. But, one by one, men retired to corners where they wrapped themselves in their capes or saddle blankets and, with saddles for pillows, were soon snoring soundly in the straw. The three boys, however, succumbed to the relative luxury of their beds and fell quickly into deep sleep.

"*Esperarse muchachos!*" A stern voice halted the three boys as they walked uphill past a small stone building. "You boys wait over there!" A mustachioed and uniformed *carabinero*[2] jerked his head toward the building from where he stood behind a fully laden burro.

It was mid-morning. The three Jerezanos had managed to sleep through the confusion and noise of early departures from the *posada* and had arisen refreshed, if somewhat stiff. Chacón had suffered most from nocturnal depredations by bloodsucking bedbugs, and he scratched persistently at numerous angry welts on his arms and legs. After breakfasting on cups of thick hot chocolate and tidying themselves up the best they were able, the boys had set out for town. They took with them only Javier's guitar, hoping it would open doors for them.

Now, with the first buildings of Arcos in sight, the boys faced customs. They watched as the *carabinero* unwrapped a bundle he had just removed from the donkey and preceded to search for taxable goods and contraband. The protesting farmer watched him assess a duty on

---

[2]*carabinero*: armed force in charge of customs and control of smuggling; named for the carbine rifles they carried.

each food item, down to the last egg. When, at last, the grumbling peasant was permitted to reload his animal, the *carabinero* strolled over to where the three boys had been impatiently waiting.

"Where are you from?"

"Jerez de la Frontera," replied Chacón and Javier almost simultaneously.

"Do you have anything to declare?"

"Us, something to declare?" said Antonio. "*Qué va...somo ma probe que las ratas!*" [No way...we're poorer than rats!]

"What's in the case?"

"Javier started to speak, but his brother interjected, "A piano...what does it look like?"

The *carabinero* fixed a hard glare on the boy and said sternly, "Open it!"

When Javier had opened the case, the *carabinero* removed the guitar, looked inside, gave the instrument a solid thump with his knuckle— a thump that made Javier wince—then handed it back to the boy. Turning to Antonio, he said, "You, *gracioso* [wiseguy], come here!"

Antonio, with a look of feigned innocence, said, "Me?"

"Yes, you." The *carabinero* patted the boy's clothing until he felt the bulge of the tobacco pouch. "Ah-hah, what is this?" he exclaimed with a tone of satisfaction. Removing the pouch, he asked, "Why didn't you declare this tobacco?"

"I didn't think I had to declare such a small amount."

"*Hombre*, this is more than a small amount. Don't you know that smuggling tobacco is a serious crime? You must declare all food or tobacco brought into the city. Just yesterday we caught one of your fellow Jerezanos attempting to pass a quarter pound of tobacco hidden inside a watermelon! Can you imagine that...a watermelon! We caught him and now he is in jail."

The crestfallen look on Antonio's face seemed to appease the *carabinero*, for, after rubbing his stubbly chin for a moment, a twinkle came to his eye and he asked, "Who plays the guitar?"

"I do," said Javier, brightening at the change of tone. "My brother is a *bailaor* and our friend sings. We have come to perform here in Arcos...that is, if we can find a place."

The *carabinero* tugged on his handlebar mustache for a moment and then said, "*Pues, mire usté!* [Well, look here!] Go to the café of *Don* Bartólome Morillas, just past the plaza, and tell him that Miguel *el carabinero* has sent you. I'm sure he will help you." Then, with a wink, he added, "And no more smuggling, eh!"

An ancient church with a tall bell tower, an Arab castle, and a palace formed three sides of the main plaza of Arcos. The fourth side lay open to a panoramic view of the river below and the fields that stretched beyond. From the plaza, a maze of steep and narrow streets, roughly paved with stones, spread like fingers in all directions. Two and three-story whitewashed homes lined the streets in the town's center, while those on the outskirts nestled into the hillside or balanced precariously at cliff's edge. Bright red and green potted geraniums and occasional black grillwork at the windows enlivened the otherwise bleak appearance of the stark dwellings.

The boys found the café just off the plaza. To their disappointment, it proved to be little more than a tavern, a small dark room with pine tables and esparto-grass chairs. A quick survey of the room revealed nothing that might serve as a stage. *Don* Bartólome, in his shirtsleeves, rose from where he was talking with two men and approached the new arrivals. It was not common in Arcos to be visited by three boys wearing suits and carrying a guitar.

Javier, spokesman for the trio when it came to business matters, explained their situation. *Don* Bartólome, enthusiastic about their proposition, assured them there was no place in Arcos better suited for the performance. He could not afford to pay them, but would certainly permit them to collect what they could from the customers. The budding artists had no choice but to accept his offer, and they made arrangements to begin at nine o'clock that evening.

Word spread quickly through the small town that three artists from Jerez would appear in Casa de *Don* Bartólome. By nine o'clock the café had filled with noisy men. Harsh, loud voices spoke the almost unintelligible dialect of the countryside. Fieldworkers, goatherds, craftsmen, and merchants mingled in an atmosphere of camaraderie and anticipation. The elegance of European fashion had not made its mark on Arcos. Yet, even the poorest wore a jacket of some sort, though it be ill-fitting, of coarsely woven cloth, or in the ancient *traje corto* style that came only to the waist. The low, wood beam ceiling trapped the thick odor of hardworking men, the smoke of cheap tobacco, and the fumes from oil lamps that dimly illuminated the room. In that suffocating atmosphere, eyes watered and lungs strained. Even the air seemed to hold its breath.

A small space in one corner had been cleared for the debut of the three *artistas*. They fought their way through the packed room to the "stage" and Javier began to play. The spectators nearest them quieted and shouted at others further back to be quiet. Cries of *"Callarse!"* brought the noise level to a new high at first and then began to take effect. But even with the sound down to a rumble of voices, clinking glasses, and shuffling feet, the guitar could barely be heard. The boys had agreed to begin with Antonio's *alegrías*, counting on the dance to attract the attention of the public and set the mood for *cante*.

Chacón began to sing the verse and the room quieted to the point where he could be heard. But when he had finished, the voices grew loud again, drowning out what little sound Antonio's boots could produce on the rough clay tiles. Then the clapping began. The wine-soaked country folk beat out erratic rhythms in an attempt to accompany the dancer. Antonio struggled to a finish. Javier tried to follow with a short guitar solo, but gave up quickly when conversation returned to full volume.

It was up to Chacón. He began *por seguiriyas*. At the first tones of this *cante*, the audience returned its attention to the performers. Even the guitar could be heard. Chacón poured his heart into *letra* after *letra* of *seguiriyas*. Ten minutes, fifteen minutes, and still he sang. When he had completed his closing verse, the audience applauded and yelled approval. The *cantaor* was drenched with sweat, as were Javier and Antonio. Jackets and the suffocating heat of the room had added to the exertions of their performance.

A loud voice called out a request for *Olé con olé*, an old popular song. Chacón attempted to explain to those who could hear him that he was there to sing the *cante flamenco*, not popular music. He asked Javier to play *por soleá*. But even as he began to warm up with his *temple*, someone cried out, *"El Gangu Gangu!"* Chacón ignored this request for the popular *tanguillo* and continued *por soleá*, but few listened. The villagers had heard enough of the gypsy *cante* and wanted songs they knew.

The performance came to an end amid noise and confusion. A tray made the rounds of the room and collected a small quantity of *céntimos* and *reales*. The boys faced a barrage of praise, critiques, and requests for more *canciones* [popular songs]. A fat, red-faced man barked at them, "Enough of that gypsy stuff. We want to hear the *cante andaluz*,³ a *tirana*, or a *rondeña* like my mother used to sing!"

Antonio Molina pulled his companions away, muttering under his breath, "*Qué tío ma pesao...ma pesao que una chinche!* [What a jerk...more bothersome than a bedbug!] These hicks don't know anything!"

Another man grabbed Chacón's arm in a steely grip as the *cantaor* passed by. "*Chiquillo, ecusha!*" [Listen boy!] He began to croak in an off-key, wine-warped voice: "*Mi yeeegua castañaaaa...*" Chacón pretended to listen for a moment and then, at the first opportunity, slipped away to join his companions.

The second show fared no better than the first. Antonio's favorite dance, the *zapateado*,⁴ focused on footwork and could not be performed on the hard clay floor. The *bailaor* had to make do with a *tango*. Chacón briefly captured the attention of the unruly spectators with his *malagueñas*, but then, in the middle of a *copla*, a florid face, crusted with several days growth of gray stubble, leaned toward him and grunted, "*Niño, la pricaora!*"

When Chacón ignored the comment and continued singing, the man clutched his arm and brought his face so close that the *cantaor* recoiled from the foul wine-soaked breath. "*La pricaora*...sing *la pricaora*..."

The boy realized at last the man wished him to sing the popular song "*La Picadora*." He attempted to explain. "I don't sing that, I sing only flamenco."

"*Sí, niño*, you sing it!"

Chacón twisted out of the man's grasp and moved as far as he could from his tormentor. The man fought to regain balance in his chair and then became preoccupied with his drink, clutching it with both hands and staring into the glass, But throughout the rest of the night sporadic garbled cries for "*la pricaora*" could be heard over the din of voices.

By eleven o'clock the café had begun to empty. It would seem an

---

³*cante andaluz*: Andalusian *cante*; in flamenco, those *cantes* that are not specifically gypsy in origin.

⁴*zapateado*: a dance without *cante*, emphasizing the display of footwork virtuosity (from *zapato*: shoe).

early hour in the bigger cities, but was to be expected in a town like Arcos. The young artists were exhausted, Javier's fingers worn from trying to force an audible sound from his strings, and Chacón's throat sore from the smoke and shouting to be heard. As they collected a meager assortment of small coins from the remaining patrons, a man entered, obviously very drunk. He offered them a *duro* [five *pesetas*, or twenty *reales*] if they would stay longer and perform for him.

The boys exchanged glances in disbelief. Five *pesetas* was more than they had collected all evening—nobody gave that much money. The man tossed the silver coin into the tray. Joy momentarily banished fatigue. Javier forgot about his aching fingers and Chacón felt strength return to his strained throat. They launched into a fiesta that lasted nearly an hour. The intoxicated patron barely noticed when the three young artists slipped out into the night.

"What a mess!" exclaimed Javier as the boys walked through the dark and quiet streets toward the *posada*.

Chacón agreed. "Very difficult! I can't sing like that."

"And the dance?" added Antonio, "It was impossible. It's like throwing daisies to pigs!"

"They didn't know how to listen, neither to the guitar nor the *cante*." Chacón felt humiliated by the whole experience. "And that *cero a la izquierda* [complete idiot] who kept asking for '*La picaora*'..."

"At least," interrupted Javier, "thanks to the drunk with the *duro* we made enough money to pay our bill at the *posada*."

"How much did we make?" asked Chacón.

"Aside from the *duro*, almost six *pesetas*...not very much considering how many people were there. By the time we pay the fifteen *pesetas* we owe at the *posada* we will be broke."

"Poorer than a door latch!" laughed Antonio. But, remember, *no hay atajo sin trabajo* [no pain, no gain]."

The following morning, as the boys prepared to leave La Posada de las Cuevas, they received a surprise visitor. It was the drunken patron of the previous night. He demanded the return of his *duro*, claiming that, being "*algo bebido*" [somewhat intoxicated], he had not realized how much he had given. Antonio Molina, furious, grabbed Chacón's *vara* and threatened the man, yelling, "*So miserable* [miserable wretch], last night you made a big show of being generous with us and now you regret having given us the *duro! Vete a la porra!* [Go to hell!] You'll get your money back the day a frog grows hair!"

Not to be intimidated, the man continued to make a scene. But when other lodgers began to gather in defense of the boys he fled in shame. Outraged, Antonio took some time to calm down. "Imagine! That *sinvergüenza* [shameless one] thought he could get his money back, after we performed so long for him last night!"

As the boys passed through the arched portal, from the cavernous gloom of the *posada* into the dazzling morning sun, eager to begin the next leg of their journey, they could already see that making a living with their art was not to be a simple matter.

At the eastern edge of Arcos, whitewashed houses came to an abrupt end. Beyond a wooden bridge lay desolate open and mountainous land, covered with shrubs and great spiked aloe cactus. Further in the distance stretched a pine-clad wilderness.

Not long on the road, the young travelers heard a hollow clanking coming from beyond a rise. The sound drew closer, accompanied by a trilled cry, *"Arrrre!"* Soon a human voice became distinguishable, calling out, *"Arrrre...arre mula, arre!"* Even before the first mule came into sight, the boys recognized the sounds of the mule train and the cries of the *arriero*, the muleteer, whose descriptive name derived from the trilled "r" he employed to keep his animals moving. The mule train was the lifeblood of Spain, the major means of distributing goods throughout the country.

The train of mules presented an impressive sight when it came into view. The lead mule wore an enormous copper bell that clanked its melancholy song against the animal's knees. Behind, in single file, came a long line of stolidly plodding mules, decorated with tassels and monotonously tinkling bells and shorn in fantastic patterns—zebra-like stripes or designs that outlined the harnesses and loads on their backs. The *arriero* came last, mounted on a donkey and dressed all in brown, his grizzled, weather-beaten face shaded by a very broad-brimmed and slouched leather hat. This tough man of the open road kept the train moving at a steady, languid pace by pelting the animals with small stones, keeping them in line by hitting their ears with great accuracy. All the while he maintained a constant harangue, his curses limited in creativity only by the extent of his knowledge of anatomical, geographical, and religious terms: *"Arre vieja* [old one]...*arre revieja* [doubly old one]...*carajo* [popular obscenity of the day]... may a dead donkey burst its bladder upon your grandmother's grave..."

The boys saluted with a wave, to which the *arriero* grunted in response. When Antonio Molina yelled out over the noise to ask where he was coming from, the rider turned in passing and replied in a voice that was barely more than a croak, "Ronda..." Then he was gone.

When the dust had settled, Antonio turned to his companions and said, "Let's go to Ronda!"

Javier looked at him questioningly. "Why Ronda? I thought we were going to go to the small *pueblos?*"

"If our experience in Arcos is an example of how it will be in the *pueblos*, we will never make money. Ronda is a bigger town and we would surely be hired by a café there."

"He might be right, Javié," added Chacón, still despondent about the previous night's experience. "In Ronda they might appreciate us more. They might know how to listen..."

"If that's what you two want...but we can't wait until Ronda to work, we're almost broke."

"We can work as we travel," said Antonio. "On to Ronda!"

"*Viva* Ronda!" exclaimed Chacón, his spirits rising once again.

The hours passed slowly, the road passing under the boys' feet with procession-like monotony. Fortunately the weather had cooled slightly, resulting in a balmy day with the occasional breeze. From time to time small crosses appeared at the side of the road, propped upright by piles of stones. Clearly, the crude crosses marked sites where people had died, but the boys were puzzled by their frequency and their old and decayed appearance.

Shortly after noon, two uniformed men seated in the shade of a scrub oak hailed the travelers. Two horses grazed on tethers nearby. The men, one bearded and the other with a heavy drooping mustache, were dressed in gray trousers and jackets over which each had strapped a wide belt holding an ammunition pouch and a saber. But what identified the *Guardia Civil*[5] at a glance was the white cap. The cylindrical cap had a small visor flipped up vertically in front and the top came to a small peak in back. A white flap hung down to the shoulders to provide protection from the sun. Two carbines leaned against the trunk of the tree.

---

[5] *Guardia Civil*: an armed force created in 1840 to guard highways, railroad stations, and small towns, and to suppress the hordes of bandits that ruled the countryside. In 1884, there were over twenty thousand *Guardia Civiles* on foot in Spain and another five thousand on horseback. They never went singly, always in pairs, and have remained to the present day as the most feared and respected of Spain's security forces.

The *Guardias* welcomed the distraction of company and invited the boys to sit and rest in the shade. Antonio offered tobacco and, as they all lit up, asked, "You're not from around here are you? You don't speak like Andalusians."

"No, replied the bearded *Guardia*, "I am from La Mancha and my *compañero* is Madrileño [from Madrid]. They always send us far from home...so that we don't compromise ourselves."

Chacón, who had been listening quietly, asked suddenly, "The crosses we have seen along the road...do you know who died there?"

"The crosses," answered the *Guardia* with the mustache, the more talkative of the two, "those crosses are from long ago. They mark the spots where people were killed by bandits. Although, sometimes the bandits, who were very clever, put up the crosses themselves in order to frighten travelers into being more cooperative during robberies. You know, only a few years ago a man would never have traveled these roads alone."

The boys had heard stories all of their lives about bandits such as José María "El Tempranillo" who, according to legend, stole from wealthy travelers and aided the poor. Bandits had become heroes to many Andalusian peasants.

"To travel these roads in those days you had to go in large caravans with armed guards. Bandits were everywhere, thousands of them, stealing and smuggling. Even in the *posadas* or pueblos you weren't safe. A *ratero* [thief] would see where you hid your money and then wait for you outside of town with his accomplices. It was very dangerous..." The *Guardia* paused a moment and then added, "A smart traveler always carried a cheap watch or some jewelry to give to the robbers...because, if the thief found nothing to steal it made him furious. If he felt that there had been a premeditated intent to deceive him, he might beat the victim, leave him stripped naked, or even kill him."

"And the *arrieros* and the coaches?" Antonio Molina, like his companions, was fascinated. "How were they able to travel in those days?"

"It is said that many of them paid a fee to the bandits who controlled the territory. That was part of the cost of doing business. And the *arrieros* can be as bad as bandits. Even today many of them are smugglers. You know, you boys are traveling on one of their favorite smuggling routes. They used to bring tobacco in at Gibraltar and then use the coastal routes. But now that we control the coast it is too dangerous for them, so they go inland, up the valley of the Genal River to Ronda. They often travel at night and take refuge in bandit towns around here...Gaucín, Igualeja, Cortes, and even Villalengua del Rosario. So, be careful...in the *posadas* you never know which *arrieros* might be smugglers."

The other *Guardia* spoke up. "Now that we control the countryside, there is little to fear from bandits. But you must watch out for smugglers...and *gitanos*..."

Chacón interrupted, "*Gitanos*? We have lived all of our lives with gypsies, why should we fear *them*?"

"*Muchacho*, you may know well the gypsies of your pueblo, the *gitanos caseros* who have settled down and adopted the ways of the *Castellano* [Castillian, i.e. Spaniard]. Perhaps they are not so bad. But those around here, the *gitanos canasteros*,[6] are evil people. They will steal everything you own, and perhaps stick a knife into you to get it!"

The *Guardia* with the mustache added, "The *gitano* steals even with his words. He does not know how to tell the truth. While he babbles carelessly, making you laugh with his foolishness, he puts *pesetas* into his pocket. They don't even speak proper *cristiano*.[7] They speak that thieves' jargon so that we won't understand their evil intentions."

The boys found it difficult to take the *Guardias* seriously. It was true that gypsies had their own way of speaking and lived differently from the *gaché*, but it was not such a bad lifestyle, and certainly not evil as the *Guardias* described.

"And they're lazy," the *Guardia* continued. "Once, we found two gypsies sleeping under a tree...up near El Bosque. I kicked one of them with my boot to wake him and said, 'What are you doing here, don't you know this is private land?' The *gitano* sat up, very frightened, and told me, 'We're gathering snails.' I asked him, 'Snails? Where are they?' Instead of answering, he shook his partner to wake him saying, '*Primo* [cousin], wake up! I thought you were supposed to be collecting snails.' The other looked around with feigned surprise and said groggily, 'I had one...but I guess it got away!'"

The two *Guardias* roared with laughter and the boys couldn't help joining in. "And the women are worse," continued the *Guardia* when

---

[6]*gitanos canasteros*: basket-making gypsies; generic name given to gypsies who wander the open road, due to the custom of women making baskets to sell.

[7]*cristiano*: Christian, implying that anything besides Spanish is heathen, improper.

he had caught his breath. "The *gitana*, when she is a baby, is carried by beggars, naked and filthy to evoke pity. Then, as soon as she can walk she begins begging on her own. When a gypsy is born, they twist her arms so that they easily go palms up for begging. By the time she is fifteen she has one baby at the breast and is about to give birth to another. They breed like rabbits, like weeds. At thirty she is an old woman, a greedy old hag who tells lies and works her evil magic until she dies at seventy or eighty…"

"And they are a filthy people…" the other *Guardia* started to say, but was interrupted by his partner.

"That's true. They don't bathe…and when they are not doing evil, they spend their time picking lice from each other. Even worse, they eat dead animals that they find on the road. No meat is too rotten for a gypsy. Around here, farmers give them their diseased carcasses."

At last the feverish pitch of the *Guardias'* tirade against the gypsies began to subside. Their final word was one of caution. "Remember, *muchachos*, don't trust them. The *gitano* does nothing for nothing. He takes payment for every blink of his eye!"

The Jerezanos had never heard such an outburst. Many of the things that had been said did not fit the gypsies they knew in Jerez. Later, on the road, Chacón said to his friends, "Do you think the *gitanos* around here are as dangerous as the *Guardias* said?"

"No way!" responded Antonio. "The *Guardias* were very exaggerated. *Gitanos* are *gitanos*…nothing more, nothing less."

Yet, even Antonio Molina felt uneasy as evening shadows began to fall over the harsh and lonely landscape, transfiguring trees and rocks into grotesque and sinister shapes. All three boys breathed easier when they reached the *posada* on the outskirts of El Bosque.

El Bosque, the halfway point between Jerez and Ronda, was an important stopover, and the *posada* had already begun to fill with travelers and *arrieros*. It was a dull and gloomy place, the covered courtyard surrounded by a vast corridor of rock arches and pillars. Men came second in what was essentially a large stable. Mules, donkeys, and horses munched contentedly on all sides. As a pig sniffed curiously at the boys' feet, the innkeeper appeared, muttered a word of greeting, and left the travelers on their own. There was no question of sleeping in one of the upstairs lofts—Javier pointed out they had only enough money to permit them to pass the night in the stable and perhaps eat a small meal the following day. They would have to make their beds in an archway near the kitchen.

All about the courtyard men cooked in scorched earthenware pots on small, crackling twig fires. They had purchased food from peasants who gathered outside the *posada* each evening to sell hares and partridges snared in the brush, or chickens and produce from their farms. When the meal was ready, the men sat back on low stools and stabbed pieces of meat with the tips of their knives or soaked up gravy with bread. As each new *arriero* arrived he led his animals past the diners, unpacked them, applied to the innkeeper for salt, straw, and barley, and went to the well for water. Drinking water was stored in large *tinajas*, conical earthen amphorae whose pointed bottoms rested in holes in a wooden shelf. Evaporation through the porous clay cooled the water on the hottest of days.

Muleteers were true lords of the open road, more respected in their dusty ways than dukes or counts. Sullen, proud, and seldom courteous, they had been able to travel in the times of the bandits where even royalty could not go with impunity. Their tanned and dust-impregnated faces were inscrutable, often fierce and scowling under stubbly black beards. Seated by fires in the *posada*, some wore beret-like caps, while others knotted dirty scarves over their matted black hair. Before eating, each offered food to his neighbor, saying in a husky voice, "*Gusta usté comé?*" When the other politely declined, the *arriero* would stab a piece of meat, bring it to his mouth, the juice trickling down his sweaty chin, and then slurp the remaining contents of his earthen platter from a spoon of wood or horn.

Chacón and the Molinas settled in a corner near the kitchen to eat their meal of goat meat in a thin tomato sauce, and the ever-present rice. They looked at the other guests with new suspicion: *Might some of them be smugglers?* The loud voices and raucous laughter of *arrieros*, coachmen, and travelers mixed with the grunts and gulps of diners and the placid chewing of animals. A huge wineskin made the rounds, the cheap country wine pouring in arching streams into parched throats. Shirtsleeves served to wipe errant drops from mouth and chin.

Later, when most had finished dining, the men pulled their stools closer to the fires and passed around a bowl of hot coals for the lighting of cigarettes and cigars. Soon, the dense tobacco smoke had diluted the robust, sweet odor of the animals and the acrid, pervasive stench of rancid sweat. Wine and laughter flowed with shared stories and coarse jokes. Inevitably, the rough dissonant voices of the *arrieros* broke into song. Theirs were songs of the mountains, songs of the hunt, of mules and horses, and of girls left behind in distant villages. Among their *cantes* were the *rondeñas*,[8] similar to the *verdiales* and therefore distant cousin to the *malagueña*, but much rougher and more primitive than either of these—especially when sung by the *arrieros*:

Cazadores de la sierra,	Hunters of the mountains,
a esa liebre no tirarle,	don't shoot that hare,
porque está haciendo en [*la tierra*]	because she is making in [the earth]
madriguera pa ser madre	a den for giving birth
y es muy sagrado lo que [*encierra.*]	and what it contains is very [sacred.]
Ví a un bicho correó	I saw a running animal
salir de la cueva El Loro;	leave El Loro Cave;
le empujé mi perra galga;	I set my greyhound bitch upon it;
clemencia le pido a Dios	I ask God to forgive me
que le dí la muerte amarga.	for giving it such a bitter death.

When Chacón's turn came, he sang *por martinetes*:

Caminito de Antequera,	On the road to Antequera,
preso llevan a un gitano,	a gypsy has been taken prisoner
porque se encontró una capa	because he found a cape
antes de perderla el amo.	before it was lost by its owner.

As the boy sang the room grew quiet, except for outbursts of surprise and approval. *Arrieros* and coachmen did not often find such a singer in their midst. "*Chiquillo!*" they yelled, "What a *cantaor* we have among us!" "Well done *muchacho!*" "He sings better than my mules!"

When Chacón had finished, the men flattered him by insisting that he continue. There was more respect for his singing among those coarse and simple men than he had felt the entire night in the café in Arcos. Javier brought out the guitar and Chacón sang *por soleá* and *seguiriya*. The singer was *a gusto*, very much inspired to sing. The effects of

---

[8]The *rondeñas* are thought by some (Mairena and Molina) to be the most primitive of the present day *fandangos* and most like the ancestral type.

fatigue and wine had freed him from inhibitions and he threw himself into the *cante*, venting his frustrations by singing better than he ever had.

As the coals of the fires began to die, men rose one by one and made their beds. There was no undressing or cleaning up. Coachmen wrapped themselves in their capes and lay down on the straw. *Arrieros* threw brightly striped and tasseled saddle blankets onto the bare cobblestone floor and curled up with their heads resting on packsaddles or saddlebags. Within moments they were sleeping sonorously.

The three Jerezanos were fortunate to have brought capes with them, for the mountain air had cooled considerably since sunset. They each scraped together a thin mattress of dirty straw and lay down wrapped in their cloaks.

"*Ozú*, how uncomfortable!" muttered Chacón as he struggled to find a sleeping position free from sharp bumps.

"*Tocayo*," mumbled Antonio sleepily, "*a buen sueño no hay mala cama!*" [for true sleepiness, there is no such thing as a bad bed!]

Fatigue had just begun to drag Chacón into oblivion when he was brought alert by an intense itching in his legs. As he scratched, the itching spread to his arms and neck. Javier, too, began to scratch. "*Carajo!*" he yelped, "I'm being eaten by fleas!"

The other Molina responded in a drowsy whisper, "Brother, he who sleeps well is not bitten by fleas!"

"That may be true," replied Javier, "but how is one who is bitten by fleas supposed to sleep at all?"

The only answer was a soft snoring. Javier and Chacón itched and scratched until they fell at last into fitful sleep.

Chacón awoke to the deafening clatter of hooves on cobblestones. Loud voices rang out in the sleepy morning. It was not yet daylight and already the *posada* was all confusion and noise as animals were fed, harnessed, and loaded. Bills were paid to the accompaniment of much loud cursing. The night had been far too short for the Jerezanos. Bleary-eyed and scratching at welts that covered their bodies, the boys dragged themselves to the fireplace. The innkeeper's wife handed each a cup of thick hot chocolate. Chacón studied his friends between sips of the restoring drink and then suddenly declared, "We look like the devil...how can we expect to find work looking like this?"

The other two stared at each other for a moment and then burst out laughing. "You're right, *tocayo*," exclaimed Antonio, *"estamos más puercos que las arañas!"* [we're dirtier than spiders!]

Indeed, four days of travel had taken a heavy toll—four days without a change of clothes except to perform, and no opportunity to wash. Fatigue was evident in the boys' sun-parched faces, and red, sleep-deprived eyes. Antonio Molina, with a thick black stubble of beard, disheveled hair, and rumbled clothes, could easily pass for a common vagrant. Javier, younger and with a lighter beard, was only slightly less disheveled in appearance. Even Chacón, now a stocky fifteen-year-old of shorter than average stature, had finally begun to display a fringe of sparse, light-colored hair on his chin and upper lip. His dark hair, fine-textured and already thinning slightly at the temples, hung shaggy and unkempt over his ears. Only the boy's prominent forehead and deep-set, intelligent eyes belied his beggarly appearance.

Antonio is right," said Javier thoughtfully. "We have to clean up before we can hope to work again. Do we use the last of our money for a shave...or do we eat?"

Chacón answered, "If we eat, it will probably be our last meal!"

"*Tocayo*," said Antonio Molina, "are you ready for your first shave?"

It was a four-hour walk to the small mountain village of Villalengua del Rosario. The Jerezanos arrived just before noon, in time to find a barber who had set up shop in the shade of a tree. Antonio volunteered to go first and settled into the rickety chair with its seat of woven esparto grass and arms polished by much use. The barber draped a tattered towel about his neck to catch the hair, and without further ceremony cropped him close with a large pair of shears, leaving an ample lock in the front. Water heated in a pot over a charcoal burner moistened his face and then a rock-hard piece of soap was rubbed back and forth over his cheeks until a froth finally appeared. The barber, talking non-stop and mostly to himself, scraped his badly chipped razor across the boy's face in short jerky movements, leaving a series of crimson nicks in its wake. A quick rinse and a blotting with a towel of questionable color finished the job.

Javier went next, and then Chacón. The barber joked about how little work he had to do on both Chacón's hair and his sparse beard. The boy winced at each nick of his skin. When finished, the boys paid the barber a half *real* each and left, feeling bloodied but refreshed.

"I'm hungrier than a blind man's dog," said Antonio Molina.

"*Tocayo*, do we have any food?"

"Only a piece of bread I saved from last night."

"How about money, Javié?"

"Ten *céntimos* [cents]. But before we do anything else, we have to see about working tonight...or we won't even have a place to stay."

Within an hour the boys had arranged to work in a humble worker's café, the sort of place that granted credit to farmers and laborers until the next harvest. As they headed out of town to find the *venta* [country inn] where they hoped to spend the night, Antonio Molina turned to his companions and said, "Give me the bread and the ten *céntimos*...I have an idea!"

Chacón and Javier watched from the road as Antonio approached the doorway of a whitewashed hut on the outskirts. They saw a white-haired head appear in the doorway, but could not hear the conversation. Moments later Antonio returned carrying a second small loaf of bread and a small clay bowl containing liquid.

"How did you do that?" asked Chacón.

"Easy, *tocayo*. I told the woman that we have only a small piece of bread to eat and asked her if she would sell us a little oil and vinegar so that we could make gazpacho. She insisted that I take more bread with the oil and vinegar. Look, she even lent me this bowl...and she wouldn't take the money!"

"That still isn't much of a meal...I'm starved as a dog!"

"*Hombre! Cuando no hay lo que sirve, sirve lo que no sirve!* [when you don't have what will do, make do with that which won't do!] Besides, we can do the same thing again."

Antonio went to a second home, out of sight of the first. He returned empty-handed. "All she said was, 'May God help you, *hermanos!*' Come on, let's try again!"

The next house yielded more bread and some cloves of garlic. Satisfied with their luck, the boys retired to the shade of a tree just outside of town. Antonio sliced and crushed the garlic while Javier and Chacón broke half of the bread into crumbs and small pieces. When they mixed these ingredients into the oil and vinegar they had a crude gazpacho.

"This is the worst gazpacho I've ever tasted," said Chacón, dipping a piece of stale bread into the bowl of tangy mush. "Where's the tomato, green peppers, cucumber, and salt?"

"*A buen hambre no hay mal pan, tocayo*. [To the hungry there is no such thing as bad bread.]. I'm so hungry that this tastes as good to me as our mother's stew."

When they had eaten, all three stretched out in the dry grass, partially shaded by the sparse branches above them, and smoked cigarettes. Antonio said sleepily, "Now let's have a little nap...and then we'll see..."

They slept soundly for over two hours.

The lonely little *venta* on the road outside of Villalengua del Rosario was an ancient one-story building with a thatched roof. An elderly blind man greeted Chacón and the Molinas, assuring them that the accommodations were comfortable. When asked about food, he replied that there was plenty of everything. "*Hay de todo*," he said.

Inside the travelers found a single room, half of it floored with cobblestones and fitted with a crude fireplace, simple furnishings, and a few cooking utensils. The rest of the room had a floor of packed earth and served as the stable. When the boys inquired of the *ventero*'s wife, asking what they might expect to eat and what it would cost, the bent old woman flew into rage. "And what am I supposed to cook? Do you think this is a café? If you wish me to cook, bring me the food and we will see..." With that she limped away, muttering to herself.

They were three hungry youths who entered the tiny café to perform that night. The evening went much as it had in Arcos, except for the addition of a crude stage created by inverting a large wooden watering trough. The raised platform was too small to accommodate more than one performer, so they had to alternate. While Antonio danced, Javier and Chacón sat in chairs behind the stage. The wood resounded with the footwork and enabled the *bailaor* to perform all of his dances.

Both Chacón and Javier found that, during their solos, they received more attention seated precariously on the platform than they had in the café in Arcos. The spectators were more attentive, but no more generous when it came time to collect contributions. The night's work, which dragged on until almost three o'clock in the morning, resulted in a collection of assorted *céntimo* coins and *reales* amounting to little more than enough to cover expenses at the *venta*.

Among the peasants gathered in the café, one man stood out. He came in late and sat quietly through the evening, smoking cigarette after cigarette and downing *cañas* of *manzanilla*. What distinguished him from the others, apart from the way he seemed to concentrate on the *cante*, was his unusually forbidding appearance. His dark-complected face was deeply etched with lines and pockmarks, and an angry scar ran from the outer edge of one eye to the corner of his mouth. Deep-set eyes peered alertly from under dark bushy eyebrows; unruly black hair, thick sideburns, and a heavy drooping mustache accentuated his fierceness.

Chacón had noticed the man enter and had been a little unnerved by the glint of crafty malice in his intense stare. Later, when the youth realized that the gypsy—and there could be no doubt that he was gypsy—was one of the few who had remained attentive, he began to direct his *cante* toward the man. At least one person was really listening!

As Chacón came down from the improvised stage for the eighth time, the gypsy stopped him and indicated an empty chair across the table. In a deeply hoarse and gravelly voice, with an exaggerated Andalusian lisp, he said, "Well done, *chaval!* [young man] How is it that you sing the *cante* of the *calé* so well...although you don't have the voice for it?"

Seen up close, the man's dress was that of the nomadic gypsy: a dark coat with black, braided ornamentation at the hem, a broad *faja* sash wrapped about his waist, from which protruded a pair of trimming shears and a wicked skinning knife, and a bright yellow scarf showing at his open collar. Against the table leaned a stout *vara*, carved from a slender tree branch with a fork at the upper end and the bark peeled to create a pattern of light and dark rings.

"I'm from Jerez. I grew up among the blacksmiths of San Miguel."

"Ah, that's it," said the gypsy, nodding his head. "And the guitarist, the same, I imagine...he plays well." The man tilted his head back, threw down the last of his *manzanilla*, and signaled for more. "I invite you and your friends, *chaval.*"

When all three boys were seated at the table in the largely empty room, the gypsy expelled a plume of smoke and said, "I am El Morrongo [The Cat]. I have come here to buy livestock for the fair in Villamartín. Fortunately, the *busnés* [non-gypsies] here have as little knowledge of the value of their animals as they have of the *cante*. El Morrongo understands both!" When the gypsy smiled, the scar gave his mouth a sinister twist. "Have you finished here?"

Antonio Molina answered after a quick glance around the almost empty room. "I think so...it's not worth doing more."

"Well then, I invite you to accompany me to where my family is camped...not far from here. We will celebrate my daughter becoming a woman...it happened this morning. We *calés* [gypsies] celebrate those things. Empty your drinks and let's go!"

Javier glanced uneasily at the other two and could see by their expressions that they were not eager to go off into the dark with this wild-looking and somewhat intoxicated gypsy. The words of the Guardia Civil weighed heavily on their minds: *The gypsy steals with his words...he does nothing for nothing!*

The guitarist said, "*Hombre!* We would love to go, but we have left our things in the *venta*."

"*Vamos!* Let's go get your things and go to my camp. My woman will make food for us and we can drink and sing the rest of the night...and all day tomorrow..."

"We're dead tired...we haven't slept in days," interrupted Antonio, "and, besides, we have already paid for our lodging."

"Sleep? Sleep is worthless, except to women, children, and dogs. You can sleep anytime. If you wish to sing and play like the *calés*, if you expect to truly feel it, you must learn to live like the *calés*. We sing because we recall what we have lived and what we have suffered."

"*Hombre*, tomorrow. Perhaps tomorrow we can go to see you..."

"There is no tomorrow, a man must live today, now!"

"Listen," continued Antonio, rising from the table, "we will come to your camp tomorrow, we promise..."

"Promise? What good is a promise?" The gypsy spat disdainfully on the floor. "You are like children. A man sings all night, until the morning..."

"Tomorrow, we'll be there, as sure as there is a God."

The gypsy continued to press his argument, but the boys persisted and prepared to leave. With obvious disgust El Morrongo finally relented, saying sarcastically, "If you don't get lost, you will find me in the forest on the road to Grazalema." The boys left him shaking his head and muttering to himself about *los busnés*, "May God give all of them three gifts in one week—jail, the hospital, and the cemetery!"

The Gypsies

A blood-red sun had just begun to peak above the rugged mountains when th eboys set out on the dusty road from Villalengua del Rosario. A full day's trek to Grazalema lay ahead. With luck they would arrive early enough to arrange work for the evening, work they desperately needed. The following day they hoped to be in Ronda.

When the Jerezanos had returned to the *venta* the night before, only a few hours before sun-up, they had to knock on the door several times before finally being admitted by the *ventero*. The blind man had dragged out three husk-filled mattresses from the corner and placed them on the stone floor as far as possible from where his wife slept soundly on a pile of burlap. A muleteer snored loudly from his bed on the bare earth. The last thing the *ventero* said to the lodgers was, "*Madrugaís?*" In spite of their fatigue, the boys had to laugh. It was meaningless to ask if you were going to rise at daybreak, for the only possible answer in a *posada* or *venta* was, "Yes, of course!"

Now, traveling with only a few hours' sleep and without breakfast, the boys were ill-humored and they trudged the hills in silence. They had gone to bed hungry, and Antonio's last words before falling into a deep slumber had done little to console them: "*Acuéstate sin cena, amanecerás sin deuda!*" [Go to bed without dinner; you will wake up debt free!]

Chacón felt miserable. Moving his feet as if in a stupor, he let his mind wander to visions of fried fish or bowls of savory garbanzo stew. It had been days since he had eaten well, and as he recalled delicious home-cooked meals he couldn't help but wonder if the trip had been such a good idea.

After only an hour, the sun made its presence felt, bathing the red, parched soil in a warm glow. "Let's rest a minute, "said Chacón, wiping the sweat from his forehead with his sleeve. He squinted into the sun's glare at his companions ahead of him. "I don't have much strength...I feel like I have one foot in the grave."

Javier and Antonio came back to join their friend as he collapsed onto a large rock. The older Molina joined Chacón, dropping to the ground and cradling his head in his hands. "My head is killing me. I drank too much last night!"

Look at this!" said Chacón in response, pulling up his sleeve to reveal an arm covered with bloody welts. Old fleabites had been scratched until they bled and formed scabs, while the more recent had only just begun to swell and were at the peak of irritability. But it was the bedbugs that had done the more lasting and cruel damage. The site of each bedbug's bloodthirsty feast had swelled to several times the size of a fleabite. Where the latter itched for a day or two, the welts of the "horses of Satan" became more and more inflamed and irritable with each passing day. Scratching made the discomfort worse, yet the boys found it nearly impossible to resist, resorting to anything that might give momentary relief.

"I don't know how much more of this I can take," said the *cantaor*. "And it seems like we are not getting anywhere..."

"*Andamos pa 'tras como er cangrejo* [We're going backwards like crabs]," said Antonio. "Shall we give it up, *tocayo?*"

"You mean go back? No, not yet. Even if we wished to go home, we would still need work to survive. And, besides, our luck has to change. What do you think, Javié?"

"I'll go along with whatever you two say. If we don't find work soon, it won't matter either way."

"Antonio?"

"Let's go! On to Grazalema!"

More and more the road was bordered by patches of the great gnarled cork oaks that formed an immense forest in the mountains south of Ronda. Where branches and trunks had been stripped bare of the cork bark the trees appeared as orange, naked skeletons in the dark woods. Because of the trees and the winding road, it was not surprising that the boys hadn't noticed a rider approaching them from behind until he was quite close.

Javier saw him first. "Someone's coming," he said. The other two turned to see a man mounted on a burro and leading a second animal making his way at a sprightly pace up the steep incline toward them.

"*Me cago en la mar!*"[1] exclaimed Antonio suddenly. "It's the *gitano!*"

The others groaned, for it was indeed El Morrongo. Until that moment he had been completely forgotten. The gypsy approached, a grin on his craggy face and his legs dangling almost to the ground on either side of his diminutive mount. He wore a scarf knotted about his head, over which perched a cheese-shaped *calañés*—a flat cylinder of black velvet that lacked the wide brim of Javier's hat.

"*Lachós chibeses, chavales!* [Good day, boys! (gypsy language[2])] I'm glad I caught up with you...you might not have been able to find my camp, which is not far from here." El Morrongo slipped off the donkey and, leading both animals, started up the road. "Come, it's just up this way."

The boys exchanged apprehensive glances. But fatigue and hunger had worn them down and they meekly fell in line behind the gypsy. As they walked, El Morrongo talked non-stop, bragging about the good deals he had made in purchasing the donkeys and berating the *busnés* of Villalengua, "...who did not understand the *cante* and did not know how to listen. Only the *caló* understands the *cante*...it is our music. No other people can understand its meaning, not even *los húngaros* [non-Spanish gypsies]. Have you heard their songs? *Los húngaros* have nothing like our *cante*..."

When El Morrongo turned off the road and headed across a small meadow toward a grove of trees, the boys hesitated and tried once more to explain that they urgently needed to get to Grazalema. But it was futile. The gypsy would have none of their excuses. His glib tongue turned the boys' every protest into helpless acquiescence. He insisted that they come "...just for a drink and something to eat," and to show his family "...the *busnés* who can sing and play like *calés*."

The camp of "Los Morrongo" was well situated, hidden from the road in a tree–lined clearing beside a trickling rocky stream—one of

---

[1] common Spanish curse; literally, "I defecate in the sea!"
[2] The language of the Spanish gypsies, called *caló*, is a mixture of Sanskrit, Romany, thieves' jargon, and Spanish. Widely spoken until the late 1800s, it had largely disappeared by the mid-1900s. There have been recent attempts to save what is left, but it is spoken only in a limited fashion by very few.

few to survive the long, dry summer. A gaunt greyhound with pathetically exposed ribs charged them, growling and threatening. But when El Morrongo raised his *vara*, the animal cowered, tucking its tail between its legs and arching its bony spine. With a dispirited yelp it turned and skulked back to its spot in the shade. Close behind the dog came two naked children, a boy who could not have been more than ten and a younger girl. Both were shaggy headed and covered with dust. "*Bato, bato!*" they cried. Their father's hard eyes softened as he bent to scoop the girl into his arms and covered her dirty face with kisses. El Morrongo handed the rope leads of the two donkeys to the boy, saying, "*Chavo*, take these *bestis* and put them with the others!" Then, when he saw the children staring at the strangers, their big dark eyes curious, yet distrustful, he laughed and said, "These are three *busnés* who wish to be *calés*."

The campsite, largely shaded by trees, was set against the backdrop of the family wagon, a dilapidated cart with two large wheels and a hooded canvas top. Tattered straw-filled mattresses and an old rug were piled near the cart, and numerous pots, frying pans, assorted clay jars, and a variety of baskets lay scattered about. Two women tended to a small fire and a pot supported over it on three large rocks. Their once colorful blouses were ragged, and dirty aprons covered the laps of their voluminous skirts. With sharp eyes they followed the approach of the newcomers.

"Dolore!" barked El Morrongo.

"Eh?" replied the older of the two *gitanas*, an arrogantly handsome woman with her hair tightly gathered back from her hawk-like face. Squatting by the fire, she added ingredients to the pot with slender fingers whose long dirty nails resembled the merciless talons of a bird of prey.

"Prepare extra food, we have guests..."

"Guests? We have many mouths to feed and little to eat...and now you wish us to feed the *busné?*" she spat. "*Estás chalao* [You're crazy], Rafaé!"

"Shut up woman!" bellowed El Morrongo, raising his hand as if to strike her. "These *busnés* are artists from Jerez and they are here as my guests. We are hungry."

The *gitana* grew sullen, but rose to her feet and walked slowly and haughtily toward the wagon. El Morrongo turned to the other woman. "Rují [Rosa], your husband hasn't returned yet?"

"No, not yet!" Rosa, a homely woman, with a round, almost Oriental face flecked with smallpox scars, had a warmth in her expression that the boys had not felt from the other. Her breasts swelled at her neckline and, from time to time, she pulled one of them forth and offered it to the infant lovingly cradled in her lap.

"Don't be worried... it's not time for him to return. Perhaps tomorrow. Where is Angu'tia?"

"She went for water."

Dolores returned with a clay jar and a handful of wild greens. The aroma from the boiling pot had already reached the Jerezanos and left them weak with hunger. Their ravenous glances had not escaped the sharp eyes of the *gitana*. She glared at them, wrinkled her nose with distaste, and sneered, "*El busnó hiede, que apesta!*" [The *busnó* smells so bad he stinks!]

It was true. The travelers and their unwashed clothing emitted a stench that even they found intolerable. The gypsies might be ragged and dusty, perhaps even dirty, and they might smell of animals and humanity, but they seldom reeked as did the three boys.

"*Chavales*, take off your shirts!" grinned El Morrongo. "If you are going to visit with us, we have to be able to breathe. Angu'tia will wash them for you. Where is she?"

Dolores yelled shrilly, "Angu'tia, come here!"

A husky, but youthfully feminine voice responded from directly behind the chagrined visitors. "I'm coming!"

The boys turned as one and, as one, were stunned motionless. A young *gitana* came toward them. Although scarcely more than a girl, her innocent sensuality left the youths momentarily speechless. She was barefoot and naked to her bronzed waist, where a red scarf tied over her ragged skirt gave emphasis to the undulations of her slender hips. Diminutive in size, she held herself like a queen, head high, shoulders back to display her youthfully firm breasts, and an arrogance in her feline stride. A mane of jet-black hair, wild and uncombed, framed the beauty of her strong features. Thick eyebrows and full lips gave her a sultry charm. When she smiled, her teeth glistened brilliant white, contrasting with her rich brown skin.

"*Sí, bato?*" the girl said, with no trace of self-consciousness in her gaze as she studied the strangers. Water dripped from her coppery arms where she held a large clay jar of water on her right hip.

"Take these shirts and wash them! *Venga, chavales*, take off those clothes!"

Feeling self-conscious, the boys fumbled with their shirts. When they finally handed them to Angustias, they couldn't help but allow their eyes to follow the girl's return to the stream, where she lifted her skirt, baring her thighs in order to tuck the garment between them.

"*Ostebé!*" cried Dolores when she saw the boy's bloody arms. "The *bichos* [critters] have eaten you alive." The *gitana* had decided to play along with her husband, for she supposed that he must want something from the young *busnés*. "Rují, bring me some mud from the stream!"

While Rosa went to the stream, Dolores fetched a bundle of herbs from the wagon. She ground the herbs in a mortar and combined them with the mud. Then she had each of the boys spit in the mixture before spreading it on their inflamed arms and legs. The cool poultice brought instant soothing relief. The gratified Jerezanos thanked her and sat down in the dry grass near where they had piled their belongings to wait for the mud to dry.

"It is obvious that you are not *calés*," said El Morrongo, lighting the twisted cigarette he had just formed from Antonio's tobacco, "you have an extra rib...we *calés* have seven and a half ribs."

Antonio Molina thought for a moment and then asked, "Have you ever counted your ribs?"

"No, but there are seven and a half. My grandfather told me, and he was a very wise man." Morrongo's tone left no room for argument.

The boys sat back in the stiff dry grass, listening to the ramblings of the gypsy. Above, a bird chirped its song while, out of sight by the gurgling stream, Angustias could be heard pounding wet clothes on a flat rock to accompaniment of her husky voice: *"Ay Dolores, ay Dolores, que huele el cuerpesito a flores!"* [Ay, Dolores, ay Dolores, your body smells of flowers!]

"*La adelfa, chavales, la adelfa!*" A thin, crackling voice rent the peaceful mountain air.

Turning, the boys saw for the first time a shapeless old woman, little more than sinews and wrinkles held together by a tattered dress. She sat by the wagon in the camp's only visible chair, from where her dark eyes, mere slits in her wizened face, had been taking in all that went on before her.

"*Chavales*, scatter leaves of the oleander about the place where you sleep and you will not be molested by *bichos!*" Even as she spoke, her bony but still agile fingers manipulated flexible reeds taken from a riverbank, forming them into what would become a small basket. Los Morrongo were *gitanos canasteros* in the full sense of the term. Not only were they gypsies of the open road who refused to submit to the laws and social strictures of the *gachó*, but part of their livelihood derived from the *canastas* [baskets] they wove during idle hours in camp, or to the rhythm of slowly turning wagon wheels while on the road.

"Listen well, *chavales*," pronounced El Morrongo, "my mother is very wise!"

Moments later, Dolores announced that the meal was ready. The Jerezanos weakly protested the offer of food—they knew that they would be taking from the mouths of the impoverished family. But their refusal lacked conviction and El Morrongo would have none of it. The men ate first, dipping into the pot with pieces of hard bread and wooden spoons to scoop up the stew of garbanzos, greens, and small bits of meat and chorizo sausage. Spiced with a great deal of olive oil and garlic, the mixture was flavorful and hearty. They washed it down with mountain water from the spout of a clay jug.

While the women ate, Morrongo and the boys sat back in the grass to enjoy Antonio's dwindling tobacco. The sun filtered down through the branches, its warmth bringing drowsiness to bodies already heavy with food. Dolores came to cradle her husband's head in her lap and began carefully going through his hair, parting it with her long, curved nails and minutely inspecting each inch of his scalp. The gypsy closed his eyes, his craggy face relaxing with pleasure. Nearby, Rosa carried out the same procedure on little Carmelita, while Angustias knelt behind her, searching her aunt's hair for tiny parasites.

El Morrongo spoke lazily. "*Chavales*, how do you like the life of the *calés?* There is nothing better than to be born a *caló*[3]...it is the best a man can wish for. We are the *señores* of the countryside, of the fields and mountains. From the trees, the vineyards, and orchards, we obtain fruit and vegetables. The mountains supply our firewood, the streams our water, the fields and forests our meat. The hard ground is our feather mattress, the rain our shower, and our sun-toughened skin protects us like an impenetrable armor. Even the dirt on our skins shades us from the sun in the summer and keeps us warm in the winter. With such a

---

[3]*caló*: a gypsy; *calí* is the feminine and *calé* the plural, although very often the incorrect plural, *calés*, was used (the same endings are seen in the older terms for the non-gypsy: *busnó* and *busné* or *busnés*). *Caló* is the abbreviated form of *zincaló*, derived from the Sanskrit word for "black man."

life, what need have we for money? *Er gusto bale ma que er parné.* [Pleasure is more valuable than money.] As the *copla* says," and the gypsy intoned softly, half singing, half speaking:

Yo soy rico	I am rich
porque toda la riqueza,	because all wealth,
la alegría, y el pan,	joy and bread [food],
lo encuentro en mi libertad.	I find in my freedom.

Chacón had been only half listening. The ramblings of the gypsy were like a series of dreams—imaginative and distorted. It was nearly impossible to dispute his dogmatic pronouncements, for he had the cunning logic of a wild animal. The boy had been watching the gypsies pick parasites from each other's scalps. With the excruciating itching of his ravaged body only too fresh in his memory, it hadn't occurred to him that, for the gypsies, the process of de-lousing was more than an act of simple hygiene—it was an intimate social interaction, a source of great pleasure. He interrupted El Morrongo. "How can your life be so good if you have to suffer those *bichos* in your hair?"

"*Hombre,*" replied that gypsy in his same drowsy tone, "one louse more or less...what does it matter to a *caló*. They suck out the bad blood...it's good to have them!"

Birds chirped in the distance, water sang in the ravine, and small insects hummed as they circled in hazy shafts of sunlight. One by one, the occupants of the wooded glade drifted off to sleep.

The sun was dropping quickly toward the mountains behind them as El Morrongo led his wife, son, and the three visitors some distance on the road toward Ronda, then off through the corkwoods to the edge of an open field. There, in the clearing, they found a number of humming beehives, each fashioned from a cylinder of cork that had been stripped intact from a small tree.

Before approaching the hives, El Morrongo collected dry grass and green leaves. Once gathered into a bundle and lit with Antonio's flint, the gypsy had a heavily smoking torch. He took a large bowl from Dolores, signaled the others to move back, and went to the nearest hive, enveloping it and himself in a cloud of smoke. The pacifying fumes would not last long, so Morrongo worked quickly, prying the cork lid off the hive, thrusting the torch inside for a few moments, and then using his knife to slice out large sections of golden sweetness. He placed several large hunks of dripping wax honeycomb into the bowl, and then, backing slowly away, with bees swarming ineffectively all about him, he yelled, "Run!" They all turned and fled.

Not until they reached the road did they stop to sample the stolen honey. For Chacón it was a sweetness he had never experienced. He chewed the wax and savored the thick nectar as it ran down his throat. El Morrongo, rubbing at the few stings he had received, laughed, "You see, I am too clever even for the bees!"

Chacón asked, "Don't you ever worry about being caught when you steal?"

"*Ca, hombre!*" replied Morrongo, lifting his hands in an emphatic gesture. "Who is going to catch me? *Los jundanaré?* [The Guardia Civil?] Those *cabrones* [he-goats; bastards] are such cowards they have to always go in pairs. I don't fear them. And, besides, the honey is there for the *calés*. The *busnó* has plenty of honey and the bees will make more. The *busnó* was put into this world to work, and the *caló* to live from his work. The *busnó* believes he is superior to the *caló*, but he is superior like the bee is superior to the cicada. The bee makes honey and wax...the cicada eats it! That's why we sing:

Bente con mangue y berá	Come with me and you will see
la gracia que hay de tené	the *gracia* you must have
pa bibir sin currelá.	to live without working.

El Morrongo spat a hunk of wax into the dust and then continued, warming to his topic. "Work is the punishment that God imposed on the *busnés* because of the sin of Adam, when he was tempted by Eve. Isn't that so?" Then, without waiting for an answer, "*Pues*, since we *calés* do not descend from Eve, but from the first wife of Adam, we are not condemned to this suffering."

The Jerezanos, with only a scanty knowledge of the Bible, could not refute the gypsy's logic.

"Besides," added Morrongo, "we *calés* owe our way of life to the mercy of the Virgin Mary. We gave asylum to the Mother of God when the Holy Family fled to Egypt. When the *calés* saw that the Virgin had no place to stay, they said to her, 'You are the Virgin Mary...*pues*, come into our home, nobody will bother you here.'

"The Virgin accepted the hospitality of the *calés* and, the next day, when she was ready to continue her journey, they said to her, 'María, now that your child is saved, what are you going to give us?'

"The Virgin answered, 'You will never again be forced to work.' "

Morrongo grinned. "And that's why we do not have to work. We eat by our wits."

"The Virgin," added Dolores, "was *calí* [*gitana*], while Joseph was *busnó*. That is why *El Señor* [Jesus Christ] was half and half."

"You have only to see pictures of the Virgin," corroborated Morrongo with authority. "She has the face of a *calí*, the face of Angu'tia."

Antonio Molina suddenly recalled something that appeared to contradict the gypsies. "Wasn't it the *gitanos* who made the nails used to crucify Jesus...and that's why they have to suffer..."

"*Hombre*, that's false...falser than Judas! The truth is what I just told you. Besides, it was the *calés* who gave *El Señor* a drink of water when he was carrying the cross. And he too said, 'You *calés* have my blessing. You will eat, but you will not work!'"

In the last light of early evening, as the countryside began to come alive with frogs and crickets, the gypsies relaxed. El Morrongo tended to his livestock while the women gathered firewood for the night, but for the most part they lay about, chattering idly.

Chacón and the Molinas passed the time watching Angustias. The girl had covered her nakedness with a blouse, more out of vanity than any sense of modesty. But the sensuousness of the young *gitana*'s body—the firm roundness of her youthful bosom, the curve of her lower back, and her proud, graceful movement—was not lost on the boys. She awakened desires in Chacón that had thus far in his life lain dormant, obscured by his passion for the *cante*. The natural innocence of her beauty appealed to his inexperience.

Javier perceived the girl as a fine instrument. His dexterous fingers could almost imagine the warm texture of her flawless brown skin. Antonio Molina, his body surging with youthful hormones, saw in Angustias a mysterious and passionate femininity, as different from the girls of Santiago as a wild feline animal was from a cultivated garden flower. Earlier, he had whispered to Javier, "How beautiful Angustias is...*tiene carita de cielo*. [she has a heavenly face.]"

It took the boys somewhat by surprise, therefore, when Angustias, passing several feet in front of them, suddenly lifted her skirt to her knees, squatted, and sent a stream of golden liquid gushing in an arc from between her thighs onto the trampled grass in front of her. When the flow had ceased, she nonchalantly straightened and strolled over to pick up her little sister, oblivious to the three pairs of eyes that followed her.

Such occurrences were not unfamiliar to the Jerezanos. In fact, they were a part of daily life in the barrios of Jerez—but only among men and children. Adult women were generally more discreet. The act had caught the boys off-guard because it did not fit the images of Angustias they had formed in their minds. It should not have come as a surprise, for the family of El Morrongo carried out the most personal of acts without the slightest attempts at privacy. They stopped in full view, wherever they might be, to perform their toilet. Modesty in the gypsy women consisted primarily of taking care to keep their private parts strategically hidden from male eyes.

When it came time for Chacón or the Molinas to take care of such personal matters, they found themselves in an uncomfortable position. Antonio's solution was to turn his back to the women, saying to his companions, "*A la tierra que fueres, haz lo que vieres!*" [When in Rome do as the Romans do!]

Reluctant to follow Antonio's example, Chacón looked longingly—and apprehensively— at the darkening woods. Without thinking, as he headed for a tree just outside the circle of firelight, he said, "I hope there are no snakes!"

Instantly a shriek of collective horror burst forth from the gypsies. Chacón turned to see Angustias and Rosa throw their arms about each other, trembling uncontrollably. Rosa's baby wailed with fright as Dolores cried out rapidly in her shrill voice, "*Lagarto, lagarto, lagarto, vete a comer esparto!*" [Lizard, lizard, lizard, go eat esparto grass!] It was an oath commonly repeated to ward off evil.

Even El Morrongo's eyes went wide, the whites reflecting the orange hues of the fire. "*Chaval*," he said sharply, "you must not say the name of the creeping one...it is not done, for it brings *los malos mengues* [evil spirits] and bad luck!"

"I didn't know you were afraid..."

"It is not fear, *chaval*...El Morrongo fears nothing...but a wise man does not tempt *los malos mengues*."

Chacón noticed that El Morrongo tightly gripped the charm that hung around his neck—a piece of horn tipped with silver and suspended by a cord of black mare's tail, "...so that no one can give me the *mal de ojo* [evil eye]."

The gypsy came and squatted near the boys. He said in a low voice so that the women, who were just beginning to recover their wits, could not hear, "To show you that I am not afraid, I will tell you of the *bicha larga* [long creature] that lived in the city of the *calés*, in Meligrana [Granada].

"She was longer than three men and lived in the Alhambra. No one ever saw her, but she was known to be there because her children, which were about as long as a man's arm, were seen often. Some men chased her away...I know this to be true because my father knew one of the men. Her children never grow any larger because it takes them a thousand years to grow. And since their mother is gone, they must always be searching for milk. At night they creep into the beds of mothers who are nursing and push the child aside. While drinking the milk, the animal...which has some sense...puts its tail into the child's mouth to keep it quiet. You can tell when this has happened because the child will have a black ring around its mouth in the morning and does not grow properly."

El Morrongo rose to his feet, saying, "Enough! It is not good for a *caló* to speak of these things." Turning to Javier, he said, "*Chaval*, get the *bajañí*...play for us!"

To calm the baby, Rosa had begun to sing softly in a high-pitched, almost Arabic, voice:

Duérmete niño chiquito,	Go to sleep little boy,
qué tu mare está a lavá,	for your mother is doing the wash,
y a la noche de que venga,	and when night comes,
la tetita te dará.	she will give you her breast.

The clear night had grown chilly, forcing the gypsies to throw more wood on the fire and sit closer. Javier returned with the guitar, and their capes, which the boys draped about their shoulders. While the guitarist trimmed his fingernails with a knife and tuned his instrument, Chacón chatted idly with El Morrongo's young son who sat on the ground beside him. Curious about the visitors, the little gypsy had stayed near them all afternoon. In spite of the chill, he still wore not a stitch of clothing.

Chacón asked him, "*Niño*, aren't you freezing with no clothes on?"

THE GYPSIES

The gypsy shook his head with a quizzical expression on his face. Then, an impish glint in his eye, he said, "No...y *ostré*, is your face cold?"

"No, of course not!"

"*Pué*," said the boy with a grin, "*yo tengo mucha cara, sabe!*" [literally, "I have a lot of face, you know!"; but the expression means "bold-faced, bold, without shame."]

Chacón and the others who had been listening laughed heartily.

Javier enthralled the gypsies with his playing. The children had never heard a guitar and, to them, it was truly something wondrous. They sat on the ground listening, wide-eyed at the movement of Javier's fingers and hypnotized by the outpouring of notes. The women were only slightly less impressed, for guitars were not common among their people and rare was the opportunity to listen to music. Only El Morrongo, who frequented cafés and livestock fairs and had seen and heard the best artists of the time, could judge the artistic merit of Javier's playing.

Feeling a little stiff and unsure from the lack of regular practice, Javier played some of the *alegrías "por rosas"* he had been composing. Little by little he had been adding original variations to the music he learned by watching Paco de Lucena. The rich *por arriba* [E-Major] chords produced a stronger sound than did the *por medio* [A-Major] key normally employed to accompany the *cante* and *baile* and provided more opportunity for melodic development.

The night air played havoc with the delicate and very worn guitar strings. Javier stopped to tune. El Morrongo grunted, *"Bien chaval!"* And then, to Chacón, "Now, *er guiyabo!* [*cante*] Sing for us the *cante* of the *calés!*"

Chacón sang at length *por soleá* and *seguiriya*. The sound of his voice dissipated in the cool night air, robbing him of resonance, but the stillness of the forest enabled him to be clearly heard. With the rapt attention of the gypsies and their uninhibited words of encouragement, the *cantaor* felt *a gusto* and sang from the heart.

"*Sí, sí... hala...eso é!*" grunted El Morrongo approvingly.

Dolores glanced questioningly at her husband and said, *"Lo chanela de verdá, no?"* [He really knows, doesn't he?]

"Yes, he knows...he sings well. He lacks the voice of the *caló*, but he knows." And then, louder, as Chacón sang a particularly strong *remate* [closing], "*Güeno, quiribó* [friend], very well done!"

Angustias sat cross-legged on the ground, listening intently. Chacón's *cante* intrigued her and held her spellbound. It sounded controlled and not as rough as her father's singing, or that of other gypsies she had heard. When the *cantaor* had finished the *seguiriyas* and stopped to take a drink from the wineskin El Morrongo offered him, the girl blurted out in her throaty voice, "*Busnó*, you sing well, but how you can sing like a *caló* with those feet that you have?"

Chacón looked down at his feet.

"All *busnés* have big feet, but I have never seen *pinreles* like yours. Your shoes look like coffins!"

Chacón blushed, while the gypsies and Javier laughed. Antonio Molina forgot to laugh. He was aware only of the shape and movement of Angustias' lips as she spoke.

El Morrongo took the wineskin and expertly directed a stream of dark liquid into his upturned mouth. Wiping his mouth and mustache with the back of his hand, he announced, "We celebrate the entrance of Angu'tia into puberty. *Chaval*, sing something so that she can dance. Angu'tia, show the *busnés or quelo de la calí!*" [dance of the *gitana*]

Javier looked at Chacón. *"Por tango?"*

Chacón nodded.

The lively rhythm began. Chacón sang. Angustias listened for a moment, then slowly rose to her feet. Her concentration revealed itself in two tiny furrows that appeared between her eyebrows above her partially closed eyes. Her hands began to move in slow circles, rising higher and higher until they were overhead. There was nothing studied or planned in her dance, only natural movement in imitation of what she had seen among her people. She was all graceful arms, arrogant expression, and proud posturing, with little movement of her feet except to softly mark the beat of the music and create a gentle undulation of her hips.

Chacón sang. Javier played. The gypsies clapped their hard hands. And Angustias danced like one possessed. Her hands and fingers were alive at the ends of arms that writhed like serpents. When she spun in a rapid turn, her skirt twirled high, jeopardizing the modesty imposed by her newly acquired womanhood. A jerk of her head tossed her hair back off her face, revealing drops of moisture on her brow and upper lip. The whites of her eyes glowed in the dark shadows of her face. The sensuous dance of the young *gitana* was spiced by that unique gift of *gracia*, the *ángel* that distinguishes everything touched by the hand of the gypsy.

The Jerezanos were completely captivated, held speechless by flashes of thigh and tufts of dark hair under upraised arms. But El Morrongo was at no loss for words. "*Ole!*" he cried, "*Así sinela or quelo de la cañí* [That is the true dance of the *gitana*]...*qué sandunga* [what *gracia*]!"

As Angustias collapsed finally on the ground near the fire, her inspiration spent, Chacón heard a cracked voice next to him saying, "You dance better than the angels in Heaven!" He looked over to see Antonio with a glazed expression on his flushed face. What was the matter with him? The girl danced well, naturally and with *gracia*, but she was not professional. She didn't have the technique of a Juana Antúnez, and she certainly wasn't of the stature of Antonio himself. Angustias was gifted, but Chacón couldn't see that she deserved to be called "without equal!" He also didn't see the glow of Angustias' eyes when she flashed a glance across the fire at Antonio and then looked quickly away. Nor could he have seen in the darkness the blush that rose to her cheeks.

El Morrongo said loudly, "My girl is now a woman. Soon she will marry. Perhaps she will find a husband in Villamartín, at the livestock *feria*...

"A good strong *caló* with many horses," added Dolores.

"And small feet," giggled Angustias.

A low, broken "*ayyy...*" rumbled forth from El Morrongo. He sat up straight on his small stool, hands on his thighs. Across the fire from him squatted his old mother. Rosa sat on the ground at the old woman's feet, holding her sleeping baby. Next to her, Dolores and Angustias. To one side, the three visitors sat draped in their cloaks, while the two younger children sprawled by the fire, sleeping soundly.

"Now *I* will sing for my daughter," said Morrongo. In his throaty, cracking gypsy voice, he began softly:

Por la Sierra Morena	Through the Sierra Morena [mountains]
va una partía;	goes a band [of outlaws]

After a momentary pause, his high-pitched wail pierced the night, raw and powerful:

va una partía	a band goes

And then, in extended and gradually descending *tercios*:

por la Sierra Morena,	through the Sierra Morena,
por la Sierra Morena	through the Sierra Morena
va una partía.	goes a band.

And finally, a chant-like passage that rose and fell:

Ayyyy...	Ayyyy...
ayyyy...	ayyy...
Va una partía.	Goes a band.

In similar fashion, El Morrongo sang the second two lines of the verse:

Va una partía;	Goes a band;
El capitán le llaman,	The leader is called,
el capitán le llaman	the leader is called
José María.	José María.
Ayyyy...	Ayyyy...
ayyyy...	ayyyy...
José María.	José María.

A different melody completed the *copla*:

Qué no será preso,	He will not be taken prisoner,
qué no será preso,	he will not be taken prisoner,
mientras su jaca torda	as long as his dapple pony
tenga pescueso,	has its pride,
mientras su jaca torda	as long as his dapple pony
tenga pescueso.	has its pride.

This *cante* resembled the songs of the *arrieros* and coachmen, both in its verse and in the rough, straightforward delivery of the melody. El Morrongo did not have the technique of a professional singer, but he did have strength and the gypsy roughness of the *voz afillá*. There was also honesty in his singing, a direct communication of emotion without the exaggeration that comes from attempting to impress an audience. And there was, again, the *ángel* of the *gitano*, that "something" that put his stamp upon a piece of forged ironwork, a basket, the sale of an animal, the playing of the bull in the bullring, or the turn of a *tercio* in the *cante*.

Chacón felt moved by the impact of the gypsy's song and admired the power of his delivery. He said to El Morrongo, "*Hombre*, that is a magnificent *cante*..."

Javier interrupted, "They are *serranas*, no?"

"*Sí, chaval*, they are *serranas*. They are the *cante* of the mountains...our *cante*, the *cante* of the *serranos*, as they call us here in the Serranía de Ronda [the Ronda Mountain Range]. Listen, here is another..." And he began to sing. Javier, who had found the tones on the guitar, placed his *cejilla* where he could play *por arriba*. He played quiet chords, not attempting to impose rhythm on the gypsy's very personal interpretation:

Es la mujer lo mismo	A woman is the same
que leña verde;	as green firewood;
resiste, gime, llora,	she resists, whines, cries,
y al fin se enciende.	and, finally, ignites.
Luego, encendía,	But then, when lit,
ni resiste, ni llora,	she neither resists, nor cries,
sino suspira.	but only sighs.[4]

El Morrongo took a drink, belched, and said, "In this *cante* nobody can top me..." After a momentary pause he added, "...although there is one who sings these *serranas* like nobody else, like an angel...a big man, a giant. He is called Silverio..."

Chacón sat up and swelled with pride at the mention of his idol.

"...but," added El Morrongo, almost under his breath, "of course he is *busnó*..." The gypsy shrugged his shoulders in a gesture of dismissal, his grimace intended to plant a seed of doubt concerning Silverio's credentials. Then he turned to Javier and said, "Another *cante*...for you, *chaval*." In the same melody, he sang:

La mujer y las cuerdas	A woman and the strings
de la guitarra	of the guitar
es menester talento	require talent
para templarlas.	to tune them.

---

[4]This is the poetic verse of the *serranas*; when sung, it is expanded in the manner of the previous example.

> *Flojas, no suenan,*   Too loose, they don't sound,
> *y suelen saltar muchas*   and many will snap
> *si las aprietan.*   if you tighten them too much.

Chacón wondered whether the gypsy improvised his words or just had a good memory for *letras*. It was all the Jerezano could do to memorize the words as he heard them, but by that third verse he had begun to sing the melody to himself, shadowing the voice of El Morrongo.

Antonio did not take his eyes from Angustias. From time to time the girl looked up and boldly held his gaze for a moment before again averting her eyes and poking distractedly with a twig at the embers of the fire.

El Morrongo's sharp eyes glanced from his daughter to the *bailaor* and narrowed slightly, flickering with a momentary glint of suspicion. "Continue with *la bajañí!*" he said to Javier, and then more sharply to the girl, "Angu'tia, listen well!"

> *No fíes en los hombres,*   Do not trust men,
> *aunque prometan;*   even if they make promises;
> *qué ellos tiran la caña*   they throw out their [fishing] pole
> *por ver si pescan.*   to see what they can catch.
> *Pero, en pescando,*   But, when they catch something,
> *ellos salen riendo,*   they leave, laughing,
> *y ellas, llorando.*   and the girls, crying.

For a moment, no one spoke when El Morrongo had finished. Only the night sounds of the forest imposed upon the inner thoughts of those seated around the dying fire in that wooded glade. Then, suddenly, the gypsy directed himself to the Jerezanos, focusing his penetrating gaze on Antonio. "Angu'tia is now *una majarí...una moza* [virgen], as you say...and we must watch her carefully. Her *lacha* [chastity] is the most precious thing she has, for, without it she cannot marry...no one would have her. You *busnés* cannot comprehend what honor is to a *calí*. Honor is everything. We ask only three things of our women...that they remain *majarí* until they marry, that they be faithful to their husbands, and that they carry on our race by bearing many children."

El Morrongo was speaking more freely with the Jerezanos than he normally would with those outside his race. The fire, wine, and shared intimacy of the *cante* had blurred the distinction between gypsy and *gachó* and had loosened his tongue. He spoke now as much for his daughter's ears as to warn the visitors.

"The *calí* must choose her husband carefully, for once married she can neither leave nor be left for another. Among us *calés* no one takes the woman of another. We live free of jealousy. But if it *should* happen that a *caló* takes the woman of another, we do not go to the justice of the *busnés*. We ourselves are the judges of our wives, and we can take her life as easily as we kill an animal. We bury her in the mountains, and no relative will seek revenge. In this way, with this fear, our women live chastely and we live with confidence and security. We share everything except our women. The *busnés*, with their foolish laws, do not understand this. Nor do they understand that a man does not become old as quickly as a woman. Among our people, when a man's wife becomes too old for him, he may leave her and select another more in keeping with his desires. Thus, we live happily."

El Morrongo took a drink, spat violently, and rolled a cigarette. His impassioned sermon had vented much of his anxiety concerning his daughter. The words of caution had been heard. Angustias had not raised her eyes even once during her father's harangue. Chacón and Javier were oblivious to the motive for the discourse, while Antonio was beyond caring, lost in his own world of desire. The *bailaor*'s only concession to El Morrongo was to be slightly more discreet in his attempts to attract the attention of Angustias.

Lowering his voice, El Morrongo said, "Some *calés* have forgotten our ways. *Los caseros* have chosen to live among the *busnés* and have forgotten that we are superior, as anyone with intelligence knows. We are brave and suffer without complaint. We do not get sick. We see things that others do not. We are loyal to our own and obey our laws. Our law is very simple, *chavales*, and we do not need books and judges. We say, 'Do no harm where you live!' That's all. Very simple. But the *busnó* cannot understand. And from that come our three laws. The first, which I have already told you, is to be true to the man, he who commands. Then, we must be loyal to our race. We look out for each other and we respect our old people and our dead. We do not offend our ancestors by cursing them as do the *busnés*. We pray to our dead and they help us. We say, 'It is your mother who is watching over you.'

"A *caló* is always true to his word...if it is given to another *caló*. That is the law. And we respect the *caló* who obeys these laws, who does not sin against his people..."

El Morrongo grew quiet and thoughtful. He realized that he had talked too much, that a *caló* should not speak of these things with outsiders. The *busnés* were his enemy. The laws and morals of the *busnés* were but creations of *busnó* imagination so far as the *caló* was concerned. Nothing that belonged to the *busné*, not their lives nor their property was worth a *céntimo*. The *caló* felt no remorse in taking from the *busnó* nor in lying to him. In fact, he felt an obligation to do so.

"*Venga cante, chavales!*" bellowed the gypsy, beginning to feel the effects of the wine. Javier put his fingers to the guitar, and the *cante* began to flow once more. Hours passed. There might never have been sleep for the Jerezanos if El Morrongo had not finally collapsed from fatigue and drink.

One by one, gypsies and non-gypsies alike rose, stretched, and wandered off into the dark to prepare their beds. Chacón heard Antonio whisper something to the yawning Angustias as he passed by her. While the gypsies spread grass-filled mattresses on the ground and huddled together under blankets, the Jerezanos put their feet toward what remained of the glowing fire and wrapped themselves in their cloaks. For the first time since leaving home, they would fall asleep free from the assaults of fleas and bedbugs. Aside from the occasional marauding mosquito, the only impediment to sleep was the persistent memory of the Guardia Civil's words, "*...and they will stick a knife into you to get it!*" Chacón consoled himself with the realization that, except for the guitar, they had nothing worth stealing.

Antonio Molina was the last to fall asleep. He couldn't escape the image of Angustias sleeping so near, the curve of her hips clearly molded by her blanket. Once asleep, visions of the *gitana* wove themselves into his dreams throughout the night, causing him to toss and turn restlessly.

In the sleepy morning, Chacón, returning from the edge of the woods, yawned and said to the gypsies gathered about the newly revived fire, "How well I slept! I even dreamed that we were..."

"*Maldito sea* [a curse upon you], *chaval!*" snapped Dolores. "Don't you know that speaking of dreams before breakfast will bring bad luck to all of us for the rest of the day?"

Chacón watched as Dolores picked up a wooden spoon and began rubbing the handle furiously. The other gypsies had each found wood to touch, The Jerezano almost laughed out loud at the comical effect produced by all of Los Morrongo rubbing wood to ward off any possible ill effect of his comment.

Antonio came up beside Chacón and asked, "Has anybody seen my tobacco pouch? I had it in my jacket last night and now I can't find it."

The gypsies all shrugged their shoulders. Dolores said, "You must have misplaced it..."

"Misplaced what?" It was El Morrongo, arriving just in time to catch his wife's words.

"I can't find my tobacco pouch."

The gypsy's face darkened with anger. Looking into the faces of his family, he bellowed, "These are my guests. They will lose nothing in my camp. You will find that pouch immediately!" He raised his *vara* in a rage, as if he would lay waste to the whole lot of them.

The women and children scurried about, appearing to be searching for the lost object. Dolores scowled, her eyes seething with malevolence, and began to look about indifferently. Her half-hearted effort further enraged her husband. When El Morrongo stepped toward her, threatening, the frightened woman raised her hands over her head to protect herself and backed away. In an attempt to placate her husband, she removed a scarf from about her neck and tied a knot in it to form a small pouch. Reluctantly, she began to search, striking the pouch against each object she passed—a wheel on the wagon, an iron pot, a large rock—all the while chanting:

San Cucofato, San Cucofato,	Saint Cucofato, Saint Cucofato,
los anres te ato;	I tie your testicles in a knot;
si la petaca aparece,	if the tobacco pouch appears,
[*te los desato,*]	[I'll untie them,]
y si no, no te los desato.	and if not, I won't untie them.[5]

Dolores continued thusly for several minutes before grumbling out loud, "Here it is...here by the wagon!" The sullen *gitana* came to where Antonio stood next to the glowering El Morrongo. "*Busnó*, it must have fallen from your jacket in the dark."

Antonio, not wishing to cause more trouble, started to say, "Yes,

---

[5]This superstition was not unique to gypsies, but was common throughout Andalucía. People still tie a handkerchief in a knot to help find a lost object, but the verse and the meaning have been lost. The legend said that the mythical Saint Cucofato was martyred by being strung up by his testicles.

that's probably what happened..." but his words were cut off when El Morrongo snatched the pouch from Dolores with one hand and with the other delivered a powerful blow to the side of her head.

"Shameless one!" he raged and would have struck her again had she not retreated rapidly to the far side of the clearing. Once at a safe distance, the enraged *gitana* began to berate her husband in a fierce volley of invective. Chaos broke out. Rosa and Angustias attempted to calm the crying children, while the old woman scolded shrilly and the dog howled.

"*Mardita sea, mala sangre* [Damn you, bad blood]...it was a bad hour when I married you!" shrieked Dolores at the end of a particularly vitriolic tirade.

El Morrongo, his anger vented, turned to the Jerezanos with a laugh. The boys had been immobilized by the suddenness of the outburst and the confusion, but the tension drained out of them when the gypsy said, "What a fiesta we had last night!" He slapped Antonio on the shoulder in what appeared to be a friendly gesture, but the steely strength of the man made it a bruising blow, an act of dominance with an underlying hint of warning.

"It doesn't surprise me that you lost your tobacco on the way to bed, *chaval*...we drank a lot of wine." El Morrongo laughed again. "What a fiesta! Let's have some breakfast. *Mujeeeé!* [Womaaaan!]"

Squatting over a cup of hot chocolate, El Morrongo listened to the Jerezanos discuss their plans for the day. They wished to leave for Grazalema immediately after breakfast in order to arrive early enough to arrange work for the evening, The following day would take them to Ronda.

The gypsy interrupted. "*Chavales*, there is nothing for you in Ronda. Why don't you come with us to Villamartín? The livestock fair is one of the best in Andalucía. There will be much wine, *alegría* [good times], and many *calés* spending the money they earn in the *feria* [fair]. Your talents would be much in demand."

Antonio, who had been strangely quiet, came to life at the suggestion. His face lit up as he said to his companions, "He's right! Ronda will be a gamble. We might be swallowed up and find ourselves out of work, just like in Jerez. The *feria* is where we can earn the most."

Chacón and Javier looked at each other. "What do you think?" asked Javier.

The other thought for a moment and replied, "Perhaps it would be better to go to Villamartín, but I think we should go ahead by ourselves to see what we can earn in the pueblos on the way."

Antonio's face dropped as Javier agreed with the *cantaor*, but El Morrongo smiled in agreement with the plan. In truth, he had not relished the idea of having to feed the *busnés* during the journey.

"When is the *feria?*" asked Chacón.

"It begins the nineteenth," replied the gypsy, whose livelihood depended upon keeping track of the days and knowing the dates of all the *ferias*.

"How many days is that from now?"

The other counted backwards on his fingers. "That will be five days from now."

"Then it's settled?" said Chacón, looking to his companions for confirmation. "We leave now for Grazalema and spend the next five days working in the pueblos on our way to Villamartín."

Javier expressed enthusiasm for the plan, while Antonio, long-faced, had no choice but to agree.

Packing was quickly accomplished by all except Antonio, who moved slowly and took every opportunity to pass near Angustias and exchange words with her. Chacón and Javier had a more pressing problem. They were troubled by their inability to repay the gypsies in some way for their hospitality. Then, Chacón came up with a solution. He took Antonio aside and said to him, "*Tocayo*, let's give El Morrongo what's left of our tobacco!"

The *bailaor* was reluctant.

Chacón argued, "It's the only thing we have to give, and there isn't much left anyway."

"But, our tobacco..."

"Do you want to see Angustias again?"

Antonio reached for the pouch without another word.

The gypsies clustered about the departing Jerezanos. Only Dolores stood back, still wondering what her husband planned to gain from these *busnés*. El Morrongo received the gift of tobacco with little comment. "*Bien, chaval*," he said indifferently, tucking the pouch into his sash without a glance, as if it were something owed him.

"*Buen viaje sus diñele Undebé!*" said the gypsies. "*Nos endiquemos en Villamartín.*" [May God grant you a good journey. We'll see each other in Villamartín.]

The boys had taken only a few steps toward the road when El

Morrongo called after them, "Wait!"

The Jerezanos turned and the gypsy gestured to Chacón, saying, "*Chaval*, come here!"

As Chacón approached, El Morrongo said to him, "A *cantaor* of your ability should have a true *ran* [*vara*], not just any old twig. Take this...it will bring you luck!" He handed the *cantaor* the carved *vara* that had seldom been out of his hands.

Speechless, Chacón grasped the forked handle and felt an inexplicable sense of power surge through him from the striped staff. He wanted to refuse the gift, but words would not come. El Morrongo, obviously pleased by the reaction, sent the boy on his way with a solid thump on the back.

As the three boys moved up the dusty road, Antonio Molina was the last to look back. Angustias stood slightly off to one side, away from the others, her large, luminous eyes fixed on him as she combed her hair back off her face with the fingers of one hand.

La Feria

A crisp, clear day proclaimed the end of summer. The three Jerezanos, invigorated by a night's rest and the cool, bone-dry mountain air, made rapid progress north toward Grazalema. Chacón had not ceased singing since leaving the camp of Los Morrongo. Enthralled by his new walking stick, he could not resist glancing down at it and swinging it to feel its heft.

Javier, striding easily with the aid of Chacón's old *vara*, interrupted the *cantaor*'s song, commenting, *"Qué bruto son Los Morrongo!"* [What rough people those Morrongos are!]

"That's true," replied Antonio. "Dolores is *má pesá que lo garbanzo* [harder to take than garbanzo beans]...and her husband, *un peaso de bárbaro* [a brute]."

The *bailaor*'s voice took on a softer tone after a pause. "But Angustias...Angustias is flour from a different sack."

"Yes, she *is* pretty, brother, but it is useless to think about her. El Morrongo would never allow you near her."

"She's more beautiful than an ounce of gold. If I could just speak with her alone..."

"You're crazy!" interrupted Javier. "The Morrongos don't want a *gachó* around...not even in a picture."

"We'll see," replied Antonio, smugly. His companions shook their heads in disbelief. It seemed to them that, overnight, Antonio had lost his sense of reality and was oblivious to both their warnings and the threats of El Morrongo. Knowing it was futile to protest further, Javier and Chacón shrugged their shoulders and continued the march toward Grazalema.

The Jerezanos gave a concert in the *casino* of Grazalema—a tiny white *pueblo* tucked into the valley between two of the highest peaks in the mountain range. As in most small towns, the *casino* was open only to members and their guests. Within its walls, men of the community passed evenings drinking and playing cards, dominos, or billiards. Gambling brought a spark to their lives and provided a respite from the otherwise tedious life of the pueblo. The concert in the *casino* earned the boys enough to pay for the night's lodging and to purchase tobacco and food for the next day's travel.

The approach to Zahara, a half-day's journey north of Grazalema, was signaled by a massive, square-towered castle perched on the tall cliffs above the whitewashed town. There, the Jerezanos worked in a café and again they earned more than their expenses for the night. Adding to their good fortune, an enthusiastic aficionado gave Antonio a pair of boots to replace his practically useless old ones.

Chacón expressed the feelings of the three the following day on the road to Algondonales. "This is the happiest I have been in my life. Our luck has changed and nothing can stop us now!"

As they walked, the boys sang and dreamed, their *alpargata*-clad feet scarcely aware of the miles. They lunched beside the road on bread, cheese, and chorizo, and before entering each pueblo, changed clothes to make themselves presentable. Good fortune followed them to Algodonales and Puerto Serrano, and they were in high spirits when they reached Villamartín on the eighteenth of September, the eve of the livestock fair.

It appeared at first that their luck would hold in Villamartín. A temporary café with a canvas roof had been constructed on the grounds of the livestock market, and the three artists were offered their first contract—seven *duros* [35 *pesetas*] for the three days of the *feria*, plus whatever they could collect from the patrons. This represented a fortune to the boys and they were elated. In addition, a second *cantaor* had been hired. El Puli, older than the Jerezanos, was an energetic, wiry little man. If he wasn't a gypsy, he certainly dressed and acted like one. He sang well and agreed to sing for Antonio's *baile*, freeing Chacón to concentrate on singing solo, *p'alante*.

The artists earned their pay, for the nights were long. Nobody slept during the *feria* and sunrise saw the performers still at work. After going on stage a dozen or more times each night, they often had to continue at the table of a drunken customer. It was usually well into morning before they could drag themselves to the *fonda* [inn] for a few hours' rest.

Villamartín had come alive with joy and merriment. The annual *feria* was one of few opportunities to put aside the cares and dreariness of daily life in the villages. Morning festivities concentrated in the livestock market, a chaotic gathering of herds of horses, mules, donkeys, sheep, goats and pigs spread out over a dusty open space at the edge of town. And where there were animals, there were gypsies. From the distant corners of Andalucía nomadic gypsies had come to sell beasts of burden, or to act as *chalanes*—mediators between buyers and sellers. They also came to be with each other, to renew old relationships, select brides, and celebrate weddings.

Young gypsies paraded horses and mules, sprinting them in the dust to show off fine points to prospective buyers. Chacón and the Molinas had to laugh when they overheard one of these *chalanes* attempt to beguile a customer into purchasing a skinny nag covered with sores.

"*Lo quié usté ve caminá?*" said the *chalán*. "Do you want to see him run? He really moves!" And then, to his accomplice, "Canino, come here. Get on this pony and take him up the road...but hold him back. Careful, Canino, *hijo mío*, be careful, don't let him get away from you!"

On all sides the Jerezanos found entertainment. On one hand, a gypsy extolled the youth of an aging horse whose teeth had certainly been filed. Here, another brought life to a pitiful animal by inserting needles into its ears. Over there, a *chalán* insured the fiery temperament of a pack mule by surreptitiously and delicately applying the lit end of a cigarette under its tail.

Fierce arguments broke out on all sides. Crowds gathered to watch and spur on lively debates between buyers and sellers. The gypsy *chalán* was a consummate actor. He knew all the tricks, how to touch the most sensitive nerves of his audience, and he almost always won out. When the success of a sale appeared doubtful, he appealed to the vanity of one or the dishonest streak in another. And he always found a joke or a stroke of genius to extricate himself from sticky situations with a touch of *gracia*.

In one such instance, the Jerezanos overheard an angry man reproaching a gypsy who had just sold him a donkey so old and thin that its protruding ribs could easily be counted. The man was saying, "...I am a traveling performer and I must have a dependable animal!"

The other replied with easy self-assurance, "You have paid for the beast and closed the deal. I don't know why your honor is complaining about the purchase, when it brings to you *en el bicho tos sus menesteres.* This animal will fulfill all your needs."

"What needs are those?"

"The orchestra, *señó...*" pointing to the prominent ribcage, "in case you ever need a harp!"

It was on the second day of the *feria* that the Jerezanos encountered El Morrongo in one of the canvas-roofed taverns erected along one side of the grounds. The gypsy had been engrossed in an animated and loud conversation when he spotted the boys.

"*Chavales*," he roared with a broad grin as he broke away from his companions and rushed toward the boys. Chacón winced when the gypsy, flushed and wild-eyed, affectionately gripped his shoulder with steely fingers. The Molinas were jolted by hearty slaps on the back. Once again, Antonio failed to grasp the message behind the forceful blow delivered between his shoulders.

"Let's have a drink, *quiribós* [friends]!" bellowed El Morongo. He was agitated and restless.

"We invite you," countered Chacón, "for we have had great success here."

"Just as I told you," replied the other. "There is much money to be made here. I too have had good luck. *Qué alegría!* The *feria* is good for the *calés*. It excites us to be around so many of our kind. We are not accustomed to it. There is a *mengue* [demon] running loose among us, making us crazy. It's the animals. You *busnés* wouldn't understand, but the smell of the animals excites the passion of the *caló*. A horse is beautiful to us...it is our life, and to see so many of them together inflames our blood..."

Glasses of *manzanilla* arrived and El Morrongo emptied the first in a single gulp. Lifting another, he said, *"A golipén e saró or burdipén!"* He paused a moment and then added, "I'm sorry! I forgot that you do not speak our language. To the health of all!" And he emptied the glass.

The Jerezanos followed suit with their drinks as El Morrongo continued.

"You know, we love these animals. When I run my hand over the flank of a good horse, I feel as I do when I touch the naked skin of my woman. With so many *bestis*, and the money, and the *alegría* [joy], the *mengue* excites our passion. There have been many *raptos* this year...many young women have been kidnapped. A daughter is taken, and the next day the boy brings her to her father and says, 'We have married. We fell in love and went to the river.' If the girl can prove she was *majarí* the wedding festivities take place."

The gypsy fell silent for a moment before he added, "We have to watch Angu'tia very carefully. She is never left alone. There have been so many *raptos*...and fights, many fights."

El Morrongo appeared to lapse into melancholy for a moment, staring down at the empty glass in his hand, but when he raised his eyes they were again alight with fire. Something caught his attention and he said in a lowered voice, "You will have to excuse me...I see that I have business to attend to."

As he moved away, he shouted back, "You will come to eat with us...tomorrow. My camp is at the edge of town, on the road to Algodonales."

The Jerezanos watched El Morrongo exchange a few words with a group of gypsies, slap backs, and then move on to where a tall, well-dressed man stood waiting. The boys finished off their drinks and returned to wander the fairgrounds.

The *feria* was a delight to the senses. In addition to the sounds and smells of the animals and the animated chatter of the *chalanes*, gypsy women assaulted fairgoers with offers of charms to protect from the evil eye or insisted on being allowed to read palms or tell fortunes. A shrew-faced woman approached Antonio, one child tied to her back in a shawl and another, clad in a scrap of cloth, clutching at her skirt. She grabbed on to the youth's shirtsleeve and wouldn't let go. "Handsome one, give me your hand! I'm going to tell your fortune. By the look on your face you are a lovesick pigeon. You have the *sacais* [eyes] of one in love and the feet of a dancer. *Anda garboso* [Go on, gallant one], pursue your loved one. But be careful, for the rose you desire is surrounded by thorns!"

No sooner had Antonio given the woman a small coin to send her on her way than another appeared, dressed in rags and bearing a pitiful child, naked and filthy. She thrust a horny hand at the boys and demanded, "*Argo pa'l niño* [Something for the child]. *Undebé se lo pague a ustés*...may God return your kindness!" The woman persisted until she received a coin.

Food vendors added to the merry chaos of the *feria* with their songs and chants. "*Agua!*" cried the water seller, a cork water tank on his back and glasses in his hands. "Fresh clean snow water from the mountains!"

Along one side of the grounds, *buñoleras* had set up their tents and portable frying cauldrons. These gypsy women, cleaned up and hair pulled back neatly for the occasion, wore voluminous skirts and aprons with fringed shawls wrapped across their breasts and tied in back. They were easy to locate by the smoke rising from the sizzling oil in the cauldrons where they fried *buñuelos* [*churros*; fritters]. It was difficult for passersby to resist the smell of the hot fried dough, and almost impossible for them to resist the persuasive cajoling of the aggressive *gitanas*, who did not relent until they had made their sale.

"*Vaya unos guñuelitos!* [What good *buñuelos*!]" they cried. If they lost their sale, their comments turned sarcastic. "*Mirozté, que son mú güenos...pa las lombrisas!* [Look here, they are very good...for your tapeworms!]"

As Chacón and the Molinas turned from smoky cauldrons, hot *buñuelos* in hand, a man in front of them attempted to ignore the gypsy women. Pursued by a cry of, *"Ande osté, caballero, una osenita!"* [Come on, gentleman, buy a dozen!], the man tripped on an uneven spot in the ground and fell flat on his face. As he rolled over on his back and made the sign of the cross, one of the *gitanas* shouted over to another, "Micaela, *anda*, go and put out the light...the *señorito* has gone to bed!" Raucous laughter followed the humiliated man until he was out of earshot.

A short time later, the Jerezanos gave in to the aroma and cry of *"Calamares fritos y calientes!"* They stopped to buy squid that had been fried in a huge pan mounted on a donkey cart. Other vendors sold peanuts, *turrón* [almond taffy], and dried fruit. Temporary taverns offered stews and *caracoles* [snails].

Entertainment could be found on all sides. Gypsies, many of them foreigners invariably labeled as *húngaros* [Hungarians], had come from afar with their trained dogs or monkeys. One family had spread an old carpet on the ground, where a gypsy woman wearing a purple velvet robe told fortunes with the aid of a raven that selected cards from a deck. Off to one side the father, wearing pink tights, balanced on a ball while his son stood on his shoulders with outstretched arms. When the boy moved up to the man's head and then did a somersault to the ground, the small crowd applauded and shouted *"Olé!"* In a loud showman's voice the father said to the little boy, "My son, what makes you do this work?" To which the boy responded, "Hunger!" A little girl dressed in rags circulated through the crowd, imploring with big sad eyes and presenting her inverted tambourine for a few coins.

"That reminds me of the *feria* of Jerez," said Antonio. "El Marrurro told me that he once heard a gypsy couple arguing in front of the entrance to a tent featuring an Italian troupe of performing fleas. The man was trying to convince his wife to go in with him to see the little creatures that everyone was praising to the skies. She was determined not to go. He says, '*Pero mujé*, why shouldn't we go to see it?' She tells him, 'Look here, Tobalo, I said no and I mean no...because I don't want the company to escape and for me to have to pass the rest of the night killing actors!' "

It was a truly happy time for the youths and they savored the afternoon until time for work. Antonio's desire to see Angustias again preoccupied him so that it took all the persuasive powers of Chacón and Javier to convince him that he shouldn't try to see her until the following day.

"**S**he did it! I can't believe it!"

Antonio was ecstatic as the boys returned from El Morrongo's camp on the third and final day of the *feria*. "She has agreed to see me alone...tonight, after we finish work. When she hears my signal she's going to come down to the river..."

The *bailaor*'s companions were dismayed. "Be careful, brother," said Javier, "the gypsy would as soon stick a knife in you as look at you!"

"El Morrongo won't be there...Angustias told me he doesn't return until morning."

Antonio had been fortunate indeed to find El Morrongo absent when they had arrived at the camp shortly after midday. Dolores had greeted them indifferently at first. Then she saw the gifts—live chickens, a large sack of garbanzos, chorizo, and candy for the children, who were delighted to see the *busnés*. Antonio found a number of opportunities to speak with Angustias out of the hearing of Dolores and the others—until the father made his appearance, returning for the *siesta* hours.

El Morrongo was courteous with the visitors, but not as warm as he had been previously. The gypsy had been on a binge of drinking and celebrating with his people for several days and he no longer felt the urgent need of companionship and music that had led him to so readily accept the company of the *busnés*. In addition, his wine-soaked brain had become obsessed with protecting Angustias. He was determined to have a say in whom she married and not allow her to run off or be kidnapped.

Thus it was that the visit had not been prolonged, and the Jerezanos found themselves returning to town in the late afternoon. On all sides, gypsy camps were awakening from the stupor of *siesta*, coming back to life in preparation for the final night of revelry. Antonio Molina was blind to all but his plan to meet Angustias.

"We must try to finish early tonight," said the *bailaor*, "so that I can see Angustias before her father returns."

"Don't expect us to help you with this foolishness," replied Javier.

"Let's get back to the *fonda*," said Chacón, ignoring the subject of Angustias. "Javié, I want to try the *serranas* I learned from El Morrongo. If we practice a little, maybe I can sing them tonight."

"Have you already learned them well enough?"

"I think so. And they should go over very well with the people from around here."

Noisy customers packed the café as midnight approached. The artists had been working for several hours when they noticed a gentleman enter, order wine and find a chair near the tiny stage. He cheered the performers enthusiastically and drank heavily. Much later, the man introduced himself and invited the Jerezanos and El Puli to drink with him. *Don* José Gonzalo had come from San Fernando to purchase livestock.

"Get your guitar," said *Don* José to Javier.

Seeing that the public had largely deserted the café, Javier brought his guitar to the table and the artists began to entertain the gentleman. Antonio was restless, anxious to be off to see Angustias. He hoped that each *cante* would be the last, or that his presence would no longer be needed. But each time he attempted to excuse himself, *Don* José gripped his arm and said, "No, *hombre*, you can't leave. It's still early. Have another drink and give us one more little dance…"

Don José ordered wine and more wine. Hours passed. Antonio, dejected and heavy-eyed with drink and fatigue, realized that his only hope was to attempt to see Angustias later in the morning. Perhaps while her father slept, Angustias could slip away to the riverbank.

At a nearby table, two men had been drinking heavily and playing cards. Suddenly, one of them stood up unsteadily, knocking his chair over backwards, and said in a foggy voice, "*Home*, you're cheating...I know you are!"

The other replied, "How can I be cheating...you're winning all the money?"

The first man looked down at the stack of winnings on the table in front of him. With a bewildered expression on his face, he said, "*Caramba*...maybe *I'm* the one who's cheating!"

Sun-up found the four artists still at work, although numb with exhaustion. *Don* José periodically nodded off, but whenever the boys stopped for a breath, his eyes would open slightly and he would thump the table feebly, saying, "No, *hombre*, continue...don't stop!" Finally, he slumped in his chair with his chin buried in his chest. The youths looked at each other, not sure what to do. Then, suddenly, the man snapped his head up, looked around in a haze, and mumbled, "*Vámono!* Let's go!"

The Jerezanos accompanied *Don* José to his *fonda* and waited expectantly while he fumbled with his wallet in the doorway. At that moment, a friend of his appeared behind him, on his way out. *Don* José pulled out a green hundred-*peseta* note and said, "Quico, get change for this bill and give ten *duros* [50 *pesetas*] to these *muchachos*."

El Quico, a gypsy *chalán* who had accompanied *Don* José from San Fernando, led the four artists to the nearby Café Sopapo [The Slap] and ordered coffee for all of them. Chacón, Javier, and El Puli wanted only to be paid and be off to their beds. The coffee and El Quico's stories of his bargaining exploits in the *feria* were of little interest to any of them, particularly Antonio, who could hardly contain his eagerness to see Angustias.

Minutes crawled by, and there was no sign that El Quico was about to pay them. Javier, growing more and more agitated, finally said, "*Señor* Quico, we appreciate the coffee, but we really must get some sleep. We were up all night entertaining your friend *Don* José. If you could just give us the money you owe us..."

El Quico replied with a smile, "Certainly..." And he began searching his pockets in an exaggerated fashion. His expression slowly changed to one of puzzlement and he said, "I don't seem to have the money. I must have lost it!"

Antonio had been building to the boiling point, and now he exploded. "Liar! *A otro perro con ese hueso!* [Tell your lie to someone else!] That cannot be true, for we have been with you all the time. So please pay us at once!"

As Antonio rose to his feet, the gypsy answered by drawing a wicked knife from his sash and lashing out. The *bailaor* avoided the lunge and, without stopping to think, picked up a large glass and slammed it into the side of El Quico's head. The glass shattered and the knife dropped to the floor. Someone shut the door to the room as Antonio threw himself on top of the bleeding gypsy and spectators yelled in a mixture of anxiety and anger.

It ended as suddenly as it had begun. El Quico, blood pouring from the wound in his head, slipped out of Antonio's grasp and out the door before anyone could stop him. Antonio, disheveled but unhurt, would have given chase if two *Guardia Civiles* had not blocked his exit from the café.

"Where are you going, *muchacho?*"

"That thief, the one who ran from here, has our money. Let me go...I have to catch him!"

Antonio squirmed in the grasp of the *Guardia*, who said tersely, "That one has escaped us, but we won't be tricked into letting you go too. The *feria* is over. Maybe a few days in the jail will cool you down. Come along!"

In spite of his continued protests, the boy was led off to jail, a *Guardia* at each elbow. His companions followed alongside, maintaining a persistent harangue of pleas and explanations. At the door to the jailhouse, one of the *Guardias* relented and agreed to accompany the boys to the *fonda* where they had last seen *Don* José.

At the entryway to the *fonda*, a heavy-set woman clad in black rose to her feet from where she had been scrubbing the stone doorstep and dashed any hopes the boys had of corroborating their story and perhaps recovering their lost money.

"*El Señor* Gonzalo left here some time ago. His companion? The other has not returned since he went out this morning."

For three days, Chacón and Javier went often to the jail, waiting for long periods outside with women who had brought food for their husbands in tin buckets or wrapped in large scarves. But no one would tell them when Antonio would be released. They passed the time wandering the streets, listless and dispirited. There was no question of working.

Villamartín was spent after three days of *feria*. The temporary cafés and taverns had been dismantled and the gypsies had moved on. The town appeared deserted and only slowly did it return to the normal rhythm of daily life.

On the morning of the third day, reason prevailed at the jail and Antonio Molina greeted his companions in the street. A broad smile beamed forth from three days growth of stubble. "Let's eat! I'm hungrier than a snail on a mirror. Then, as soon as I get cleaned up I want to find Angustias..."

"Calm down, *hermano!*" Javier was relieved to see his brother, but disappointed that he was still obsessed with the gypsy girl. "Angustias is gone...the Morrongos left days ago. Forget about her. We have to decide what *we* are going to do."

The *bailaor*'s face dropped. He had held on to the hope that El Morrongo would not leave immediately after the *feria*. "I don't care what we do now," he muttered and then fell silent.

Javier looked at Chacón and said, "I think we should return home. Things aren't going as we planned. What do you think?"

More and more, the Molinas had begun looking to Chacón for leadership. The *cantaor* replied, "I think we should go on. What has happened here is not going to happen again. If we leave here today, we can be in Sevilla in two days and then in Zafra for the *feria* in the fifth of October."

"Zafra? Zafra is very far..."

"Yes, but we have enough money now to take a coach from Sevilla, and the livestock fair of Zafra is one of the biggest. El Morrongo said..."

"That's right!" interrupted Antonio, brightening at the mention of the gypsy. "El Morrongo spoke of Zafra. Angustias will be there..."

Two hours later the boys walked north out of town, past the remains of what had been gypsy camps, where now only flies rejoiced over the trampled vegetation, charred fire pits, piles of garbage, and the scattered wastes of man and animal. Antonio, with renewed vigor, babbled on about his jail experience. "To pass the time in there, the prisoners gamble. And since they have nothing to gamble with, they scratch a circle on the floor, place lice in the center, and bet on which one will leave the circle first..."

El Café de Silverio

The trip from Villamartín to Las Cabezas de San Juan was a full day's trek from the mountains down onto the fringe of the *dehesa*, the wide plain that spread out from the Guadalquivir River between Jerez and Sevilla. For much of the way, the boys followed an ill-defined *camino de herradura* [bridle path] through dense chaparral, a route traveled primarily by mule trains. By late afternoon they had reached great expanses of grazing land, home to vast herds of cattle, horses, and fighting bulls. Darkness and fatigue overtook them as they entered the town of Las Cabezas. There could be no question of looking for work, here or the following night in Utrera. Flush with money, the Jerezanos were anxious to reach Sevilla.

The three youths left the dusty white pueblo of Utrera early in the morning, feeling stiff but refreshed. Shortly after midday they stopped at a lonely *ventorillo* [country tavern] located at the junction of the road to Dos Hermanas. Little more than a simple hut, constructed of cane with a roof of palmetto fronds, it had a crude sign nailed to one support post that read: *AQi SEBENdE bino* [*Aquí se vende vino*: Wine sold here]. In front, hitched to a two-wheeled cart, a donkey stood in the hot sun, head drooping, eyes closed. The animal's closely-sheared skin twitched periodically to send small clouds of flies buzzing in frantic circles, only to settle once more in the same spots they had vacated a moment earlier.

Inside, the Jerezanos joined a crusty old Sevillano and the proprietor at the wooden plank that served as a bar. The boys lifted a moist clay jug high to drink, water from its spout running over their chins, cooling them both inside and out. Red wine, served in unwashed glasses, was sour and diluted. The Sevillano coughed deeply and spat often: clearly his health was not good. Curious about three young men traveling with a guitar case, he asked about their journey. When he learned that they were on their way to Sevilla, to see it for the first time, he said, "*Quién no ha visto a Sevilla, no ha visto a maravilla*" [He who has not seen Sevilla has missed a marvel] and offered to take them in his cart.

The sun had begun to set low on the horizon to the left of the road when the driver pointed ahead and grunted, "*Theh-bee-zhuh.*" [Sevilla]. At first the boys could see nothing in the purplish haze, but as the minutes passed they began to make out a tiny spire. "That's the Giralda of the Cathedral," said the old man. "The tower is so tall that, to see all of it, you have to come back a second day!" He chuckled to himself at his cleverness, then broke into a coughing fit, spat, and added, "And the Cathedral is...it's so big that you have to ride a donkey from one chapel to another!" In actuality, the old man had never been inside the Cathedral of Sevilla. Like many Andalusian men, he believed the church to be the domain of priests, women, and tourists.[1] But the sheer bulk of the structure had impressed itself upon his imagination.

The tower continued to grow in size above the unseen city until, at last, the travelers came up over a slight rise and saw Sevilla for the first time. The still distant shaggy outline of walls, buildings, and spires were barely discernable in the dusky light. As they came closer, they could make out the square tower of the queenly Giralda dominating the skyline, soaring several hundred feet above the city, and surrounding it, the lacework of gray stone flying buttresses that supported the Cathedral.

The cart entered an open meadow spreading out from the city wall to greet them. "El Prado de San Sebastián," said the old man. "Here is where we have the fair in the spring. You should see it...*las casetas* [tents] of many colors, the livestock market, much to eat and drink...everything you can imagine. It's the best fair in Spain, right here in this meadow." Then, in a lowered voice, "It was here, too, in the Inquisition, that many people were killed, burnt to death."

---

[1] It may seem strange to mention tourists during this period, but U.S President Ulysses S. Grant wrote, upon his return from Sevilla in 1878, that the city had been ruined by tourism.

The boys looked around, wide-eyed as they envisioned such a terrible death. "And what's that?" asked Chacón, pointing off to the left. At the edge of the meadow of San Sebastián, an immense building loomed out of the dusty haze. "Is it a palace, or the government?"

"No, *hombre*, it's the tobacco factory. Thousands of women work in there making cigars and cigarettes."

"It must be like heaven inside, no? With all those women!" Antonio Molina couldn't resist fantasizing."

"*Hombre*...I pity the man caught in there alone...ah, here we are."

The cart pulled up before an arched gateway in one of the few remaining fragments of the high, red clay wall that only a few decades earlier had surrounded Sevilla. "Here you are, La Puerta de la Carne. If you enter here you will be in the Barrio de Santa Cruz."

"Are we near the meat market?" asked Javier. "Is that why it is called the Gate of Meat?"

"*Qué va, hombre!* No way! On Holy Saturday, during Easter week, sheep are sold here, in this part of the meadow. Then the *gitanos* come...many *gitanos*. They build a small city of huts and shacks, and butcher sheep over there by the wall. That's why we say 'La Puerta de la Carne.'"

"And the postal coach?"

"In Triana, as I told you before. Go through the Barrio de Santa Cruz, past the Cathedral, and continue on until you reach the river. There you will see the bridge to Triana. In Triana, ask and they will tell you where to find the postal coaches. But, be careful, Triana is a dangerous place. The *gitanos* there will cut the throat of a *gachó* for his purse."

"How about Silverio's café?" asked Chacón, as the old man paused to cough and wipe bloody spittle from his mouth. "Can you tell us how to find it?"

"Calle Rosario...El Café de Silverio is on Calle Rosario. You will hear the best *cantaores* there, but watch yourselves and hold on to your money ...it's not a place for decent people at late hours. *Pos, vayan ustés con Dió*...I have to go this way, to enter through the Puerta de Osario."

The boys watched the old man encourage his tired donkey down the road to the left, the wheels squeaking loudly, then they turned to enter the city.

Once past the wall they found themselves in a labyrinth of very narrow streets between whitewashed two-story buildings whose wrought-iron balconies almost met overhead. The fronts of the homes were painted in grays and browns to shoulder height, hiding dirt splashed on the walls by passing animals and pedestrians, as well as protecting clothing from the chalky whitewash applied each spring to the rest of the building. Wrought-iron gates permitted the boys a peek into cobbled or tiled patios surrounded by columns that supported second floor hallways and balconies. Ornate tile mosaics decorated the inner walls. Potted geraniums, crimson oleanders, and even small orange trees, combined with canaries trilling in their cages and the gurgling of water in the occasional fountain to create a cool and peaceful retreat from the blistering summer heat. Families had moved chairs, sofas, and even pianos to the patios, avoiding the oven-like upper floors as much as possible in the hot season. High above, at roof level, a canvas canopy shaded the patio, but could be drawn back at night to allow passage of the cool evening air.

As the travelers passed each entryway, drafts of refreshingly cool air swept over them from the patios. The aroma of hot olive oil, saffron, and frying chicken reminded them that they had not eaten a full meal that day. They hurried through the narrow, twisting streets, often flattening themselves against the face of a building to allow a donkey to pass. Everywhere children played, women talked in small groups, and old crones dressed completely in black stared from their doorways.

When the youths found themselves in the same tiny plaza for the third time, they asked directions for a way out of the confusing maze. They were directed through an arched gate and another plaza and then, finally, the immense bulk of the Cathedral rose before them. "*Caray*, what a marvel!" exclaimed Antonio Molina. "It's bigger than the churches of San Miguel, Santiago, and La Colegiata all put together!"

It took some time to circle around the huge monolith, with its external arched flying-buttress bracing and the attached Patio of the Orange Trees. Just past the Cathedral a major street bustled with coaches of all descriptions, horses, donkey carts, and pedestrians out for the evening *paseo*. The boys marveled at the tall four and five-story buildings. They crossed the street and continued westward down side streets wider than some of the main streets in Jerez. As they walked, the air began to take on the scent of the sea, the sharp, tangy smell of fish mixed with the pungent odor of tar. They came around the corner of the bullring and, suddenly, there before them lay the Guadalquivir River.

The great river flowed green and sluggish after a long, dry summer, far below its high-water line. Sailing vessels, large and small, docked at the river's edge from beyond a squat, octagonal Moorish tower on the left to the bullring on their right. Some distance past the bullring a bridge of ornate ironwork stretched more than a hundred yards across the water to the smoky, low-lying buildings that lined the far side. According to what the Sevillano had told the Jerezanos, that had to be the barrio of Triana.

The three youths stood in awe of all they saw—the sheer magnitude of the city and its buildings, the majestic river and its ocean-going ships, the elegant bridge, and the throngs of strollers and vendors milling about the tree-lined waterfront. The last light of day had turned the sky lavender and tinged wispy clouds a fiery orange. Behind them the Giralda glowed a deep pink as the sun disappeared into Triana. A new moon appeared and hung like a scimitar just above the tower.

The Jerezanos made their way to the bridge and crossed into Triana, dodging mules, donkeys, carts and pedestrians. The bridge brought them to a plaza formed by the confluence of four streets. To the right a stairway led down from the bridge to the food market, a half-buried maze of stalls in what appeared to be the foundation of an ancient castle. Descending from the bridge into Triana, the boys entered a world of dirt and stench. Two-story buildings lined the streets of rough and broken cobblestones. Flowers on second-story balconies added a touch of color to the drab barrio, but the streets were poorly lit and largely buried under dust and dirt. The barrio's sewage flowed freely down the middle of the streets to create swamps of foul smelling mud. Gypsies were everywhere, some barely distinguishable from the *gaché* with whom they mingled, others standing out in their bright *faja* sashes and *calañés* hats.

For Chacón and the Molinas the atmosphere reeked of intrigue and excitement. At first opportunity they stopped a man whose bearing suggested he could be gypsy and asked where they might find lodging for the night. The man looked them up and down and said, "*Miroztés*, you had best look over there in the *Cava de los Civiles* [the neighborhood around the *Guardia Civil* headquarters]. There, among the *gaché*, you should be able to find something. If you come over here, to the gypsy side of Triana, you are likely to find only trouble."

A short time later the Jerezanos left their belongings in a guesthouse on Calle Castilla and found their way through darkened streets to the

Parador de Patrocinio where they arranged to ride with the mail coach the following morning. Then they set out to explore the city—although Chacón had only one thing on his mind: the Café de Silverio.

The Salón de Silverio—popularly known as the Café de Silverio—was the most highly revered *café cantante* of the day among aficionados and artists alike. Chacón knew that every flamenco artist aspired to appear on its stage. Not only did Silverio hire only the best, but he also had a reputation for treating them with unaccustomed respect and dignity. He had resisted the trend seen in many other cafés of sandwiching flamenco between variety acts that included magicians, popular singers, acrobats, and comedians. And of course, there was the attraction of the great man himself, the legendary Silverio, although it was said that he no longer sang in the café.

Chacón's excitement was contagious and the Molinas were soon caught up in his quest. Near the bridge they stopped to eat. A fish vendor dipped fillets of sole and mullet into flour and slid them into a deep vat of hot oil. When the fish had fried to a golden brown, the vendor scooped the fillets from the oil, drained them, and put them into cones of rolled paper. Eating the crispy, flavorful fish as they walked, the three Jerezanos crossed the river into Sevilla. Straight off the bridge, the youths continued up the wide Calle de los Reyes Católicos, with its bars and hotels. Asking directions, they turned right on Méndez Núñez and two blocks later made a left turn into the narrow darkness of Calle Rosario. Chacón's heart beat faster as they found Number 4 and stepped into the doorway.

El Salón de Silverio, like many cafés, occupied what had formerly been a luxurious private home. Marble columns formed arcades around the perimeter of an enormous patio and supported second-floor hallways leading to small rooms reserved for private parties. Pine tables and crude wooden chairs with seats of woven esparto reeds filled the patio around a central fountain, while box seats with wooden railings lined the side walls at stage level. The renowned stage, framed by heavy drapes, protruded from the back wall.

The air was thick with the acrid smoke of black tobacco and the deafening noise of many conversations, laughter and shouts, the clinking of glasses and bottles, and from the stage, the sharp beating of *palmas* and the pounding of feet on the wooden stage. A glass skylight covered the ancient patio, enclosing the heady atmosphere and creating a dizzying effect upon the Jerezanos. Little by little the boys' eyes adjusted to the dim light and they found their way to a table.

On stage a young woman danced, her figure illuminated by ornate gas lamps and reflected in gilt-framed full-length mirrors behind her. The curves of her hips strained the fabric of a tight *bata de cola*, the stiff percale of the train dress rustling loudly with each movement. When she turned, the dress lifted to reveal fashionable low-cut shoes and an intriguing amount of bare leg. In her hair she wore a cluster of flowers and a delicately carved *peineta* comb. Behind her, at center stage, the house guitarist followed the rhythms of her feet with bored indifference. He seemed to focus his attention on accompanying the *cantaora*, a portly gypsy woman with a husky, penetrating voice. Eight women posed haughtily in the other chairs lined up along the back of the stage, bulky embroidered shawls wrapped about their upper bodies with the long fringe spread out over their laps and ruffled skirts. While they waited their turn to dance, the seated women smoked, teased each other, joked with friends in the audience, and occasionally got to their feet to look into one of the mirrors and arrange their hair. In between, they found time to accompany the dancer with *palmas* and *jaleo*—shouts of "*ole*" and wisecracks filled with *gracia*.

The audience applauded wildly each time the dancer stamped out a burst of footwork, and their eyes followed the curves and magic spirals traced by her bare arms in the air. When she arched her back and twisted to one side, the lines of her bosom swelled at her neckline and the long silk fringe of her airy shawl fell loose and trembled about her waist.

Chacón and the Molinas were entranced. The cafés of Jerez were neither as large nor as opulent as this one, and they generally featured fewer artists in the *cuadro*. Yet, in spite of their sense of awe and the beauty of the dancer, the boys were also aware of the more technical side of the *soleá* she danced, of the interplay of the *cante* and the *toque* with the dance.

Three glasses of *manzanilla* arrived at the table, along with some greasy olives and *tapas* of spicy salami.

"You play better than that, Javié," said Chacón to his friend.

"Maybe," replied Javier, "but this guy knows what he's doing...follows the dancer well. He just doesn't have a lot of technique or imagination."

Chacón had been looking around the room, as if searching for something. "Do you see Silverio anywhere?"

EL CAFÉ DE SILVERIO

The room was filled with noisy spectators—peasant farmers in coarse cloth jackets, craftsmen wearing cloth caps, merchants in derby hats and well-cut suits, and gypsies with brightly colored scarves knotted about their heads under their *sombreros calañés*. Yet, there appeared to be nobody present who fit the description of Silverio Franconetti, said to be a large and imposing man.

"It's still early, *tocayo*," said the older Molina. "He may not have come in yet. Look, Javié, in the last chair on the right...isn't that Juana la Macarrona?"

"You're right. I haven't seen her in years." Seeing the questioning look on Chacón's face, Javier explained. "Antonio, you see that woman at the end, wearing white?"

Chacón looked and saw a young gypsy woman, perhaps in her early twenties, with harsh features and a large pointed nose.

Javier continued. "That's Juana la Macarrona, María's sister. Do you remember María, the one who danced in El Palenque? I saw Juana dance once, before I began to play in the Vera Cruz. Then she left to dance in Málaga and never came back. I heard that she became an important figure in Barcelona."

"*Tocayo*, you have to see this woman dance!" added the other Molina. "As well as she danced before, imagine what she must be like now!"

On stage, the dancer had finished her voluptuous performance and was replaced by another, a pallid and frail girl, but with an inner fire that revealed itself in her black eyes and provocative movements. She, in turn, was followed by an arrogant *gitana* with a curvaceous body and cherry-red lips, and then a tall and sculptured Gaditana [from Cádiz] who could have danced on the steps of a Greek temple. Finally, an aristocratic sylph rose from her chair. She had white skin, a delicate and sensuous neck, a rounded and well-formed bosom, and a waist as thin and flexible as a reed.

No sooner had this last dancer taken possession of the stage than a voice rang out. "*Esa*, that's her! What beauty...what *gracia!*" The voice was almost a moan, filled with trembling passion. All three boys looked in the direction from which it had come. Seated at the far end of their table was a young man with an agreeable face and elegant carriage, obviously a gentleman, *un señorito*. The man stood up, blocking Antonio Molina's view of the stage, and wailed, "Esperanza [Hope], you were once a treasure of virtues and now I find you a pearl in the mud..."

Antonio leaned over to his companions and said with a grin, "*Está tó tajao*, he's so drunk he doesn't know what he's saying." Then in a louder voice, "Hey you, I can't see!"

The man turned to see who had addressed him, fell back into his chair, and said, "Esperanza is like a sister to me...her memory is connected with the best days of my existence. How beautiful she is!" With that, he returned his full concentration to the figure on stage.

The Molinas and Chacón looked with renewed interest at the object of such devout attention. The dancer seemed out of place among the flamencos. In spite of the provocative nonchalance with which she wore her rich, cream-colored dress, she struck a note of discord in that chaotic room. While her dancing was in some ways more sensuous than that of her companions, there was also something refined, distinguished, and even romantic about her. She might easily have been a prima donna in silk slippers.

The rowdy spectators rewarded the artistic gifts and originality of the dancer by applauding noisily. The *señorito* did not remove his eyes from her for a moment, demonstrating by his cries the impatience that was devouring him. Esperanza returned to her chair. There remained one other dancer yet to perform.

Juana la Macarrona rose from her chair slowly, with majestic dignity, arrogant as a queen. To the *compás* of the *soleá* she raised her arms overhead as if she were blessing the spectators, weaving patterns and forming shadows over the darker shadows of her smoldering eyes. From the depth of the stage she advanced straight forward, doubling the pounding of her feet on the wooden boards and raising a cloud of dust upon which she appeared to float. Slowly, with an almost religious cadence, she lowered her arms like two serpents, crossed them at waist level, and advanced further to the front with sinuous movements of her hips. She seemed to focus inward, oblivious to the audience, as she balanced on one leg, gripped the ruffles of her skirt in both hands and brushed the floor with her other foot.

Chacón could see La Macarrona clearly now. Her face was dark and rough, seeming almost dirty, and crossed by shadows between which flashed the aggressive whites of her eyes. Her lips parted slightly to reveal white teeth tinged with red. In her dull black hair, a red carnation had already begun to wilt and fall to pieces from the force of her movements.

The *señorito*, oblivious to La Macarrona, continued to mumble,

"Esperanza, *qué lástima de mujer*...poor unfortunate woman...what beauty..."

Juana la Macarrona suddenly spun on one leg and kicked with the other, sending the white train of her *bata* flying into the air, expanding over the stage like a great wing that seemed to hang in space. She was transformed into a white peacock, magnificent and proud. The exquisite line of her body swept away the harshness of her face and left the audience breathless and silent. A sudden rapid burst of footwork and her feet, clad in tiny red shoes, began to beat out the *compás* of the dance.

"*Qué taconeo más bárbaro*," uttered Antonio, "what footwork!"

The *señorito* moaned.

Desplantes [variations], sudden stops, *gracia* in her movements, gypsy to the core in appearance and style—Juana la Macarrona had everything necessary to reign as a queen in the *café cantante*. When she returned to her chair, accompanied by the final *tercios* of the *cante*, Chacón realized that what the Molinas had said about her paled before the reality of what he had just seen.

The dancers descended from the stage to share drinks, according to custom, with the regular customers. The *señorito* waved to Esperanza, who, with graceful courtesy, came over to his table. "Arturo," she said with a show of great joy in seeing him, "I'm so glad to see you!"

The two of them launched into an animated conversation, seemingly centered on memories of their youth. Suddenly, Esperanza looked over at the other three occupants of the table. "Arturo, you're not going to allow your friends to drink like that are you?" And without waiting for an answer, she reached over, collected the glasses in front of Javier and Chacón, and emptied them onto the floor. "We don't drink like that here," she said as she motioned to a waiter. "*Niño, una cañera de cién* for this table!"

Almost as if by magic a large circular double tray made of brass appeared at the table. The upper circle had round openings for one hundred slender, cylindrical *caña* glasses containing *manzanilla*. Arturo, with proverbial Andalusian gallantry, made no protest, bowing to this feminine generosity at his expense. *Cañas* of *manzanilla* were passed out left and right. When the hundred *cañas* had disappeared, another hundred followed, and then another. Two more sirens wrapped in brightly colored shawls appeared at the table. One of them, a dark-eyed *gitana*, reminded Antonio Molina of Juana Antúnez. Unseen by

Arturo, the women took small sips from each glass and then surreptitiously poured the remainder on the floor, or passed glasses to customers behind them.

Meanwhile, the intimacies of Arturo and Esperanza had taken on such tenderness that their new friends could not help but be moved upon listening to them. The two old friends recalled the afternoons of the past, when they played in the patio of their *casa de vecinos*, and the nights under a full moon, when they sat in the doorway of the patio and sang the children's song, *Luna catuna cascabelera*. Then there was the sudden death of Esperanza's mother—the first time they cried together.

"What a beautiful handkerchief you're wearing, Arturo!" The capricious girl had spied a bit of blue silk with red trim protruding from Arturo's jacket pocket. The young *señorito*, who would have denied Esperanza nothing at that moment, placed the handkerchief around her neck without hesitation. "Oh, Arturo, what happy days those were!" The enchantress continued to lavishly distribute wine, and it wasn't long before Arturo's diamond tiepin had joined the blue and red scarf.

Hours passed. The three youths, drinking more than they were accustomed, lost their awareness of time. The lights went out on the stage and most of the customers made their way to the street the best they were able. To continue, it was necessary to move to a *reservao* upstairs. Javier and Chacón were reluctant to join the party, but Antonio, with the dark-haired "Juana" on his arm, pleaded with them to accept Arturo's invitation.

The festivities continued in a small room furnished with a table, a number of chairs, and a sofa—to be used by the intoxicated to snooze briefly, or couples who needed a moment of privacy. Several other new "friends" of Arturo had joined the party and a guitarist quietly slipped into the room and began playing in the background. Esperanza had not left Arturo's side. He, in turn, pampered her as if she were a child, attentive to her every whim, in spite of the growing fatigue that led him to occasionally drop his head into his arms on the table. Esperanza caressed his right hand, on which sparkled a beautiful diamond ring, while emptying another glass of *manzanilla* onto the floor.

The girls sang. Chacón sang. Arturo sang. Under the influence of drink everyone became a singer. The hours flew by. As the first light of day began to creep in through a window, it was Javier who suddenly realized the hour and whispered to Chacón, "Antonio, the postal coach, it leaves at sun-up. We have to hurry!"

EL CAFÉ DE SILVERIO

At that moment the door opened and the obese *montañés* [café manager[2]] entered. He went to Arturo, now alone with his head on the table, and tapped him on the shoulder.

Arturo lifted his head groggily and asked, "Eh...do you love me, *niña?*"

The answer was given by the *montañés* when he demanded payment of over three hundred *pesetas* for the evening.

"Esperanza, where is she?" asked the confused Arturo, turning an imaginary ring on his now naked little finger.

"Anda, anda! Esperanza? Échela usted galgos!" exclaimed the *montañés* as he picked up the money Arturo had taken from his pocket. "Esperanza is long gone...even greyhounds couldn't catch up with her now. She's an honorable mother with a family and she is picked up here *every* morning at daybreak."

---

[2]*montañés*: a man from Asturias in northern Spain. Many bars, taverns, and cafés in Andalucía were owned or operated by *montañeses*, who were considered to be especially skilled in the business of selling food and drink.

Salvaoriyo

Chacón and the Molinas, somewhat unsteady on their feet, hastened through the streets in the early morning light. After retrieving their belongings from the boarding house they hurried to the Parador de Patrocinio. Fortunately the coach had not yet departed, for they could not have afforded to remain in Sevilla waiting for the next mail coach to Zafra.

They would be traveling *sillas correo*, that is, in the few seats reserved for passengers on the postal coach. In addition to the mail, the sturdily built coach carried a load of sacks of dried cod and one other passenger, a *quincallero* on his way to Zafra to sell his *quincallería*—pins, needles, nails, and other hardware, much of it newly purchased from the gypsy blacksmiths of Triana.

Heading west toward the pueblo of Camas, the bells of the Giralda chiming six o'clock behind them, the exhausted boys found that they would not be traveling in the luxurious comfort they had anticipated. Antonio Molina rode on top with the driver, while Javier and Chacón occupied worn leather seats inside the coach with the *quincallero*. Javier's guitar quickly became a concern, for the coach moved at great speed, hitting bumps with bone-jarring force and swaying and groaning on its leather springs. The passengers were tossed against the wooden sides of the compartment and bounced from their seats at each large pothole. All Javier could do with the guitar was to pad the case with clothing and hold it close.

On the up hills, the *zagal*, a youth of perhaps fifteen, leaped from his perch at the side of the coach and ran alongside the four mules, pelting them with stones and verbal abuse. On a particularly steep incline, he beat the animals mercilessly with a club as they humped and clawed at the road in their attempt to pull the heavy coach upward. At one point Chacón noticed a loud scraping sound above the din of rattles and creaks, the clatter of wheels against rocks, and the sounds of the mules and their drivers. Looking out the window, he saw that one of the brakes dragged uselessly against its wheel. He leaned out as far as he could and yelled to the driver that the broken brake was preventing the wheel from turning easily. The driver leaned over the side and shouted back, "I know, but it's not so bad on the down hills!"

Chacón gave Javier a look of apprehensive resignation and settled back in the jouncing seat. The *quincallero*, a dour type with a perpetual frown, watched his fellow travelers in silence for a while and then said abruptly.

"Where are you boys from?"

Javier answered. "Jerez de la Frontera…"

"We're artists," interrupted Chacón. "We're going to work in the *feria* of Zafra."

"The other raised a skeptical eyebrow, noting the frayed and rumpled clothing, and asked, "Have you been working in Sevilla?"

"Sevilla?" replied Chacón, somewhat deflated. "No, we didn't work in Sevilla. We're in a hurry to get to Zafra." Then after a moment's silence, he couldn't help but add, "Sevilla is not an easy place to work…it's so big, so many people!"

"Big? It's not as big as it was," grumbled the *quincallero*. "Last year *el minuto*[1] [cholera] killed one person of every three or four. One minute you were speaking with a friend and then, sixty seconds later, he was dead."

Chacón and Javier were only too familiar with these epidemics that carried away so many friends and family members. Children died and were replaced so often that there was a common saying: *"Angelitos al cielo y ropitas al arca."* [Little angels to heaven and their clothing back in the chest.]

Before conversation could continue, the mules picked up speed on a stretch of flat and a cloud of choking dust filled the coach.

---

[1] *el minuto*: the minute, cholera; epidemics of cholera, typhoid fever, smallpox, and from the colonies of America and the Philippines, malaria and yellow fever, had devastated the population of Spain. Sevilla, a city of 300,000 under Moorish rule in the 11th century, was down to about 120,000 in the mid 1800s.

Not long on the road, Javier and Chacón began to feel queasy. With each bounce of the coach their stomachs lurched up into their throats. It was an unfamiliar sensation for the youths. Chacón turned pale, almost green, and sweat began to pour down his face. *El minuto* passed through his mind. Then, without warning, he vomited. With a look of surprise on his face he turned quickly, sending most of his stomach contents toward the window. The smell was the last straw for Javier who lunged toward the window on the opposite side just in time to avoid befouling the interior. As Chacón wiped his mouth on his sleeve, the *quincallero* said dourly, "The next time you take a coach, remember to take this seat that I have, nearest to the front and the driver...it bounces the least." But he made no offer to trade places with the suffering boys. Chacón never adjusted to the motion of the coach and would suffer throughout the trip.

The day wore on monotonously. The boys tried to sleep, nodding off for moments only to be abruptly awaked by a bone-jarring lurch or the sharp, brittle crack of the driver's whip. There was a brief respite in the tiny pueblo of La Algaba—just time to stretch and rinse dust-choked throats with a glass of wine.

After Las Pajanosas, where there was a longer stop for lunch, a welcomed nap, and a change of mules, the road began to wind and climb into the foothills of the Sierra Morena. Another stop in the late afternoon, in El Ronquillo, for a fresh mule team. Progress slowed in the mountainous terrain and the sun lay low on the horizon when the driver announced that they had passed out of the province of Sevilla and entered Huelva.[2] They arrived at the *posada* outside of Santa Olalla in complete darkness. Beaten and bruised and coated with a thick mantle of red dust, the travelers could only brush themselves off, wolf down a meal of eggs and cod stewed in tomato sauce, and throw themselves onto the evil-smelling straw bed they shared with the animals. They fell asleep immediately, despite the strong odor of manure and the swarms of fleas and bedbugs.

Before daylight the following morning the young *zagal* shook the passengers awake and then set to laying out harnesses on the ground and hitching the mules one by one. The groggy travelers savored their

---

[2]Spain is divided into regions, the southernmost being Andalucía. Each region is made up of provinces, Andalucía having eight—Huelva, Sevilla, Cádiz, etc. Zafra is located in Extremadura, the region lying north of Andalucía and adjacent to Portugal.

cups of hot chocolate before boarding the coach for another grueling day of bouncing over rocky roads. By mid-morning they had left Huelva behind and entered the region of Extremadura [*extrema*: extreme; *dura*: hard].

The road led through a sun-baked desolate and wild land, each hill seeming higher and bleaker than the previous. They would travel miles without seeing a soul and then pass a solitary shepherd with his flock. Deserted villages of crumbling mud testified to centuries of emigration to the American colonies and to northern cities in search of work. Extremadura had supplied most of the soldiers for Spain's almost constant warfare. Occupied villages were seldom more than clusters of wretched rock hovels with thatched roofs. Woman stared from doorways at the passing coach, dull, stolid expressions on their faces, while mangy dogs and immense swine mingled with naked children in the dust and dung.

The trip to Fuente de Cantos, with its primitive *posada*—seemingly intended for catering to animals only—was shorter than that of the previous day and they arrived before dark. The next morning the coach was again on the road before dawn. Rocky and barren land gave way to stretches of cork forest, olive orchards, and fields of parched corn stalks. Late in the afternoon, the driver announced the arrival to Zafra by pointing out ancient castle ruins looming over the town.

The Jerezanos splurged the last of their money on a room with beds, water for a bath, and having their clothes laundered. As they attempted to make themselves presentable, Chacón made a pronouncement.

"We are not going to work for nothing here in Zafra. I want us to earn at least ninety *duros* during the *feria*."

"*Hombre*," said Javier, "you're dreaming! Four hundred and fifty *pesetas* is a lot, especially considering that we are not artists *de cartel* [with our names on a poster, i.e. well-known]...and we're broke. We have to take what we can get."

"You're crazy, *tocayo!* You don't even believe what you're saying," added Antonio.

Undaunted, Chacón just said, "We'll see."

It was Friday night and, on an obscure and dirty street, the Jerezanos found a café filled with locals and visitors arriving for the fair. To their surprise the sound of *cante* hit their ears even before they entered. After a moment of watching from the back of the dingy room near the door,

Antonio Molina whispered to the other two, "As bad as we are, those guys are even worse!"

Chacón nodded in agreement and added, "Maybe we can work here. Javié, why don't you find the owner and ask."

It turned out that the man in charge was on stage. He didn't perform, but kept time with a *vara* and did *jaleo* for the others, all while smoking cigars and throwing the butts onto the stage. From time to time he nodded condescendingly to entering customers, and when friends in the audience sent him a glass of wine, he sipped a little, then spit most of it out to the side of the platform. It was some time before Javier saw an opportunity to speak with the man.

When Javier returned, he said they could try out when everyone else had finished. Their turn came about an hour later. Chacón and Javier went up first onto the cramped stage tucked in between a corner wall and a wooden post supporting the beamed ceiling. Chacón seated himself and, to the pulse of Javier's music, began to tap out the rhythm of the *soleá* on the floor with his new *vara*. Holding the style stick about a third of the way down, between his thumb and forefinger as if it were a writing instrument, he tapped 1,2,3…7,8…10…1,2,3… After tuning his voice with some low-pitched *ayes*, he launched into the *soleares* of El Mellizo:

Compañerita de mi arma,	Girlfriend of my soul,
la que me ha mandao Undebé,	you who was sent to me by God,
que por orvidarte hago, ay,[3]	the things I do to try to forget you,
y no se me orvida tu queré.	but I just can't forget your love.

He changed to a different melody by the great *cantaor* from Cádiz, shorter and more intense:

Le pío a Dios	I beg God
que me alívie estas duquelas,	to free me from this pain,
duquela e mi corazón.	pain of my heart.

When he had exhausted his repertoire of *soleares* in this style, he finished by lightening the mood with a *letra* from another great singer from Cádiz, Paquirri el Guanté:

---

[3]This line is a bit unclear in its original form; later singers have changed it to "*lo que hago yo por olvidarte*" which is how I have translated it.

Metío en cañaverales, *Perched in the reeds,*
los pajaros son clarines *the birds are buglers*
al divino sol que sale. *for the divine sun that rises.*

The audience had hushed during the performance and cheered the singer when he finished. Determined to maintain his grip on the emotion in the room, the *cantaor* followed immediately with *seguiriyas* of *El Señor* Manuel Molina and El Marrurro, and then the *malagueñas* he had learned from Fosforito. With each *cante* the applause grew louder and longer and the audience more attentive. Chacón had been imperceptively maturing in vocal power, technique, and knowledge. There had been little time for study or practice while they traveled, but performing almost nightly had refined and strengthened the singer's command of his repertoire. It all came together and bore fruit that evening in Zafra—in spite of fatigue and days without singing. Gone was the broken, undecided voice, and in its place, an instrument with a rich and powerful sound. Chacón did not have the rough *rajo* of the gypsy, yet his voice was full and very flamenco in tone.

Javier, also without practice for several days, required only a short while to begin playing better than he ever had. He demonstrated his growing technique and artistry when, after Chacón had finished to a warm applause, Antonio mounted the platform to dance *por alegrías* with *falsetas* [guitar melodies[4]]. Both dancer and guitarist performed as never before. Delighted with the response of the public, the owner invited the three youths to work for the duration of the *feria*.

Two nights later, on the first night of the fair, an incident occurred that left Chacón puzzled. The *cantaor* had just finished singing a number of gypsy *cantes* of Jerez, *por seguiriyas* and *soleares*, when one of a group of rough looking gypsies addressed him. The man, like his friends, was dressed in the ostentatious manner of the old-time *calés*, from the tip of his *calañés* to his knee-high leather spats. Seated near the stage, the group had listened attentively throughout Chacón's performance. Now, late in the evening, one of them, a man with a large mustache and a stubbly face, asked in a voice so deep and hoarse as to be little more than a croak, "*Chaboró*, enough *cante* for *los gachés*...now sing something for us *calés!*"

---

[4]*falsetas*: melodic variations on the guitar. In those times it was common to refer to a dance as "such and such *cante y falsetas*," presumably because the dance was done to the *cante* and the guitar *falsetas*.

Chacón was dumbfounded. He protested that he had just sung the most gypsy of *cantes*. The other shrugged his shoulders and shook his head, as if to say, "What can one expect from a *gachó*," spat disdainfully, and said something to his friends that brought forth a burst of laughter. The four gypsies rose to their feet and, amid yawns and belches, disappeared into the night.

Chacón felt humiliated. He assumed the man had meant he didn't sing "gypsy" enough. He knew that his voice was not well suited to the *cante gitano*, but he also knew that knowledge and technique could compensate for this deficiency, and he had been growing in confidence as his audiences continued to respond more and more enthusiastically to his singing. He tried to shrug off the incident, but it continued to eat away at him throughout the night.

The following morning, toward noon, as boys wandered the fairgrounds, Antonio Molina kept an alert eye out for El Morrongo. "Over here," he said to his companions as he headed in the direction of a small group of men gathered around an old white horse. But the transaction had been unsuccessful and the crowd was already disbursing. The gypsy *chalán*, holding the halter of the decrepit animal, yelled after the departing buyer, "This horse is perfect for you, *caballero*...."

The gentleman turned and retorted, "I told you, I'm looking for a black horse."

To which the gypsy replied, "I'll throw in some black shoe polish...then you will have two horses for the price of one!"

"*Qué gracia!*" laughed Antonio. But it was another comment that had the boys laughing until tears ran down their cheeks. A rebuffed *chalán*, indicating the scrawny burro by his side, yelled out for all to hear, "*Oigazté, compare* [Listen friend]...if this ass is not good enough for you, go get your mother and father to make one to suit you!"

Antonio, always ready for a laugh, was dead serious about his search. "Look, there is a good-sized gathering. Maybe it's El Morrongo."

Chacón and Javier rolled their eyes and followed their lovesick friend to where two gypsies were haggling over a horse.

"*Mirosté* [*Mire usted*: Look]," said one gypsy, "it's an animal as fine as silk. It grieves me to part with him." Placing his hand on the shoulder of the other, he continued, "For you, a friend and a very likable person, someone who knows how to make a deal, I will let it go for only forty *duros*."

The other responded, "Since you are so generous, I will ask for only a small reduction. Twenty-five and *trato hecho* [a done deal]."

The first gypsy went into a theatrical display of gestures and grimaces. "*Mare de Dios* [Mother of God], haven't you seen the animal well? Even if I had stolen it, I couldn't let it go for that!"

"Twenty-five and no more."

"Take another look at the beast. *Córralo usté pa velo!* [Run it so you can see!] What grace, what pace!"

"Twenty-five."

"Look here! I'm going to do what I would do for no one, I swear, not even my own father. Thirty-five *duros*."

The buyer turned to go.

"Thirty-three, and for the health of your children, don't say no! I'm trying to be reasonable."

Without turning, the other said, "Twenty-eight."

"Neither my price nor yours...thirty," said the other, offering the reins, "and I don't earn a thing!"

The other returned. They spit on their hands and shook, clutching the handshake with their free hands. "*Compare, qué boca pa un trato!* [Friend, what a mouth you have for making a deal!]," said the first gypsy. "Let's go have a drink...this was your lucky day!"

And so it went, on into the early afternoon and the break for siesta. As the youths ate their meal in a tent café, Antonio lamented his inability to find Angustias. Javier attempted to console him, saying, "It's pretty far from Villamartín to Zafra. Perhaps the gypsy just couldn't make it in time. But you never know, he could show up anytime. There is still one day left."

Antonio, brightening somewhat, said to Chacón, "*Tocayo*, did I ever tell you about La Karaba?"

"La Karaba?" replied the singer. "What's that?"

"La Karaba...spelled with a 'k'. It was in the *feria* of Jerez a few years ago. You were probably too young to go see it. Some gypsies had set up a tent with colored rags covering the entrance, and they put up a sign that said, 'La Karaba.' For less than a *céntimo* you could see it. While a little boy beat on a drum, the gypsy yelled to attract a crowd. When he had gathered sufficient customers and collected the money, he pulled back the curtain and there was nothing but an old mule, barely able to stand."

"So, where was La Karaba?"

"Listen! The crowd began to yell and complain, 'That's not La

Karaba, it's just an old mule.' And the gypsy answers, 'You think that is not La Karaba? She's old now, but I assure you that she once was...' And here the man slowed his speech and spoke very carefully, '...*la que araba!* [...she who used to pull a plow!].''

Javier had heard the story before, but Chacón laughed. Suddenly his laughter was cut off by the sound of singing. He looked around and located the source in a group of gypsies gathered near the entrance of one of the temporary taverns. The men stood drinking, while several women sat on the ground to one side surrounded by baskets of various sizes that they had brought to sell. One of the men, dressed similarly to those that had been in the café the night before, sang an unfamiliar but infectious melody, while the others beat out a steady but rather sedate rhythm with hard, calloused hands:

Está visto y comprobao	It has been seen and proven
que él que bebe vino tinto	that he who drinks red wine
está gordo y colorao.	is fat and red-faced.

When the man finished, all of the women chimed in with a chorus of shrill, nasal voices:

Al entrar en La Picurina,	On entering La Picurina,
lo primero que se vé,	the first thing you see
a los gitanos en cueros	is the gypsies without clothes
y a los niños sin comé.	and the children without food.

Toa la noche en la escalera	All night on the stairway,
esperando el porvenir,	waiting for the future,
y el porvenir nunca llega.	and the future never comes.

Chacón went to listen. After a moment, he tapped the shoulder of an old man who stood back a little from the group.

"Excuse me," Chacón asked when the man turned his head, "do you know what they are singing?"

The man looked at the youth a moment, as if not grasping the question, and then replied, "Why, the *cantes gitanos*,[5] of course! They are gypsies from Badajoz...from the Plaza Alta..."

Suddenly it became clear to Chacón. *Of course! The gypsies of*

---

[5] These *cantes* are known today as *tangos extremeños*.

Extremadura had their own cantes *and had not recognized that which he had sung the night before, any more than he had recognized what they sang. Flamenco might be popular in the large towns of Extremadura, but the gypsies distinguished it from what they considered to be the true* cante gitano—*their* cante gitano.

On the last night of the livestock fair, after a long and exhausting night of working in the café, the three young flamencos walked slowly toward the *fonda*, smoking cigarettes in the quiet of predawn. The stars seemed to twinkle in *compás* with the cicadas and in the distance a horse's hooves clattered on cobblestones.

Antonio Molina walked in silence, ruminating on his inability to locate El Morrongo and Angustias. He had searched each day, investigating each crowd and entering each tavern looking for the gypsy. There had been no sign of the family. At first he had been disappointed, but slowly had become resigned. In truth, his image of the vagabond gypsy girl had lost some of its luster. Time and frustration had taken their toll on his ardor—aided by the memory of a torrid evening in Sevilla with the "Juana" of the smoldering eyes.

Chacón broke the silence, speaking softly. "How much have we earned, Javié?"

Javier exhaled a plume of smoke. "I think we have saved about thirty *duros*."

"*Ojú, qué bien!* That's fifty *pesetas* each...more than my father earns in a month!"

"It's not the ninety *duros* you wanted, *tocayo*," said Antonio, "but it's enough for us to live on for quite awhile. What should we do now...go back to Sevilla?"

Both of the Molinas looked at Chacón, who said without hesitation, "We didn't earn the ninety *duros*, but we earned enough to live well, and we received genuine respect as artists. Let's go back toward Sevilla, but from pueblo to pueblo, and see if we can continue to work."

It was agreed. They would leave Zafra on foot in the morning. All three were relieved not to be facing another ride in the mail coach.

The Jerezanos arrived in Bienvenida late the following afternoon, having slept until almost mid-day and then walking all afternoon through seemingly endless cornfields and olive groves. Their entrance to the village was greeted, as was usually the case, by barking dogs and equally noisy children.

No sooner had they made their way past the threat of nipping dogs and curious urchins when a low rumbling seemed to shake the very earth beneath their feet. Dogs and children disappeared into doorways as the three boys looked around for the source of the disturbance. At the very moment they spied the cloud of red dust, a seething mass of charging brutes appeared from around the corner of a row of buildings. An unstoppable herd of grunting and squealing pigs hurtled down the street, barely giving the boys time to flatten themselves against the wall of a dwelling, where the great beasts brushed their legs and crushed them against the rocks.

"What a scare!" said Antonio Molina with a grin as he dusted himself off. "Now I know why they call this the land of the *jamón serrano* [Spain's famous cured ham]." The boys watched as small clusters of animals broke off from the main pack and individuals entered doorways up and down the street. Later they learned that each morning the *porquero* went house-to-house collecting the pigs. When the owners heard the bell of the lead animal, they let their pigs out to join the herd. After a day spent foraging in the woods and fields, the herd returned each evening, trampling everything in its path as the pigs hurried home to dinner.

No matter whom the Jerezanos asked for direction in Bienvenida, the answer was always the same: "You have to go to see Manuel Mejías!"

Mejías,[6] a retired matador and an avid aficionado of flamenco, was thrilled to have the young artists in his pueblo and immediately began to make arrangements for a concert in his home that evening. In conversation it came out that Mejías had often included Manuel Hermosilla in his *cuadrilla*. Hermosilla was a familiar figure to the youths because he had gone on to become a full matador of some renown and had, in turn, included the *cantaor* Enrique el Mellizo as *puntillero* in his *cuadrilla*.[7]

The concert in the home of Manuel Mejías was a success, resulting

---

[6] Grandfather of the matador Ignacio Sánchez Mejías, who was eulogized in García Lorca's great poem *Llanto por Ignacio Sánchez Mejías*, and would later play an important role in flamenco.

[7] *cuadrilla*: the bullfighter's team of assistants; *puntillero*: the one who administers the coup de grace to the bull with a short, pointed knife.

in a satisfactory profit for the boys. The following day they walked to the town of Llerena where they performed in the *casino*. In the *posada* they arranged to ride the following day with an *arriero* who was going in the direction of Guadalcanal with his mule train. At daybreak the heavily loaded mules filed out of the *posada* amid a cacophony of clanking, jingling bells, grunts and wheezes, and volleys of curses and insults. Everyone, including the *posadero*, yelled and pitched stones at the animals. The Jerezanos rode toward the back of the train, seated on crude saddles of folded blankets that gave only partial protection from the sharply protruding backbones of their mounts.

Not far outside of Llerena, the *arriero* came up behind Chacón's lagging donkey and gave it resounding smack on the flank. Unprepared for the animal's startled lunge, Chacón tumbled backward and fell, hitting the ground headfirst. The Molinas had a moment of fright when they saw their friend lying motionless, but by the time they reached his side he had recovered consciousness. Dazed and bleeding from a cut on the back of his head, the youth required a few minutes of recovery before resuming travel.

The remainder of the journey to the silver and lead mining town of Guadalcanal was uneventful, and the boys performed that evening for a social club. Then it was on to Cazalla, El Pedroso, and other small mountain towns of the Sierra Morena, working in cafés, *casinos*, and anywhere they could get permission to gather a small audience. If they earned little in one place, they made up for it in others. Occasionally they were held over for several days and paid a small salary on top of what they could collect from the public.

When they arrived in Sevilla on the first of November, the Molinas asked Chacón, "What do we do now? Should we go home?"

The *cantaor* replied, "We're just beginning to have success. If we go home now, we'll be right back where we were before. Let's make a tour of the province of Huelva."

"*Camarón que se duerme, se lo lleva el corriente*," said Antonio in agreement. [The shrimp that sleeps is carried off by the current; we have to keep moving forward.]

Early the following morning the boys boarded a train for the first time. The third class coach, constructed of wood and painted a bright green, had four compartments, each with its own door to the outside. The Jerezanos stashed their luggage as securely as possible and found places on the two wooden benches that faced each other across the compartment. The benches filled rapidly to their capacity of ten passengers. A heavy woman, breathing hard from the effort of climbing into the coach with a bundle of clothes and two small children, settled next to Chacón. Antonio Molina would later say, "That *harta de ajos* [garlic stuffed woman] had stretched her skin so tight from eating that she could only close one eye at a time!"

Across the compartment, on the other bench, sat a well-dressed man wearing a dark gray cape about his shoulders and a peasant who had wrapped himself in a blanket with a collar and a hook sewn to it to fashion a rudimentary cloak. Two brown-garbed priests and a man who carried a ball of cackling chickens strung together by the legs completed the passengers squeezed into that small space.

A deep, powerful huff, a chorus of clicks and hisses as steam billowed up from the immense smokestack funnel, and the coaches lurched forward. Wheels screeched as they caught in sand applied to the rails for traction, couplings groaned and creaked, and with one burst of the ear-piercing whistle, the train was underway.

The passengers were soon like a big family, conversing and smoking among the many bundles, sacks of produce, jugs of water, and livestock. Cold morning air blew in through the glassless windows, at times carrying with it suffocating clouds of smoke and ash. Whenever someone sneezed, the peasants mumbled almost in unison, *"Jesús, María, y José!"* [Jesus, Mary, and Joseph!] In spite of the cold, the fat woman flung her fan open every few moments from force of habit and sent a draft of cold air over Chacón. Then realizing where she was, she would heave a vast sigh, moaning *"Ay de mí!"* [Poor me] and let the fan fall shut.

The train moved slowly westward toward the province of Huelva, screeching to frequent stops for wood and water. After each stop the ticket collector made an appearance through the outside door to check tickets. When one of the passengers inquired about the danger of traversing from car to car on the outside running boards, the man said, "You get used to it...but I have to be careful to watch for tunnels!"

The three young artists stared out the windows at the panorama of fertile foothills and floodplains that stretched between two great rivers. The wide Guadalquivir River meandered south from Sevilla to the immense tidal swamplands of Las Marismas and the coast, while, far to the west, the red Río Tinto flowed down from the mountains to the sea at Huelva. Scattered across this vast agricultural belt were small sparkling white towns, each clustered about a stone cathedral with its tall gray tower rising above the rust-colored tiles of the surrounding rooftops.

Sanlúcar la Mayor, crowning a hilltop like a white jewel set in the dark gray-green of surrounding olive groves, was larger than many of the pueblos, with several thousand inhabitants. Chacón and the Molinas found lodging in a *fonda* and arranged for a concert in the *casino*. That evening they were warmly received by the *arperchineros*, as neighboring pueblos called the Sanluqueños in reference to the oil-producing olive mash, *alpechín*. Although the boys earned little more than enough to cover expenses, they were satisfied with their performance, as they were the following days in Benacazón and in Escacena del Campo, where they worked in a café.

Manzanilla, in the province of Huelva, lay in lush grasslands where large herds of powerful fighting bulls roamed freely, awaiting their date with destiny in the bullring. Here, the Jerezanos met *Don* José Marquez, a skilled guitarist with a very flamenco personality. *Don* José took a liking to the youths and brought them to see the concierge of the *casino*. During the evening, the concierge demonstrated that he could more than hold his own in the *cante* and was, in fact, applauded much more than Chacón. However, this took nothing away from the performance of the latter and the Jerezanos had no complaints about their reception in Manzanilla.

Not so in Palma del Condado, a picturesque pueblo among the orchards and vineyards of the river valley of the Río Tinto. It seemed like a good idea to use an empty bodega for the concert, in spite of its large size. To the surprise of the artists, the cavernous and musty hall quickly filled to capacity with boisterous and unruly fieldworkers who soon became drunk and out of control. The frightened artists had no choice but to go through with the concert, although performing was all but impossible. Neither the guitar nor the *cante* could be heard above the din, and the loud complaining only made the situation worse. The boys felt fortunate just to make it through the night and escape with a handful of coins.

It was suggested that the Jerezanos might have better luck in Trigueros. Although this town was somewhat out of the way, to the north of the city of Huelva, the people there were said to be "very flamenco" and the boys hoped they would be able to stay several days. In Trigueros, they were directed to continue on the train a short distance through the rolling hills of olive and fruit trees to Beas, a tiny pueblo whose low white buildings radiated downhill in all directions from the church.

The concert in Beas began as soon as sufficient members had gathered in the *casino*. Later, after the boys had collected what money they could and were preparing to return to the *posada*, a man approached them.

"*Muchachos*," the man said, "I am the stationmaster here. If you would accompany me to the train station, I will give you tickets for the return to Trigueros...and it won't cost you a thing!"

The boys agreed among themselves and Chacón said, "Wait here for us while we get our things from the *posada*."

The train station of Beas was isolated more than a mile outside of town, a considerable walk for the tired Jerezanos at that late hour. The man accompanied the youths to the station, where he asked them to wait while he went for the tickets. He disappeared inside and closed the door. A quarter of an hour passed.

"What could he be doing?" said Antonio Molina.

"I can't imagine," replied Chacón. "Maybe he fell asleep...he had a lot to drink. Let's knock on the door!"

Persistent beating on the door brought no response. Since daylight was not far off and the ticket window would soon open for the early morning train, the boys settled down to wait.

Chacón was just nodding off when Javier's voice broke through the haze of his fatigue. "Wake up! The ticket window has opened."

The three staggered groggily to the window.

"Are you going to give us the tickets?" asked Antonio.

"What tickets?" came the curt reply.

"The tickets you said you would give us if we accompanied you here to the station."

"I don't give away tickets. Whoever wants tickets has to pay for them!"

Antonio was growing angry. "Liar! We lost a night's sleep to accompany you here..."

"What you do is not my concern."

"*Qué malange!* [Malicious one!] If you weren't hiding behind that little window, I would make you remember your promise...*sieso* [asshole]...*sieso manío!* [rotten asshole!]..."

The window slammed shut as Antonio ran off a string of obscenities, ending with "...*a tos tus muertos!*" [and all of that on your dead ancestors, too!] The livid youth turned from the closed and silent window, saying, "*Caray, qué tío*...if I could just get my hands on him! A liar is worse than a thief!"

It took some time for the anger to subside, but at last Javier said, "Now what are we going to do?"

Chacón, with calm logic, replied, "We can't stay here, and I don't feel like walking all the way back to Trigueros. I would rather buy tickets than give that man the satisfaction of knowing that, on top of everything else, we had to walk all that distance."

"But..."

"*Hermano*, as you would say, '*Agua pasá no muele molino.*' [Water already gone by cannot turn the mill wheel.] What's done is done and we need to get some sleep."

Reluctantly, Antonio agreed, and the boys paid their way to return to Trigueros, where they were well received and stayed for three days.

The final stop before Huelva was San Juan del Puerto, a stark white pueblo whose unusually straight and parallel streets led down to what had once been the waterfront. When the Río Tinto changed its course, the town was left high and dry, with railroad tracks where there had once been docks. The performances in a café were highly successful, thanks to the enthusiasm and generosity of a large group of barrelmakers from Jerez, many of them friends or acquaintances of the artists. It was a happy reunion for all.

At the end of a chilly November the Jerezanos boarded a train in San Juan del Puerto and made the short trip to the provincial capital of Huelva. A reserved and intimate fishing town of about ten thousand inhabitants, Huelva huddled along the bank of the Odiel River near where it merged with the great Río Tinto and flowed into the Atlantic Ocean.

From the train station, the boys walked along the waterfront, turned up the narrow Calle de la Marina,[8] and found comfortable lodging in a *fonda* on Calle Gravina. They asked in the *fonda* for possible cafés where they might find work.

"I know of no *café cantante*," said the innkeeper. Then beaming with self-satisfaction, he added, "But you are in luck, for you have

---
[8]Today, General Franco.

come to the right person. I know just the man you must see. *Don* Salvador García knows more about the *cante* than any other around here."

"Where can we find this *Señor* García?" asked Javier.

"I don't know where he lives, but you can find him in his fish stall in the market."

That was all the information the boys needed. After cleaning up the best they were able and shaking the dust out of their travel-worn clothes, they found the market and inquired at the first fish stall. The vendor shook his head. He was not *Señor* García but would be glad to introduce them. After wiping his hands slowly and deliberately, with great ceremony, he ducked under his counter and the led the boys several paces to the booth directly across from his own.

"*Don* Salvador," the man said loudly, with much self-importance, "I believe these boys are looking for you."

A short, heavy-set man turned from his cutting board. He appeared middle-aged, but the sadness in his face and the dark circles under his eyes may have added years to his actual age.

"*Buenos días, Señor* García!" As usual, Javier spoke for the trio. "We have come from Jerez…"

"Jerezanos!" The fish vendor's face brightened into the semblance of a smile. "Welcome to Huelva." He spoke in a deep voice that suited his bulky stature. "I too am from Jerez, from the barrio of San Miguel…"

"San Miguel!" said Chacón, thrilled to meet someone from his barrio. "My father is a *zapatero* in the Plaza Orellana."

"I don't recall a *zapatería* in the Plaza…"

"We used to live on Calle Sol."

"Oh yes, I know it well. You must be a Chacón."

"Antonio Chacón, at your service."

"Pleased to meet you Antonio Chacón."

"And these are my friends from Santiago. Javier Molina is an excellent *tocaor* and his brother Antonio is a phenomenon in the *baile*."

A young boy had appeared and stood by the fish vendor's side staring at the strangers. The man looked down at him.

"This is my son, also called Salvador." Turning to the boy he said, "*Niño*, look after the stall while we go for a drink."

The vendor removed his apron, picked up a highly polished walking stick, and led the youths a short distance to an open-air bar located within the market. Over glasses of *manzanilla*, *Don* Salvador listened with interest to the adventures of the three artists. Upon hearing of Chacón's success in one of his performances, he turned to the young *cantaor* and said, "*Muchacho*, sing something for me, something to remind me of my homeland."

Wanting to impress the man, Chacón tentatively began the *soleares* of El Loco Mateo. When he saw the eyes of the vendor brighten with approval, he continued with growing confidence.

"*Bien, muchacho*," said *Don* Salvador. "And *los cantes de sentimiento* [the songs of feeling]...do you sing *por seguiriyas?*"

Without hesitation, standing at the bar and accompanied only by the tapping of his *vara* on the clay floor, the young *cantaor* launched into the *seguiriyas* that began, "*Nochesita oscura...*"

A faraway look came over the vendor's gaze and then he let his eyes close. At the finish of the *letra*, he looked up. "That is the *seguiriya* of Silverio, and well sung. But that is not exactly how the maestro does it. Listen!"

Don Salvador gripped his polished walking stick with meaty fingers and began to rap the three fast and two slow beats of the *seguiriya*. At the first *ay* of his *temple* [tune-up] Chacón felt a tingle in the back of his neck. The sound was completely unexpected. No *gachó*, least of all a fish vendor in Huelva, sang like that, in a deep and resonant voice with just a hint of the highly desired gypsy *rajo*. *Don* Salvador's face flushed and the veins stood out at his temples as his *letra* unfolded. The sobbing anguish in the *quejíos*[9] and the profundity of the melody made it clear to Chacón that his own version had lacked the subtleties that brought such beauty and emotional impact to the *cante*.

Don Salvador paused a moment to catch his breath and then said, "Here is another from the great Silverio:

Tóos le piden a Undebé	Everyone asks God
salú y libertá;	for health and freedom;
yo le pío una buena muerte	I ask Him for a good death
y no me la quiere dá.	and he doesn't want to give it to me.

The three youths were transfixed, thoughts of finding work momentarily forgotten.

"How can this be?" exclaimed Chacón. "I have never heard singing

---

[9]*quejíos*: weeping *ayes* inserted between the words of the *cante*.

like that!"

The older man smiled his sad smile and said, "It comes to you directly from the maestro himself. Some years ago I sang regularly with Silverio in Sevilla, in his café. I was in charge of the *cuadro* there...in the Café Botella as people called it. In those days I was known as Salvaoriyo..."

"Sarvaoriyo!" The three boys cried out almost in unison.

Chacón was speechless for a moment. He should have known at the first sound of the voice...a Salvador from San Miguel who could sing the *cantes* of Silverio.

"*Don* Sarvaó," the boy said at last, "I have dreamed so long of meeting you. It is said that you know the *cantes* of Silverio like no one else."

"It's true. When I returned from America, in the year '72..."

"You have been to America?"

"Yes. In fact my boy was born in Havana. When I returned here, I went to Sevilla and sang beside the maestro for many years."

"Why did you leave? Why did you stop singing?"

The *cantaor* grew quiet. When at last he spoke, there was a detectable catch in his voice.

"The *cante* is something wondrous, a mystery. Often, when I sing, something happens to my body that I don't understand. The *cante* will always be part of me. But to live by the *cante* is difficult...very difficult. One goes days without eating or sleeping. You drink and lose track of time, of where you are...always drinking. And for what? In the end there is no money."

The man fell silent again and then added, softly, "When I returned from America my wife was ill. If I had spent more time with her, cared for her better, perhaps..."

His voice trailed off. It was apparent that he had suffered a great deal, that he kept dark secrets bottled up inside.

"So I decided to retire and come here to Huelva with my son. I became a partner in the fish business and it has been good to me...I have no complaints. But it is true that nobody knows Silverio's *cante* as I do. In fact, I know the maestro's *cante* so well that he used to come to me to remind him of songs he had forgotten."

Chacón blurted out, "Would you teach me?" Then, realizing how forward he appeared, he blushed slightly.

Salvaoriyo looked long at the boy. He felt a deep need to pass on his knowledge and, while his son showed some promise, he did not seem to have the natural talents of this young Jerezano. Finally he spoke.

"To become somebody in the *cante* you must know and master all of the styles. It is not an easy thing. But...come to my home this afternoon and we will see if you can learn a few things. Now, let's hear that *seguiriya* again..."

Chacón had found his first real teacher. Salvaoriyo took the instruction very seriously and proved to be a great *seguiriyero* with a wide knowledge of different styles. When he sang *por seguiriyas* there was a desperation in his outcry that seemed more than human, expressing some deep remorse eating at his insides and tearing him apart. It appeared that, if he had been unable to exhale his pain through the *cante*, he would have succumbed under the weight of bitter memories. Even when not singing, Salvaoriyo seemed to carry a heavy burden upon his sloping shoulders. One moment jovial and joking, the next he would appear to recall something and stare off vacantly into the distance. Then he would recover his composure and advise Chacón.

"In the *seguiriya* you must give everything. If you have sung correctly you will be broken, spent, exhausted emotionally and physically when you finish. Nowhere but in the *seguiriya* can we express such personal pain. There are only a few lines of words, but the *quejíos*, naked and filled with inconsolable grief, can say so much. The *seguiriyas* are the tears of the *gitano*. In this *cante*, a *cantaor* who has not suffered is like a guitar without strings!

"I am reminded of a time when Silverio went to Cádiz to contract artists. His good friend Enrique Ortega, a master of the *cantes* of Cádiz, had died not long before. The two men had been intimate friends and Enrique had also become an extraordinary singer of the *cantes* of Sevilla, especially those of Silverio. Silverio's grief renewed itself each time he went to Cádiz and he was in low spirits as he traveled with friends to nearby San Fernando. On passing through Puerta Tierra[10] the maestro suddenly ordered the carriage to halt near the cemetery and he sang this single *seguiriya*:

---

[10]Puerta Tierra: The area just outside the fortified walls of Cádiz that separate the city from the strand leading to the mainland and San Fernando.

> *Por Puerta Tierra*
> *no quiero pasá,*
> *porque m'acuerdo de mi amigo*
>   *[Enrique]*
> *y me echo a llorá*
>
> Through Puerta Tierra
> I don't want to pass,
> because I remember my
>   [friend, Enrique]
> and I begin to cry.

"The others in the carriage felt their hair stand on end and some began to cry..."

"Was that Enrique el Gordo [The Fat]?" asked Chacón.

"It was the father of the El Gordo who is singing now, El Gordo Viejo [The elder]."

"What genius to be able to create a *cante* like that, at the moment!"

"Yes, Silverio is a genius. But I will tell you a secret. He did not really create that *cante* at the moment. That *letra* came from Silverio's teacher, El Fillo, who was called the 'king of all *cantaores*.' All Silverio had to do was change a few words. Listen." And he sang:

> *Por la iglesia mayor*
> *no quiero pasá,*
> *porque m'acuerdo de la mare*
>   *[de mi arma]*
> *y me echo a llorá.*
>
> Through the main chapel
> I don't want to pass,
> because I remember the mother
>   of my soul]
> and I begin to cry

"Of course, with his immense abilities, the maestro gave the *cante* new melodies and grief-filled *quejíos* that tore at the hearts of those around him."

Chacón took in all he heard and his alert mind saw how it was possible to create by building upon existing tradition. Salvaoriyo continued to speak of El Fillo.

"Silverio sang many things of El Fillo, even to the point of imitating that deep, hoarse voice. Since El Fillo was considered to be the king of all *cantaores*, everyone wanted to sing with that *rajo* [raspiness] of his, with the *voz afillá* as we say now. Listen, here is another *seguiriya* that Silverio learned from El Fillo."

With that, Salvaoriyo sang an especially plaintive *seguiriya* in the tones of *martinete*,[11] a majestic *cante* with long flowing *tercios*:

---

[11] In the Major mode rather than the usual Phrygian mode of the *seguiriya*.

Mataron a mi hermano	They killed my brother,
e mi corasón,	the brother of my heart,
y los chorreles que l'han queaíto	and the children he left [behind,]
los mantengo yo.	are taken care of by me.

"Those are *cabales*, aren't they?"

"*Sí muchacho*, we call them *cabales* today. Do you know why we call them *cabales?*"

Chacón thought for a moment before replying. "Is it because the *cantaor* must have so much knowledge, be *cabal*, in order to sing them?"

"It is true that they are difficult, but Silverio told me that they were first called *cabales* because of something that happened to El Fillo. It seems that El Fillo had sung a long series of these *seguiriyas* for the bullfighter Paquiro and was rewarded with a one-ounce gold coin. Later, the *cantaor* discovered that the coin had been shaved. He sought out the torero and said to him, 'Tell me maestro, was there anything lacking in my *cante*?'

"Surprised, Paquiro assured him that there had been nothing lacking. But El Fillo was not satisfied. 'Were not the *seguiriyas* I sang yesterday *cabales?* [true; faultless?]' Again the torero affirmed that they were, to which the *cantaor* responded, '*Bien*, I have given you good money, a *cabal* coin, for which you have given me a false one...'

"Since that time those *seguiriyas* of El Fillo have been called *cabales*."

"And Silverio is the greatest singer of those *cantes* of his teacher?"

"Yes...well, there was another...Tomás, Tomás el Nitri."

Salvaoriyo settled back into his chair, while Chacón leaned forward in anticipation of another story.

"El Nitri was El Fillo's nephew. His name was Vargas too, Tomás Vargas, while El Fillo was Ortega Vargas. Tomás was just a child when Silverio left for America.[12] You know, there are those who say that Silverio was forced to leave Spain...because of El Fillo's brother. There were two brothers, both formidable *cantaores*. Curro Pabla, a giant *por seguiriyas* and *cañas*, went off with a married woman and was killed by her husband. Juan Encueros [Juan the Naked] was stabbed to death by a *cantaor* and it is said by some that Silverio was involved. It

---

[12]Recently, a supposed birth certificate was found for El Nitri in Puerto de Santa María, dated December 14, 1850.

may be true, for after that El Fillo began to sing this *seguiriya* in which he used the *tú*, as if he were speaking to a close friend:

Mataste a mi hermano;	You killed my brother;
no te he de perdoná;	I don't have to forgive you;
Tú lo mataste liao en su capa	you killed him as he lay wrapped [in his cape]
sin jacerte ná.	having done you no harm.

"In any case, when Silverio returned to Spain, he found that El Fillo had died and the family no longer welcomed his company. El Nitri, who had grown up with El Fillo, had not only mastered his uncle's *cantes*, but had improved them. Tomás was a strange gypsy, *mu raro*...more bohemian even than El Fillo. He was very nervous and restless, and he couldn't stay in one place for long, even though, with his abilities, he could have lived comfortably anywhere he wished. He wandered from town to town, always a stranger among strangers. You can feel his loneliness in *seguiriyas* like this:

La Pastora divina	Divine shepherdess,
venga a mi compaña;	come keep me company;
que me veo sin calor de naide	I find myself without the warmth [of anyone]
y en tierra mu extraña.	and in a very strange land.

"Incredible *por seguiriyas!* Maybe even better than Silverio. But *mu raro...mu juerguista* [very eccentric...a lover of fiestas] and very extravagant. He earned a great deal of money, even though he never performed for the public, but he spent it all on clothes and fiestas. Although very handsome, Tomás had little interest in women, except for his aunt, La Andonda. La Andonda...how that woman can sing *por soleá*...La Andonda had been El Fillo's lover until he died. But she was closer to El Nitri's age and took up with him until he too died. Tomás was *tísico* [had tuberculosis] and died very young...it is said that he died choking on his own blood while singing *por seguiriyas*...a victim of his art."[13]

Salvaoriyo sat up suddenly and looked intently at Chacon with his

---

[13] 1884, at age 34 (see appendix).

sad eyes. "I must warn you, Antonio Chacón, that the art you have chosen can kill you!"

"What?"

"It's true. The *seguiriya* demands more than the human body has to give. Only an exceptional man, a titan, can withstand its demands. And even those who are superior to normal men, who have greater strength and endurance, end up falling sick. It is inevitable that nine out of every ten *cantaores* will become *tísicos*. The *seguiriya* eats away at even chests and throats of stone. The lungs and throat spend themselves with a rapidity that is frightening. And those *cantaores* who don't die from tuberculosis, like Juan Encueros, who was saved from the horrors of the disease by a knife thrust, they die from heart failure or go deaf like *El Señor* Manuel Molina. We don't exaggerate when we say that the *seguiriya* is a formidable *cante*...frightening. It eats at the insides of he who sings it and grips and shatters the hearts of those who listen.

"And if the effort of singing the *seguiriya* does not destroy a man's lungs, the power of its sentiments will devour him, dry out his heart and destroy his nerves. Only a man condemned beforehand by fate can feel the pain, the indescribable anguish, the infinite yearning, the unbearable memories of the past and terror of the future...all of that formidable mixture of profound emotions that are expressed in the *seguiriya*. This *cante* is a devouring fire that consumes a man and eventually leaves him empty, spent and useless. Listen to this *seguiriya* of El Nitri:

Por una ventana	Through a window
que al campo salía,	that faced the countryside,
yo daba voces a la mare	I used to cry out to the mother
[*e mi arma*]	[of my soul]
y no me respondía.	and she never answered.

"*Qué cante ma formidable!*" exclaimed Chacón. "If everything El Nitri sang was that formidable, he must have been as great as Silverio!"

"There was no one like him *por seguiriyas*, but he was *mu corto*, very limited. He specialized in the *seguiriya* and a few other *cantes*. Silverio sings everything...he is the most complete *cantaor* who ever lived. Yet, one of his obsessions was to hear El Nitri sing, to find out if the *cantaor* was as good as people said and to refresh his memory in the *cantes* of El Fillo. But El Nitri refused to sing for him and Silverio never heard him."

"Because of the bad blood between the families?"

"Perhaps. But it is also possible that Tomás was jealous of Silverio's great success. Why should he wish to help Silverio recall the *cantes* of his uncle? And, because Silverio was *gachó*, the *gitano* may not have trusted him. You know, Silverio was the first *gachó* to dominate the *cante gitano* and many *gitanos* resent him for exposing their *cante* to the public in his cafés and concerts. There are still many *gitanos* who will not sing in front of any *gachó*."

With his lively imagination, Chacón had been completely captivated by Salvaoriyo's tales. Awe glistening in his eyes, he said, "What a singer El Nitri must have been. I wish I could have heard him!"

Salvaoriyo smiled. "You *and* Silverio! But there *are* those who have heard him, and some who know his *cante* well. Perhaps someday you will have a chance to hear Agustín Talegas. El Nitri lived with him in Alcalá for several years and he sings much of the *cante* of Tomás. And Juan Junquera has heard El Nitri many times. In fact, one time El Nitri was in a fiesta with Junquera and all the best singers of Jerez...*El Señor* Manuel Molina, Paco la Luz...all the best. It was one of those rare moments for the unpredictable Tomás, when he became truly inspired and drove the others to cry and tear their clothes. He was crowned "king of *cante jondo*" and presented with a *llave de oro del cante* [golden key of the *cante*]. He was even photographed holding a large key."[14]

"But isn't Silverio the king of *cantaores*?" asked Chacón.

"This all happened in the '60s, before Silverio had returned and reestablished his reputation. Silverio is *más largo*, he sings all of the *cantes*, while El Nitri was *corto*, but a great *seguiriyero*."

"I want to be just like Silverio. *Don* Sarvaó, will you teach me those *cabales* that you sang?"

The great *cantaor*, impressed once more by the boy's insatiable curiosity and capacity for learning, heaved a great sigh of acquiescence and plunged anew into the lesson.

The days passed and there was no work for the Jerezanos. For a while,

---

[14]This photo still exists, and the key has been formally presented twice since, in 1926 and 1962 (see appendix).

the boys were content to rest and live off their recent earnings. They visited a tailor and ordered new suits in the latest fashion. All three now sported stylish *sombreros vaqueros* [ranch hats], flat-crowned hats with broad circular brims.[15] Antonio Molina constantly checked his hat with both hands to assure that he had the brim tilted at the proper rakish angle. Chacón immersed himself in study and saw Salvaoriyo almost daily. Often, he went to the fish stall in the late mornings to be with his mentor. It was during one of those visits, accompanied by both Javier and Antonio, that Salvaoriyo suddenly stopped in mid-sentence and pointed toward the far end of the marketplace.

"Do you see that man...the one in the blue cape?"

The boys looked and saw a man who was well dressed, but whose clothes were not the current fashion and had clearly been cleaned and repaired too many times.

"That is *Don* Eugenio. Every week he comes to buy sardines. You will see. He'll come and speak of the *cante*, praise my singing, and order a half-kilo of sardines. Then, after I've weighed out the half-kilo, as I'm about to wrap them in paper, he'll pick out one more fish and throw it in with the others, saying, *"Pa el niño!"* [For my little boy!]"

Salvaoriyo shrugged his shoulders. "What can I do...it has *gracia!*"

A few minutes later *Don* Eugenio appeared, just as Salvaoriyo had predicted. He greeted the vendor, saluted the boys, and, throwing the noticeably worn cape back off his shoulders to free his gesturing arms, began to speak with exaggerated drama.

"How you sang the other night Salvador! What *soleares*, what *seguiriyas*...give me a half-kilo of sardines...there is no other who can sing like that!" Turning to the Jerezanos, he continued, "You should hear this man sing..."

All of this while Salvaoriyo weighed the sardines. When he had removed them from the scales and was about to fold the paper around them, the other stopped him with a gesture of his hand. Selecting a large, fat sardine, *Don* Eugenio tossed it in with the others as he winked at the youths and said, *"Pa el niño!"*

Antonio Molina turned away, barely able to contain his laughter, while Javier and Chacón didn't dare look at each other. When *Don* Eugenio had gone, Salvaoriyo shrugged and said, "What could I do...it has *gracia*, no?"

---

[15]Similar to today's *sombrero cordobés*.

A week later, the boys were again with Salvaoriyo as he was preparing to close his stall for the afternoon siesta. The vendor was telling them of his other mentor in the *cante*.

"Paco la Luz is the *gitano* I most like to listen to *por seguiriyas*..."

Javier interrupted, "Paco la Luz is from my barrio, from Santiago. His family, the Valencias, live not far from me. I used to like to listen to the daughter, Maria, sing her father's *cantes*, but then she went to Sevilla where I hear she is a *figura* [a star]..."

"And don't forget Juana, *la Sordita* [the little deaf one]," added the other Molina. "She is a wonder in the dance, even though she can't hear very well...and what a beauty she is going to be!"

Salvaoriyo smiled at the *bailaor*'s preoccupation with girls. In the weeks he had been with them he had come to know and enjoy the three young Jerezanos.

"I haven't seen the family in years," said the *cantaor*, "but they are all artists. Even the grandmother, María la Luz she was called, used to sing very well..."

"Look, it's *el de las sardinas* [he of the sardines]!" Chacón had spotted *Don* Eugenio approaching the fish stall.

"*A ver!* [Let's see what happens]" said Antonio Molina with a grin. Anything that smacked of *guasa* or practical jokes appealed to him and he found Salvaoriyo's predicament very funny.

"*Buenas tardes*, Salvador, how goes it?"

Don Eugenio nodded to the three youths, "*Muchachos*," and turned back to Salvaoriyo. "Salvador, remember that time in Casa Pepe when you had everybody weeping with your *seguiriyas?* What a night...give me half a kilo of sardines...I'll never forget it...what *seguiriyas*, what *soleares*..."

Salvaoriyo weighed out the half-kilo of fish and was about to wrap it when he stopped, leaned toward his customer, and interrupted the stream of flatteries by saying, "Excuse me *Don* Eugenio, will that be *with niño* or without?"

There was a moment of stunned silence, the boy's faces frozen in wide-eyed suspense. Then *Don* Eugenio, proving he could take as well as he gave, let out a burst of thin laughter. "*Qué angel*, Salvador," he said, catching his breath, "you have as much *gracia* in your business as in the *cante!*"

The tension broken, everyone laughed, while Salvaoriyo threw an extra sardine in with the others and invited *Don* Eugenio for a drink.

SALVAORIYO

Salvaoriyo was a master of the *cantes* of Paco la Luz. He and Chacón worked long and hard on the difficult *seguiriyas* of this gypsy genius who, although he performed in public on occasion, preferred to sing in gatherings of friends and knowledgeable aficionados. The slow, solemn delivery of this *cante* made it especially dramatic and heart-wrenching, and greatly increased its difficulty, especially in the long third line. Over and over they worked on the *letra* that went:

Mi hermana Alejandra	My daughter Alejandra
a la calle me echó.	threw me out of the house.
Dios se lo pague a mi	May God reward my brother
[*hermano Curro*]	[Curro]
que me arrecogió.	who took me in.

"No, Antonio," reprimanded Salvaoriyo, "that's not the way. You have to dominate the long line if you want it to come out. If you don't have it completely under control, you will never be able to connect it to the last line. Try it again!"

This time, Salvaoriyo stopped his student halfway through, saying, "You're rushing, Antonio. Slow down and be careful with your *compás*. I'm reminded of a time when Silverio was testing a young *aficionado* [amateur] in his café. It was his custom to allow unknown *cantaores* to come in and show what they could do after the regular shows had finished. One night an aspiring *cantaor* came in from a nearby pueblo. Silverio felt the youth was singing too fast and told him again and again, 'Slower...sing slower!' When the *aficionado* continued to ignore the advice, singing faster and faster, Silverio said to him, '*Bueno, mira* [look here]...go back to your pueblo, and when you learn to sing in the rhythm I'm trying to teach you, come back. Because it is one thing to sing, and quite another to sell lottery tickets!'[16]

"Silverio was very demanding when it came to the *cante* and he might dismiss a singer for the smallest error. He couldn't bear to listen to a *cantaor* who, instead of singing '*mi mare*' [my mother], said '*mi maresita*' [my dearest mother], because he felt it lightened the mood and destroyed the *aire* of the *cante*. So you see that we must pay careful attention to detail."

After many attempts, Chacón began to understand the intricacies

---

[16]Referring to the auctioneer-like chant of street lottery vendors.

of the melody and the subtle syncopations of the *compás* of the *seguiriya* of Paco la Luz. It was a demanding *cante*, but with a compelling beauty and passion that validated the widely held esteem of its creator.

Days stretched into weeks; weeks became a month. Christmas came and went and still the Jerezanos had not worked. As their savings dwindled, the Molina brothers began to pressure Chacón to leave. They were no longer in a mood to compromise. After a long New Year's Eve night of drinking and *cante*, they found the *cantaor* drinking coffee with Salvaoriyo.

"We have to do something, Antonio, our money is almost gone." said Javier.

"What do you want to do? Where would we go?" replied Chacón, realizing that he could not put his friends off much longer. In truth, the thoughts of all three boys had turned toward home during the holiday season and they were growing restless in Huelva.

"We can work our way toward Jerez the same way we got here..."

"Why don't you go to La Higuerita?" said Salvaoriyo, who had been listening in the background.

"Where?" asked Chacón.

"La Higuerita...Isla Cristina, as they call it now. The people there are great aficionados of the *cante* and guitar. You would earn good money every night."

The boys looked at each other. Isla Cristina was located near the border with Portugal, in the opposite direction from Jerez.

"I'm telling you, there is a fortune waiting for you there. And it's easy to get there...you can go by sea. Fishing boats go all the time and they will take you for little more than nothing."

So it was that the Jerezanos departed from Huelva that very night. Young Salvador could barely hold back tears as he said goodbye to Chacón, who had become his idol and had excited his enthusiasm for the *cante*. In the darkness of the pier the artists boarded a *pareja* and set sail for Isla Cristina. The small fishing boat, of a type used in pairs to set out nets, was tossed about roughly by the angry sea, forcing the three frightened passengers to take shelter under a heavy canvas tarp where they huddled, terrified and seasick.

Gray light had just broken through the chilly morning mist when the *pareja* docked in Isla Cristina, a tiny pueblo set on a point that jutted out into the Atlantic. At that early hour the waterfront bustled with activity as men and boats prepared to sail in search of sardines and tuna. The Jerezanos, unsteady on their feet and stinking of fish and vomit, stopped to clean up in the first tavern they encountered on the docks. The tavern owner, without even knowing what caliber of artists they might be, not only permitted them to make themselves presentable, but invited them to a meal and said, "Come tonight or tomorrow night and you can begin work right here."

Everything Salvaoriyo had said about Isla Cristina proved to be true. The three artists performed the following night and never lacked for work thereafter. The fishermen were great aficionados of the *cante* and *toque* and had money to spend. There were very few concerts with the unpredictable passing of the hat, for they had as many private fiestas as they could manage. When it wasn't one group of fishermen, it would be another. In those days, a payment of five *duros* was an extraordinary gift—and there were many such gifts for the young artists.

Night after night the boys worked, earning and saving money while refining their skills. Such was their luck that one night a butcher who had been listening to them invited them to stay with his family and save the cost of lodging. For the remainder of their stay, *Señor* Rojas cared for the boys as if they were his own sons. The visitors, in turn, became attached to the family, especially the daughter, a tiny thing with a beautiful face who was completely paralyzed from the waist down and had to drag herself about the floor.

From Isla Cristina the Jerezanos easily made day trips to neighboring towns without the burden of luggage. In Lepe they performed after a traveling theater company and were applauded with such fervor that Antonio Molina had to dance his *zapateado* a second time. Ayamonte, on the Portuguese border, was also the scene of a number of successful concerts. It was during the return from one of these that Chacón had time to reflect upon the overwhelming success of one of his *cantes*.

He realized that Salvaoriyo had to be given credit for the applause he had received in the café in Ayamonte. Several days before leaving Huelva, Chacón and the Molinas had been with Salvaoriyo and friends in the tavern where they often gathered in the evenings. It had been late and, in a quiet moment, Chacón unexpectedly began to sing the *serranas* he had learned from El Morrongo months earlier.

Salvaoriyo's eyes had widened slightly, but revealed little. When the youth had finished, he asked, "Where did you learn those *serranas?*"

"From a *gitano* in the mountains near Ronda," replied Chacón.

Shaking his head the other said, "They are not correct. You have the idea, but that is not the way the *serranas* are sung. Listen to how Silverio sings them."

Salvaoriyo then sang, *a palo seco*:

Yo crié en mi rebaño	I raised in my flock
una cordera;	a lamb;
de tanto acariciarla,	from so much caressing,
se volvió fiera.	she turned wild.
Y las mujeres,	And women,
contra mas acarician,	the more they are pampered
fieras se vuelven.	the wilder they become.

The *cante* was similar to that which Chacón had sung, but more carefully crafted. Where the gypsy from Ronda had sung with raw power and bare emotion, Salvaoriyo delineated the melody with detail and subtlety. In that moment Antonio had felt a helpless sense of futility. It seemed that Salvaoriyo found fault with everything he attempted. There was so much to learn.

The following day the study of the *serranas* had begun in serious.

"The *serranas* are not a *cante* of *gitanos*," Salvaoriyo had said. "You can tell by the *letras*. They are more educated, more formal, with a philosophy that is different from that of the *gitano*. Here is one that could never have been created by a *gitano*...

Las mujeres de ahora	The women of today
son como libros:	are like books:
que por nuevos se compran,	you buy them thinking they're new,
y están leídos.	and find they've been read.
Y muchos de ellos	And many of them
están remendados y	have been repaired and
pasan por nuevos.	pass for new.

"Do you see, *muchacho?* They are very formal. The *serrana* is a *copla* of four lines, two long and two short. Like this..." And the *cantaor* recited the following as he tapped out seven pulses [syllables] for the long lines and five for the short:

SALVAORIYO

Si el amor que te tengo	If the love I have for you
fuera pecado,	were a sin,
no podré de esta culpa	I would never, for this sin,
ser perdonao.	be forgiven

"And then we answer this with three more lines of five, seven and five beats:"

Nunca ha sío	Never has
perdonao er pecao	a sin been pardoned
no arrepentío.	that has not been repented.

"Do you understand?"

"Yes, *Don* Sarvaó, but why did the *gitano* tell me the *serranas* were of his people in Ronda?"

"What *gitano* ever told the truth? The *serranas* may have been a *cante* of the mountains at one time...a *cante* of bandits and smugglers, of *arrieros* and shepherds. But, you know, they sing the *serranas* here in Huelva, too...in the mountains where the smugglers go between Portugal and Spain. Yes, they love the *serranas* here, as you will see. And since Silverio made that *cante* popular it has become a *cante* of the towns and cities. We no longer have to sing only of the mountains."

Salvaoriyo sat up suddenly and said, "Enough talk! Your *serranas* were *esparrabáas* [not in *compás*]. They should have the *compás* of the *seguiriya*, but slower, more relaxed, with more flexibility. Javié!"

The guitarist looked up from where he had been half listening as he bent over his guitar. "Eh?"

"Put the *cejilla* on four and play por *seguiriyas*, but in tones of *la caña* [a predecessor of the *soleares*]." Turning back to Chacón he continued, "You see, Antonio, the *serrana* has a great deal of *la caña* in it...the *compás* of the *seguiriya*, and the tones and *aire* of *la caña*. Listen!"

For the first time the Jerezanos heard the *serranas* with proper guitar accompaniment. So skillfully did Salvaoriyo weave the long and solemn *tercios* with his powerful voice that Javier had no difficulty maintaining the *compás* and following the tones. At the end of the *letra*, the *cantaor* signaled for Javier to continue playing and a moment later launched into a long, gut-wrenching *seguiriya*:

Dice mi compañera	My girlfriend says
que no la quiero;	that I don't love her;
cuando la miro, la miro	when I look at her, I look at her face,
[*a la cara,*]	
y el sentío pierdo.	and I lose my mind.

Flushed and perspiring profusely, Salvaoriyo caught his breath and said, "*Leche*, what a difficult *cante*...the *seguiriya* of María Borrico that Silverio uses as the *cante de cambio* [song of change], the *macho* [ending] for *serranas*. Have you heard María Borrico sing?"

The others shook their heads.

"She's old now and doesn't leave Cádiz so often, but she can still sing. What a voice...a man's voice, very *afillá*. And very good *por seguiriyas*. Antonio, you must learn this *seguiriya de cambio* for the *serranas*. It is a beautiful *seguiriya*, between the old style of El Fillo and the way we sing today."

They had worked, day after day, until Chacón began to grasp the subtle nuances of the *serranas* and the *cambio* of María Borrico. Just when he thought he had mastered the *cante*, Salvaoriyo deflated him.

"It's time to learn the rest of the *cante*."

"The rest of the *cante?*" stammered Chacón in disbelief.

"Of course! If you wish to sing the *serranas* as Silverio does them, you must prepare the *cante* with the *livianas*."

"*Livianas?*" Chacón knew of the old *livianas* and had heard them sung a few times, but had not associated them with the *serranas*.

"Yes, the *livianas*. It is a *cante* of the mountains and the countryside, like the *serranas*, and has the same *letra*. Just as the *serranas* fall between the *caña* and the *seguiriyas*, the *livianas* are between the *seguiriyas* and the *serranas*...although they have more of the *aire* of the *serranas*. Because they are a *cante liviano*, lighter and easier to sing, they are used to prepare the voice and the listener for the *serranas*. Just as the lead donkey, *el liviano*, guides the others, the *livianas* lead the way to the more difficult *cante*."

Chacón learned a *letra* that went:

Ventanas a la calle	Windows to the street
son peligrosas	are dangerous
pa las madres que tienen	for mothers who have
sus hijas mozas.	maiden daughters.

SALVAORIYO

With the addition of the *livianas*, Chacón had a *cante* of epic proportions. Opening with *livianas*, then singing the *serranas*, and closing with the *seguiriyas de cambio* of María Borrico, created not only an intense emotional experience for the listener, but an awesome display of vocal strength and virtuosity.

On New Year's Eve, Salvaoriyo, filled with pride and deeply moved by his student's rendition of the *serranas*, had approached the youth as if he were about to embrace him.

"Antonio, take this as a gift, you have earned it."

The older man held out his *vara*, an elegantly slender staff highly polished from years of use. "This *varita* was given to me by Silverio many years ago and has been my companion ever since. It has never failed me."

Chacón felt a surge of emotion that held him motionless, unable to grasp the slender staff.

"Take it, Antonio! It carries the spirit of Silverio and will help you. This *vara*, along with your dedication to learning, to mastering all the styles, will carry you to great heights in the *cante*…"

The arrival of the carriage in Isla Cristina snapped Chacón out of his reveries. He gave a last silent thank you to Salvaoriyo for having made possible the tremendous success he had just experienced in Ayamonte with the *cante por serranas*.

In early May, after four months of artistic and financial success, the Jerezanos began to feel the pull of home, a desire to be in Jerez in the spring. They rationalized that it would be wise to leave Isla Cristina before people tired of them. After a tearful good-bye to the Rojas family, with promises to return at the earliest opportunity, Chacón and the Molinas boarded a galleon destined for Cádiz. Since they knew all of the crew and the officers, having performed for them many times, they were charged nothing for their passage and received such attention that their trip was pleasant and uneventful.

From the sea, Cádiz appeared as a brilliant gem on the horizon, a gleaming pearl as white as crystalline salt set in the deep blue of sky and ocean. Tall whitewashed buildings clustered at the end of a silvery strand that ran off to the right to connect to the distant mainland. The galleon sailed around the high seawalls into the bay and docked amid the many seagoing vessels berthed in the busy port.

The Jerezanos, anxious to be home, made immediate arrangements for a coach and left Cádiz the following morning for Jerez. Their trip had been all they had dreamed. Along with money and the outward trappings of success, they had matured considerably as artists, having honed their abilities through constant performing under difficult conditions. Yet they faced the next phase of their lives with mixed feelings. In spite of their confidence as artists, they knew it would not be the same for them in their hometown. As Antonio Molina put it, "Nobody is a prophet in his homeland."

The *bailaor* didn't overly concern himself with worrying about work. His thoughts were of the little gypsy dancer Juana Antúnez. But Javier wondered if there would still be a place for them in the Vera Cruz and whether his old guitar students would come back for lessons. The guitarist had become increasingly anxious about his family. He knew that the money he had saved would be welcomed, but would not last long. It was essential that he find work as quickly as possible.

Chacón found himself growing uneasy as he neared Jerez. Was he returning to the same life he had left? Had the whole trip been for nothing? In spite of a growing self-assurance, the young boy in him had begun to raise doubts. He feared being rejected again by Junquera and then left on his own when Javier and Antonio returned to the Vera Cruz. And he didn't know if he even wanted to work for Junquera, whose words, "You won't do, *nene!*" still burned as freshly in his mind as the day they were said. His dream of escaping from singing *p'atras* in the *cuadro* seemed as distant as ever—he had no promise of *any* work at all. And behind all these doubts and questions nagged the persistent fear of his father's demands and criticism. After nine months of freedom, Antonio did not think he could endure living as he had before. Would the success he had found in the *cante* be enough to impress Papa Chacón?

The appearance of the golden dome of the Colegiata on the horizon announced the approach to Jerez and the imminent answers to the boys' questions.

María

Jerez de la Frontera, late spring, 1885

"That's all I can give...not a *céntimo* more! Four *pesetas* a night is a good salary, more than my husband ever earned!" The woman speaking was a burly matron, dressed in black with thick black hair pulled back tightly into a bun.

Antonio Chacón could barely conceal his elation behind a mask of feigned indifference. Four *pesetas* was indeed a good salary in a time when the average fieldworker of Jerez earned less than half a *peseta* for a long day of backbreaking work.

"Will I sing *p'alante?*" asked the youth.

"We'll see. At the moment we have Marrurro, Manuela, and Miguel to sing *p'alante*. You will sing in the *cuadro* for three functions each night."

Tomasa was an astute gypsy businesswoman. It was not without reason that Juan Junquera felt confidence in his sister's ability to direct the Café de la Vera Cruz while he attended to his newest *café cantante* in Utrera and managed an ever-increasing number of artists.

Chacón glanced over to where his two friends sat at a table in the largely deserted café. Javier and his brother had already agreed to terms. The three boys had just returned from Medina Sidonia in the foothills of Cádiz. A contract for three week's work in the hilltop town had been fortuitous, as there had been nothing for them in Jerez when they first returned from Isla Cristina. Buoyed by success in the pueblo, the three had returned home to find openings for them in the Vera Cruz. Chacón had been spared a confrontation with Juan Junquera and having to face the conflict between his desire to work and his resentment of the impresario's harsh words the year before. Although he had promised himself that Junquera would have to beg him to sing, he felt no such reluctance about working for Tomasa. At the same time, he realized that he was in no position to be making demands and was fortunate to be receiving the generous offer of four *pesetas*.

"I *must* sing *p'alante*," grumbled the sixteen-year-old *cantaor* to his companions as they strolled away from the Vera Cruz. "I wasn't meant to sing in the *cuadro*. How am I to become known if I must always sing behind the dance?"

"Be patient, *tocayo*," said Antonio Molina, "*con el tiempo y la esperanza, todo se alcanza!*" [all things come with time and hope!]

"Yes, you have to be patient," added Javier. "You're lucky to be working at all...and earning four *pesetas*, at that! Look at the singers they have...Antonio Marrurro sings almost as well as his brother Diego, and Miguel Frascola is a monster *por alegrías* and *malagueñas*. And what about La Fernández...Manuela sings *por soleá* and *seguiriya pa rabiar* [to drive you crazy]. *Hombre*, you sing well, but do you expect to put those people out of work?"

"Besides that, *tocayo*, you can sing all you want in the *cuartos* [private rooms] after we finish work. You're sure to be hired often for fiestas."

"I will *have* to work in the *cuartos*. Now that my father is too sick to work, I need to earn as much as possible."

"How is your father?"

"Not well. He can't work at all."

Chacón had returned to Jerez to find his father too ill to be concerned with his son's choice of profession. In the spring of 1885, a virulent epidemic of Asian cholera had descended upon Spain, entering the east coast at Murcia and Valencia and spreading westward through Andalucía. The disease lurked in food and water contaminated by human waste, striking down its victims with debilitating fever and fatal gut-wrenching dehydration. Hundreds died each day and many more were left weak and invalid. The elder Chacón had survived the disease, but remained bedridden and deteriorating day by day. His son had assumed the role of provider for the family.

Café de la Vera Cruz became Antonio Chacón's university. Unlike in the pueblos where the young *cantaor* stood out in contrast with second-rate singers—drunks and bohemians who eked out a meager existence going from town to town—in the Vera Cruz, Chacón found himself surrounded by the artistic cream of Jerez and the best artists from Sevilla and Cádiz.

Gone from Jerez were some of the dancers from the year before. Juana and Fernanda Antúnez were in Sevilla, as was María, the young sister of Juana la Macarrona. But the voluptuous La Chorrúa remained, along with Gerónima la Morenita, excellent in the *soleá*. The comedic *bailaor* Antonio Moneo delighted audiences with his renditions of *El Pericón* [The Fan] and *El Oso* [The Bear], while Paquiro Ortega, potbellied and balding, brought the *gracia* of Cádiz to his *bailes por alegrías* and *tangos*. Chacón sang *alegrías* for his friend Antonio Molina and *soleares* for the powerful gypsy dance of Juana Peña.

Salvaoriyo had said: "To be somebody in the *cante*, you must know and master all the styles." This advice drove Chacón to make the most of his time in the café, in spite of the disdain he felt for singing *p'atras* in the *cuadro*. Listening night after night to the *cante* of Miguel Serrano "Frascola," the youth absorbed new *letras* and melodies for the *alegrías*. He developed the ability to anticipate the dancer, to inspire the *baile* with *cante* at precisely the right moment, and he learned which *letras* suited the dramatic parts of the dance and which supplied strong rhythm and excitement.

Dancer after dancer, Frascola and Chacón alternated in the *cante*. Then, El Marrurro or Manuela Fernández went out *p'alante* to sing with Javier, who had surpassed the abilities of Junquera's son-in-law, Luis Juanero, and become first guitarist. Later, the artists of the *cuadro* huddled near the bar over drinks or mingled with customers, hoping to arrange private fiestas for later in the night. The *cuadro* would return for two more shows, finishing after one in the morning.

Hour after hour the *compás* pounded in Chacón's ears. The endless cracking of hard hands, the staccato rhythm of pounding feet, and the driving pulse of the *cante* continued to reverberate within him long after leaving the stage, becoming as much a part of him as his own heartbeat.

When the aching feet of the final dancer had pounded out their last *redoble* [short footwork combination] and most of the clientele had filed out, staggering home to sleep off the wine for a few hours before another work day, the artists who had made arrangements retired with their customers to the *cuartos*, where the *cante* would continue through the night. As much as Chacón resented having to sing in the *cuadro*, he dreaded even more the fiestas in the *cuartos*. But, night after night, he lingered at the bar with the women and the other artists, hoping to be included in a last-minute arrangement. Even if he could have afforded to pass up the money, he had little choice in the matter, for the café's owner insisted that the artists be available for fiestas.

Sun-up often found Chacón arriving home after a night of waiting, a night spent smoking and drinking with fellow artists. The more experienced and well-known *cantaores* were hired first. If Chacón were taken for a fiesta, his role was generally to break the ice, to set the mood for the other *cantaor*. The intelligent aficionado knew that he could not command a Marrurro or Joaquin la Cherna to sing a particular *cante* at a given moment. To get the best from these *cantaores*, it was necessary to ply them with wine and employ a lesser singer to inspire and challenge them.

In the best of these *reuniones* [gatherings[1]], a *señorito* and a few of his friends retired to a *cuarto* with a couple of veteran *cantaores*, a guitarist, and perhaps a novice singer like Chacón. In the small rooms set aside by the café for *reuniones* were a few chairs, a small table, and occasionally a sofa for the use of passed-out drunks or lovesick couples. There was nothing to distract from the purpose of the gathering—to drink and listen to *cante*. If the *señorito* were an *aficionado cabal*, one who understood and appreciated *cante* and who knew how to do more than live extravagantly off the rents of his father's land, he might win the respect of the artists and be considered a patron. If he knew how to allow the *reunión* to develop at its own pace and how to encourage the artists with praise, wine, tobacco, and fried fish or slices of smoked ham, the magic of the *cante* might occur. *Venga vino, venga cante!* Wine and song through the night—six, eight, ten hours, or more.

This was Chacón's school. In that environment, he learned what it meant to give from the heart, to fight with the *cante*, to suffer the anguish of the *cante*. If the *cantaor* were successful, he would sing not only his own feelings, but, vicariously, the feelings of the others. In identifying intimately with the *cantaor*, the spectator would experience the *cante* as his own. In that shared expression and communal catharsis lay the power of the *cante* to grip a man's soul and drive him to seek its solace time and time again.

---

[1]*reunión*: in flamenco, a term generally reserved for gatherings of friends and aficionados; *fiesta* is a more general term, while *juerga* was a more contemptuous term used to refer to drunken orgies.

When the gathering broke up in full daylight, payment was surreptitiously slipped to the exhausted artists in a handshake, the amount determined by the prestige of the artist and the generosity of the *señorito*. Chacón was normally paid half of what the others received.

The *reunión* of *cabales* was a rarity. More often, the *señoritos* were what the flamencos called *sabiondos*, know-it-alls who demanded *cantes* from the singers and pompously displayed their ignorance in order to impress the women. On one such occasion, Chacón could barely contain himself when a particularly offensive *señorito* said to Joaquín la Cherna, who had just sung *por soleá*, "What good *martinetes*, Joaquín!" Without batting an eye, La Cherna replied, "You are really knowledgeable, because those were some very unusual *martinetes* that I have put into *soleá*."

Later, La Cherna had told Chacón, "If the *señorito* says black is white, we have to lower our heads and agree." The comment rankled in Chacón. He didn't think he would ever be able to bow before the ignorance of the *señoritos* the way others did, to praise their attempts at singing or laud their popularity with women.

Worse yet were the *mangones*, the hangers-on who paid nothing, but had to be endured because they were friends of the *señorito*. The artist who wished to be paid had no choice but to bear their outrageous demands, crude behavior, and condescending smirks.

And always, in the back of the artist's mind, the gnawing fear: *Will there be money at the end of this, and how much?* Once, while walking toward San Miguel in the early morning, Chacón asked El Marrurro, "Why must we wait until the fiesta is over before we know what we are to be paid? Why can't we agree upon an amount ahead of time?"

"It's just not done," replied Marrurro. "We have always been paid at the end. Look, Antonio, if we knew what we were to receive, we would have no reason to work hard. When we know that we will be paid according to how we sing, we give our best. And sometimes the reward is greater than expected...wine can loosen a man's purse strings."

"That may be true, but I still don't see why we can't be paid as others are paid, an agreed upon amount..."

" It wouldn't work. We're not like them."

Worst of all were the all too common *juergas*, arranged by men who were out for a night of merriment. One of these had fallen to Chacón shortly after he began at the Vera Cruz. Four men, well-intoxicated even before entering the *cuarto* (*Maybe they will pass out early*, Chacón had thought, hopefully), had selected from the artists who were left—Frascola, Chacón, two women from the *cuadro* and two others, and Juanero on guitar.

As the least experienced, Chacón sang first, *por soleá*. No one listened. The men were preoccupied with small talk and pairing off with the women. Chacón struggled, until one of the men, wishing to impress the women, wagged a hand of dismissal at him, saying, "*Muy bien, muy bien!* Enough of the popular stuff...now sing some *cante jondo* [deep song]! He exaggerated the gutteral "j" sound in imitation of the flamencos' pronunciation of *hondo* and laughed sarcastically at his cleverness.

Chacón flushed with anger and thought: *He wants cante jondo, I'll give him jondo!* He said, "Luis, put it on two, *por serranas!*"

A short guitar introduction and a warm-up with the *livianas* as Salvaoriyo had taught him. Then he threw himself into the *serranas* of Silverio:

"*Yo crié en mi rebaño* [I raised in my flock], *una cordera* [a little lamb]...*una cordera...una cordera...*" He strained with the difficult *cante*. "*Yo crié en mi rebaño, yo crié en mi rebaño...una cordera...ay, ay...una cordera...*"

No sooner had he begun the second part of the *letra*, repeating again, "*Una cordera...*" than he was interrupted by a drunken croak, "*Una cordera?* [One lamb?]...There are enough sheep there to feed a regiment!"

The *cuarto* broke into riotous laughter and shrill giggles. Chacón was stunned to silence. Frascola, seeing his predicament, prevented an impetuous action by quickly saying, "Antonio, let me sing, I'm in the mood! Luis, *por tango*."

Chacón slouched in humiliated silence, listening to Frascola struggle to be heard over the boisterous voices and incessant giggles. Anger replaced hurt, and when he could contain himself no longer, he leaned toward the nearest man, touched him on the arm, and said with barely controlled rage, "*Señor*, if you would just quiet down a little, everyone might be able to hear."

The man looked over in a stupor and replied in a foggy voice, "You just worry about your singing!" Turning back to the woman by his side, his hands resumed their out-of-sight explorations.

The noise increased. A man tried to dance, but lost his balance and staggered backward into Juanero, knocking the guitar against a table corner with a sickening crack. The others laughed, *"Qué ángel!* Look at Eduardo...*qué precioso!"* An olive pit hit Chacón above the eye. The door to the next *cuarto* slammed angrily, announcing that the *reunión* there had ended in frustration after numerous requests for quiet and loud poundings on the wall.

Hours later, when the last client had stumbled out the door, the artists received the final affront. The money was given to Frascola in a lump sum, leaving to him the unpleasant task of dividing it among the artists. Chacón, disappointed with what he received, would always wonder whether Frascola had kept more than his share."

By mid-morning Chacón reached home, where he would sleep a few hours, nap again in the afternoon, and then return to the Vera Cruz to face another night.

As always, the Vera Cruz closed for the month of August, when oppressive heat brought everything to a standstill. September, with its *vendimia* and harvest festivities was a lucrative time for the flamencos. Chacón was not rehired when the Vera Cruz opened once more, a victim of the normal rotation of artists. After a stint in the Café de Rogelio, he had to resort to sporadic work in nearby pueblos.

On a crisp morning in late November, Chacón sipped coffee at his usual table in front of a café on Jerez' central Plaza Arenal. He couldn't help overhearing conversation at the next table.

"The poor man, may he rest in peace," one of a group of men was saying. "He died because he was so good..."

Chacón could guess the subject of the man's comments. Even he had heard about the sudden death of King Alfonso XII.

"Good?" interrupted another. "How can you say *good*, the way he treated us here in Andalucía? Those in Madrid don't care about us...they treat us like one of the colonies, to be taxed and robbed..."

"*Hombre!* What about the new railroad? And don't forget the improvements in the road to Sevilla, or the schools..."

"Schools? Of what use are schools if people don't have enough to eat?"

"*Hombre*, those are things of government, but Alfonso, may he rest in peace, was a good man. Did you read how he died?"

"I've heard he had tuberculosis."

"*Qué va, hombre!* Read the paper, it's all there. The good man went to Aranjuez to try to help the many who were dying from this cursed epidemic. They didn't want him to go, but he went anyway. Imagine going in among all of those sick?"

"*Qué valor!* [What bravery!]"

"It says in the paper that, a few days later, he went with the Queen Mother and the Queen to the countryside. Imagine this, they were laughing and chatting around a fire when Alfonso, may he rest in peace, suddenly became very serious, very sad, and he said, 'A nice way to spend my birthday!'

"Nobody knew what he meant...there was still a week until his birthday! But, can you believe it, three days later, yesterday, he was dead!"

"*Qué barbaridá!*"

"Now what will happen?"

"That remains to be seen. When the Queen's child is born, if it's a boy, he'll be king. They say that the daughter, Mercedes, will be queen until then, with her mother ruling for her as regent..."

"A woman should not rule! We are in for hard times, wait and see. Perhaps the anarchists are right when they say we would be better off with no government."

"*Al carajo* with the anarquists...trouble makers, murderers...thank God the *Guardia Civil* has put an end to their strikes and marches..."

"That's not so. I have heard they still hold meetings and as long as taxes are so high and workers are starving they will be able to organize against the landowners and the government."

"*Hombre*, to try to help is one thing, but to attack the Church is another. My cousin in San Fernando told me they tried to change the name of his town. They wanted to remove the 'Saint' and call it just Fernando. *Qué tontería!* [What an idiocy!] And they tried to get people to say *'Salud'* [Health] in place of *'Adiós'* or 'Go with God'..."

The argument droned on. Chacón had given little thought to the world outside of Jerez and its neighboring *pueblos*. The journey through Andalucía had widened his perspective, but Madrid and the workings of government were beyond his conception. He knew only that his father complained incessantly about the burden of taxes, and that in the pueblos, farmers grumbled, "After taxes and rents, we can't afford even the bread made from our own wheat."

"*Una limosna, por favor*, alms for one who has not eaten today!"

Chacón looked up. The pitiful plea had come from the toothless mouth of an old man. The humble figure, stooped from a lifetime of working in the fields, the tattered clothes, and the tobacco-stained beard were all familiar.

"Churri! You don't recognize me, but I used to listen to you sing in the *taberna* of Chícharo, in Santiago. Sit down and have a coffee?"

"*Gracias, joven* [young man], God will repay you!"

No longer able to work, Churri made the rounds of the *tabernas* each evening, begging coins in exchange for his painful attempts to sing. As the old man clutched his coffee, savoring each sip, he muttered bitterly, "One cannot live today. We work all our lives for what? One cannot earn enough to live on...nor even enough to die with dignity! *El gobiesno* [*gobierno*; government] has forgotten us. That's why we have to sing..." And in a broken voice, scarcely more than a raspy whisper, he sang:

Me has despreciado por pobre	You have scorned me for being poor,
y cuatro palacios tengo:	when, in reality, I have four palaces:
el asilo, el hospitá,	the asylum, the hospital,
la carcel, y el cementerio.	the jail, and the cemetery.

Chacón watched the fragile old man shuffle off, the monotonously intoned, "Alms, for the love of God, I have had nothing to eat today," as much a part of him as his stale, unwashed odor. Vowing to avoid a similar fate, the young *cantaor* renewed his determination to escape the ignominy of singing in the *cuadro*.

"Antonio, what's up?" The arrival of the Molina brothers shook Chacón from the depths of thought. "When did you get back? How was it?"

"I came in last night. *Hombre*, what a mess! It was like some of those places we worked last year...lots of work, very little money. Lebrija is not like here, not like working in the Vera Cruz. How are things there, when do you think I might be able to go back?"

"I asked the other day," replied Javier as he and Antonio pulled chairs up to the table. "Tomasa told me there might be room for you after Christmas."

"*Bien*, I need work. Antonio, there is something I want to ask you."

"*Sí, tocayo?*"

Chacón seemed somewhat flustered. It took him a moment before he blurted out, "There is a girl I like...and I'm not sure what to do!"

Both Molinas sat up grinning. Antonio reached over to thump

Chacón on the shoulder. "A girl? *Hombre*, it's about time!"

"Who is it?" asked Javier.

Chacón turned red. "It's María, the daughter of the bread man. Her parents have the *panadería* [bread bakery] over on Campana. I saw her this morning for the first time in years...she has grown up to be very pretty. But I don't know what to do next..."

"*Hombre*, you have to *pelar la pava* ["skin the turkey": court her]..."

"*Hermano*, you don't know!" interrupted the older Molina. "Before he can begin to court her, he has to meet her and arrange it. Listen, *tocayo*, here is what you do." He leaned in toward Chacón and said in a conspiratorial tone, "Go by the *panadería* every chance you get. When you see her, smile and give her a complement. Say, 'Blessed be the priest who baptized you,' or, 'Your eyes are bigger than your feet!' You're lucky, because you can go to the *panadería*...you don't have to wait for her to come out with her mother. Go there and buy bread, and if she will speak to you, you can ask her, '*Niña*, can I come to talk with you?' If she says yes, then you can go to see her, to *pelar la pava*."

Chacón followed instructions. He visited the *panadería* at every opportunity, sometimes buying bread twice in a one day. Mama Chacón had willingly sacrificed the social pleasures of her daily stop for bread in the hope that her bohemian son might settle down with the breadmaker's daughter. The young suitor soon came to associate the warm fragrance of the golden bread loaves with the object of his desire, until the least hint of that rich aroma immediately stirred appetites stronger than hunger.

María, a short, plain brunette with an olive complexion and generously developed bosom and hips, helped her mother wait on customers. At first she spoke freely with Antonio when he came for bread, but when his flushed, lovesick stares and fumbling attempts at conversation revealed his intentions, she fell silent, neither waiting on him, nor looking in his direction.

On the advice of Antonio Molina, Chacón continued to pass back and forth in front of the *panadería*, or waited hours on the corner of the street where María lived, hoping to see her go out with her mother or appear on the balcony. If María came to the balcony, as she did with increasing frequency, and always accompanied by her younger sister, the youth would stroll casually by, smile up at her, and say, "*Buenas tardes!*" Or he would sing in a voice loud enough to be heard as he passed by:

Manojitos de arfileres,	Handfuls of needles,
chiquiya, son tus pestañas;	girl, are your eyelashes;
qué, cada vez que me miras,	each time that you look at me,
me los clavas en el arma.	you pierce my soul with them.

In a burst of giggles, María would coyly avert her eyes, blush red, and attack her vegetable peeling or stitchery with renewed vigor. As he became bolder, Chacón began to ask, "*Niña*, when are you going to allow me to speak with you?"

After almost two weeks, Chacón's persistence was rewarded when the sister came to the balcony alone, leaned over the railing, and said in a shouted whisper, "Listen, *muchacho*...my sister says for you to come to the window tonight, at eight o'clock."

Chacón's heart pounded with joy, and panic. He rushed to Antonio. "What do I do now? What do I say to her?

"*Hombre*, say anything! Tell her how pretty she is, or how you count the minutes until you can see her. Don't worry, she'll take care of the talking."

Seven o'clock that evening found Chacón wrapped in a gray cape against the chilly night and pacing nervously in the dark street across from María's window. Behind the heavy iron grillwork, the window appeared ominously dark. An hour crept by, the shrouded figure flattening against the wall at every sound—it wouldn't do to be seen by one of María's brothers or her father. He thought to himself that he was fortunate to be waiting by a ground window. Many courtships were carried out long distance, in whispers between the street and a second-story window. Or, even worse, through the *gatera*: Chacón recalled the times he had passed a figure sprawled upon the ground, attempting to converse through the hole used by the cat.

Eight o'clock came and went. In the cold darkness, the minutes passed painfully slowly. When the Colegiata bells sounded nine o'clock, Chacón gave up, slinking home dejected and discouraged.

The following day he went angrily to the *panadería*, intending to vent his rage and be done with such foolishness. But when María whispered, even before he could speak, "I couldn't. But if you come tonight I can talk with you," his anger dissolved and he was overcome with guilt at having doubted her. Seven o'clock found him again anxiously watching the grilled window on Calle Campana. After an hour, he had just begun to grow agitated when a soft "Tsst!" came from the window.

With an apprehensive glance up and down the street, he crossed to the window, where he found that the shutter had been cracked open and María's shadowy features were just distinguishable in the dark interior.

"Here I am," she whispered tensely, eyes darting about like a timid animal, ready to flee at the slightest hint of danger.

"I came, like you said," replied Chacón.

"You were late!"

"Late? I've been here a long time."

"I know, but you were late."

"But..."

"You don't have to explain...I understand. You probably had something more important to do than be with me."

"There is nothing more important than you!" Chacón could feel her silent satisfaction in response to this admission.

María talked on about her family, of her brothers and sisters, and her friends, which of them had found *novios*"[2] [fiancées] and which she was certain would never marry. "Can you believe it, Mari Carmen is fifteen and she hasn't fallen in love yet! Rocío is so lucky, her *novio* has declared himself to her. Do you know Eugenia...the daughter of Francisco, the *tonelero*? She's getting married next Wednesday...You know, you can't get married on Tuesday, *en martes, ní te cases, ní te embarques* [on Tuesday, you can neither marry nor set sail]...she's so lucky I can't stand it...I can't wait for the wedding. You know, weddings are contagious...out of one wedding come others." She asked Chacón about the shoe business and his father—who had been growing weaker daily—but whenever Antonio tried to bring up his singing she changed the subject

At the nine o'clock bell, they separated for dinner, but, in what was to become a nightly routine, they were back at the window an hour later. The conversation soon became intimate: Did Antonio like brunettes? Did he think she was too tall? Too heavy? Too talkative? Did he wish to have a big family? When Antonio insisted that he had had no previous *novia*, María refused to believe him. In response to being asked, "Do you believe in God?" Antonio had answered, "How could I not believe in God? Now, it's one thing to believe, and another

---

[2]*novio*: boyfriend, fiancée; in that time, the term *novios* was reserved for those who had entered the *noviazgo*, the period of courtship and engagement that could last for years.

to be in church every single day..." In reality, Chacón escorted his mother faithfully to Mass on Sundays, but, like most men, he stood in the back after seating her, where he could slip outside to talk and smoke. Many men felt that they had fulfilled their obligation if they just peeked in the door.

Chacón lived for the nightly ritual. Although he dreaded the endless small talk and the hours of standing on rough stones until his feet ached, his passion consumed him; it filled every moment of his day and kept him awake through the short nights. He wasn't singing, and he didn't care.

During the day he tried to see María whenever possible. They arranged signals using flowerpots. A medium size pot placed at the right side of the balcony meant she would be going out in the afternoon. A larger pot next to it signified that she would be accompanied by her mother and that Antonio should station himself where he could watch her pass by without being seen. A smaller pot indicated that her younger sister would be with her and Antonio would be able to walk with them briefly.

Each night was the same. Antonio would invariably be accused of arriving late. After protesting in vain and finally apologizing, he would be forgiven, only to be subjected moments later to a fit of jealousy: "I would kill myself if you were unfaithful to me. Don't you dare pay attention to other girls!"

After the bells had sounded eleven o'clock, María would begin to comment, "It's late, I'd better go. It wouldn't be proper for us to be seen together at this hour." But, when Chacón agreed with her, she came back with, "Why are you in such a hurry to leave me?" It seemed that María could always find something to anger her. If Antonio showed remorse, she became forgiving and coquettish, but if he protested too strongly or became angry, she accused him of not caring about her and tears poured down her cheeks until he relented. Her last words each night were, "Now you're going to go off to visit those bad women, aren't you. Don't say you aren't...I know you are. You better not, or I'll never speak to you again!"

Eventually they began to speak of engagement. But whenever Chacón yielded to María's persistent pleas and agreed to speak to her parents, she became hesitant, saying, "Not yet, I'm afraid of my father."

Churning with frustration, Chacón lay awake nights envisioning the softness of María's skin. But, when he dared to slip his hand through the iron bars one night and attempted to grasp María's hand where it lay seductively on the sill, she jerked away.

"What are you doing, Antonio?" she snapped.

"I just wanted to hold your hand. We're almost engaged...I should be able to kiss you now!"

"What would people say? If I let you touch me, then you'll leave me..."

"María, I wouldn't leave you, *juro por la leche que mamé* [I swear by my mother's milk³]... "

"Antonio! Don't talk to me like that...is that all you think of me? And you *would* leave me. If I give you what you want, you will leave me and nobody will ever want me... I'll never be married."

"But... "

"Shhhh! Be quiet, Antonio! If anyone hears us, we'll never be able to talk again."

Chacón, increasingly frustrated with his inability to discuss his career with María, decided to give her the news. "María, I'm going back to work in the Vera Cruz...I won't be able to come see you at night for awhile."

"Antonio, don't tell me that!"

"It's true. I can't put off my singing any longer... "

"But, what about the shoes... and our dream of having a *zapatería* near here, near my family?"

"That's your dream, María. I'm not going to be a shoemaker. I haven't worked with shoes for years. I am an artist, a *cantaor de flamenco*... "

"That can't be! You can't raise a family on *gitanerías* [gypsy foolishness], that's not an honorable life for a woman. You must be joking."

"It won't be like that, María, listen to me... "

"Tell me you're joking!"

"It's not a joke. *Carajo!* I'm telling you the truth!"

"Don't use that language with me... I am not like those people you call your friends... those *gitanos* and... and who knows what! Can't you see? It can't be... my parents will never allow it."

The soft sound of sobbing lasted but a moment before the dull but final thud of the shutter left the street in silence.

The following day, María was not in the *panadería*. Chacón's

---

³This was an oath of the lowest classes and particularly offensive to middle and upper classes, considered an affront to the mother.

inquiry was met by an icy retort from her mother. "She is home, where she belongs!" He kept watch all day, hoping to see her go out or appear on the balcony. That night, he waited in vain by her window for over two hours. At last, convinced of the futility of his vigil, he turned to leave, but looked back one last time toward the balcony that had meant so much to him. There in the gloom, in its familiar place at the right was the flowerpot. *Empty and upside down.*

Chacón never spoke with María again. Devastated and despondent, he threw himself into his work. Sometimes while singing he experienced a rush of bitter remembrance and his voice would choke with emotion. Often, in those moments, some good aficionado would say, *"Olé!"*

Carnaval came and went, followed by the somber season of Lent and its crowning Holy Week, with days of processions leading up to Easter. Then festivities of the spring fairs. In May, King Alfonso XIII was born and celebrated, although he would not rule until he turned sixteen. It was also in May that Chacón, frustrated by the slow progress of his career, astonished his friends with an announcement.

El Canario

"But Antonio, you can't just leave like that!" Javier pleaded with his friend, exasperation evident in his voice.

Chacón shrugged in a gesture of futility, "What am I supposed to do, Javié? I'm not getting anywhere here."

"Is it because of María?" asked Antonio Molina. "If so, you have to remember, *el amor es un pasatiempo que pasa con el tiempo* [love is a pastime that passes with time]...you'll get over her."

"It's not that, *tocayo*. I've been in the Vera Cruz for months and still they won't let me sing *p'alante*. I need to go someplace where I'll be appreciated."

"*Hombre*, what do you expect? It was easy in Isla Cristina, but here, with so many good artists, you have to be patient..."

"Patient! For how long, *hombre*...for how long?"

Javier shrugged. "You're making good money, you can't quit..."

"Good money? With my father sick, four *pesetas* is barely enough for us to survive on. The other day, Frascola told me that when Juan Breva was in Madrid a couple of years ago, he sang in three places at the same time and earned five *duros* a day in each of them. And he demanded to be paid in *gold!* Imagine, Javié, I earn four *pesetas* and he was making *twenty-five in each place*...and the Imparcial even gave him a house for his family!"[1]

"*Hombre*," interrupted Javier, "you can't expect to be paid like Juan

---

[1] In 1884 Breva performed in the Príncipe Alfonso Theater, the Café del Barquillo, and the Café Imparcial.

Breva. Four *pesetas* is a good salary, more than most of us earn, and look what you sometimes make in the fiestas!"

"Fiestas!" spat the other. "What do they give us? I sing all night on stage and then go into a room with some drunks and sing until morning, until my voice is gone, and what do they give me? Maybe a few *reales*...if they can't find a way out of it!"

"What do you expect? That's the way it is with us artists. We have to take what work we can find..."

"Not me! I won't spend my life in the *cuadro* and singing for drunks who don't appreciate the *cante*. If they won't allow me to sing up front here, I'll go elsewhere."

"Where?" chimed in Antonio. "Where can you go...except back to the pueblos, where you will earn even less than you do here? Be careful, *tocayo, antes que te cases, mira lo que haces!*" [before you marry, look at what you're doing; look before you leap!]

"Sevilla...I'll go to Sevilla," Chacón blurted out without thinking.

"Sevilla? You're crazy..."

Three weeks later, in late May and just after his seventeenth birthday, Antonio Chacón stepped off the train in Sevilla's Estación de San Bernardo. Ignoring the four-mule *omnibús* that transported passengers from the station, the youth walked the short distance to the city. He followed the path he had taken with the Molinas, passing through La Puerta de la Carne and into the narrow, twisting streets of the Barrio de Santa Cruz. He quickly found room in a *fonda* and then set out to learn what he could of the *cafés cantantes*.

The warm spring air was thick with the fragrance of orange blossoms and jasmine mixed with the acrid yet enticing smell of charcoal smoke and frying olive oil. Chacón felt at home in the intimacy of the Barrio de Santa Cruz. But even the heavy chiming of the bells of the Giralda, so ominously near, did little to prepare the youth for the noise and confusion of the heavy traffic that assaulted him upon emerging from a narrow passageway onto a major thoroughfare. Tall buildings and bustling throngs of people, animals, and carriages pressed in upon him, while off to his left rose the mountain of stone that was the Cathedral.

Antonio had forgotten how big the city was. Now, confused and somewhat intimidated, he fought his way through the horde of beggars that swarmed about the Cathedral. Sevilla was a beggar's town. Many of the *pordioseros*—so-called for the "*por Dios*" that began their persistent supplications—were crippled or blind. But just as many were able-bodied soldiers or desperate peasants who had come in from the countryside to escape starvation. And children. Everywhere in the streets and cafés, tattered and filthy ragamuffins imitated their elders, pleading "Alms for the love of God," and rewarding the gift of a few *céntimos* with, "May God repay you!"

Asking directions, Chacón made his way down the broad Avenida de la Constitución, past the government buildings and into the undulating passageway appropriately named Calle de las Sierpes [Street of the Serpents[2]]. This narrow lane, several blocks in length and closed to vehicles, was the center of Sevilla's social life and almost always congested with vendors and their donkeys, soldiers, peasants in *calañés* hats and faded woolen jackets, and the ever-present beggars. In chairs so numerous as to almost block passage in front of the many cafés, men sat smoking and drinking. They stared in silence or talked ceaselessly, debates growing heated in the afternoon *tertulia* gatherings. People came to see and be seen. Pigtailed and flamboyantly dressed bullfighters drank with their followers, while moneyed *señoritos* lounged in the doorways of the *casinos*, shoeshine boys crouched at their feet. Behind the windows of the *casinos* the members sat motionless through the afternoons in their leather armchairs, absorbed in the deep satisfaction of being themselves. Under a high canopy, drawn over the street on hot afternoons, ranchers and businessmen closed deals, bullfighters signed contracts, and olive merchants haggled over prices. It was on Calle de las Sierpes that the business of Sevilla was transacted.

Chacón made his way in wonder past the Café Nacional, the grand Café Suizo with its café, restaurant, billiard parlor, pastry shop, and hotel, and mentally noted the location of the Café Teatro del Centro, where he thought he might look for work. A short distance further and Calle de las Sierpes ended in the Plaza de la Campana. The youth crossed the plaza and passed through the adjacent tree-lined Plaza del Duque with its two imposing palaces. Just beyond the Palace of the Duke of Medina Sidonia this plaza gave way to a maze of narrow streets where the youth found a number of *cafés cantantes*, among them the renowned

---

[2]Actually named for the House of Serpents that stood at one end.

Café del Burrero, Café Filarmónico, and the Salón Oriente dance hall. Satisfied with having located the cafés that interested him, the Jerezano wandered the streets of Sevilla through the afternoon, amazed and bewildered by the size of the city and its many novelties.

That evening, Chacón began his quest in the Salón de Silverio, on Calle Rosario, not far from Calle de las Sierpes. Noise assaulted him even before he slipped by two old *gitanas* selling wilted flowers and garishly colored matchboxes in the entryway. Once inside, he found himself surrounded by the boisterous confusion of that smoky patio, with its stately white columns and azure-tiled fountain contrasting sharply with the crude wooden tables, rickety chairs, and sand covered floor. In spite of his previous visit and his experience singing in the Vera Cruz, Chacón could not help but feel that familiar debilitating sense of awe, the tightness in his throat and the knot in the pit of his stomach. In the world of the *cante*, the name of Silverio had been venerated since before the Jerezano was born and his cafés long associated with the best the art had to offer.

Squeezing into a vacant spot at the bar, Chacón soon found himself wide-eyed as the cream of Sevilla's artists paraded before him on the raised stage. La Macarrona, more regal than ever, sat at one end of a row of women indifferently beating out *palmas*. The persistent drone of the handclapping accompanied a figure at center stage, a heavy woman whose animated dancing depended as much upon humor as upon gracefulness to evoke approval from the captivated audience. The *bailaora*'s generous hips were swathed in yards of white fabric, a pattern of vertical green stripes running down to the row of tiny ruffles bordering the hem. The spectators loved her, cheering her on with laughter and cries of "*Viva la del Macaca*" and *"Ole el flamenquísmo puro!"* ["Long live she of Macaca" and "*Ole* the pure flamenco-ness!"] The woman personified *gracia*, her comic gift accentuated by the expressiveness of her pretty face and the contrast of her bulky figure with a delicately pointed nose and the tiny knot of hair gathered at the top of her pointed head.

But it was the *cante* that riveted Chacón's attention. A small, wiry man wearing tight striped pants, a red sash about his waist, and a short jacket over a white ruffled shirt filled the salon with a variety of *alegrías* styles. His driving rhythm propelled the dancer through her movements. "What *compás!*" Chacón thought to himself, feeling a sudden twinge of inadequacy.

"Who is that singing?" the youth asked of the bartender.

"*Er cantaó?*" responded the man behind the bar. "Miguel Macaca...the dancer is his wife, Enriqueta."

The name "Macaca" suited the singer, for his intense, narrow-set eyes and black slicked-back hair gave him the appearance of a macaque, the baboon-like monkey found along Spain's southern coast. The feminine form of the nickname suggested that it had passed down from a woman in the family.

Chacón was overwhelmed, thinking: *If great singers like El Macaca cannot escape the cuadro, what chance do I have?* But the youth had little time to battle his growing insecurity before the *cuadro* had finished and the first singer to perform *p'alante* moved to center stage with a guitarist. To the Jerezano's great delight the singer proved to be none other than María Valencia, daughter of Paco la Luz and better known as La Serrana. Chacón did not recognize her at first, for she had already gone to Sevilla before he began to visit Barrio de Santiago. In her early twenties and already an imposing figure, she had the audience in her hands even before she began to sing. Her dark gypsy face, round and pretty with just a hint of a double chin, radiated serenity and confidence. A large red rose perched just above the bun of her tightly gathered hair, while an immense black shawl, heavily embroidered in white floral patterns, draped her body in thick black fringe and concealed most of a white train dress down to the tiny pleated ruffles at its hem.

The first notes from La Serrana transported Chacón back to his lessons with Salvaoriyo. There could be no doubt about the origin of that *cante*. In a throaty voice with more power than might be expected from a woman, La Serrana sang *por seguiriyas*:

Yo le pido a Dios	I ask of God
que tú me mires con los	that you look at me with the
[*mismos oijitos*]	[same eyes]
que te miro yo.	with which I look at you.

Chacón thought to himself that La Serrana was a worthy successor to her father and would bring great fame to the name and *cante* of Paco la Luz.

A familiar figure replaced La Serrana on the hazy stage. The humble bearing and tiny pug nose of El Chato [the Snub-nose] of Jerez was unmistakable. Sebastián el Chato, in his late forties, excelled in the *cantes* of his fellow Jerezano, the enigmatic Loco Mateo. *Gachó*, yet with a potent voice suited to the *cante gitano*, he was a modest and gentle man who never lacked time to encourage an aspiring young singer. Chacón revered the great *cantaor* and had pestered him on several occasions in the Vera Cruz, asking about the early years when he had sung with Silverio and, it was said, held his own. With unassuming simplicity and honest spontaneity El Chato lived his life and expressed his art. Incapable of vain ostentation or useless extravagance, he had a naturalness that was reflected in both the notes and the words of his favorite *cantes*.

El Chato de Jerez, seated beside the guitarist on the stage of the Café de Silverio, tapped his *vara* firmly against the worn and splintered boards and, with few preliminaries, laid bare the depth of his soul in the cry of the *seguiriya*:

Carita de rosa,	Little face like a rose,
quién te ha pegao, quién te ha	who has hit you, who has
[*hecho daño,*]	[done you harm,]
que estás tan llorosa?	that you should be so tearful?

Chacón, the wounds of love still raw, was touched deeply by the *cante*. As simple and natural as a tender caress, it said more to the heart than could any empty display of virtuosity or pompous theatrics. The second *letra*, following the other so closely, moistened the eyes of many in the audience:

Yo no quiero a naide;	I don't want any other;
con tus oijitos, serranita mía,	with just your eyes, my little girl
	[of the mountains]
tengo yo bastante.	I have all I need.

It was disheartening. Chacón felt he would never be able to sing like that. In simplicity, El Chato de Jerez had found the secret of supreme beauty.

A commotion at the back of the café caught Chacón's attention. The huge bulk of a man filled a doorway, shuffled to a table, and, with effort and the aid of a stout *vara*, eased heavily into a chair. A waiter rushed to tend to him, while a rustle of whispers ran through the room: "Look, it's Silverio...That's the great Silverio who has just come in!"

Chacón tried to study Silverio across the smoke-filled café, but could only make out that he was a large man, quite heavy, his massive head seemingly glued to his body with no hint of a neck. In spite of an air of resignation and fatigue in Silverio's bearing, there remained something regal and commanding about his presence, about the manner in which he held his head high and slowly surveyed the room. Chacón knew he should take advantage of the moment, a moment he had anticipated for so many years, but he couldn't move. Intimidated by all he had seen and heard that evening, his confidence shaken, he dared not imagine even asking to work in the *cuadro*, let alone as a soloist. Unable to approach Silverio, he slipped out into the street, torn by disappointment and frustration.

Lost in thought, the Jerezano's feet carried him to Calle de las Sierpes, past the gaiety and noise of brightly lit cafés and taverns, and into the relative quiet of the Plaza Campana and the darkness of the Plaza del Duque. With the realization that he was headed for the *cafés cantantes* of Calle Amor de Dios, Chacón brightened and rationalized that he could always return to speak with Silverio. Perhaps it would be more practical to set his sights a little lower, to start with a less prestigious café.

The sign near the junction of Calles Tarifa and Amor de Dios read, *Salón Cantante de Manuel Ojeda*. Chacón knew this as the Café del Burrero, in reference to the nickname of its owner, Manuel Ojeda "El Burrero." By the light of flickering candles, the youth climbed the narrow wrought-iron stairway that spiraled steeply to the second floor, and experienced a tremor of renewed excitement on entering the now familiar atmosphere of loud voices, clinking glasses, suffocating smoke, and the penetrating odor of spiced foods and stale humanity. A gypsy woman and a guitarist were descending from the small stage to the last remnants of applause as Chacón found a seat at a small table.

The café of El Burrero was quite different from that of Silverio. Located on an upper floor, it lacked the great size and the marble columns of a courtyard café, but made up for it with increased intimacy that forced people into closer contact and generated human warmth and enthusiasm. The rowdy clientele defied the attempt to create a sense of opulence through large mirrors and paintings hung in gilded frames on the musty walls. *Señoritos* wearing flat, wide-brimmed hats or fashionable derbies occupied prominent tables, ordering *manzanilla* in *cañeros* of fifty glasses or sipping sherry and cognac. At other tables, boisterous merchants and craftsmen downed *cañas* of *manzanilla* or *aguardiente* [anise; brandy] while howling their approval of the women on stage. Toward the rear stood a motley group of peasants in *calañés* hats, down-and-out flamencos looking for work, and tattered derelicts hoping for the offer of a sip of red wine with a *tapa*—a bit of sausage or a couple of olives to serve as the evening meal. Several women, overly made up and dressed in clothes that had once been elegant, circulated from table to table seeking to arrange trysts for the evening. While the male artists congregated at the bar for drinks, the women of the *cuadro* mingled with the customers, enticing them to drink.

Chacón spotted Juana Antúnez at a table where an impassioned group of admirers competed for her attention. At age fifteen the young dancer had blossomed into a beautiful and sultry young woman. If Juana is here, thought Chacón, then Fernanda must be nearby. But he did not see the protective older sister until the artists of the *cuadro* had returned to take their seats along the back wall of the raised stage.

Chacón recognized several others in the *cuadro* of El Burrero. Among the dancers were the venerable Antonio el Pintor and his young son, Lamparilla. Two singers seated in the middle, a man and a woman, were unfamiliar, as were the guitarists. Chacón looked around for someone who might be able to identify the artists for him. The table to his right was occupied by a group of ruffians. On the left a man seated at a table by himself seemed a more likely candidate. His bored look and the way he leaned back casually in his chair gave the impression that he was no stranger to the café.

Chacón said to him, "Excuse me, can you tell me the names of the guitarists?"

The man looked the youth over for a moment and then said, "José Luis Gallardo at your service. I've been coming here since Manuel opened the place some five years ago." Seeming eager to show off his knowledge, the man scooted his chair over a little toward Chacón and continued, "The guitarist wearing the *calañés* is the great Maestro Antonio Pérez..."

"I've heard of him," said Chacón, guessing the guitarist's age to be somewhere in his forties.

"...and the other is the maestro's student, Paco Robles...and that's Paco's daughter, that dancer over on his left."

Chacón thanked the man and turned his attention back to the stage. But the man wasn't finished.

"...and that's Concha la Carbonera there on the right...surely you have heard of her."

Chacón had, in fact, heard of this famous dancer from Málaga. She had become a legend throughout Andalucía.

"Wait until you see La Concha dance...it's something you won't soon forget..."

Chacón was beginning to regret speaking with the man.

"...and there by her side...you see that man? That's Concha's lover, La Escribana [female scribe or court clerk]..."

Chacón spotted the effeminate man seated next to La Carbonera.

"...and I assure you that the only thing she has of a man is her clothes...although some would say otherwise. La Escribana is a wonderful singer of *cantiñas* de Cádiz, and those two *comadres* [girlfriends] provide us with many laughs."

Chacón tried to shut the man out and focus on the stage. Antonio el Pintor stood, removed his jacket, and assumed an arrogant pose at center stage. With his arms raised at an angle above his head, where they would remain throughout the dance, he proceeded to put on a display of footwork that did not stop until he was ready to sit down. His grimacing smile did not relax even for an instant.

For Chacón, the revelation among the dancers was Lamparilla. Although only in his early teens, the diminutive boy was already a veteran *bailaor* and a respected artist. The picture of elegance, he dressed impeccably in a short gray jacket with black velvet lapels, a white ruffled shirt buttoned at the collar, and well-tailored high pants fit snugly at the hips. His poses were arrogant and strong, arms always in harmony with the movement of his body, fingers together and held straight or in the classic hook with the wrist broken inward to add grace to the movement of the arms, and his tasteful footwork was perfect and sure, without the slightest faltering in his very difficult *escobillas*, *falsetas*, and *desplantes*.[3]

The others in the *cuadro* spurred the boy on with cries of "*Bien bailao, mi arma...Eso é, guapo...Salero, chiquillo!*" [Well-danced, my soul...That's the way, handsome...What style, boy!] A man in the audience yelled out, "*Qué vivan los gitanos de La Alameda,*" implying

---

[3]*escobilla*: extended footwork; it is unclear what *falsetas* referred to with regard to the dance in those times, whether it was dancing to guitar *falsetas* (melodies) or some sort of filigree done by the dancer (see Appendix B for more). *Desplantes* are rhythmic variations.

that the *bailaor* was gypsy and from the flamenco neighborhood of Sevilla's Alameda. Lamparilla was handsome, almost pretty, Chacón thought, with a childish round face and short black hair combed up in a high wave at the forehead. The boy was the most complete *bailaor* Chacón had ever seen. He had everything: style, grace, strength, and speed, combined with creative and sensitive artistry.

Chacón's intense absorption in Lamparilla's dance was shattered by raucous laughter. One of the *bailaoras* had cried out, *"Qué planta, Dios mío! Lastimita que no fuera más hombre!"* [My God, what posture, what good looks! What a shame that he isn't more of a man!] The precocious *bailaor* redoubled his efforts in an attempt to establish his masculinity.

Lamparilla was followed on stage by Juana Antúnez. The young *bailaora* had matured in both her beauty and the creation of a personal style of dance. Her *baile por alegrías* was complemented by the powerful singing of a dynamic *cantaora*, identified by Chacón's new "friend" and shouts from the *cuadro* as La Juanaca. Chacón had never heard of La Juanaca, but she proved to be a formidable dance accompanist, with the strength to be heard above the din of *palmas* and noise from the rowdy public, and a sense of *compás* that compelled the dancer to give her best. In the conclusion of the *alegrías*, the voice of La Juanaca stood out above the *palmas* and the dancer's pounding footwork as she brought the crowd to a frenzy with a festive and witty *cantiña*:

Cómpreme usté esta levita,	Please, mister, buy this coat from me,
usté, gue gasta castora;	you, with the top hat;
es prenda que da la hora,	the garment can be stylish again
volviendola del revés.	if it is turned inside out.
Le quite usté la solapa,	You take off the lapels,
le pone un cuello bonito,	put on a pretty collar,
pareserá un señorito,	and you will look like a *señorito*,
como un figurín francés.	like a French dandy.[4]

But it was in the *soleares* for Fernanda Antúnez that La Juanaca demonstrated her consummate skill as a *cantaora* for the dance. Fernanda, heavier than her sister and perhaps not as elegantly beautiful, radiated sensuality with her languid dark eyes, full lips, and deep olive

---

[4]*Cantiñas* are similar to *alegrías*, but lack its formal structure. This *copla* has been sung in modern times as a *cantiña* of El Pinini de Utrera.

complexion. Her brown hair was just light enough in color to earn her the nickname *La Rubia* [The Blond]. She proved to be an extraordinary *bailaora* who needed extraordinary *cante*.

Fernanda remained seated while Maestro Pérez set the mood of the *soleá* with his strong *toque*. The guitarist, a small, intense man whose large head seemed out of proportion to his slender body and short legs, wore a dancer's high-waisted pants, vest, ruffled shirt, and short jacket. His deeply lined face was a study in angles, with high cheekbones and a square jaw. Deep-set dark eyes smoldered with fierce concentration. He supported the guitar at an upright angle with his left thigh, which he raised by hooking his boot heel on the rung of the chair. A cigarette dangled from his mouth as Maestro Pérez attacked the strings with his thumb, wresting forceful melodies from the instrument and finishing with a flourish to call for the *cante*.

La Juanaca warmed up her voice with a *temple*. Fernanda rose slowly from her chair. It was immediately apparent that Fernanda's *baile* would be very gypsy, earthy and strong. The *cante* pierced the smoke and noise, bringing a hush to the room. Fernanda closed her eyes in concentration, arms spiraling upward, head raised, aloof and distant, her gaze focused inward. Creases between her brows and the firm set of her mouth betrayed her apparent serenity, hinting at inner struggle. From the waist down the *bailaora* planted herself into the floor. Where Juana had been coolly elegant, Fernanda was passionate and forceful. Her sublime art appeared to Chacón to be torn between heaven and earth, rooted in the pain of life, yet seeking solace and liberation from above.

As the *cante* soared, Fernanda moved her arms and hands slowly and gracefully, yet never raising them much above eye-level. Her body twisted and arched, head held high. At the end of the *letra*, a flurry of movement sent the long fringe of the *bailaora*'s immense shawl flying about her compactly rounded body. When Fernanda marked rhythm with her feet, the floor shook and someone yelled, "She's an earthquake!" More *cante*, *escobillas*, and again the *cante*. Maestro Pérez leaned in toward the dancer, his right hand a blur, eyes on fire beneath his dark protruding brows and slicked-back mane of hair. The cigarette had long since gone out, dropping ashes over the guitar and down the front of his clothes.

Suddenly, the guitarist leaped to his feet. Without ceasing to play, he thrust the guitar behind his back and began to dance with Fernanda, escorting her off the stage to the right. It was a grandiose effect—the swirling power of Fernanda, the almost acrobatic antics of Maestro Pérez, the *cante*, the rhythm, and the accompanying handclapping and shouting. The audience rose to its feet with applause, cheering, and incredulous laughter.

Chacón, like others who had not seen it before, was moved by the masterful performance. But when the exhilaration of the moment had passed, the Jerezano felt a sudden burst of insecurity. Who was he to dare to compete with these great artists? It was as if he were again a little boy, looking up at the godlike figures who performed on the stage of the Vera Cruz. Juan Junquera's crushing words, *You won't do, child*, rang in his ears. Clearly, he was not yet ready for Sevilla.

The *cuadro* left the stage. In an unusual move, due to the large number of singers, the Burrero presented a second *cuadro* made up of singers and guitarists only. Two guitarists, two women Chacón did not know, and two familiar figures from Jerez mounted the platform. Paco Robles dragged a chair to the front edge of the stage, took his time to sit down, then lit a cigarette, crossed his legs, smoothed a lock of hair into place, and began to tune the guitar. A second chair appeared at the side of the guitarist and the first soloist to sing *p'alante* was introduced as La Bocanegra from Málaga. She was a tiny woman, obviously not gypsy, with frizzy hair gathered in bun, and close-set small eyes that squinted out from a chubby, pinched face. Paco Robles' sure fingers brought forth crystalline notes in an introduction for *malagueñas*, while the *cantaora* assumed various poses and coughed to clear her throat.

Chacón did not take the woman seriously at first. The *ays* of her *temple* demonstrated a clear, sweet voice that held little promise for serious *cante*, but the first *tercio* [sung line] of her *copla* captured the youth's complete attention. She sang, "*De tu pelo*," in serene and sustained tones. Chacón waited for the completion of the phrase, but it never came. Instead, La Bocanegra went on to the second *tercio*, a powerful descent sung at full lung, and then continued with the *copla*:

Por las trenzas de tu pelo,	Up the braids of your hair
un canario se subía,	climbed a canary,
y se paraba en tu frente, ay,	and it stopped at your forehead, ay,
y en tu boquita bebía,	and drank from your mouth
creyendo que era una fuente.	thinking it was a fountain.

Chacón had never heard anything like it. Although there was an underlying resemblance to the *malagueña* of Juan Breva, this *cante* had a deliberate and serene majesty that was unlike that of the great *cantaor* from Vélez-Málaga. The intensely brilliant second *tercio* and the powerful fourth, which was extended by the addition of an *ay*, alternated with short and tender *tercios*, to build to an emotional climax in the greatly prolonged final line of the *copla*.[5]

La Bocanegra sang more *coplas*, each with a slightly different melody, but always beginning with a short *tercio* of two or three words. Chacón was fascinated, for he had never heard such a thing done before. He also wondered why so many of the *coplas* were sung from a man's perspective. Far too soon, the *cantaora* from Málaga left the stage, to be replaced by another.

Concha Peñaranda, with the guitar of Maestro Pérez, sang a style of *fandango* foreign to Chacón. Yet, in spite of its unfamiliarity, her *cante* impressed and deeply touched the Jerezano. The voice was clear, clean, and admirably employed with delicate artistic taste. One *letra* stayed with Chacón:

Son las tres de la mañana;	It is three o'clock in the morning;
donde estará ese muchacho?	where can that "man" be?
Estará bebiendo vino,	He must be drinking wine,
y luego vendrá borracho.[6]	and later he'll come in drunk.

The woman was extremely popular with the customers, who cheered her, called her La Cartagenera, and pleaded for *copla* after *copla*.

Paco Robles returned to the front chair, followed by a man and woman Chacón had recognized from Jerez. It was El Loco Mateo and his sister, La Loca. Loco Mateo,[7] handsome and elegant in a fashionable three-piece suit with a silk handkerchief in the jacket pocket and a gold watch chain dangling from his vest, appeared surprisingly youthful

---

[5]In most *malagueñas* (and *fandangos* in general) the first *tercio* is sung using the second line of the poetic verse. The second *tercio* of singing goes back to the first line and the song continues through to the end of the verse. Thus, five lines of verse become six lines of song. In the style described here, the first *tercio* consists of only the last three words of the first line of poetry.

[6]This is one of the most popular verses sung today *por tarantos*.

[7]Mateo Cano Cauquí.

for a man who had been competing with the best in the *cante* for more than two decades. Angustias, better known as La Loca Mateo, was so diminutive that her embroidered shawl draped her body to the floor. But that shawl disguised a stout and sturdy body and her mouse-like appearance belied the strength with which she interpreted the *cantes* of her famous brother.

La Loca sang first, *por soleares*, with Mateo encouraging her and accompanying her with a gentle tapping of his ornately carved *vara*. Chacon had heard her sing on several occasions and admired her ability, but was impatient to hear the genius of her brother. When his turn came, Mateo asked the guitarist to play *por seguiriyas* on the third fret and then demonstrated why, in spite of being *gachó*, he was the equal of any in the profound forms of the *cante gitano*. It was well known that the *cantaor* was high strung to the point of eccentricity. He sang always of his mother and felt his art with such passion and intense torment that he often broke down under the strain of the *cante*, tears pouring down his contorted face. This sensitivity earned him his nickname, but by the time he had completed the following three *letras por seguiriyas*, Mad Mathew was not the only one in the Café del Burrero on the verge of tears:

Llamarme al méico,	Call a medic for me,
llamarme un dortó,	call me a doctor,
pa que l'alivie las duquelas	to alleviate the suffering
[*a la mare*]	[of the mother]
é mi corasón.	of my heart.
M'encargó mi mare	My mother asked me
antes de morí,	before she died
que le dijera una misa de	to have a Mass said for her
[*limosna*]	
en San Agustín.	in the church of San Agustín.
En aquel rinconcito,	In that little corner,
dejarme llorá;	let me cry;
que se m'ha muerto la mare	the mother of my soul
[*é mi arma*]	[has died]
y no la veo má.	and I will see her no more.

Chacón swallowed hard to suppress the lump in his throat. No matter how many times he heard El Loco Mateo, he never failed to be stirred by the moving delivery or to be impressed by the melodious richness of the man's *cante*. But on this occasion it was too much for him. The aspiring *cantaor* had lost all sense of his own ability and had abandoned any thought of singing in Sevilla. Needing to be alone, he left the noise behind and slipped out into the night.

The darkness pressed down on the Jerezano as he wandered slowly through the narrow streets, shoulders drooped and head lowered in thought. His dream had been shattered and he did not know where to turn, what to do next. He emerged in the dimly lit Plaza del Duque, turned right just past the imposing palace, and plunged once more into the dingy gloom of tiny streets. The night was silent except for the chirping of crickets, and the streets deserted except for the many gecko lizards scurrying about the walls hunting insects near the few isolated lanterns, and the bats that sailed blindly over the rooftops. Twice, Chacón stumbled over sleeping bodies that grunted and cursed him, but he paid little attention and permitted his legs to carry him where they would. In the silence of the night, his head spun with all he had seen and heard, with despair for his future, and, above all, the feeling of self-doubt and helplessness.

A wide, lamp-lit street, identified as Los Reyes Católicos by black tile lettering high on the side of a building, took Chacón to the right until he found himself facing the bridge that crossed the Guadalquivir River to Triana. The sluggish flow of the water, visible only in occasional flickers of light on its placid surface, soothed the youth, so he turned left to follow the waterfront on the Paseo de Cristóbal Colón [Walkway of Christopher Columbus]. Ahead, he could make out the silhouettes of steamships and sailing vessels docked in front of the Maestranza bullring and the Torre del Oro.

The light of an open-air bar caught Chacón's eye. Without thinking, he approached a man who was stacking tables and chairs and asked, "Can I get a drink?"

The other shrugged and said, "I'm closing, but have a seat over there." He indicated a table near the bar.

Chacón slumped into a chair beneath a sign that read in large weathered letters, *EL CHINO*, and underneath, *nevería*. It was still too early in the year for the sale of ices and cool drinks made with snow brought by mule train from covered pits in the mountains of Grazalema. As the youth waited, a fragment of *malagueña* floated through his mind. It was a melody that had been haunting him since he heard it earlier. He had been impressed by the way it began so simply, appearing out of nowhere with just a few words that set the mood instantly for the powerful and majestic *tercios* to follow. Softly, almost under his breath, Chacón attempted to recreate that opening *tercio*: "*De tu pelo...*"

"El Canario," a voice said over Chacón's shoulder, startling him. The bartender placed a *caña* of *manzanilla* on the table and repeated, "The *cante* of El Canario... that was his *malagueña* you were singing."

Recovering from his surprise, Chacón asked, "And how is it that you know the *cante* of El Canario?"

"How could I not know it? Manolo[8] sang it here every night."

"Here?" Chacón looked around incredulously.

"Of course! This *nevería*, called by many El Café Sin Techo [The Café without a Roof], was a flamenco café all last summer, an open-air café operated by El Burrero. You must know how El Burrero favors the *cante* from the East, from the Levante...not like Silverio, who prefers the *cante gitano*. Well, that's why we had so many *cantaores* from Málaga...La Bocanegra, La Rubia de Málaga, El Canario...and even a *cantaora* from Cartagena, Conchita la Cartagenera.[9]

"Right over there," the bartender continued, pointing toward a raised platform stacked high with tables and chairs, "El Canario and his rival La Rubia competed every night."

"But El Canario is dead, isn't he?"

"Yes, he's dead, murdered over there by the bridge. I was here, I saw it." Chacón's eyes widened. The other, seeing his interest, said, "Just a minute!" He went behind the bar and returned a moment later, unfolding pages of yellowed newspaper. "Do you read?" he asked.

Chacón nodded. The man handed him the pages and the youth read with difficulty in the dim light of an oil lamp:

> *El Porvenir*: Sevilla, August 14, 1885. Homicide. Ever since a *café cantante*, of the flamenco variety, was established in the vicinity of the Puente de Triana, all of the press of Sevilla has been alerting the governor concerning the kind of shows and the type of people who gather there, especially in the late hours of the night...Now, it is said that in the crowded barrio of Triana the lethal influence of that *café cantante* has been felt. Fathers arrive home without their small wages;

---

[8]Manuel de los Reyes Osuna "El Canario," born 1855 in Álora, Málaga.
[9]Cartagena is a coastal city far to the east of Andalucía, in the region of Murcia.

youths, who should be helping their fathers, lose everything, to the last *céntimo*, without those at home being able to determine where nor how they have squandered the fruit of a week's work...According to my colleagues, it was, and is, dangerous to pass the night in the neighborhood of that center of recreation, and there is some truth in those sensible observations, for yesterday, at dawn, there appeared, stabbed to death, a man who was said to be a *cantaor* by profession.

The second sheet was from the Sevilla paper, *El Progreso*:

At quarter past five in the morning yesterday, an hour that daily sees the completion of the edifying shows of the flamenco *café cantante* of El Burrero located next to the Puente de Triana, that theater was the site, as on almost all days, of a terrible drama. In that center, a heated argument had started a few minutes earlier between one of the *cantaores* known as El Canario and the father of one of the artists of that establishment. The brawl gradually took on greater proportions in spite of the intervention of some of those present, and they left the place, determined to play it out to the end. Then, great confusion, shouts, shiny weapons flashing with feverish agitation, a body, and a murder.[10]

Chacón looked up. "What happened? Why was he killed?"

The bartender pulled up a chair, glad to escape the boredom of a slow night in an establishment that would not blossom until the long hot nights of summer. "You had to know El Canario. He first came to Sevilla as a youth, years ago, singing in the style of Juan Breva. But the public here was not impressed. Sevilla was not well prepared for the *malagueñas* at that time, and besides, Breva did it better. Manolo told me that he went back to Málaga and began to create his own *cante*. He changed the songs he had learned while growing up in Álora by putting into them things he learned during his stay in Almería...You know, he sang often of Almería[11]...do you know this one?" And he recited:

Tengo que poner espias,	I have to place lookouts,
para ver si mi amante viene,	to see if my lover is coming,
al pie de Torre García.	at the foot of García Tower.
No se para mi que tiene	I don't understand my fascination
el camino de Almería.	with the road to Almería

---

[10]Blas Vega, *Los Cafés Cantantes de Sevilla*, p 44.
[11]Almería is the coastal capital of Andalucía's easternmost province of Almería.

"A woman called La Bocanegra sang that one tonight," said Chacón.

"Yes, La Bocanegra! She imitates El Canario, sings all of his *cantes* very well. She is from Málaga, too. Now, as I was saying, Manolo created this new *cante por malagueñas*. Then he went to Madrid, to sing in the Café Imparcial, and when he returned to Sevilla last year, he was an immediate success...the public went crazy. Of course, we were better prepared for his *cante* because of another singer from Málaga, La Rubia Colomer. La Rubia had captured the hearts of Sevillanos with her voice and her beauty.

"But when the aficionados switched their allegiance to El Canario and his new *cantes*, La Rubia had no choice but to follow his path, to imitate his style. She had her own *cante*, very sweet, very plaintive, but she had to copy El Canario because the public demanded it. So they competed, *mano a mano*, night after night in the Burrero and right over there on that stage. Now, you have to know El Canario...*muy juergista*, he loved fiestas and sang because he loved the *cante*. For him it was not just a business, as with so many others. Manolo was a happy person, adored by the public and pursued by women. He enjoyed his popularity, to the point of being vain. So when others began to copy his *cante*, he couldn't accept it and lost no opportunity to humiliate them. La Rubia was the best of the imitators and, on some nights, due to her beauty and her great soul, she even eclipsed Manolo and took away some of his luster.

"El Canario declared war. Night after night, he played up La Rubia's lack of originality, her lack of shame in imitating him, and her lack of artistic personality. Rivalry became hate. Manolo went so far as to seek out opportunities to sing where La Rubia sang just to belittle and humiliate her. Vanity does not forgive and he was relentless in venting his hatred. There are those who say that La Rubia was in love with Manolo and that he would go with other women to make her jealous, but I don't believe that...and I saw them here every night. In any case, the father of La Rubia took to heart the insults directed at his daughter. Tired of her crying, he challenged the *cantaor*, calling him all sorts of names.

"Manolo laughed and said to his friends, 'This old man, look how lame he is!'

"When the exchange grew heated, the men were restrained and led outside. As they left the *nevería*, El Canario gave the father a shove and knocked him to the ground. '*Pero, hombre*,' said the old man, 'is that the kind of man you are? You would leave me here on the ground? Give me a hand and I'll show you who I am!'

"Manolo replied, '*Anda hombre!* Go away and leave me alone!' But he answered the other's challenge by offering his hand to help him up. Then, as La Rubia's father came up off the ground, he was ready with a large knife and plunged it into El Canario's groin, killing him..."

After a moment's silence, Chacón asked, "What happened to La Rubia?"

"La Rubia? The public turned on her. Those who, before, had received her with such affection on the stages of the Burrero and the Café de Silverio refused to applaud her. The best woman's voice that has been heard in Sevilla was driven from the city. It is said that she went to Madrid."

A short time later, Chacón found himself once more in the empty streets, heading for his room in the Barrio de Santa Cruz. From the darkness behind him came the cry of a *sereno* [night watchman] on his nightly rounds, *"Ave María Purísima, la una ha tocao!"* It was one o'clock in the morning. Chacón had been thinking again of the *malagueñas* of El Canario, fragments of melodies persistently repeating themselves in his head, or tantalizing him by floating just beyond his grasp. The cry of the night watchman had reverberated so mournfully through the stillness in the narrow canyons of Sevilla's streets that the *cantaor* began to repeat it to himself, to a melody of the *malagueñas*: "It's one in the morning and I'm thinking of you..."

No, that didn't work. Perhaps, he, thought, a bell sounding one o'clock. "At one in the morning, the sad bell tolls..." Better. Now, what to rhyme with *campana triste?* Memories of María flooded him with sadness. "At two o'clock I was thinking about how you left me, *te fuiste*."

Chacón's spirits rose as he experimented with words and melodies. By the time he reached the *fonda*, a complete *copla* for *malagueñas* had taken shape. Before an ornate iron gate he clapped his hands twice, the sharp pops echoing in the silence of the deserted street. He listened, clapped again, and waited. At last, from off in the distance behind him, drifted a faint *"Ya voy!"* [I'm coming!] While he waited in the darkness, the youth sang to himself:

Dando en el reloj la una	The clock sounds one
de aquella campana triste,	with that sad bell,
hasta las dos estoy pensando	until two I am thinking
el querer que me fingiste,	about the love you pretended,
y me dan las tres llorando.	and three finds me crying.

It was a childish verse and it had strayed somewhat from El Canario's melody, but Chacón was thrilled with his creativity. The pounding of a staff on the cobblestones and the jangling of a ring of huge keys announced the arrival of the *sereno*. The ancient gray-clad watchman held up a lantern, rested his staff with its wicked looking blade against the building, and used a large crude key to open the front door of the house. Chacón dropped two small *céntimo* coins into the man's outstretched hand and ascended to his room. With the realization that he wasn't ready for Sevilla and the decision to return home, a great burden had been lifted from him. Even the new *malagueña* was unable to keep him awake for long, and he slept soundly until noon the following day.

El Mellizo

Antonio Chacón hesitated, then edged nervously into the noisy room. The stifling closeness, thick with heavy smoke and raucous male voices, enveloped him, took his breath, and stopped him just inside the door. The back room of the tavern on the Plaza del Progresso in Jerez shook with rough laughter and the guttural jargon of gypsy men.

A man standing with his back to the newcomer struggled for attention, croaking in a voice as harsh as that of an old rooster, "Listen! *Callarse cabrones*. Be quiet and listen to this...and then dare to tell me that Manuel Hermosilla doesn't have *gracia!*"

More laughter. But then curiosity began to subdue the din. The men who sprawled about the long table were almost all gypsies. Some, like the speaker, were dressed in the old gypsy style—short pants tied at the knee over silk stockings, short satin jackets, and *calañés* hats. Others wore three-piece suits of fashionable cut, elegantly adorned with gold watch chains and silk handkerchiefs.

"It was El Gordito and Chicorro who were going to *torear*[1] [work the bull] with Manué...Gordito and Chicorro, in Málaga. And the impresario of the bullring comes to the *fonda* where we were staying and asks to see Manuel Hermosilla..."

Chacón had recognized Hermosilla immediately. Seated at the near end of the table, the celebrated matador wore an elegant dark gray suit.

---

[1] *torear*: from the word *toro* (bull) and meaning "to work the bull." The term "bullfight" is completely antithetical to the Spanish concept of the ritual of the bulls (*la corrida de toros*) and it would be out of place here to speak of "fighting" the bull.

Short and stockier than most *toreros*, with a prominent hooked nose, down-turned mouth, and baleful eyes, only a carefully braided pigtail at the nape of his neck revealed his occupation.

"So the impresario says to Manué, 'Manuel, we are going to announce in the posters that Gordito will place the *banderillas* while sitting in a chair, and Chicorro will do the *salto de la garrocha* [vault over the bull aided by the lance used to control the animals]. What shall I tell them to say about you, as a promotion? What will you do?'"

The room hushed as that deep voice continued. "Manué didn't like that impresario, didn't trust him when it came to money. So he looks at the man for a moment, thinking, and then says very seriously, '*Pues*, tell them to announce that Manuel Hermosilla will collect his money *before* dressing for the *corrida*...and if not, he won't enter the ring!'"

Amid the burst of laughter and backslapping, Manuel Hermosilla muttered to himself, "*Carambita*, what was I supposed to do? That *sinvergüenza* [shameless one] wasn't going to pay me!"

Chacón felt the tightness in his chest begin to relax. One of few non-gypsies in the closely packed room, he found himself very much outside the obvious shared intimacy and camaraderie of men who faced fear in the bullring and celebrated with abandon. But he began to single out familiar faces in the confusion. The matador Hermosilla, of course, and from Jerez, Enrique Sánchez, *picador* for Hermosilla. Chacón spotted his friend Joaquín la Cherna in animated conversation with a man who immediately became the object of his attention. There could be no mistaking that long, somber face with its heavy, underslung jaw, the immense hooked nose, or those protruding flaps that served as ears. Enrique el Mellizo was every bit as ugly as they said. But even from across the room Chacón could feel the warmth and sincerity that radiated from that clumsily constructed countenance. And he was much younger than Chacón had imagined. Instead of the wizened maestro the youth had expected, he found a man in the prime of life.[2]

Chacón recognized the great *cantaor* from the previous day, when El Mellizo had carried out his duties in the bullring as *puntillero*, approaching the mortally wounded bulls cautiously to administer the coup de grace by severing the spinal cord just behind the head with a small knife. If done correctly, the animals shuddered and slumped

---

[2] Enrique Jimenez "El Mellizo" was born Dec. 1, 1848, making him 37 years old when Chacón first met him.

immediately to the ground in death. Enrique's occupation as *matarife* [slaughterman] in Cádiz served him well in carrying out this duty in the bullring.

Chacón had attended the *corrida* of July 25, *El Día de Santiago* [St. James Day] with great anticipation, for it was expected to be among the best of the year. The bulls had always fascinated Chacón, even though he had not been as adept as some of his childhood friends at imitating the cape work of the torero, and more often than not he had been relegated to playing the part of the bull. Now, for the first time, the youth could afford to enter the *plaza de toros* legitimately, with a ticket. This year, the fiesta of Santiago had featured two left-handers, one of them the renowned Manuel Hermosilla, the other a newcomer, Felipe García. Chacón had been thrilled to learn that Hermosilla was coming, for he had heard it was likely that his *puntillero* would be Enrique el Mellizo.

During the afternoon *corrida*, Hermosilla had proved to be a courageous, if somewhat crude, torero, short on repertoire, but with a *gracia* in his *adornos* that brought approval from the highly vocal crowd. When it came time for the moment of truth, for the kill, he fared badly. Even Chacón could see his error. Hermosilla set the bull up well—few could do it better—and went in over the horns *volapie*, with the sword well directed. But his left hand was the enemy, carrying the *muleta* [cape] so that the animal saw the trick and fell apart. The thrust invariably came up short. Chacón felt that he should have received the bull, let it come to him. The matador had the skill for that.

With his second bull, Hermosilla's sword barely pierced the animal between the shoulders and had to be withdrawn for another try. The second attempt failed completely when the sword hit bone. The crowd grew restless as the third thrust hit shoulder bone and sprang out of the matador's hand and into the air. A gypsy seated near Chacón rose to his feet and yelled, "*Pero, home* [*hombre*], what do you think you're doing...eating olives?"

It was Hermosilla's bravery, reputed to have resulted in frequent gorings, that won over the aficionados in Jerez but almost led to his undoing. The newspaper summed it up the following day: "The plaza was very well attended, the livestock excellent, the fifth bull standing out. The *espadas* [swords; matadors] were good and received much applause, each distinguishing himself with his first bull. In killing the fifth, Hermosilla was reached by the animal during one of his passes, tearing his pants, but with no more serious consequence."

Chacón had received word the day after the *corrida* that Tomasa Junquera wanted to see him. It seemed that Hermosilla wished to celebrate his success and his escape from harm by inviting the *cuadrillas* of both toreros to dinner. Tomasa had been asked to supply artists for the event. She hired Chacón, unemployed at the time, La Cherna, and the guitarist El Lolo, sending them to La Rondeña, a tavern operated by Junquera's competitor, the owner of the *café cantante* "El de Rogelio."

A little after ten o'clock that evening Chacón had entered the tavern of Rogelio and now stood indecisively just inside the door. Attention had shifted to where El Mellizo had those nearest him holding their sides with laughter as he spoke solemnly, as if revealing a profound secret.

"…this *gitana* in my barrio, in Santa María, used to go to the church every morning. As soon as the priest opened the door, there was the *gitana*. She would get down on her knees in front of the figure of Christ and say, '*Ay, Pare mío* [my Father], how beautiful you are…what dark eyes you have…can there be anyone more beautiful in the world? Please *Pare mío*, tell me of what I am going to die!'

"And, of course, Christ said nothing. What was he going to say?"

The serious tone of this explanation had the others in stitches.

"And the *gitana*, when she finally tired of begging for an answer, rose to her feet and said, 'You won't tell me today, will you, *Pare mío? Güeno*, until tomorrow, handsome.'

"The next day the same. As soon as the priest opens the door to the church, the *gitana* is on her knees in front of the *paso* [procession float holding the figure of Christ] saying, 'Ay, today you are even better looking than yesterday. I have never seen a face like yours, with that slender nose, that mouth…what a beautiful face! Please tell me *Pare mío*, how am I going to die?'

"And, of course, Christ continued to say nothing."

By this time El Mellizo had everyone in the room laughing and hanging on his every word. He was one of those natural storytellers whose manner of telling is more entertaining than the story itself.

"And so it went, day after day. Until one day the priest said to himself, 'Enough of this! If she comes today, she will see. If she comes today she won't come back again!'

"The *gitana* arrives, drops to her knees in front of the *paso*, and s begins her supplication. 'If there is no one in the world more beautiful than you, why won't you tell me how I am going to die...and then I will be at peace?'

"The priest, who had hidden behind the *paso*, suddenly called out in a loud and resonant voice, god-like, 'YOU WILL DIE BY HANGING!'

Chacón and the others jumped, startled by the sudden volume of Mellizo's voice.

"How that *gitana* jumped! You had to see it to believe it. She leaped up and ran as fast as she could toward the door..."

El Mellizo paused a moment before adding, "...but just before going out, she turned and yelled angrily back at the Christ, 'Who told you that, clod-face?' "

Pandemonium.

As he wiped the tears from his cheeks, Hermosilla leaned toward where El Mellizo sat smoking as if nothing had happened and said, "*Qué ángel, compare* [friend]! How about giving us some more...*por soleá?* I'm in the mood for *cante*."

At that moment, Joaquín la Cherna noticed Chacón for the first time. Approaching the youth, he smiled, "Antonio, come in, come in!" Then, turning to Hermosilla, "Manué, this is Antonio Chacón. He sings very well, *mu gitano* [very gypsy]."

Hermosilla rose and greeted Chacón with a hard handshake. He had a day's growth of black stubble—his last shave would have been the day before, on the morning of the *corrida*. The matador looked the youth up and down, taking in the rumpled black suit and soft features. In an effort to appear older, as well as to hide his prematurely receding hair, Chacón had not removed his *sombrero vaquero*. But the weight he had put on, and his smooth, round face, betrayed him, making him appear even younger than his seventeen years.

"A *gachó* who sings like a *gitano?* That I have to hear!"

"Let him be, Manué!" It was the voice of El Mellizo. "If Joaquín says he sings well, he must sing well. *Chaval*, come join us for a drink!"

Chacón accepted a glass from El Mellizo. The first deep swallow hit his throat with a sharp searing pain, throwing him into a fit of violent coughing and bringing tears to his eyes. He had not expected the potent cognac and the laughter of those around him brought a flush of shame to his cheeks, adding to his discomfort. El Mellizo slapped his back a forceful blow and said with a laugh, "*Chaval*, you're going to have to learn to drink like a man!" More howls of delight.

Amid the laughter and renewed drinking, the young *cantaor* was soon forgotten. That is, until Hermosilla recalled that he was in the mood for *cante* and turned to Chacón, saying, "*Chiquillo*, let's see what you can do. *Venga cante!*"

Chacón knew that, as the youngest artist present, he had been hired to break the ice, to create a mood that would inspire the others. But he was reluctant to begin, feeling intimidated by the presence of El Mellizo. If only Javier were there. Javier knew how to bring out his best, where to place the *cejilla* and how to anticipate him or wait for him if necessary. But Javier was busy in the Vera Cruz. Instead, Tomasa had sent El Lolo, a respected guitarist in Jerez, but unfamiliar with Chacón's *cante*.

Unable to escape Hermosilla's goading, Chacón asked El Lolo to place the *cejilla* on the fourth fret and play *por medio* for *soleá*. Then he threw himself into a series of *soleares*. Nervously at first, but with growing determination to demonstrate his ability, he fought through several *letras* of El Loco Mateo, finding inspiration in the great *cantaor's* emotion-filled melodies. His confidence grew as he realized the guitarist was staying with him, supporting his *cante*. He changed to *soleares* of Paco la Luz. Some of the gypsies grunted approval, but seemed unsure, as if waiting for a cue from Hermosilla or El Mellizo.

Chacón glanced toward El Mellizo. He appeared to be listening thoughtfully, his deep, narrow-set eyes gazing off into the distance, but it was impossible to read his reaction. Could that awkward and simple man really be a great and sensitive artist?

More *cantes por soleá*. The young *cantaor*, in an attempt to please, sang perhaps longer than he should have. A scattering of comments greeted the closing guitar chord: "Not bad, *hombre!*...*Bien!*...Well done!"

El Mellizo spoke up. "Well sung, *chaval*. Those *cantes* of El Loco and Paco la Luz are not easy...and you sing them with heart."

Hermosilla grunted, "Very pretty, *chiquillo!* Well sung for a *gachó*, for one who does not have it in the blood, who has not the voice for the *cante gitano*. I don't suppose you dare to sing *por tóo lo jondo?* [the maximum profundity]"

Chacón felt trapped. It was not his place to be singing *por seguiriyas* when there were veteran *cantaores* yet to sing. And he could not please Hermosilla, no matter how well he sang. He emptied his glass of cognac to stall for time. Then, swallowing his anger at the challenge, he said,

"I will leave that *cante* to those at whose feet I humbly sit, to Joaquín and the maestro, Enrique."

"Well said, *muchacho*," replied the matador with a smile of satisfaction.

"Antonio!" It was Joaquín la Cherna. "Sing them! Sing for us *por seguiriyas!*"

Chacón looked around the room and saw mischievous delight on the swarthy gypsy faces. When El Mellizo nodded agreement, the youth said to the guitarist, "Leave it there, *por seguiriyas*." And, gently tapping his *vara* in the alternating rhythm of the *seguiriya*, he threw himself into the *cante*, determined to give all he had from the very beginning of the *ay* of his *temple* [warm-up]. *Cantes* of Paco la Luz and El Marrurro. The young *cantaor* strained with effort, sweat pouring down his cheeks. In an interval, while the guitarist played to allow him to catch his breath, Chacón removed his hat to wipe his brow. Led by El Mellizo, the gypsies warmed to the *cante* and voiced their approval. *Seguiriyas* of *El Señor* Manuel Molina, and then, in a moment of sudden inspiration, he finished with the *cabales* of Silverio.

El Mellizo, who had become increasingly enthusiastic about the youth's singing, came over to where Chacón sat and gripped his hand. "Very well done, *chaval*. You have sung those *cantes machos* very well, *por derecho* [correctly]. You have only to learn to conserve your strength. You must not force your voice, but allow the sound to come naturally from your lungs...and from your heart."

"*Venga cante!*" It was Hermosilla, looking to save face. "Joaquín, it's your turn."

La Cherna indicated to the guitarist that he should continue *por seguiriyas* on the same fret. Such was the mournful intensity of La Cherna's *temple* that his first cry was met with sudden and complete silence. The raw gypsy voice poured forth its pain in a torrent of emotion: "*Día grande, mare...*" The gypsies grunted and cried their approval. La Cherna sang *letra* after *letra* until finally he collapsed, exhausted.

Deeply moved by the *cante* of his friend and mentor, Chacón felt both intimidated and inspired. Lightheaded with drink and *cante*, he was bursting with the need to sing and could barely hold back while Hermosilla sang *por soleares*, defending himself well in the styles of Cádiz with a rough but expressive voice. Then, at first opportunity, Chacón followed with more *soleares*, displaying a confidence that had been lacking in his earlier attempt. Relaxed now, he allowed his voice to project naturally, unforced, finding new power and expression.

El Mellizo couldn't contain his growing enthusiasm for the young Jerezano's *cante* and became somewhat exaggerated in his praise. "*Recarambita*, look how this *gachó* sings! He's going to be a monster in the *cante*." The veteran *cantaor* appeared to enter into Chacón's singing, contorting his face and body with the strain of each *tercio*. When Chacón had finished, El Mellizo slumped in his chair as if exhausted. "Very well sung, *chaval*. You have made me feel the *cante* as few others can...*Díos mío!*" And then he seemed to drift off into thought, staring vacantly at the floor, perhaps feeling the effects of the long night of drinking.

Worried expressions appeared on the faces of those who knew El Mellizo well, who knew that at any moment he could withdraw into himself, become uncommunicative and distant. But then the *cantaor* lifted his head slowly to face his anxious companions. He extended a hand to silence the guitarist. With his round-brimmed black hat set back halo-like on his head, a short black jacket, white shirt buttoned high with a black cravat crossed at the neck, and his morose countenance, El Mellizo appeared about to deliver a sermon.

The *cantaor* cleared his throat, coughed, and spat noisily to the floor. He tested his voice and then burst forth with a *salida*[3] unlike anything Chacón had heard before:

Perdón, Dios mío;	Forgiveness, my God;
perdón y clemencia;	forgiveness and mercy;
perdón e indulgencia;	forgiveness and leniency;
perdón y piedad.	forgiveness and piety.

El Mellizo had employed this verse as a warm-up, in place of a *temple*, but its power and majesty brought a reverent hush to the boisterous gathering. Chacón had never heard such a *salida*, an invocation delivered in a god-like voice, deep and hoarse, yet full of warmth and rich tones. The *cantaor* continued, shattering the almost sepulchral silence with a moving *malagueña* of immense proportions:

---

[3]*salida*: the opening *tercio* or section of a *cante*.

Ay, de la pena;   Ay, of sorrow;
Ay, yo ví a mi mare vení,   Ay, I saw my mother coming,
ayiii...ayiii...ay, ay, ayiii,   ayeee...ayeee...ay. ay, ayeee,
en el carrito de la pena.   in the cart of sorrow.[4]
Se me occurió el decí,   It occurred to me to say,
'Siendo mi mare tan buena,   'My mother, being so good,
no se debía de morí.'   should not have died.'
Ayiii...ayiii...ay, ay, ayiii...   Ayeee...ayeee...ay, ay, ayeee...

The room erupted with impassioned cries: "*Ole!...Mi arma!...*Enrique, what a *malaguena!...Vaya la malagueña doble!*"

The words "*malagueña doble*" stuck in Chacón's mind, for the *cante* had indeed seemed "double"—twice as long as other *malagueñas*. The descending cadences of "ay" created extra *tercios*, extending the *letra* and giving it liturgical magnitude. Chacón thought back to what Fosforito had told him, of how El Mellizo would stop in the cathedral on his way home from the slaughterhouse. Listening now to El Mellizo's incantation *por malagueñas*, it was easy to imagine the great *cantaor*, with his paper of fish, listening to the singing of the priests and then repeating what he had heard as he walked the narrow streets toward home.

As El Mellizo continued with more majestic and solemn *letras*, Chacón was held spellbound by the musicality of his voice, the subtlety of its shadings—at times little more than a raspy whisper, then suddenly erupting into *rajo*-filled cries of anguish or supplication:

Se la llevó Dios   God has carried off
a la pobre mare mía.   my poor mother.
Porque se la llevó Dios?   Why did God take her?
Si era que El la quería,   If it was because he wanted her,
eso lo respeto yo,   I can respect that,
pero s'ha llevao toa mi   but He has taken all of my
              [*alegría.*]   [happiness.]

Una pena lenta y mala   A slow and terrible suffering
se llevó a la mare mía.   took my mother away.
Hasta la cama temblaba   Even the bed trembled
de ver lo que me decía   upon witnessing what she told me
y el consejo que me daba.   and the advice that she gave me.

---

[4] cart of sorrow: a horse-drawn hearse; in times of plague, carts used to collect bodies.

In their rapture, some of the gypsies had become wildly demonstrative. One threw his hat to the floor and was demolishing it with his feet, while another, tears in his eyes, drained his glass and shattered it upon the floor. Hermosilla rushed to embrace El Mellizo, saying "*Ole! Bendita sea la mare que te parió, cabrón!* [Blessed is the mother who gave birth to you!⁵] You have made me cry!"

Chacón was stunned. In spite of all he had heard, he had not been prepared for the impact of El Mellizo. Moved by the *cante* and dazed by drink, he could not control the tears that welled up in his eyes and poured down his cheeks. "I am nothing before this man," he mumbled to himself. Rising from his chair and lurching to where Hermosilla was pinching El Mellizo's stubbly cheeks, the youth dropped to the ground and attempted to wrap his arms about the *cantaor*'s knees. El Mellizo broke free from Hermosilla and looked down at Chacón. Gripping the youth's shoulder forcefully, he said, "*Chaval*, don't do that!"

Chacón lifted his gaze to meet the flashing, narrow-set eyes of his idol.

El Mellizo continued, "A *cantaor* of your promise has to bow before no one." Then, rising unsteadily to his feet, he bellowed, "Listen! Listen everyone! Quiet!" He pulled Chacón to his feet, leaving a heavy hand about the boy's shoulder. Chacón turned away from the intensity of the man's burning black eyes, but was never to forget the words he heard him pronounce with the majesty of a king: "Son, listen to what I say. One day they will call you the Pope of the *cante*. I, Enrique Jimenez, tell you this...and I know very well of what I speak!"

---

[5]*cabrón*: usually an insult; used here as a term of affection.

Patiño

Cádiz, August 1886

Shimmering lights arched overhead, whimsical patterns of brilliance running off in all directions. Gas lamps by the thousands illuminated the Alameda de Peregil[1] above the exuberant crowds that thronged to the Velada de Nuestra Señora de los Angeles. The Velada, born as an attraction and diversion for summer visitors, was second in popularity only to the spring fair in Sevilla. It stretched across the western end of Cádiz, from the Castle of Santa Catalina at the south, to the Bulwark of Candelaria and its battlements on the north, occupying the broad space between the formidable wall that enclosed the city and the seawall that dropped precipitously down to the pounding waves of the Atlantic Ocean.

"Antonio, the boss wants to see you!"

Now what? thought Chacón. *I've worked only two nights, and I thought it was going well.*

Two days earlier, Antonio Chacón had passed under a decorative arch over Calle Sacramento and entered a world of festivity such as he had never imagined. It had been early evening, yet the gardens and the wide, tree-lined Alameda already vibrated with joyous people. Along the walls and down the center of the Alameda stretched rows of identical *tiendas* [*casetas*] each built on a raised wooden floor with a railing in front and slender poles supporting a peaked roof and sides of red and white striped canvas. The *tiendas*, occupied and decorated by families, businesses, or social organizations, filled to capacity each

---

[1]Today, Parque Genovés.

evening with friends and family members. A number of larger canvas structures broke the monotony of the rows of private *tiendas*. These were the *tiendas* of government organizations: the Department of Medicine, the Department of Water, the Department of Gas Manufacture, the Círculo Mercantil, and the Municipal Employees. That of the *Ayuntamiento*, the municipal government, was the most magnificent—regal and sumptuous in its decoration. But the favorite *tienda* of the people was that of the Casino of Cádiz, a huge tent where young people and foreigners gathered to dance polkas, waltzes, and rigadoons. Chacón had tried to enter, but retreated before the unbearable heat and the tightly packed bodies that left little room for dancing. It seemed, however, the place to be—to be, and to be seen.

Music came from all sides in a clashing of chaotic sound. Blaring bands in the larger structures all but drowned out pianos in the private *tiendas*. Vendors filled the streets with cries in praise of peanuts, dates, toasted garbanzos, or *turrón* candy. The water seller, much in demand with his sugar and egg-white meringue sticks that sweetened glasses of water, sang in shrill tones: "*Ayiii...agüitiii fresquitiii...bibi, bibi, bibi...*" [Ayeee...fresh water...drink, drink, drink...] Gypsy *buñoleras*' cries of "*Calentitos!*" combined with the irresistible aroma of frying *churros* wafting from cauldrons of boiling oil to entice passersby. Customers packed the open-air cafés and the *neverías* selling iced drinks. Adding to the color and the confusion were game booths, circus acrobats, and the endless parades of horses, bicycles, and people. It was a magical scene set against a background of black night and the thunderous crashing of waves against the seawall.

It had been one week exactly since Enrique el Mellizo had given Chacón his blessing in the tavern of Rogelio. Life had not been the same for the Jerezano since. The second day after the fiesta he had received a visitor. The man said, "I am contracting artists for the Velada de los Angeles in Cádiz. Enrique el Mellizo told me, 'I met a *cantaor* in Jerez who is sure to please. Ask him if he would like to work here a few days and offer him seven *pesetas* a day.'"

Trembling with excitement inside, Chacón had feigned indifference, bluffing as he responded, "I accept...on the condition that I be permitted to sing *p'alante*."

The other raised an eyebrow, staring at him a long moment before replying, "I think that can be arranged."

When Chacón had tried to convince the Molina brothers to accompany him to Cádiz, Javier had protested, "Antonio, we can't give up our jobs at the Vera Cruz."

"But Javié, look how much you can earn during the Velada...and you will become better known!"

"A bird in hand is better than a hundred in flight," responded the older Molina. "At least we know we have work here..."

"You'll never get anywhere if you don't take a chance, if you stay here, working for nothing."

"*Anda, hombre!* In this thing of flamenco one is fortunate to have work. One day you will have to stop dreaming, you will understand what it means to be an artist. We must accept our lot...there is no other way."

"*A ver*, Javié, we'll see!"

Little did the three youths realize that, with this separation, they were embarking on paths that would carry them in very different directions.

From Jerez, a coach had carried Chacón to the sea and then turned south to follow the coast through the port towns of Puerto de Santa María and Puerto Real. After San Fernando— "*La Isla*"[2] to locals— the road led west toward the peninsula, passing through seemingly endless salt flats and immense shallow beds of seawater. Here and there, towering mountains of grayish salt glistened in the sun, salt that had been deposited in the flats by evaporation of seawater, then collected, and transported by donkey. From the coach, workers could be seen opening channels to allow fresh seawater to enter the beds, starting the cycle over. In Cádiz it was said that the salt did not come from the sea, but from the wit of the Gaditano [inhabitant of Cádiz]; in Cádiz, everyone was a *salero* [saltshaker].

From the salt beds of La Isla, the road turned north onto a narrow tongue of sand that headed out to sea. The sharp, salty air and the dazzling reflection of the white sand heightened the anticipation of those in the lurching coach. Here and there, small white houses with tiny green gardens relieved the monotony of tufted dunes and clumps of prickly pear cactus. Far in the distance, at the tip of the peninsula, shimmered the crystalline brilliance of Cádiz, "*La Tacita de Plata*," [The Little Silver Cup] as it was called by the Moors.

---

[2]La Isla de León: The Island of León, ancient name of San Fernando, which is, in fact, cut off from the mainland by ocean channels.

The sandbar widened, and little white *ventorillos* [country taverns] increased in number. In the shade of cactus hedges or grape vines, the *venteros* awaited customers for a lunch of fried fish or the shrimp known as *bocas de La Isla*. Ahead, the white buildings of the city rose up behind an immense fortified wall. To enter Cádiz from the mainland, it was necessary to pass through La Puerta de Tierra [The Gate of the Land]. A narrow, raised roadway crossed the wide waterless moat in front of the wall and entered an ornate, columned archway under the central tower. The coach halted under the archway for customs, where a *carabinero* began a search of the luggage that ended only when the passengers had scraped together enough money to satisfy him. As the coach continued into the city, one of the passengers said to Chacón, "Don't get caught outside the gate at night...La Puerta de Tierra is closed at ten o'clock!"

Cádiz never failed to impress visitors. Enclosed by the sea, it could only expand upward, with buildings of no less than three stories and often towering as high as six, all whitewashed, with vermilion stripes separating stories and dividing houses. In Moorish fashion, all but the main streets were extremely narrow, impervious to the rays of the sun except at midday. In every direction streets ended at the city wall, beyond which an outer avenue looked out over the sea wall and the battlements to a vista of ocean and endless space.

Chacón had been nervous before his debut in Cádiz. Not only was this to be the most important opportunity of his short career, but he also feared being judged by the knowledgeable aficionados of that city. However, all had gone well the first two nights. As he had been promised, he was permitted to sing *p'alante* once each night after singing for the *cuadro*. He had taken full advantage of the opportunity, his clear, deep voice and maturing *cante* winning him applause *por soleares* and *seguiriyas*. El Mellizo's generous praise of the Jerezano had insured a warm reception among aficionados.

On this, the third night, Chacón had strolled down the festive Alameda, dodging fairgoers while brightly colored fireworks exploded above him. He had been looking forward to singing. But that was earlier. Now he nervously sought out his employer. The café was just off the Alameda and, like other temporary cafés of the Velada, constructed of poles, boards, and canvas. While not as grand as the big public *tienda* on the Alameda, where six hundred people could be seated under crystal chandeliers, the café had chairs for up to two hundred set about the dusty floor of hard-packed earth, and a piano at the foot of the raised stage.

Chacón passed the bar at the side, where a dozen young waiters lolled about awaiting the evening crowd. He found his employer seated at a table.

"*Señor* Martínez, you wish to see me?"

"*Ah, buenas tardes*, Antonio. Have a seat…what will you drink?"

Chacón, hat in hand, sat down. "*Manzanilla*, thank you."

"Listen, Antonio, we have been pleased with the response of the people to your *cante*, but we feel we must make a change. Smoke?"

Antonio took the black cigarette in a trembling hand. It was a treat to smoke a manufactured cigarette.

"Beginning tonight, and for the remainder of your two-week contract, you will sing *p'alante* twice and your guitarist will be Maestro Patiño. But you will still have to sing for the *cuadro*."

Silence from Chacón, who had stopped inhaling mid-breath.

The other continued, "If you accept, we will raise your salary to ten *pesetas* a night. What do you say?"

Chacón coughed and began breathing again. "That will be fine *Don* Luis, whatever you say. *Gracias!*"

Maestro Patiño! Chacón's only contact with this patriarch of guitarists had been an initial introduction and a couple of nods of greeting. The Jerezano held the old man in awe, for the name of Patiño was legendary. Javier always spoke of El Maesto Patiño with reverence. It seemed that the best guitarists were all disciples of Patiño, including Paco el Barbero, Paco de Lucena, Juan Gandulla "Habichuela", and El Pollo of Cádiz. Only El Maestro Pérez and his students in Sevilla could be considered outside the school of *toque* of Patiño, and even they had felt his influence.

Chacón guessed José Patiño to be in his fifties, although he seemed older, from a different era. Still sprightly, with quick and nervous movements, he gave the impression of one who clung to the past, dressing as he did in the short jacket, the *sombrero calañés*, and a faded blue cape worn with indifference to the heat. Even his tiny antique guitar was of a type no longer played by professional guitarists. Yet, the sound that he coaxed from the ancient instrument was magic—precise, melodic, and always in perfect harmony with the *cantaor*.

Chacón found the old man behind a canvas partition, tuning his guitar. "Maestro," he said diffidently, "excuse me! It's me, Antonio. *Don* Luis has told me that you are going to play for me tonight."

Patiño grunted acknowledgement without ceasing to adjust the wooden tuning pegs of his instrument, testing the tone of each string by snapping it forcefully with his bony, tobacco-stained thumb.

Chacón watched the brown, claw-like thumbnail, fascinated by its thickness and the way it grew out twisted. After a moment of awkward silence, he said, "Ah...I thought that perhaps you might want to rehearse a little..."

Patiño continued to tune. When, at last, he seemed satisfied, he looked up with an air of resignation and said dryly, "*Niño*, do you know how to sing?"

"Of course!"

"And I know how to accompany...so why rehearse?"

Taken aback, Chacón fumbled for words. "Well, Maestro, I sing *por soleares* with the *cejilla* on the fourth fret."

"Yes, yes, the fourth!" The old man studied the youth before him, letting the guitar drop to his lap. "You know, the *cantaor* did not always have it so easy. Before, when I was young, you could not tell me to put the *cejilla* on the fourth fret...there was no *cejilla*...*sabe?* [you know?] The *cantaor* could only say, 'play *por medio*' or 'play *por arriba*'...*y pare usté de contá* [and stop counting]. He had to adjust his voice to those tones...although for some *cantes* we also had this tone, *por abajo*." To illustrate, Patiño formed a D chord and strummed crisply down across the strings with his thumb.[3] Sometimes we even had to change the tuning of the guitar, loosening or tightening the strings to change the pitch.

"So, the *cantaor* had to force his voice, to sing higher or lower than he wished. He had to fight with his voice as well as the *cante*. You had to be a real *cantaor* to sing with guitar in those days. Many singers had no choice but to use the *voz farsete* [falsetto] that we still hear so often. Or the strain roughened the voice...and gave us this *rajo* we have in the *cante*. Voices that were naturally hoarse adapted better to singing in difficult tones. One of the best was El Fillo, with a voice *mú ronca* [very hoarse] and when others began to imitate him, people would

---

[3] *por medio*: (in the middle) keys based on the A-Major chord; *por arriba*: (above) keys based on the E-Major chord; *por abajo*: (below) keys based on the D-Major chord; named for the relative positions of these chords as they appear on the fingerboard.

say, 'He has the voice of El Fillo, *una voz afillá*.

"One day, long ago, Paquirri said to me...do you know Paquirri?"

Chacón shook his head., "I sing some of his *cante*, but I have never met him."

"Paquirri el Guanté...he used to make *guantes* [gloves]...a monster *por soleares*. Paquirri says to me, 'José, I've been thinking. There must be a way to raise the tones of the guitar so that we can sing better, without forcing our voices so much. It is enough to fight with the *cante*, without having to fight the guitar also.'

"Paquirri plays the guitar...*sabe?* And not badly. So he understands the instrument. I saw his idea immediately. We tied a little piece of wood across the strings...and it worked phenomenally. But, of course, it could not be easily moved. Later, I thought of this little peg and cord to hold it in place. At first everyone thought it was just a gimmick, a passing whim, but soon they began to copy me and now it is an indispensable part of the guitar. That's why you can say to me, 'Put it on the fourth,' and sing without effort, like a canary!"

A voice interrupted the guitarist. "*Vámonos*, it's time!"

The gas lamps had been lit, the tent was half-filled with customers, and the piano at the foot of the stage had silenced. Chacón went onstage with the *cuadro*. Afterward, he returned alone with Patiño to sing *por soleares*. Singing with the guitar of Patiño proved a revelation for Chacón. Not only did the maestro follow every nuance of the *cante*, but he seemed to merge with the *cantaor*, to anticipate his every whim, coaxing the best out of him and encouraging him to take chances. Patiño appeared pleased, enjoying the collaboration. He never took his eyes off the *cantaor* and, from time to time, mumbled, "*Bien!*" or "*Así é!*" [That's the way it's done!]

Chacón recognized that Patiño did not have the technique of Paco de Lucena, or even Javier, for his was the *toque corto*, short on technique and repertoire, and the *toque p'abajo*, the thumb driving downward in a forceful attack on the bass strings. But the music inspired with its choppy syncopated rhythms and creative melodies that burst forth in dry staccato notes at just the right moment. The *cantaor* felt exhilarated and performed at his best, the public responding and applauding enthusiastically after each *letra*. He lost track of time, oblivious to all except the magic communion of *cante* and *toque*. Only a whisper from Patiño was able to bring him back to reality, "*Ya, hombre*, that's enough!"

Chacón received congratulations at the bar. Behind him a well-known *cupletista* had taken the stage with her popular songs, to be followed by a humorist.

Two hours later, after Chacón had again fulfilled his obligation with the *cuadro*, he reappeared on stage to sing solo. As he took his seat, Patiño leaned toward him and whispered, "Look who has just come in!"

Chacón looked up and gasped, "Mellizo!" It had taken only a glance toward the entrance to spot the unmistakable figure of Enrique el Mellizo. Clustered about him, a half dozen gypsies stood out in the now crowded *tienda*.

"And Enrique Ortega..."

"El Gordo?" Chacón felt his heart begin to pound.

"*El mismo* [One and the same]..."

There was no mistaking Enrique el Gordo, his bear-like body brutally squeezed into a rumpled jacket held closed by two straining buttons. Even at a distance, the disdainful arrogance of the man's bearing bore down heavily upon young Chacón.

"...and Mellizo's brother Mangoli...and El Pata..."

Chacón froze, overcome by a wave of insecurity. Who was he to sing *por seguiriyas* in the presence of these giants of the *cante gitano?* At last, he managed to say to Patiño, "I can't sing *por seguiriyas*...I'm too embarrassed!"

"Then what do you want to sing, *armamía?*" [*alma mía*; term of affection]

Chacón hesitated a moment before answering, "Play *por malagueñas* for me!"

He sang the first thing that came to mind, the *malagueña* that he had composed that night in Sevilla, "*Dando en el reloj la una...*"

The applause was overwhelming, unlike anything he had experienced previously, and he was forced to continue with *malagueñas* until he had exhausted his small repertoire.

Later, in his bed and unable to sleep, Chacón reflected upon his success. The *malagueñas* came easily to him, unlike the *cantes gitanos*, and adapted themselves well to his voice. And the most acclaimed *malagueña* that evening had been the one he had created. Already his head was spinning with ideas for new *letras*. By the time the first light of morning had broken through the cracks in the heavy wooden shutters, Chacón was singing a *letra* in the same melody, but based upon the somber and moving verses he had heard from El Mellizo less than two weeks earlier. *This will really get to them*, he thought to himself:

En la tumba de mi mare,	In the tomb of my mother,
a dar gritos me ponía,	I began to cry out,
y escuché un eco del viento:	and I heard an echo in the wind:
"No la llames," me decía,	"Don't call to her," it was saying,
"que no responden los muertos!"	"because the dead don't answer!"

Chacón and Maestro Patiño developed a warm friendship. The young *cantaor* won over the old guitarist with his enthusiasm, his knowledge, and his respect for the traditions of the *cante*.

"I played for all the best," Patiño said early one evening, "for El Nitri, El Fillo, and Silverio before he went to America...and later in the Café de Cagajones [horse dung] and the Cafe de Triperas [the tripe seller], all gone now. In fact, it was I who arranged the fiesta for Silverio when he returned to Cái [Cádiz] after having been gone for so many years. That was more than twenty years ago, in '64 I think, but I remember it as if it had just happened.

Chacón felt like a child again, listening to tales of Silverio told to him by his *Tío* Juan. He smiled, encouraging Patiño to continue.

"The first thing Silverio did upon disembarking was to find me and ask me to arrange a fiesta. So I called together the best gypsy *cantaores* I could find...El Gordo Viejo, Curro Durse, María Borrico...en fin, *una baraja* [a full deck] of the best we had. No one recognized Silverio...*hombre*, he had been gone for eight years, and he had a full beard, expensive clothes...they thought he was a wealthy Cuban. Late in the evening, after everyone had sung, Silverio says to me, 'Now it's my turn. Play *por seguiriyas!*'

"You can imagine the commotion. You know how it is with *señoritos* when they have had too much wine...they all want to sing. We are accustomed to that, and it can have *gracia*. But, *por seguiriyas?* Everyone laughed and made faces behind the big *señorito*'s back...until he opened his mouth in a powerful *temple*, with that *rajo* and that echo of his. The *gitanos* were stunned. And their astonishment grew when he sang:

La malita lengua	The evil tongue
que de mi murmura,	that gossips about me,
yo la cogiera por en medio	I would grasp it by the middle
la dejara muda.	and leave it mute.

"The *gitanos* asked among themselves: *'Quién es ese tío?'* [Who is that guy?] *'Cómo puede ser que este gachó tan raro cante tan bien, con esa voz tan afillá?'* [How can it be that this strange *gachó* sings so well, with that voice so *afillá?*] They looked for some flaw, something to explain or in some way justify the impossible. Finally, María Borrico, already an old woman, stepped forward and exclaimed, *'Canta mu bien, pero tiene los pies mu grandes!* [He sings well, but he has very big feet!]"

Chacón laughed, "*Qué gracia*, Maestro!"

"...and, later, when they wanted La Borrico to sing, all she would say was, 'How can you expect me to sing when that bearded *gachó me ha estemplao* [has put me out of tune, out of sorts]?' "

Patiño laid a gaunt hand on Chacón's forearm. "*Joven*, have you heard María Borrico sing?"

"No. I have learned her *cambio por seguiriyas*, but I have never met her."

"She is ancient now, older than seven parrots, but you must listen to her. To hear a woman sing like a man, *cante macho* with a voice as hoarse as that of a donkey, *muy afillá*, is a thing of wonder. There is talk of a benefit to be held for her. We'll see...but you must hear her."

"What happened after that, maestro? Did you continue to play for Silverio?"

"Did I play for Silverio? *Hombre*, I was his preferred guitarist. We worked everywhere when he first came back. Everyone wanted him. You know, Silverio was the first to sing everything well. Before him *cantaores* were either *gachó* or *gitano* and they sang one way or the other...and only a few *cantes*. Silverio, with that privileged voice, sang everything...*cante andaluz, cante gitano*...they even tried to talk him into singing opera! Because he was a *gachó* who sang the gypsy *cantes* so well, people began to accept the gypsy style. He is an intelligent man, a musical genius. He polished the old *cantes* without destroying their primitive bitterness, enriching the *coplas* without damaging them. Yes, Silverio overshadowed all the others."

The old man sucked on his cigarette and continued, "I recall that shortly after his return, perhaps the following year, we performed in Jerez..."

"*Ozú*, that was before I was even born!" muttered Chacón.

"...and it was something extraordinary for flamenco...although we didn't call it flamenco in those days, we said '*cante andaluz*.' Silverio was the first to announce his *cante* as *flamenco*, but that wasn't until much later. In Jerez we performed in a theater. Imagine that! Nobody worked in theaters. Only Silverio could do that. It was something quite extraordinary. First the orchestra played. Then actors presented a play. Then Silverio and I went out to do *la caña*, *el polo*, and *seguiriyas*. After more acting and a couple doing some sort of dance, we went out again for more *cante*...*rondeñas*, *serranas*...and I don't recall what else. The public loved it, but the newspapers called it monotonous warbling and said that for three nights the dramatic arts and their muses had been in mourning! Can you believe it? But they also had to admit that Silverio had filled the theater to capacity three nights in a row... something that had not been done for a very long time.

"We returned to that same theater, the Teatro Principal, two years later. By that time Silverio had really established his reputation throughout Andalucía. He was in a position to make demands. He believed that our music should be given the same respect as other kinds of music. He was the only one to call his performances 'concerts...*conciertos de cante andaluz*'...and he insisted that we all be listed in the program as *Don* [Sir]. He called us *professors* of guitar...*Don* José Patiño and *Don* Francisco Cantero..."

"Francisco Cantero?"

"Yes, Paco el Barbero was with us. Do you know Paco?"

"I have heard a great deal about him. He was my friend Javiér's teacher."

"Well, he was there, we played together for Silverio. It was the same as before...orchestra, plays, comedies, and us. Then, at the end, they announced the 'grand competition of guitar" and Paco and I went out to compete with guitar solos. I remember I played my *zapateado de las ochenta y dos variaciones* [*zapateado* with eighty-two variations]. The audience went crazy for this competition. And you can be sure that, this time, the press did not criticize Silverio."

"I taught them all...and look what they do with it!" Between shows, Maestro Patiño was haranguing Chacón on his pet subject—the loss of purity and tradition in the *toque* of young virtuosos. "The guitar should be for nothing but to accompany the *cantaor* and to collaborate with him and with his *cantes!*" Chacón had heard this numerous times during their brief acquaintance.

"But maestro, you told me that you played solos at one time..."

"That's true. I was the first to give guitar recitals...the others have all learned from me. But that was the foolishness of youth. The guitar was made to accompany the *cantaor*..."

"What do you think of El Barbero?"

"You mean Paco?"

"Yes."

"That one learned a great deal from me and we have performed together often. I told you about when we were with Silverio, and throughout the '70s we played everywhere, even in Madrid. He knows how to play, but more and more he has left the *toque puro*, playing those *tonterías* [foolish things] of Arcas..."

"And the other Paco, also a barber?"

"You mean that youngster...El Niño de Lucena. He plays very fast, *tira p'arriba como nadie* [plays scales with the fingers better than anyone] and plays solo a great deal. That is not what the guitar was made for. I never taught him, but he has learned from me by listening. He is very clever...and *muy sinvergüenza* [shameless]. He listens to me play and, later, I hear him playing my things. He claims to have created the *alegrías por rosas*, but that is mine. And imagine this, he had the nerve to tell me, José Patiño Gonzales, me who created the accompaniment for the *cante* the way it is done today, that I was missing a tone in *la caña*. *Qué caradura!* [What nerve!] That one has no shame, to tell me that I was missing a tone, a tone needed to guide the voice within the *compás* and *cuadrar* [square off] the *cante*. The guitar does not guide the voice. We are the servant of the *cante* and follow its lead."

Patiño was livid, veins throbbing at his temples. "These young guitarists can devour the guitar. They play phenomenally. But in the hour of accompaniment, the guitarist has to stop, to listen to the *cantaor*. Not like some who, when the *cantaor* finishes his *temple*, they begin *p'arriba, p'arriba* [faster and faster]...to get attention. It is not that way. We are second to the *cantaor*. The *cantaor* is the matador, and the guitarist is the *banderillero*. You have to let them sing. If the guitarist wants to show off, let him play a couple of solos afterward, so the public will know he is somebody..."

In an attempt to calm the old man, Chacón asked, "Maestro, who, beside yourself, are the best guitarists?"

"*Ojú!* There are some from here, from Cái, who have learned from me. Manuel...we call him El Pollo [The Chicken]...who plays very well and knows all the *cantes*. And Juanito...Juanito Gandulla ...Gallego[4] like I am. They call him *Habichuela* [Green Bean]. That is a youngster who knows how to play *como Dios manda* [as God commands], how to help the *cantaor* do what he has to do, without putting in long *falsetas* or *cosas raras* [strange things]. He is playing in Sevilla now."

Patiño paused a moment in thought, then added, "There aren't many more. Pérez, in Sevilla, plays well for the dance...you know, he is the only *gitano* who plays well. All of the best guitarists are *gachó*. I don't know why that should be...perhaps the *gitano* does not have the discipline for study. Other guitarists? Here in Cái, Enrique García was a giant in his time...he used to play for Silverio. El Maestro Tapia has his *cositas* [little things], but he is very old-fashioned. No, there aren't many...and they all have copied me. I am the one who began to accompany the way we do today. In the *malagueña*, we used to do it this way, *mu corrío* [running], the way Juan Breva likes it." Patiño demonstrated the rolling strum of the *fandangos*. "Now we do it like this, with more *aire*." This time the guitar produced simple, swinging melodies that softened the pulse of the music, allowing the *cante* room to breathe while still suggesting the ancestral dance rhythm of the hills around Málaga.

"Very pretty, Maestro. It is your playing that has helped me to be successful with the *malagueña*."

"The *malagueña* suits you well, *muchacho*. It comes easily to your voice, more easily than does the *cante gitano*. If you follow the path of the *malagueñas*, you are certain to find success. Try to learn from El Mellizo...he is the best in this new *malagueña*, although, with that voice of his, he sings everything well. While you are here in Cái, learn all you can, for this is where you will find the true *cante*. Nowhere else do they sing with our feeling and *gracia*."

"*Viva Cái!*"

---

[4]*Gallego*: from Galicia in northern Spain. *Gallegos*, known for their business acumen, owned or operated most of the fried fish businesses, while *montañeses* (from Asturias, also in the north) controlled most of the taverns and cafés. Patiño and Habichuela were born in Cádiz of Galician parents (according to Pericón de Cádiz).

Curro Dulce

During the second week of the Velada, Chacón's following in the café continued to grow. Some aficionados came nightly to listen to the Jerezano, their shouted requests for the *malagueña* starting early in the evening. Fiestas came Chacón's way with increasing frequency, and mornings often found him still singing in one of the many *tiendas* on the Alameda.

Late one night, Chacón felt a hand on his shoulder as he stood at the bar. A familiar voice sounded behind him, "Antoñico, what's up *hombre?*"

He turned to find Paquiro Ortega, the comic dancer who had worked with him in the Vera Cruz. The two embraced with much backslapping as Chacón asked, "*Hombre*, it's good to see you...but what are you doing here?

The gypsy laughed. Middle-aged and balding, his generous belly draped over the sash that held up his baggy pants. "*Chiquillo*, how could I not be here? My family is here." The deep, broken voice crackled like dry leaves. "From the Vera Cruz I went to Málaga, to the Café de las Siete Revueltas, then back to Jerez. Now I'm down here to escape the heat. *Viva Cái! Hombre*, how goes it for you?"

"*Bien!* I'm defending myself. Come, have a drink!"

The two drank until Chacón's turn to sing. Later, Chacón arranged to include Paquiro in a fiesta, where the Gaditano proved to be an animated *festero*, his humor, *gracia*, and comic dance insuring that there was never a dull moment. The sun had climbed high in the sky the following morning before Antonio and Paquiro left the *tienda*, lightheaded with drink and the feel of money in their pockets.

"*Vamo pa Santa María, Tonio*," rasped Paquiro. "Let's go over to the Santa María neighborhood and have coffee...I want you to meet some of my family."

"Let's go!" Chacón had no thought of sleep. The fiesta had been one of the rare ones, organized by aficionados who knew how to listen to *cante*. The Jerezano had sung well and enjoyed himself. The *cante*, the good company, and the generous payment had left him exhilarated and rejuvenated, ready to face another day.

At the southern end of the Alameda de Peregil, the two men passed through a break in the wall into the heart of the city. "This is the Barrio de La Viña...all *gitanos*," explained Paquiro. "At least everyone is considered to be *gitano*, even if he is not. La Cachuchera was from here...what a singer of *martinetes* she was...even Silverio was crazy about her *cante*. All of the Cachucheras were good singers and dancers, almost as good as we Ortegas. Did you ever see La Mejorana dance, Antonio?"

Chacón shook his head.

"You must have been too young. Rosario Monje was her name, but they called her La Mejorana. She was the niece of La Cachuchera. What a beauty...and an extraordinary talent in the *baile*. She was only sixteen when she first went on stage, but in less than three years she had captivated half of Andalucía. But then, back in '81 I think it was, she married the torero's tailor Victor Rojas and abandoned her career. What a shame...you have never seen such beauty...pale skin and light brown hair, almost blond, with green eyes...you never forgot those eyes. *Caray, qué peaso de mujer!* [what a hunk of woman!] Face, figure, *gracia*...she had it all. You should have seen the public when she came out on the stage of the old Café de Silverio. Some came early to get a seat near the stage, hoping to catch a glimpse of more than just her tiny feet...but they could stay until four in the morning and they never succeeded. She used to come out dancing, then stop completely at center stage, like a sculpture in her train dress and fringed shawl to sing her *cantiñas*."

Paquiro had stopped in mid-street to demonstrate the pose of La Mejorana. "She often sang this *letra*:

Yo soy blanca y te diré	I am light-skinned and will tell you
la causa de estar morena:	the cause of my dark tan:
que estoy adorando a un sol	I am admiring a 'sun'
y con sus rayos me quema...	and he burns me with his rays...

"*Hombre*, more than one Christian had to wipe the drool from his mouth four or five times on listening to her. Then, while the *cantaor del turno* [*cantaor* whose turn it was] sang the second *cantiña*, Rosario brought the house down with her *baile*. What dancing...only in Cái do they dance like that! La Mejorana was the first to raise her arms overhead...before that they seldom raised the arms more than this." Paquiro demonstrated, with arms curving upward to about eye level. "La Mejorana lifted them almost directly overhead, with extraordinary *aire* and majesty. Tonio, you should have seen the other dancers. They said it was a scandal, that a woman of modesty should not dance that way. But within months they were all doing it, copying her...because the public, and the intelligent aficionados, loved it. *Ole la gracia de Cái!* And Rosario was from here, from La Viña. But La Viña is nothing compared to the Barrio de Santa María. You'll see."

The friends continued up the narrow Calle Cardoso to where it opened into a large and busy plaza. "La Plaza de la Libertad," said Paquiro. Around the perimeter of the plaza, marble columns recalled earlier civilizations, and in the center a cavernous building housed the market with its rows of food stalls bustling with activity. Amid the chaos of sounds and savory smells, the bounty of the sea was laid out to tempt the appetite, from glistening anchovies and sardines to immense slabs of swordfish, shark, and tuna; from octopus and tiny *puntillitas* squid to larger *calamares* and immense rotund and tentacled *chocos*. Among the seemingly endless varieties of shellfish were tiny *camarones* shrimp "alive and fresh," larger *gambas* and *gambones*, crayfish-like *cigalas* and *galeras*, lobsters, and bright red *carabineros*.

"Let's have some breakfast here," said Paquiro, indicating a café on the plaza where they could sit at an outside table to sip their steaming *café con leche*.

As they sat watching the lively theater of the marketplace, Chacón felt the first heavy weight of fatigue. But, by the time he had finished his second cup of coffee, he had recuperated sufficiently to continue on toward Santa María. Paquiro led him back out of the city streets to follow the seawall of El Campo del Sur along the oceanfront. The crisp, salt-laden breeze from the sea, the brilliant sunshine, and the crashing of the surf on the rocky beach below combined to complete Chacón's rejuvenation.

Where a massive cathedral loomed up just inside the wall, Paquiro turned once more into the city, leading the way to a plaza in front of the structure.

"The new cathedral," he said. "They have just completed it...after working on it for more than a hundred years." From the plaza the two men passed under a narrow medieval archway between two ancient buildings. "El Arco de La Rosa," explained Paquiro.

"Does this arch have anything to do with the *alegrías por rosas* of Patiño?" asked Chacón.

"Could be...Patiño is from here, from the Barrio de Santa María, which is just ahead. But, right now we are in El Barrio del Pópulo, the old Cái."

Streets that were little more than roughly cobbled alleys twisted in a confusing maze between houses that appeared as old as time. At a turn in a passage so narrow that the walls on either side could be reached with outstretched arms, Paquiro explained, "From here to the walls of La Puerta de Tierra is the Barrio de Santa María, home to us gypsies and very flamenco. They all live here...my family, the Ortegas...the Espeletas, the Fernández, Enrique el Melliso and his family...Patiño is from here, Paquirri el Guanté, Francisco la Perla, Miguel Macaca, who is singing in Sevilla...all of them. Stop any young man on the street and he can sing or dance for you. El Barrio de Santa María is *arte...arte* and *gracia*.

"This way," gestured Paquiro, "I want you to meet my brother José."

The path widened, leaving behind the perpetual sunless gloom, and opened onto a small plaza shaded by a church. "The Church of Santa María," explained Paquiro, "where El Melliso sometimes stops on his way home from the slaughterhouse to listen to music."

The Gaditano led his companion to Calle Miraflor, which ran straight for several long blocks to Puerta Tierra. As the two men followed a long expanse of blank wall, Paquiro explained, "My brother José... they call him El Águila [The Eagle]...is a *banderillero* by profession, but you have to hear him sing...he sings all the styles of Cái well. All of his family are artists. His daughter Rita is dancing in Sevilla. Carlota is only sixteen, but she has been performing here in Cái since she was eight years old. The younger ones all show promise, even little Manolito, who is fascinated by the *cante*...he spends more time in the home of El Mellizo than he does with his own family..."

Paquiro stopped before a cavernous entryway, where a cluster of shrill voiced gypsy women bartered with a country peasant for the herbs that spilled from a large basket:

"*Sí señora, la luisa* is what you want for your stomach."

"Then give me a handful..."

"And if your canaries won't sing, the *pili* flower will turn them into nightingales."

A flurry of interest by the women.

"And the herb *militi* for the woman who is expecting..."

Paquiro called loudly over to the women, "*Oiga osté*, give me some of that *militi!*" He patted his potbelly suggestively. Laughter accompanied him as he guided Chacón into the entrance of an ancient *casa de vecinos*.

A familiar stench assailed Chacón's nostrils from overflowing toilets and piles of accumulated garbage. Inside, several stories of dilapidated balconies ran around the patio on three sides, the fourth side enclosed by a high blank wall of crumbling brick and plaster. Behind the rusty iron railings of the balconies, rows of half-doors led to the dwellings of the *vecinos* [neighbors]. The courtyard rang with the sounds of children and barking dogs.

Just inside the entrance, two young boys played earnestly at bullfighting, one of them guiding the movements of the other, who played the bull, with the tattered remnant of what had once been a *muleta* [cape]. When the "bull" stopped to argue a point in the interest of fair play, Paquiro called out, "Enrique, if you stepped in front of the bull that way, he would catch you."

At the foot of a massive wooden staircase, dusty gypsy children, barefoot and half-naked, beat out *palmas* to accompany the dance of a diminutive and disheveled form. Shrill voices cried out "*Así...asa...Ole, Rosario*...It's your turn, Rita!"

"*Salero, guapa!*" croaked Paquiro, attempting to join in the *palmas*. But he only succeeded in bringing the fiesta to a halt, the tiny ragamuffins racing to clutch at his pant legs, yelling, "*Tío* Paquiro, *Tío* Paquiro!" The *bailaor* shooed them away, making them laugh by marking a dance step with an exaggerated sway of his hips and jiggling of his belly. Indicating a dark-skinned teenager seated on the stairs, Paquiro said, "Antonio, this is Carlota, the one I told you about. She is already a professional dancer...you should see her dance!" The frizzy-haired young girl blushed with pleasure and averted her eyes.

Paquiro led Chacón up the rickety stairs to the second floor. Birdcages of wood and wire hung everywhere from walls and railings, each containing a canary, bullfinch, or lark, and most barely larger than the bird itself. Men and women greeted Paquiro affectionately at almost every step. Picking their way along the balcony, cluttered with cages, dogs, and the occasional chicken, Paquiro told Chacón, "Many of my family live here...this is where we were born. Juan still lives up there on the next floor where my mother and father lived. Out of eight brothers and sisters, three live here with their families." Paquiro interrupted himself to call into an open doorway, "José...Rufina...It is I, Paquiro!"

A stubbly face, still creased and puffy from sleep, appeared at the open upper half of the doorway. A shirtless José "El Águila" greeted his brother and welcomed Chacón. Rufina attempted to pat her thick black hair into place while apologizing for the lack of space in the two tiny cluttered rooms that housed their large family. One room was taken up with a bed and several sleeping mats, while the other barely accommodated a small table and several chairs.

Chacón and Paquiro were not the first visitors of the day. Seated at the table was a man whose age was hard to discern in the dim light, but he appeared to be well into his sixties. The lines of his face revealed a lifetime of experiences, but there was no sign of gray in his hair. The erect posture and firmness of grip on the *vara* between his legs denoted a man of strong character.

"Tonio, have you met Curro?" asked Paquiro.

"No, I don't believe I have."

El Águila intervened. "Antonio, this is my father-in-law...Rufina's father...Curro Fernández."

Paquiro completed the introduction. "Curro, Antonio Chacón is from Jerez...he sings very well."

As they shook hands, Curro looked Chacón up and down, as if appraising the possibility that any worthwhile *cante* could come from the unlikely *gachó*. His only comment was, "Everybody sings these days!"

Paquiro laughed and slapped Chacón on the back. "Don't pay any attention to him, Antonio. Now you know why we call him 'Durse' [*Dulce*; Sweet]."

The instant that Chacón heard "Durse," the pieces came together, leaving him stunned. Curro Durse! It couldn't be. It was too unexpected at that moment, in that place. Curro Dulce, more of a legend than a reality in the mind of the Jerezano, a name from his childhood, from conversations overheard in taverns, and pronounced with reverence by gypsy blacksmiths. While Curro did not in any way exceed El Mellizo or Silverio in reputation, he was more mysterious as a person. Chacón had always expected to meet Silverio and El Mellizo one day, but, since Curro did not perform publicly and was little known outside of Cádiz, it was his music, especially his *cante por seguiriyas*, that had influenced most singers in some way. Chacón had never stopped to think about the man, whether he still lived, as if the music had just always existed. To have Curro Dulce appear to him as the father of a gypsy wife in a humble *casa de vecinos* caught him completely off guard. Speechless, he just stared, trying to assimilate, to put together the man and the myth.

"*Vamo*, José, let's go have a *copita* [drink]," said Paquiro.

"*Vale* [Okay]...give me a moment to get dressed." El Águila took a last puff on his cigarette before dropping it to the floor and extinguishing it with his foot. He cleared his throat and targeted a generous wad of phlegm at the crushed butt. Chacón noted with approval that El Águila had barely exited the room before the tile had been wiped clean by Rufina.

"*Oye*, where's my nephew Manoliyo?"[1] asked Paquiro of no one in particular.

It was Rufina who answered, "He's probably with El Mellizo...he's always over there!"

"*Qué gitanito con más ley*," added Paquiro, "He's a real little *gitano*, Tonio...the *cante* is all he thinks about. How old is he Rufina?"

"Five."

"Five years old, and he already knows the *cante...una barbaridá!*"

"With the blood of the Ortegas and the Durses, how could he not sing well?" said José el Águila as he slipped on a jacket in spite of the summer heat and adjusted his hat. "Curro, let's go...we're off to visit the *sagrario!*" [holy sanctuary; tavern]

Curro Dulce, who had not spoken a word since being introduced to Chacón, rose with a grunt and the aid of his stout *vara*. Chacón still

---

[1] Manuel Ortega Fernández, eventually to father the great 20th century *cantaor*, Manolo Caracol.

could not take his eyes off him. The four men descended the stairs and passed through the communal cooking area where women talked a running stream as they cleaned fish and wrung the necks of chickens.

In a dim passage nearby, the men entered a dark and musty tavern. Aside from the crude bar, several wine barrels, and the braids of garlic and smoked hams hanging from the smoked-darkened ceiling, the sparse furnishings consisted of one small table and several rickety chairs. The tavern-keeper, engrossed in conversation at one end of the bar, nodded in greeting to the newcomers. Tall and corpulent, with a black sash wrapped to swath him from his chest to below his immense belly, he was being subjected to a long-winded diatribe:

"There is nothing more I can do about it. The company has sent you many bills and notices, to which you have not responded. If they do not receive some satisfaction, they will greatly regret having to take action against you."

It soon became clear that the speaker represented a winery. The tavern-keeper, a *montañés*, remained unperturbed behind his heavy mustache, several days' growth of beard, and wildly bushy eyebrows. He drew forth a pouch from his sash and offered tobacco to the other, while shouting back to a tiny kitchen, "Pepa, show the *señor* the drawer of regrets!"

A timid woman appeared and submissively opened a drawer filled to capacity with folded letters. The tavern-keeper, while lifting a glowing tinder to a newly rolled cigarette, said to the winery representative, "Open whichever you wish...they all say the same thing, 'We greatly regret...'"

Before the representative could react, or the newly arrived customers break into open laughter, the *montañés* slapped the other on the back and said, "Let's talk about this over a drink...*niño*, bring us some olives and ham." *Caña* glasses of *manzanilla* appeared, along with complimentary *tapas*, introductions were made, and the winery representative found himself chatting amiably with the Gaditanos and sharing news of Jerez with Chacón. The *montañés*, a hunk of chalk tucked over his right ear, to be used to scrawl on the bar the arbitrary and illegible charges accrued by each customer, winked at the Ortegas and said, "*Venga cante*, José, Paquiro...show Juanito what it means to be Gaditano!"

Paquiro needed little encouragement. With a grin, he rapped a hard knuckle on the tabletop, snapped a horny fingernail against the wood, and the droning rhythm of *soleares* resounded through the tavern. Paquiro tested his voice several times, found the croaking to his satisfaction, and launched the fiesta with a *letra* that could only come from Cádiz:

Salero! Viva er salero!	*Salero!* Long live *salero!*
Salero! Viva la sal!	*Salero!* Long live the salt!
Qué tiene usté más salero	You have more *salero*
que er salero universal.	than the universal saltshaker.

Paquiro was no singer. He delivered his *cante* in an almost spoken voice. But his was a *cante* that derived its impact from its *gracia* and its ability to relax and inspire the others. Incapable of remaining still, he punctuated his *cante* with fragments and gestures of *baile* without leaving his seat.

José el Águila took over from his brother, continuing *por soleá* in the styles of his father (El Gordo Viejo), Silverio, and Enrique el Mellizo. The hour of the siesta came and went. While most of Cádiz ate and slept, wine and *cante* flowed in the tiny tavern in the Barrio de Santa María. Renewed by drink, Chacón sang *por soleá* at great length, winning glowing approval from El Águila and the others. Only Curro Dulce sat stone-faced, without reaction.

Juan, the wine representative, began to order round after round of drinks. Laughter and *cante* greeted the neighbors of Santa María as the barrio came to life once more in the late afternoon. The tavern began to fill with customers. Some came and went; others stayed. Everyone knew each other. Paquiro sang and danced *por tangos* to the beat of *palmas*. "Paquiro, *viva tú... ole, el arte de Cái!*"

As Paquiro settled breathlessly into a chair, El Águila gripped Juan's arm and stated, "Cái is where they dance the best, *sabe!* It's because of the sea. Here, we know only the sea...no snow, no green fields or forests, no mountains, streams, or rivers...just the sea and the waves. Watching the sea gives us our joyous sense of rhythm, and dances that are sun and salt, personality and temperament, *gracia* and *compás*. We know how to enjoy ourselves with music. And here in Santa María, they dance the best of all."

Paquiro chimed in, "And we Ortegas have the dance in our blood. All of us dance. Our sister Gabriela was the greatest *bailaora* in the cafés until she married Fernando el Gallo. José's daughter Rita is now the talk of Sevilla, and the younger ones, Carlota and Rosario are going to be famous one day. Even as far away as Málaga the name of Ortega is well known in the dance. When I was there some years ago, dancing in the Café de las Siete Revueltas, our sister Rita may she rest in peace, was the queen of Café de Chinitas...everybody loved Rita Ortega in Málaga."

While Paquiro spoke, El Águila called over the tavern-keeper's son, a dirty-faced youngster who, when he had not been busy serving drinks, had watched the fiesta with rapt concentration. "*Oye, niño*, go to the home of my brother El Gordo and tell him to come...*anda*, run!"

"Rita danced like a goddess...I often went over when I had a chance, to watch her. All the men were attracted to her beauty, but there was one who cared more for her than the others. She married Paco el Guarriro, *un gitano de pura cepa* [a gypsy of pure heritage], and what a *gitano* he was! El Guarriro[2] owned two butcher stands and a small *café cantante*. He lived in luxurious comfort and gave help and advice to any *gitano* who could sing or dance a little. But he was *mu raro* [very eccentric] and showed off his wealth in original ways. You should have seen how he dressed, *carajo!* He ordered suits of fine wool from the best tailor in Málaga...and by the dozens. But always without a jacket. Imagine, high-waisted pants, flared at the bottom, and a silk-lined vest. He never wore a shirt, only an undershirt of bright silk from Valencia. Not only did he not wear boots or fashionable spats, but he insisted on going everywhere in kidskin slippers with socks that matched his undershirt. Indoors or out —they say he was bald as a quince fruit— he wore a black alpaca cap and a white silk scarf knotted around his neck."

Paquiro was out of his chair, modeling the imaginary clothes as he spoke. "El Guarriro went everywhere in his shirtsleeves, unless the cold forced him to put over his shoulders a magnificent cape, elaborately embroidered with touches of diamonds and a scarlet velvet lining. He never buttoned the vest, but held it together with his watch chain, a thick gold chain from which dangled his lucky charms—two large gold coins, a horseshoe of diamonds and sapphires, the hand of Fatima made of pink coral, a little marble elephant, and a tiny agate hunchback."

---

[2]According to Carlos de la Luna (p.108), *Guarriro* derives from the gypsy word meaning "to laugh."

The others laughed in disbelief when Paquiro said, "No one ever saw a stain or a wrinkle in his clothes...he went for a shave and changed his socks twice a day. May my children die if it's not true! Almost every Sunday he showed off a new suit. Many of the *gitanos* in the Barrio de la Cruz Verde dressed well in the weekly cast-offs of Paco el Gaurriro.

"That was the husband of our Rita. When they married they lived downtown on Calle San Juan, and, of course, Rita left the stage. What a couple they were, she in her elegant fringed shawl and jewels to the point of excess, and he with his Cuban cigars. Everywhere they went people stopped to stare at them. They went nightly to the cafés and never missed a *corrida*...they reserved the same two seats in the bullring every Sunday. Rita was crazy about the *toreo* of Cuchares.

"This was some years ago, for, one night back in '81, La Mejorana came to Málaga to dance in Café de Chinitas. Tonio, you remember what I told you about Rosario la Mejorana...well, she was at the height of her fame..."

"*Malhaya sea la Mejorana!* [Damned be La Mejorana!]" cursed Curro Dulce. "If it weren't for her, Rita would still be alive! And she had no shame. If my woman were to raise her arms like that, I would beat her until she could no longer lift them!"

"*Hombre*, times change," said El Águila. "Everybody dances like that now. Even the Ortegas have copied her..."

"In my day, women knew how to dance with tradition, and modesty. You won't see my daughters dancing like that..."

Paquiro interrupted, "*Hombre*, La Mejorana was the most important figure of her time, after the retirement of Gabriela and Rita... *guapísima* [beautiful], *un peaso é mujé* [a real hunk of a woman]. She was dancing in El Chinitas and she challenged Rita from the stage. Rita accepted the challenge. She removed her shoes, mounted the stage, and the two of them went at it *mano a mano* [in hand to hand combat]. First one, then the other, with the crowd taking sides...El Guarriro and the Malagueños cheering for Rita, foreigners and those taken by the beauty of Rosario supporting the Gaditana. Neither would give in...until Rita suddenly fell to the floor in a faint. At first they thought it was only the strain of the unaccustomed effort, but with time she grew thinner and weaker."

Paquiro grew pensive with his memory. "In July of the next year, our Rita ceased to exist. Málaga mourned her, and Paco el Guarriro retired, grief-stricken, to his butcher shop. He never returned to the Plaza de la Malagueta, but reserved their customary front row seats for every *corrida*. Even when the plaza was sold out, the two seats remained empty behind a black shawl with white embroidery draped over the railing...that's how much he loved her and grieved for her. Before he died, El Guarriro composed this *copla* that they still sing in the Café de Chinitas:"

Ya se murió mi Rita bonita;	My pretty Rita has died;
ya se murió mi tesoro de oro;	my treasure of gold has died
no tengo quien me diga:	now I have no one to say to me:
"Paco, llévame a los toros!"	"Paco, take me to the bullfight!"

After a moment of respectful silence, Paquiro, seeking to lighten the mood, said, "Come on, José, sing some *cantiñas* for us."

José, only too happy to show off his specialty, began to rap out the rhythm of the *alegrías* on the table top with his knuckles and fingernails: Then he sang:

El sentío me da vueltas	You are driving me crazy
compañerita de mi arma;	girlfriend of my soul
el sentío me da vueltas;	you are driving me crazy;
yo me arrimo a las paeres	I have to hold onto the walls
que hasta que llego a tu puerta.	until I reach your doorway.
Que con el aire que lleva	For with that air that you have
que cuando va navegando	when you go "navigating,"
que y el farol de la cola	that lantern in your "stern"
tú me lo vas apagando.	is being extinguished on me.

"José, that *juguetillo* [little plaything[3]] is not yours," said Paquiro.

"No, *hombre*, of course not! That is one of La Mejorana's. Here is another one of hers that has a lot of *gracia*:

Yo tiré un limón por alto	I threw a lemon into the air
por ver si coloreaba;	to see if it would change color;
subió verde y bajó verde,	it went up green and it came down [green;]
qué las fatigas me ahogan.	I'm drowning in sorrow.

---

[3]Early *alegrías* were called *juguetillos*; later, the word referred to lively four-line verses tacked on to the end of the *alegrías letra* (the last four lines of this song). Today they are called *coletillas* [little endings].

"And *por alegrías?*" asked Chacón, fascinated by skill of these Gaditanos in the *cante* of their homeland.

"The one who really sings the *alegrías* is El Mellizo...he's the one who first began to sing the *jota de Cádiz*," continued José. "There was a woman who used to come around with her husband and two children and she was always playing a triangle and singing the *jota*.[4] Well, Enrique said, 'I'm going to sing that for dancing,' and he came out singing the *jota por alegrías*, like this:

Qué no quiere ser francesa;	She doesn't want to be French;
la Virgen de Pilar dice	the Virgin of Pilar says
qué no quiere ser francesa;	she doesn't want to be French;
qué quiere ser capitana	she wants to be captain
de las tropas aragonesas.	of the troops of Aragón

Paquiro interrupted José, "What about Quiqui? Some say Enrique learned from him."

"No, *hombre*, he learned from Enrique."

"Antonio, do you know Quiqui?" asked Paquiro.

Chacón shook his head.

"He's a *gitano* with a lot of *gracia*. The other day he and I were having drinks when this gentleman, a friend of his comes in, very serious, and says, '*Hombre*, Quiqui, can you do me a favor?'

"Quiqui says, 'Whatever you wish, *hombre*.'

"'Look, does this seem right to you, Quiqui? Do you think this is right?'

"'*Pero*, what's going on, *hombre?*'

"The *señorito* takes out a folded piece of paper and opens it. Quiqui can't read but he can see that it contains a long list of names with a number after each one. 'Look, Quiqui, this guy owes me fifty *reales*, this one five *pesetas*, Juan here owes me twenty *reales*, this guy forty...'

"Quiqui listened without saying a word until his friend finished reading the list and asked, '*Amigo* Quique, I don't know what to do.'

"The *gitano* thought a moment, then said, '*Bueno, hombre*, that's all well and good...*pero*, why don't you lend me twenty *reales* and put

---

[6] *jota*: a folk song from northern Spain danced by groups and couples with soft shoes, a lot of jumping, and castanet playing. When put to the rhythm of *soleá*, the *jota* gave the *alegrías* its verse structure, melodies, accompaniment for footwork, and the part of the dance called the *silencio*.

me at the bottom of the list?'"

Laughter. A fresh plate of sliced ham arrived at the table. The tavern-keeper, fearing a let-down in the festive mood, sought to keep the drinks flowing—at the expense of the winery representative, each round carefully noted in chalk on the bar.

Suddenly a dark shadow filled the doorway of the tavern. El Gordo Ortega stepped into the room and it immediately seemed smaller. "What's going on?" he said as he settled his ample girth into a chair.

"Enrique, we're here with the Jerezano people are talking about."

El Gordo's eyes slowly adapted to the dim light and he noticed Chacón for the first time. "Antonio, how's it going?"

"You know each other?"

"*Hombre*, we met last week in the place where he's singing. El Mellizo took me there. He sings well."

While the men made small talk, Chacón studied Enrique el Gordo. Only middle aged, he already personified the epitome of the gypsy patriarch. With the passing of his father, El Gordo Viejo, only a few years earlier, he had become the head of the Ortega clan of gypsy *cantaores*, *bailaores*, and toreros. He sat erect in his chair, head held high with a look of arrogance that dismisses, eyes peering out from under a wide, flat-brimmed hat. Dark coppery skin, a strong nose, and full lips indicated a true member of the gypsy race. His fleshy neck bulged over a white shirt closed at the collar, and the buttons on his rumbled jacket strained to contain his bear-like body.

Conversation went on for some time, family members getting caught up with each other and mentioning names unfamiliar to the Jerezano. Then El Águila turned to Chacón and said, "*Chaval*, sing something for us. Sing those *soleares* again, for Enrique."

Chacón sang *soleares* of Loco Mateo and some of El Mellizo. When he had finished, El Gordo said, "Well sung, *chaval*. Those are not easy, those new *soleares*. But I still like the old *soleares*, the ones you can dance…the *soleá jaleo*, as we used to call them. Like those of Paquirri el Guanté and the way Silverio used to sing them. You know, my father and Silverio were very good friends."

Without further words, El Gordo rapped his *vara* on the rung of the chair between his open thighs and tuned his voice briefly with some short *ayes*. The voice was rich and deep, with just a touch of *rajo*. He leaned in toward Chacón, resting a meaty hand on the Jerezano's thigh, and sang:

Dises que soy mar gachó,	You say I am an evil *gachó*,
siendo yo má gitaniyo	when I am more gypsy
que las costiyas de Dió.	than the ribs of God.
Chiquiya, tú eres mu loca;	Girl, you are very crazy;
eres como las campanas	you are like the bells
que toíto er mundo toca.	that everybody rings.
En un cuartito los dos,	If we two were in a room
veneno que tú me dieras,	and you were to offer me poison,
veneno tomara yo.	I would drink the poison.

El Gordo sang softly and calmly, almost as if speaking. The flamencos had the saying, "*decir el cante*," speak the *cante*. The singers in Cádiz did not forge their *cante* on stage, in noisy cafés where strength was essential to being heard. They did not shout their *cante*, but pronounced it gently and delicately, savoring the melodies in their mouths almost as if tasting the words. The *reunión* was an intimate ritual in which they sang to each other. The *cantaor* leaned in toward his neighbor, his hand resting on the other's thigh or shoulder briefly, as if to say, "Listen to this!" He sang as if confiding in the other, as if sharing a secret. When finished, he sat up straight, beaming, and perhaps turned to the man on the other side to offer another *letra*.

Sometimes they competed, exchanging *letras* one after the other, faces close enough to feel each other's breath. This closeness confined and built the heat of the *reunión*, sometimes creating a vortex that spun into moments of communal ecstasy and frenzy.

These men had sung the same *cantes*, the same verses, for each other dozens, if not hundreds, of times. Yet it was always new, as if for the first time. Details changed, melodies evolved, and new ideas sprang forth. Sometimes, in moments of inspiration, something completely new appeared, as if by magic, as if taken from the air. Those were the moments they waited for, the reason they continued to gather and to sing.

El Gordo's verses, already filled with the bitterness of unrequited love typical of the *soleares*, took a downward turn as he continued:

De pena me estoy muriendo	I am dying from this suffering,
al ver que en er mundo bibes	seeing that you live in this world
y ya, para mí, t'has muerto.	while, for me, you have died.

> *Cuando paso por tu puerta,*   When I pass by your door,
> *te reso un Ave María,*   I pray an Ave Maria,
> *como si estuvieras muerta.*   as if you were dead
>
> *En er simenterio entré;*   I entered into the cemetery;
> *lebanté una losa negra,*   I lifted up a black tile
> *y me encontré con tu queré.*   and there I encountered your love.

The gathering grew silent for some moments, a natural lull brought on by the *cante*, food, and drink. Caught up in the tranquility of the moment, Chacón began to sing softly, almost under his breath, one of Silverio's *letras por siguiriya*:

> *Me desían a mí*   They used to ask me,
> *que si te quiero güena compañera;*   if I love you, dear girl friend;
> *yo digo que sí.*   I say yes.

It was a simple verse, sung simply. A *cantaor* often used these short three-line verses to catch his breath. For Chacón it was a way to warm-up. He followed with another:

> *Déjame que vea*   Allow me to see
> *los ojos grandes e mi mare*   my mother's big eyes
> *una ves siquiera.*   one more time, if you will.

The subject of the verse had deepened, as had the *cantaor*'s interpretation. The others in the room began to respond, saying softly, "*Eso...bien, hombre!*"

Now at full voice, Chacón continued:

> *A las dos de la noche*   At two in the morning,
> *los campanilleros, con el ruío*   the *campanilleros*, with the noise
> *[de las campanitas,]*   [of their little bells,]
> *me quitan el sueño.*   won't let me sleep.

When Chacón threw himself into the *seguiriyas* of Manuel Molina, "*Dices que duermes sola...*" with its huge *ayes* and tortuous *tercios*, he carried the whole room with him. Paquiro leaned close, patting the rhythm on his thigh and whispering, "*Ala, Antonio...eso, viva Jeré!*" Others did mute *palmas* or twisted in their chairs and contorted their faces as they fought through the *cante* with the singer. Only Curro Dulce sat impassively.

When Chacón had finished and slumped in his chair, there was only a soft *"Bien..."* from Paquiro, and then silence. Chacón took the silence as a compliment. He had been accepted into this circle of gypsies from the Barrio de Santa María.

"Chaval, where did you learn the *letra 'Dices que duermes sola'?"* It was Curro Dulce, who had remained stone-faced and silent throughout much of the afternoon.

Startled, Chacón replied, "It is the *seguiriya* of *El Señor* Manuel Molina. I learned it in Jerez..."

"Certainly not from Manolo himself, may he rest in peace...from La Cherna, perhaps?"

"No, from Juan Torre."

"Ah, El Torre! Do you know that *letra* is mine? Manolo did it his way, but he learned it from me..."

El Gordo interrupted, "You know *chaval,* Molina used to come here often. He and Curro were good friends at one time. We have a *cante por soleá* that says:

Juntitos íban los tres:	The three used to go together:
Curro Durse, Vallares,	Curro Dulce, Vallares,
y Molina er de Jerez.	and Molina, he of Jerez.

Curro Dulce was not through. "And the *letra* of *los campanilleros,* that is mine also..."

"But I was told that it is Silverio's..."

"If Silverio sings it, then he got it from me. He has a good ear and we were often in fiestas together."

"Tonio," interrupted Paquiro, "have you heard what Silverio said about our Curro? *Mira,* when someone asked Silverio 'Who sings better than you?' he replied, 'Better than me? Better than me, nobody!' But when the other continued to press him, saying 'Well then, who is next best, after you?' Silverio answered, 'After me? Sometimes Curro Durse.'"

"Silverio!" grunted Curro in a tone of dismissal. *"Ese gachó canta que le parte los huesos a su puñatera mare, pero no tiene el gusto de que yo le diga ole!"* [The way that *gacho* sings is enough to break the bones of your damned mother, but he'll never have the pleasure of hearing me say *ole!*]

Curro vented his anger on the clay tile floor, rapping it with his *vara* to the *compás* of *seguiriyas*. Then, unexpectedly, he came forth with a tremendous "*Ayyyyiiii...*"

Chacón was stunned. Such power from the old man. And then the gypsy repeated the two verses that Chacón had sung. He began each with a short and sober *tercio* and then followed with a very long and difficult *ay*. The remainder of each *letra* developed with minutely ornamented details—complex, yet filled with bravura, suffering, and dark beauty. The melodies of these two verses clearly bore some similarity to those that Chacón had sung, but there could be no doubt that Curro had a unique style all his own. The Jerezano was mesmerized. Here was the voice that he had, without realizing it, been searching for throughout his travels. There was no trace of the gypsy *rajo*. The man sang as clearly as any *gachó*, with a natural voice. Here was the *cante gitano* sung with intense emotion and expression, but without the *voz afillá* that branded the style of most gypsies.

Curro Dulce continued:

Ay, ay...y era una madrugá	Ay, ay, it was the dawn
de Santiago y Santa Ana;	of the holiday of Santiago [and Santa Ana;]
ay, ay...a eso de la una	ay, ay...at about one o'clock
[*las fatiguitas grandes le diñaron*]	[they gave this great suffering]
a mi mare, Curra.	to my mother, Curra.
Hermana mía, Dolores,	My sister, Dolores,
dile al hermano Diego	tell our brother Diego
que me llame un confesorcito;	to call me a confessor;
confesarme quiero.	I want to confess.

The gypsies in the room wound themselves into a frenzy listening to these last two *cantes*. Paquiro had ripped the buttons from his shirt and was clawing at his chest. El Águila leaped from his chair and began stomping his feet, squeezing his head between his hands. Glasses shattered as men yelled, "No, no, it's impossible...Mother of God, help me...What is this...It can't be!" These men had heard Curro sing many times, but the man had gone beyond himself on this occasion...and the long afternoon of drinking had been building to this moment.

Chacón, moved to tears, felt all of his self-doubts swept aside. If

Curro Dulce, with his clear, clean voice, free of *rajo*, could be so expressive and moving, then he, Antonio Chacón, a *gachó*, had nothing to apologize for. He had been criticized often for the deficiency in his voice, yet here was one of the most revered *cantaores* singing in a natural voice. Curro had it all—rich tones, expression, and a sweet musicality that had earned him the nickname *Dulce*. Chacón knew he had to learn from the man. At the first opportunity, he said, "Maestro, I am moved by your singing...you are a giant in the *cante*. There is so much I could learn from you."

Curro remained aloof and did not respond to the hint. Hesitantly, Chacón tried again. "Maestro, would you teach me?"

The old man studied the Jerezano a moment before responding. "*Chaval*, you sing well. In some ways you remind me of myself when I was your age. But, I teach no one...no *gachó* and no *gitano*...except for my sons." Then he raised his glass to his mouth and turned his attention elsewhere.

Chacón knew he had been dismissed and there would be no further discussion of the matter. He was heartbroken. He had found the *cante* he had been seeking, but it was beyond his reach.

Seated next to Chacón, the winery representative had slumped in his chair. Clearly feeling the effects of all he had drunk, he had fallen into a despondent mood. He muttered to himself, "Everyone's dying in these *cantes!*" After a moment of thought, he added, *"Pues, muertos al hoyo, vivos al bollo!"* [dead into the hole, the living back to eating!]

Then, out loud, "*Oiga*, bring some more ham and bread, and another round of drinks!" The *montañés* brought out the food and drinks, then plucked the piece of chalk from behind his ear and carefully added to the bill scribbled on the bar.

Chacón glanced around, hoping no one had heard the comments, but he needn't have worried for suddenly a loud snoring attracted everyone's attention. Paquiro had fallen dead asleep, his head thrown back against the wall. At the sight of his friend, Chacón felt a sudden wave of fatigue settle over his body. He was completing a second day without sleep, and he still had to go to work.

"Work, *Dios mío!*" he exclaimed. "I have to go to work tonight. What time is it?" He reached into his vest pocket and withdrew the large brass watch he had purchased earlier in the week. "Nine o'clock...I have to go!" He started to get to his feet, saying, "*Señores*, with your permission..."

"No, *hombre*, don't go!" said El Águila. "You can't leave now."

"I'm late for work."

"Forget about work," mumbled Juan from the winery, just before his head drooped once more to his chest.

"Don't be such a *gachó*," grunted Paquiro, who had awakened with the commotion. "Have another drink to help you stay awake!"

"No, I must go," Chacón replied, breaking free of Paquiro's grasp on his arm.

The last thing the Jerezano heard as he made his way on unsteady feet toward the door was the *montañés* saying to the drunken winery representative, "*Hombre*, you have had a lot to drink. Come, let's take care of the bill and then I'll have my boy get you a carriage…"

Two nights later, Chacón, standing at the bar, watched as Paquiro and another man entered the café and headed toward him. The second man looked familiar, but the *cantaor* was certain they had not met.

"Antonio, I want you to meet someone," said Paquiro. "Juan, Antonio Chacón, the Jerezano I was telling you about. Antonio, Juan Fernández, Curro Durse's eldest son. He has just returned from Sevilla."

"Juan, I'm so pleased to meet you," exclaimed Chacón, thrilled to meet anyone connected with El Dulce. The man's strong resemblance to his father explained the sense of familiarity.

"I've spent a lot of time in your city, "said Juan. "Twenty years ago my father and I performed in Jerez, in the Teatro Principal, with La Cherna, El Barbero on guitar, and I don't remember who else. I've been back often since."

Before Chacón could respond, he was called to go on stage. Later, when he had finished singing, he found Juan waiting for him at the bar.

"*Muy bien, hombre!*" said the Gaditano. "Your *cante* reminds me of my father when he was younger. You may be lacking the touch of the *gitano*, but you have a clean sound and a lot of ability. Well done!"

"Your father's *cante* is something very special. I have never heard anything like it. I hope I have the chance to listen to him again. I'm done here…why don't we go somewhere else and have some drinks?"

In the days that followed, Chacón and Juan Fernández formed a warm friendship. They met and sang together often. Juan sang in a style very similar to that of his father and knew all of Curro Dulce's *cantes*. Unlike his father, he felt no reluctance to share his *cante* with

Antonio, and the Jerezano soaked up *soleares* and *seguiriyas* like a sponge.

One day, Juan asked, "Antonio, do you sing *la caña?*"

"Sarvaoriyo taught me the *caña* of Silverio. He told me that it is in the style of El Fillo."

"According to my father, there are few today who can sing *la caña* the way El Fillo did. It demands exceptional abilities, a lot of chest, if it is to come out well. In the old days the knowledgeable aficionados considered it a test of the *cantaor*. The *caña* of El Fillo was very long and gallant...and as a *macho* to finish the *cante* he would sing the entire *polo*. A lot of *cante*, and very difficult. I don't believe Silverio sings them that way now. He prefers *la caña* as they sing them here in Cáis, with the *aire* of José el Granaíno. José was a good *cantaor*, from Sanlúcar...in fact, the matadors Paquiro and Chiclanero took him with them more for his *cante* than for his abilities as a *banderillero*. Silverio learned this way of singing *la caña* from Enrique el Gordo and my father. Here is a *letra* that Silverio got from my father."

And with that, Juan launched, *a palo seco* [a capella], into a powerful and dramatic *cante*. Its link with some religious chant in the distant past clearly evident in the long descending *tercios* and melodies built on extended syllables. It lacked completely the wailing sobs and pain-filled *ayes* of the gypsy *cantes*. The liturgical lineage was further evidenced by prayer-like lament of *ay* that rose and fell at the end of the second and fourth lines of the verse:

El que siembra in mala tierra,	He who sows in poor soil,
que es lo que espera cojé?	what does he expect to reap?
Ay, ay, ay, ay, ay!	Ay, ay, ay, ay, ay!
Que el trigo se vuelva piedra	The wheat turns to stone
y no puea prevalesé.	and cannot thrive.
Ay, ay, ay, ay, ay!	Ay, ay, ay, ay, ay![5]

"Before Curro Durse," said Juan when he had finished, "they always sang '*Ah, ah, ah, ah, ah,*' or '*O, o,o,o,o,*' for the lament that follows the *letra*, but my father changed it to *ayes*, which are much more flamenco.

---

[5]This *caña* differed from that sung today in its livelier tempo, the repeat (when sung) of the entire first line rather than just the last word, and the way the lament of the *ayes* was connected to the preceding *tercio*; in the modern *caña*, the song stops completely before going into the *ayes* in a plodding, monotonous fashion.

He also told me that he remembers when the lament was sung in chorus by everyone present, but that was before my time. And we no longer sing the entire *polo* to close the *caña* as El Fillo did. El Gordo Viejo was the first to use only the ending of the *polo*...like this:

Arza y viva Ronda,	Long live Ronda,
reina de los cielos;	queen of the heavens;
y que no puea prevalecé,	and cannot thrive,
Ay...	Ay...

Catching his breath, Juan added, "You notice that you must always repeat the theme of the *caña* in this *macho por polo*."

The discussion of *cañas* and *polos* went on through the night. Juan passed on knowledge he had inherited from his father, about how these songs had been the mainstay of a *cantaor*'s repertoire when Curro and Silvero had been young men, along with the disappearing *tonás* that were predecessors of the *martinetes* and *seguiriyas*. "There were many styles of *cañas* and *polos*...from Jerez, Triana, Cáis, Los Puertos...and every *cantaor* had his own personal variation. But these days everyone prefers to sing *por soleá*, especially young people, and the old songs are being lost.

It saddened Chacón to think of the old *cante* disappearing, and he vowed to himself to learn all he could and to attempt to preserve and improve the old, pure songs.

Junquera

Chacón found El Mellizo in the patio of his home on Calle Miraflor, surrounded by a captivated audience of youths and ragged children. The *casa* showed traces of its former glory in the decorative ironwork, a massive hardwood staircase, and the marble columns that supported the upper floors. Like many of the *casas de vecinos* in Cádiz it had once, in some earlier century, been a palatial home. Time and poverty had reduced it to a communal home for a number of gypsy families. The carved railings were now chipped and broken, and a general aura of decay emanated from the dirt and clutter.

El Mellizo's mulish face broke into a broad smile at the sight of the Jerezano. "Antonio, *qué hay?* It's good to see you." He rose to embrace the Jerezano affectionately. "Come in, come in...I was just trying to pound some education into the heads of these *churumbeles* [children]."

Chacón found himself the object of intense scrutiny. A teenage boy slumped languidly against a marble column eying him with curiosity, while another studied him from his perch on the stairs. Some of the bevy of younger boys had risen from the dust to openly gawk at the visitor.

"Let's go have a drink," said El Mellizo.

A tiny voice interrupted the *cantaor* as he reached for his jacket. "*Tío*, you didn't finish the story."

El Mellizo looked down at the young boy tugging at his trousers. Placing a massive hand on the shoulder of the frail, dark-skinned child, he said in a gruff but kindly tone, "*Chiquillo*, I have a visitor..."

"But you promised..."

El Mellizo explained to Chacón. "This is Manoliyo, the son of El Águila." Then, looking down at the dirty face, he asked, "How old are you *niño?*"

The boy shrugged his shoulders.

"Well, he's five or six years old and already he's crazy about the *cante*. *Niño*, would you like to sing for us?"

The child shrugged again and said, "But aren't you leaving?"

El Mellizo laughed. "Antonio, let me finish the story. Then we'll get Manoliyo to sing for us and, afterward, we'll go have a drink. All of these children are aficionados of the *cante*." Indicating a boy of about twelve, he said, "This one is mine. Antoñito, come here and shake hands with your *tocayo* from Jerez. Perhaps someday you will sing as well as he. And Enrique, my youngest...we call him Hermosilla, after his godfather...he already has his *cantecitos*."

Pointing out two other teenage boys, El Mellizo continued, "Those two *chavales* are of my wife's family, the Espeletas. They are sons of El Pata." Indicating the fair-skinned youth leaning against the column, he added, "José, *el rubio* [the blond], sings well, and the other, there on the stairs, Ignacio, has *gracia* you can't imagine."[1]

Chacón couldn't help reflecting upon the fact that he was about the same age as the older Espeleta boy, yet there were years between them in experience. The Jerezano felt a smug satisfaction when he compared his jacket and vest with the threadbare clothes of the *gitanos*.

"You know," continued El Mellizo, "we are all one big family here in Santa María...the Jiménez, the Espeletas, and the Ortegas. *Mira* [Look here], José el Águila's woman, Rufina, is from the family of Curro Durse...Fernández and Espeleta. José's brother Juan is married into my family, to Carlota Jiménez. My woman, Ignacia, is an Espeleta. So all you hear in Santa María is Ignacio, Enrique, Rosario, Rita, Carlota...my mother was Carlota, and if I have daughter she will be Carlota..."

"The story, *Tío*," interrupted Manoliyo.

"*Sí, niño*, right now. Antonio, have a seat over here. I was telling

---

[1] This is the next generation of important *cantaores* in Cádiz: Antonio el Mellizo (twelve years old) and Enrique "Hermosilla"—to become deformed later into "Er Morcilla" [blood sausage] due to the inheritance of his father's unfortunate physical appearance—(nine years old) and the sons of Ignacio "El Pata" Espeleta, José *el Pollo Rubio* (seventeen) and Ignacio (fifteen).

these *churumbeles* that when I was a boy, a man showed me a book that said:

> In 1512, in *1512*, someone wrote flamenco sheet music...*flamenco sheet music!* On one sheet he put *soleá*, and on another, *seguiriya*, and on another, *malagueña*...
>
> And in that same year, in that same year of 1512, a schooner docked in the Bay of Cái. They began to take out the cargo that was destined for Cái, and when they had finished they discovered a strange trunk with no indication of origin or destination, *ni ná*. So they said, 'What can this be? What can it be? What can it not be? Let's see what it is!
>
> So they broke into the trunk and saw that it contained flamenco sheet music. *Flamenco sheet music!* 'Eh?' 'Oh!' *'Cante flamenco!'* And they took from the trunk all the best, *lo mejorcito*. Then they closed the trunk and sent it upriver to Jerez. In Jerez the same thing happened. They took out more flamenco sheet music, the best of what remained.
>
> In the same way, the trunk continued upward, *p'arriba, p'arriba*, to Sevilla, to Córdoba, to Málaga...until the trunk was empty. But the best of the trunk remained in Cái. That's why we sing better in Cái than any other place in Spain, and why the best artists have come from Cái and its province.[2]

Later, in a café on Calle Santa Elena, tucked in behind the bulwarks of Santa Elena that overlooked the bay near La Puerta de Tierra, Chacón and El Mellizo stood at the bar, where the Gaditano was saying, "That *malagueña* you sang the other night, the one of *la campana triste*, it reminded me of one of mine. Listen!"

And with that, the *cantaor* clutched Chacón's arm and sang directly into his face a *malagueña* with a short simple melody filled with sentimental sweetness. Unlike the intense grief shouted out in many *cantes*, this was like a sorrowful caress, with only the most subtle of adornments:

A mi me daba sentimiento,	It gave me such deep emotion
de querete toa mi vía.	to have loved you all of my life.
Pero yo paso el tormento	But I live with the torment
de que sé que no eres mía;	of knowing that you re not mine;
así voy pasando el tiempo.	thusly, I pass the time.

---

[2]J.L. Ortiz Nuevo, *Las Mil y Una Historias de Pericón de Cádiz*, p. 20.

Chacón had never heard anything so beautiful, so simple in its sentiment and delivery. The gentle but haunting melodies had fallen effortlessly from El Mellizos lips like tears.

Warming up and responding to the encouragement of others in the café, El Mellizo threw himself into a much grander and more intense *cante*, the *malagueña doble*:

Loco…y no sentir.	Crazy…and unfeeling.
Yo quisiera del momento…	I wish in this moment…
ayiii…ayiii, ayiii…	ayeee…ayeee, ayeee…
estar loco y no sentir.	to be crazy and unable to feel.
Porque sentir…porque sentir	Because to feel…because to feel
[*causa pena*]	[causes suffering,]
ayiii…ayiii, ayiii…	ayeee…ayeee, ayeee…
tanto que no tiene fin,	suffering so great it has no end,
y el loco vive…sin ella…	and the insane man lives without that…
ayiii…ayiii, ay, ayiii…	ayeee…ayeee, ay, ayeee

The drama and intense beauty of this *cante* left the listeners emotionally drained and almost as exhausted as the *cantaor*. Chacón, with moist eyes, said, "Maestro, what inspiration! Where do you find those melodies?"

"I don't know *chaval*, they just come out of me."

"In this *cante grande* that you have just sung, you began with only a piece of the verse, like El Canario…"

"Yes, with the broken first line, in the manner of El Canario. How beautiful, *verdad?* [isn't it so?]…to sing them like that, beginning with just a few words. *Loco y no sentir*…and everything is prepared for the rest of the *cante*. El Canario was a genius, a revolutionary. He sang here in Sevilla only one year before he was killed, but in that one year he completely changed this *cante* of his homeland. I went as often as I could to listen to him…"

"Was he more important than Juan Breva?"

"Breva? El Breva never sang *malagueñas*. He sang those *fandanguillos* of his and he went to Madrid where they called them *malagueñas*, because he came from Málaga. No, El Breva never sang *por malagueñas*."

"If El Canario was only here for a year, how did the *malagueña* come here, to Cádiz and Sevilla?"

"*Hombre*, El Canario sang for years in Málaga before he came here. Many others learned from him and brought his *cante* to us...surely you have heard of La Bocanegra, Concha la Peñaranda, La Rubia..."

"Yes, I have heard them in Sevilla..."

"They brought us the *malagueñas*, along with others who went from here to sing in Málaga and learned the *cante* there. But El Canario was the best. What a shame he had to die so young...may he rest in peace! Have you heard this *letra* of his...he sang it when he came back to Sevilla from Madrid?"

El Mellizo sang:

Las gentes...	People...
Por el hablar de las gentes	According to what people say
olvidastes mi querer,	you forgot my love;
pero ten por entendido	but understand
que me va a costar la muerte	that having known you
el haberte conocío.	is going to cost me my life.

The lyrical beauty of this *cante* touched Chacón deeply. He said, "That was beautiful maestro...please sing it again!"

El Mellizo responded, "It is a good *cante* for you to know. It can teach you a great deal."

El Mellizo sang. Then Chacón imitated him. Teacher and student alternated through the afternoon, oblivious to those around them in the café.

Chacón was entering the most creative period of his life, exploding with ideas that had been fermenting in his fertile mind and now found release through his contact with El Mellizo. Within days of his meeting with the maestro, he had created two new *malagueñas*, based upon those he had heard in the café on Calle Santa Elena. The first was patterned on the simple *copla* the Gaditano had sung that afternoon. The melody had haunted him during the days and awakened him at night until, while wandering through the gardens of the Alameda during the final days of the Velada, he found his own words to express it:

> *Yo entré en el jardín de Venus* I entered the garden of Venus
> *a buscar la flor que amaba,* to search for the flower I loved,
> *y me encontré a la lis morena,* and I found a dark-skinned fleur-de-lis,
> *que era lo que buscaba,* the one I had been seeking,
> *la que me aliviara la pena.* the one that would alleviate my
>   [suffering.]

The flow of the song and its gentleness were like the *cante* of El Mellizo, but in Chacón's flexible voice the melodies found new shapes, with subtle variations and moments in which they took flight like gentle gusts of breeze and then settled softly to rest at the ends of the *tercios*.

Chacón was determined to create a *malagueña grande* as majestic as the *doble* of El Mellizo, yet without imitating his maestro. He experimented with developing each *tercio* to the maximum, extending them and filling them with melodic tension. He exploited the device of the sudden rise and fall of melody at the end of the *tercios* and used held vowel sounds to embroider his phrases with elaborate adornment. The painful memory of María served to inspire a passionate verse for this *cante*:

> *Que te quise con locura.* Never in my life will I deny
> *Yo en mi vía...* that I was crazy with desire for you.
> *a...negaré* Look at what a love it was,
> *que yo te quise con locura.* That I still feel the heat
> *Mira que* that I had for your love.
> *cariño fué...é*
> *que siento...o*
> *la calentura...*
> *que tuve po...r tu queré...*[3]

Enrique el Mellizo, flattered to be the source of Chacón's inspiration, listened with awe at the manner in which the young *cantaor* carried out his ideas. The voice was full, resonant, and powerful, with complete control of subtle nuances. Equally important, the melodies were developed with intelligence and creativity. For his part, Chacón was relieved to have El Mellizo's confirmation that he had created something worthwhile and original.

---

[3] In the Spanish version of this *letra*, I have attempted to give a rough picture of how Chacón created nine *tercios* out of five lines of verse. To attempt this in English would have been awkward at best.

By the end of the Velada, Chacón had completely immersed himself in the *cante* and the flamenco atmosphere of Cádiz. "You must learn and master all the styles," Salvaoriyo had said. With that motivation, Chacón sought every opportunity to listen to the Ortegas and Curro Dulce. He never tired of listening to Curro, convinced that in the *cante* of the venerable *cantaor* lay the key to his own success in the *cante gitano*. Curro's *seguiriyas*, in particular, were especially suited to the natural way of singing, without the *rajo* of the *voz afillá*.

Rare was the day that Chacón did not find himself in the home of El Mellizo. Often he had to wait hours for the *cantaor* to return from the municipal slaughterhouse located near the barrio. Many of the gypsy men of Santa María did the difficult and dirty work in the slaughterhouse, while their wives and daughters worked in the tobacco factory. In the streets and cafés in the mornings, gypsies sold *destrozos*, the rejected parts of the cattle—head, feet, and entrails. The first time Chacón heard a gypsy woman cry out, "*Carne de bragueta*" [meat of the trouser fly], he had to ask the meaning. El Mellizo's wife, Ignacia, explained: "In the slaughterhouse, when the foreman is not looking, our men slice off a piece of beef...the best parts, you know...and put into their fly. It falls down to their ankles, here where their underpants tie at the ankles. *Aluego* [later], they bring it home to the women and we sell it as 'fly meat'...the best meat there is, for much less than it costs in the market."

Often El Mellizo arrived home late, after stopping in the Church of Santa María or the cathedral to listen to Mass, or passing the evening in that other sanctuary, the local *tienda*, for the ritual of a glass of wine. Once, he disappeared for three days. But such was his enthusiasm for his new student that, more often than not, he kept his appointments with the youth.

Late one afternoon, Chacón entered the now familiar corner room, with balconies on Calles Miraflor and Botica, to find a surprise that elicited a broad smile of delight. "Francisco, *hombre!* What are you doing here?"

Fosforito had changed in the three years since Chacón had last seen him. No longer a gangly youth, he appeared much older than his seventeen years. "Antonio, *qué hay, hombre?* It's been a long time."

The two embraced. Chacón strained his neck to meet the gaze of his friend. Fosforito had grown even taller.

"What are you doing here? How long have you been in Cái?" asked Chacón.

"*Hombre*, my family lives here. I have a break before I go back to work, so I came for a visit. I've been hired by Manuel Ojeda to sing in the Burrero when it opens in September. Yesterday I heard that you were in Cái...and here I am!"

Chacón felt a pang of envy on hearing that his friend would be singing in the prestigious Café del Burrero in Sevilla. When would his turn come? At the same time, he thought he detected something that he did not remember in Fosforito. Behind the broad smile, his face had matured and revealed the struggle to survive as an artist. But there seemed to be something beyond that. In the heavy drooping brows and the downturned mouth, a serious note belied the easygoing joviality of the Gaditano.

The two exchanged stories until El Mellizo joined them and insisted that they bless Fosforito's return with drinks. Throughout the evening and into the night there could be no topic of conversation other than the *cante*. Scarcely did one youth finish singing a *letra* than the other could not hold back and burst into song.

In the days that followed, the Mellizo home became a genuine academy of *cante*. El Mellizo would listen to them, coach them, correct them, and accept nothing but complete honesty in their singing. He told them, "The *cante* is feeling. In the *cante* the only thing of value is the gush of emotion that is so strong that it hurts inside. Whether one sings well or poorly, according to one's abilities, is not so important. He who feels the *cante*, will cry with the *cante*. El Viejo de la Isla... Antonio, do you know El Viejo...Pedro, María Borrico's brother? No? Well, you must learn his *seguiriyas*...El Viejo used to say, 'You don't have to do all those things with the *cante*, making it fancy and complicated. You have only to *quejarse* [sob, moan with grief].'"

When Fosforito learned of Chacón's experiments with the *malagueña*, he became caught up in the fervor of creativity. For days there was thought of nothing but *malagueña*. *Coplas* were created, improved, or rejected in an exchange of ideas and melodies. However, in spite of this interchange of influences, the *malagueñas* of Chacón and Fosforito never came to resemble each other. Where Chacón's music displayed virtuosity and imagination, Fosforito developed a sweet musicality, emphasizing bass tones and saturated with profound melancholy. Chacón began to see that his friend had lived through experiences that deeply influenced his *cante*. It was especially true in his *letras*. When Chacón express grief or sadness in a verse, there was almost always hope of resolution or a clever twist in the poetry. Fosforito was obsessed with sadness, but not the sadness of grief, pain, or desperation. Out of grief, pain, and desperation can come strength and hope, but Fosforito's *cante* expressed the profound sadness of melancholy, of indifference, a negation of all hope. Out of weary indifference can come nothing.

Thus, Chacón sang:

En la tumba de mi madre	At the tomb of my mother
a dar gritos me ponía,	I began to cry out,
y escuché un eco del viento:	and I heard an echo in the wind:
"No la llames," me decía,	"Don't call out to her," it was saying,
"qué no responden los muertos!"	"for the dead don't answer!"

While Fosforito came back with:

Yo canto de noche y día;	I sing night and day;
mi voz a naide conmueve.	my voice touches nobody.
Soy como el ave fría	I am like a cold bird
que canta sobre la nieve,	that sings in the snow,
llorando las penas mías.	crying out my grief.

Yo soy como el arbol solo	I am like a lonely tree
que está en medio del camino;	on a road far from anywhere;
no tengo calor de naide;	I have the warmth of no one;
maldito sea mi sino,	cursed be my fate,
que a sufrir, no hay quien	for, in suffering, no one can
[*me iguale.*]	[equal me.]

From the sharing of ideas came similar verses. Chacón sang:

Si tú no me has de querer,	If you are not going to love me,
a que tanto me consientes?	to what end do you string me along?
Mátame ya, de una vez,	Kill me now, all at once,
porque yo te perdono la muerte,	because I can forgive you for the death,
qué ya no quiero padecer.	but I don't want to suffer any longer.

Fosforito responded with:

Si me dan en mi agonía   If, in my final agony, they offered
la vía por aborrecerte,   me life if only I would hate you,
yo no lo consentiría.   I wouldn't agree to it.
Prefiero mejor la muerte   I would prefer death
a vivir sin tí en mi vía.   to living without you in my life.

This theme appeared again when Fosforito created his *malagueña grande*. The profound melancholy of this *malagueña* moved Chacón and El Mellizo to tears of admiration. Chacón held his breath as Fosforito pushed his lungs to the bursting point in order to crown the second-to-the-last *tercio*, a *tercio* of marvelously varied modulation, as unusual in its conception as it was perfect in its execution:

Desde…que te conocí,   Ever since I met you,
mi corazón llora sangre;   my heart cries blood;
yo me…quisiera morir,   I wish that I could die,
porque mi pena es tan grande   because my suffering is so great
que no puedo vivir sin tí.   that I can't live without you.

Darkness permeated Fosforito's *cante*—not the shadows of night, but the shadows of the grave, from which there could be no hope of return. His *cante* was a funeral hymn of the soul, of a soul isolated and consuming itself. From the content of his *letras*, Chacón came to suspect that the sobriety and sadness he had detected under the *cantaor*'s jovial exterior was the result of bitter experiences with love.

After Fosforito left for Sevilla and the Café del Burrero in early September, Chacón began to accompany El Mellizo on evening strolls along the wharf. The city of Cádiz sloped downward toward the bay to meet the gently sweeping curve of the waterfront. Here, facing the placid water of the harbor, docks replaced the steep sea walls that held back the waves crashing in off the Atlantic Ocean.

Leaving the labyrinth of the Barrio de Santa María, the two men would enter the wide Plaza de San Juan de Dios, an immense, open cobbled space, bordered on three sides by four and five story government buildings, hotels, and cafés. They usually traversed this plaza at a leisurely pace, for El Mellizo inevitably encountered acquaintances among the many loiterers occupying iron benches that ran in two long parallel rows down the center. From the plaza, the gateway of La Puerta del Mar offered passage through the city wall onto a broad expanse of cobblestone that curved gently along the waterfront. Directly in front of the gateway, two tall marble columns supported statues of the patron saints San Servando and San Germán. According to El Mellizo, the area served as an underground exchange. He pointed out several shady characters huddled about the base of the statues, speaking in hushed whispers, and he assured Chacón that they were almost certainly negotiating the barter or passage of contraband goods, with ever an eye cocked for the *carabinero*. Legitimate sales took place further up, along the wall near Puerta de Sevilla and the customs house, where prices were regulated for the sale of goods that arrived in port—coffee from Puerto Rico or Columbia, sugar, cacao, and spices.

Behind the two *cantaores*, tall white buildings and the domed towers of the Cathedral rose up beyond the crenellated fortifications of the city. In front of them, tall sailing ships rocked gently in their moorings, dwarfing the tiny *falucho* fishing boats that dotted the harbor, their gracefully curved, swept-back masts reminiscent of ancient vessels of the Nile.

On a tranquil and balmy late summer evening, Chacón and El Mellizo chatted over drinks in an open-air café on the pier. The moon had come up over the mainland to silhouette the riggings of the ships and reflect with an unearthly shimmer on the calm water. Several groups of men celebrated noisily over wine and oysters, all but drowning out the sound of water lapping at ships hulls and the occasional cry of sea birds. El Mellizo jerked his head toward one of the groups.

"*Mira*, you see that man...the one doing all the talking?"

Chacón nodded. A slight, well-dressed man was the center of attention at the next table.

"That's El Nene...a *pupilero*."

"A what?"

"He brings clients to the *casas de muchachas* [brothels]...here we say *pupilero*. Most likely, he has already had success today, when the ship came in, and he's back looking for more business."

Almost as if on command, the group of men paid their account and filed out of the café behind El Nene.

"The man has *gracia*," continued El Mellizo. "When a ship comes in, he finds out as much as possible about the voyage and then mingles with the passengers as they disembark, pretending to be one of them. He says, 'What a good crossing we had...although there for a while there, in the gulf, I thought I might not see my Cái again!'

"The passenger says, 'Ah, you know Cadiz?'

"'*Sí, hombre*, I know Cái like the palm of my hand...in fact, I seem to recall that right over there, nearby, was a house where we could find some women and enjoy ourselves for a while...'

"Then, they agree and go to the house, where the madam offers them a room, brings in the girls and the wine, and sends for a *cantaor* and a guitarist. *Venga muchachas, venga vino, venga cante*...until the *pupilero* says, '*Bueno, señores*, that is enough fiesta for today. Let's settle the account.' The madam brings the bill and the *pupilero* divides the amount among all involved, including himself. They pay and go their separate ways, but a half hour later the *pupilero* is back at the house to recover his money, along with a commission."

"*Qué gracia!*" And then, after a pause, " Maestro, I need to ask your advice. It's time for me to find work and I don't know if I should look here or go back to Jerez."

"Antonio, I have an idea. I know the owner of a *café cantante* near here, over on the Plaza del Cañón. Let's go and see if he will hire you."

The owner of the café had heard Chacón sing and conceived the idea of presenting him in competition with El Mellizo. Enrique, reluctant to surrender his independence, resisted the idea at first, but relented when he realized what the opportunity would mean to his young disciple. So it was that, in early September, the two singers appeared nightly in the Café de la Paz. First, Chacón would go out with Maestro Patiño, and then El Mellizo with his favorite guitarist, Manuel Pérez "El Pollo." Enthusiastic friends and supporters of El Mellizo often drowned out the final *tercios* of his *cantes* with their impassioned applause. Yet, in spite of hometown favoritism, there could be no denying the impact of the young Jerezano. Many a knowledgeable aficionado had to shake his head in amazement at the originality, the emotional sensitivity, and the vocal virtuosity of Antonio Chacón. In the intervals between the performances, aficionados hotly debated the merits of each *cantaor*.

Early one evening, Chacón sat lost in thought at a table in the café. Although he was pleased with the progress of his career, it had occurred to him that he had no idea what he might do next. The sound of his name roused him from thought and he looked up to see a man coming toward him. There could be no mistaking the portly figure of Juan Junquera.

"Antonio, *qué hay, hombre?* It's been a long time." Junquera gripped Chacón's hand firmly while giving his shoulder a squeeze of familiarity.

"How are you *Señor* Junquera?" replied Chacón with cool correctness. "Sit down and have a drink. What brings you to Cái?"

"Looking for artists, as always. I need to speak with Patiño. Your friends, Javier and Antonio send their regards."

"How are they?"

"Well. They just went back to work in the café, in the Vera Cruz. Excellent artists...hard working and dependable."

After a round of drinks and more small talk, Junquera said, "Antonio, I need someone for my café in Utrera, during the Feria de la Consolación, which begins in a couple of weeks. I think you can handle it...and I'll pay you whatever they are paying you here."

"I don't know," replied Chacón indifferently. "I'm very contented here, and they pay me well. Utrera is far away, too far to go for a few day's work...and then what?"

"I'm sure I could find you something else afterward. Of course, if you are not interested...there are many others looking for work who would jump at the chance to become better known..."

"That's true, *Don* Juan. You shouldn't have any trouble finding someone."

Junquera emptied his glass and made as if to rise from the table. Then he dropped back into the chair and laughed, "You drive a hard bargain, Antonio, but for old time's sake, and because you are a *paisano* [from same city], I will pay you twelve *pesetas* a night...that's more than anyone is earning. What do you say?"

Chacón barely heard these words. They were drowned out by the stinging memory of other words: "You won't do, *NENE!*" It took a moment for him to realize that Junquera was asking him a question.

"Can I count on you, Antonio?"

"*Hombre,* it's not the money. It just doesn't interest me...I like it here in Cái." Chacón didn't know what Junquera had heard about him to create such interest, but he was reveling in the power he felt at the moment.

The young *cantaor* glanced toward the bar, nodded his head in that direction, and then directed himself once more to Junquera. "With your permission, *Don* Juan, it's time for me to go on. Thank you for the generous offer!"

As Chacón seated himself on the stage beside Maestro Patiño,

Junquera was struck by the realization that this was not the Antonio Chacón he had known. The young *cantaor* radiated success in his manner and the elegance of his dress. The erect posture of the stocky body, head held high, and the firm rap of his *vara de estilo* on the floor suggested a strong sense of direction, commitment, and confidence.

Chacón sang *por soleá*, with a warm reception from the rowdy public. It was evident that he had won some regular admirers in Cádiz. But when he began *por malagueñas*, to a roar of approval, Junquera sat up. The impresario sensed that something out of the ordinary was happening in the Café de la Paz. He couldn't be certain exactly what it was, but the clear tenor voice, powerful, flexible, and expressive, the unfamiliar melodies, original and delicately flowing in cascades of notes, and the intense emotional impact of the delivery, convinced him that he was witnessing the birth of something significant in the *cante*.

When Chacón returned to the table, he found a changed Juan Junquera. Gone was the air of self-importance and the commanding condescension.

"*Muy bien*, Antonio, very well done! You have come a long way. I would like you to come and sing for me. I will pay you fifteen *pesetas*...nobody earns that much...and I will guarantee you work afterward."

Chacón had not intended to work for the man who had dismissed him so rudely, but fifteen *pesetas* a night was a fortune for an artist. After a moment of thought, he replied, "Fifteen *pesetas?* With no obligations to you afterward?"

Junquera winced. "If you insist..."

"And I don't work in the *cuadro*..."

This last demand was almost more than the impresario could stomach. He stared intently at Chacón, hoping to see a sign of weakness, a hint of uncertainty. But there was only the steady return gaze of unblinking dark eyes. If he had not heard what he had heard that night in the café and did not have complete confidence in his instincts as a judge of talent, he would not have tolerated the impertinence of the youth. He heard himself say, "As you wish," as he offered his hand and ordered a round of drinks.

Silverio

The staccato clacking of many pairs of castanets greeted Antonio Chacón as he entered the café. When his eyes had adjusted to the dim light, he saw that the Salón Filarmónico, located on Calle Amor de Dios not far from the Café del Burrero, was quite different from the others he had seen in Sevilla. In place of tables and chairs, rows of theater seats rose up from the stage, where, at the moment a bevy of colorful ballerinas swooped and sashayed to the rhythm and melodies of the *sevillanas* pouring forth from an upright piano. Attached to the back of each seat, a small table provided a place for customers in the next row to place their drinks. Closer to the stage and around the sides of the room, box seats catered to the more affluent patrons.

Chacón headed for the bar, but before he could inquire, he recognized a familiar figure and called out, "José..."

José Patiño turned, and his lined and leathery face broke into a broad grin. "Antonio, what are you doing here?"

Chacón took the hand of the old guitarist. "How goes it, Maestro? I had a night off after the *feria* in Utrera, so I escaped here to Sevilla. I recalled that Junquera had contracted you to work here in the Filharmónico..."

"*Bien*, it's good to see you. And Utrera...how was it?"

"I can't complain. It's not Cái, but the people seemed to like my *cante*..."

"And why shouldn't they? Listen, I want to introduce you to the owner, he might be able to help you."

Patiño led the Jerezano to where a man with a full, drooping mustache presided over the café from one end of the bar. The man appeared concerned as he surveyed the sparse crowd.

"*Don* Andrés," said Patiño, "I wish to present a friend of mine, the *cantaor* Antonio Chacón, from Jerez de la Frontera. Antonio, *Don* Andrés González."

Don Andrés shook Chacón's hand firmly, at the same time measuring the youth with obvious skepticism. The soft young man with the receding short-cropped hair presented an unlikely image for a *cantaor*. Yet, the arrogant bearing, the well-cut clothes, and the obvious intelligence reflected in the steady gaze of the youth, could not be denied.

"Chacón, eh! *Mucho gusto!* [My pleasure!] I have heard your name. I think Junquera mentioned you recently...seemed to feel you show promise. Would you like to sing for us tonight?"

"Well...I don't know..."

"*Venga*, Antonio," encouraged Patiño, "show him what you can do!"

Chacón shrugged. "As you like, *Don* Andrés."

"Good! I'll announce you in a little while. See if you can liven this place up a bit..."

"Antonio, please excuse me," said Patiño, "as soon as Maestro Pericet finishes with his dancers, I have to go on. I'll see you later on stage."

Even before Chacón could be announced, several customers recognized him from Cádiz. One of them, obviously feeling his drink, shouted, "*Qué cante* Antonio Chacón!" [Let Antonio Chacón sing!] Another came to invite the *cantaor* for a drink. Almost immediately, Chacón regretted accepting, for he was to spend the next hour listening to exaggerated praise of his singing and persistent requests for him to sing. At last, to his great relief, *Don* Andrés announced from the stage that a guest *cantaor*, Antonio Chacón, from Jerez, would sing with the guitar of Maestro Patiño.

The half-full house responded warmly to Chacón's *cante por soleá*. *Por malagueña*, the public seemed hesitant at first. But, by the end of the second *copla*, people began to grasp the novelty of what they were hearing and applauded enthusiastically. The fervor grew with each *malagueña* until it overwhelmed the room, forcing Chacón to repeat several *coplas*.

Don Andrés, barely able to contain himself, greeted Chacón's descent from the stage with arms open in a grand gesture. "Marvelous, marvelous Chacón...you must come to work for me at once!"

"But I'm under contract to Juan Junquera," replied the *cantaor*.

"Bah, don't worry about that! You know, since we opened as a *café cantante* this year Juan has been hiring our artists. I'll fix things with him."

"I don't know..."

"Here, take this as an advance." *Don* Andrés thrust five gold coins into Chacón's hand.

Chacón, still uncertain, responded, "Are you sure it will be okay with Junquera?"

"Don't worry! Just show up for work tomorrow night!"

The opportunity to work in Sevilla blinded Chacón to all further concern. He became distracted as the customers began to file out of the café. The hour was early, so he asked *Don* Andrés, "Where is everyone going?"

The other explained, "All of the patrons must leave after each session. If they wish to see their favorite artist a second time, they can return for another session and buy another drink. We have three sessions each night and many patrons return for all three."

The following evening, when Chacón arrive at the Salón Filarmónico, Juan Junquera was waiting for him at the bar.

"Antonio, you have to be in Cádiz tomorrow. You know you have a contract to sing there."

"I'm sorry *Don* Juan! *Don* Andres said it would be okay with you, and I thought..."

"I know, but you are under contract to me. What you do later is your concern."

So, rather than make his debut in Sevilla, Chacón found himself back in Cádiz, singing in the Teatro Infantil [Children's Theater] at a salary of fifteen *pesetas* a night. At the completion of that contract he had intended to return to Jerez for one more job, and then he planned to ask Junquera to send him to the Filarmónico in Sevilla. But fate intervened. Enrique el Mellizo convinced him to remain in Cádiz for a few days to attend a dinner being arranged by two gentlemen, good aficionados of the *cante*, with the help of some of the gypsy artists from the barrio of Santa María. Chacón calculated that, if he left promptly the morning after the fiesta, he could just make it to Jerez in time to fulfill his next commitment.

On the designated evening, a number of horse-drawn carriages filled with gypsies traveled from Cádiz down the length of the strand to San Fernando. Amid salt beds that stretched to the horizon, the "salt" of Cádiz assembled in a café in that small white pueblo to honor the great *cantaora* María Fernández Piña "La Borrico" [The Donkey]. Among those present were María's brother, Pedro, El Gordo Ortega, José "El Águila" Ortega, Paquiro Ortega, Ignacio "El Pata" Espeleta, Enrique el Mellizo and his brother Mangoli, Curro Dulce and his son, Juan, Francisco la Perla, Antonia la Loro and Andrés el Loro [The Parrot], as well as the younger singers Chele Fateta, the brothers Ignacio and José Espeleta, and Antonio Chacón.

Almost overshadowing the guest of honor was none other than Silverio Franconetti, down from Sevilla with Maestro Patiño to pay homage to his old friend, María Borrico. During the hubbub of Silverio's arrival, Chacón had stayed back out of the way, eyes fixed on his idol of so many years. Up close, the huge man seemed to tower over the youth, although in reality he was not nearly as tall as Juan Torre or Fosforito. Silverio moved his massive body with effort, supporting himself on a stout *vara* and stopping often to catch his breath. A strong patrician nose, intense black eyes, and black slicked-back hair without a trace of gray, hinted at his Italian heritage. A roll of fat obscured a short neck and bulged over the velvet lapel of an elegant jacket buttoned high over a white shirt and cravat. The heavy jowls and barrel chest testified to the reputed power of the man's *cante*.

When, at last, Chacón was introduced, Silverio eyed him up and down, before declaring gruffly, "So this is the Jerezano I have been hearing about! *A ver*...we'll see how you sing." Although rough and edged with fatigue, the voice resonated with a deep echo and rich timber.

Chacón struggled for a moment to find his voice. "As you wish, *Don* Silverio...but I am nothing compared to others here."

Silverio laughed harshly at the youth's deference. "*A ver*...it's true that in this room *terelamos er mejón der guiyabo cañí* [we have the best in the *cante gitano*]." He spoke in a brusque, uneducated manner, employing a liberal sprinkling of gypsy language. In that environment, the veneer of the genteel businessman had fallen away and Silverio had slipped back into the habits and manners of his youth, when he had moved freely and comfortably in the underbelly of Spanish society. In many respects the great *cantaor gachó* became more gypsy than those gathered around him.

Silverio dismissed Antonio by directing his attention to El Gordo, but then something caught his eye and he turned back suddenly. "*Chaval*, where did you get that *ran?*"

He had used the gypsy word for *vara*, but Chacón instantly grasped that it was his style-stick that had provoked Silverio's interest. The carved *vara* had long ago lost its novelty and had become a part of the youth, a faithful companion in his journey through the world of the *cante*.

"I was told that this once belonged to you, *Don* Silverio. It was given to me by Sarvaoriyo…"

"Sarvaoriyo! *Hombre*, how can that be?"

"I was with him in Huelva a year ago…he was my teacher."

"*Hombre*, you could have no better teacher than he. *Hostias* ["Host" wafers used in communion], it has been years since I last saw him!"

By the time Antonio had told of his experiences with Salvaoriyo in Huelva and Silverio had extolled the virtues of his former disciple and friend, the distance between the two *cantaores* had vanished. Through their shared love of the *cante* a bond had formed between the two men—one young and enthusiastic, his life and career ahead of him, the other tired, in poor health, riding the mantle of his fame and only able to look back at what had once been. Chacón remained in awe of the older man, but felt accepted to the point that his nerves had calmed and he eagerly anticipated singing for Silverio.

María Borrico occupied her crude pine chair as if it were a throne. The old *gitana* carried her many years with erect dignity and, head held high, scanned the room with eyes that had seen so much change in her art over the course of the century. She seemed uncertain about the commotion around her, not really grasping the purpose of the gathering, content to watch while sucking on the black tobacco cigarettes that had permanently stained her fingers and few remaining teeth.

By La Borrico's side, her brother Pedro—Perico to those close to him, but widely known as El Viejo de la Isla [The Old One of San Fernando]. Younger than María, the slight, white-haired old man leaned on his *vara* and studied with stern silence the gathering of gypsies around him. According to El Mellizo, El Viejo was "*un gitano de mucha ley*" [a gypsy true to the law] who resented the loss of the old ways and the degeneration of the *cante* in the hands of the *gaché*. Like many gypsies he had mixed feelings about Silverio, reluctantly respecting his art—as true to the gypsy tradition as any—but suspicious of the man's motives and business dealings. Silverio's name had long been synonymous with exploitation of the *cante* in the cafés, and Perico Piña had never been able to resolve his respect for the *cantaor* with the rancor that seethed inside him.

Dinner proceeded with little formality. The customarily light evening meal was more drink and talk than heavy eating. Later, as the room filled with thick, acrid tobacco smoke, and cheap wine flowed freely, it fell to the younger *cantaores* to evoke the muse of the *cante*. When his turn came, Chacón sang *por soleá*, demonstrating his mastery of the styles of his homeland, especially those of Loco Mateo and Paco la Luz.

In that gypsy atmosphere, thick with guttural gypsy language, brutally direct and often childish humor, and an often narrow view of the world from a gypsy perspective, even those close to Chacón could not help but feel a sense of separation from the *gachó* stemming from racial pride. Many of the gypsies of Cádiz had been settled in that city for generations and mingled daily with the *gaché*, forming business relationships and friendships, yet the racial memories of centuries of persecution were not to be forgotten over the course of a few generations. Gypsies congregated in barrios like Santa María, where they clung tenaciously to tradition, adopting the customs of the *gachó* only gradually and with reluctance. The gypsy flamencos gathered there in the café in San Fernando were not conscious of their conflicting emotions, but the presence of so many of them in one place altered their perception of the *gaché*. On a one to one basis with a *gachó* such as Chacón, a gypsy could accept and even admire the ability of an outsider to master their *cante*. There was an element of flattery in imitation. But when a gypsy looked around that humble café and saw the quality of those around him, racial pride put the *gachó* in a different light, as a person distinct from him in almost every way.

Silverio found himself caught between two worlds. The Silverio who had huddled as a child by the gypsy forge, absorbing the *cantes* of the blacksmiths, who had mastered the difficult *cantes* of the legendary El Fillo, who had rejected offers of formal music instruction in order to wander through Andalucía seeking out enclaves of gypsy *cantaores*, overcoming their resistance to his intrusion through the power of his personality and a *cante* so *rancio* [musty and old, with the bitterness and bite of aged wine] and faithful to *café* tradition that it admitted no possibility of criticism...that Silverio, like the gypsies, felt the tension in the room, felt resentment toward Chacón, an outsider attempting to capture the essence of expression of a soul that was not his, was not a reality of birth and experience.

But the other Silverio, the *gachó* tailor who had risen to unprecedented popular success, the first to give recitals of *cante gitano* in far-off Madrid, and eventually perform throughout Spain, earning the title "King of *Cantaores*," and who operated the most renowned *café cantante* in all of Spain...this Silverio saw in Chacón a young version of himself, although perhaps without the same natural faculties and predisposition for the life and *cante* of the *gitanos*. Chacón shared with Silverio an obvious dedication to his art, a love for the *cante*, a lust for knowledge, and an innate creativity.

A lukewarm respect pervaded the café as Chacón sang...until he began *por malagueñas*. Before he had completed the first *copla*, the atmosphere had changed completely. The gypsies, freed from the deep-seated attachments and prejudices evoked by their own music, were able to marvel at the astonishing accomplishments of the Jerezano in the *cante andaluz*—the *cante gachó*. The powerful, rich tones of the young *cantaor* struck deep in the soul of Silverio, replacing his doubt with profound and emotional admiration. He muttered to himself almost non-stop, "*Qué barbaridá!*...What is this I am hearing?...*Hostias*, how can this be?...*Bien chaval!*"

It was El Viejo who summed up the feelings of many of the gypsies. "*Chaval*, you have sung well, *mu bonito er cante* [your *cante* is very beautiful]...your voice is a marvel. But you don't have to do all of those things with the *cante*, making it fancy and complicated...you have only to *quejarse!* Look..." And without guitar, the old man broke into *cante por seguiriyas*, his cracked voice straining in difficult passages:

Fragua, yunque, y martillo	Forge, anvil, and hammer
rompen los metales;	break metals;
er juramiento que yo a tí t'he hecho	the vow I have made to you
no lo rompe naide.	will be broken by nobody.

Entre una y dos	Between one and two [o'clock],
logré mi gusto, logré mi gusto,	I had took my pleasure,
[*con mi compañera,*]	[with my girlfriend,]
solitos los dos.	the two of us being alone.

"My God," Chacón thought to himself, *"qué lástima de cante!"* [What a shame of a *cante*—meaning just the opposite.] In spite of the rough and broken delivery and the weak and strident tone of the old man's voice, the force of his effort in the *seguiriya* had brought forth the dense shadows and tragic undertones of his gypsy echo. In the second *letra*, El Viejo had done something Chacón had never heard before. When he repeated the phrase *"logré mi gusto"* without pausing, it created a spine-chilling emotional emphasis. Once more the youth fell victim to the familiar intimidation he invariably experienced when it seemed that in every corner he encountered gypsies who, with natural ease and an untrained voice, could tear at his heart and wrench tears from his eyes as easily and naturally as speaking. But his passion for the *cante* won out over the sense of futility and he determined to add another *seguiriya* to his growing repertoire—the *seguiriya* of El Viejo de la Isla.

With the force of the *seguiriya* set loose, the *reunión* warmed and gathered momentum. One by one they sang: El Pata, El Gordo, Curro Dulce... Chacón sat near Curro and fell once more under the spell of the gypsy's voice. In that gathering, Curro Dulce was the only gypsy to sing without the *voz afillá*. His *cante* was strong and mellow without being pretty, biting and grief-filled, but natural, without *rajo*:

Los méicos de Cái	The doctors of Cádiz
a mí me dijeron:	said to me:
"La enfermeaíta que tu	"The illness that your sister has,
[*hermana tiene*]	
no tiene remedio."	has no cure."

"*Ole* Curro!...*Ole er cante güeno!* [*Ole* the good *cante*]...Curro, *mi arma!*" [my soul!]

María Borrico, joy clearly evident in her toothless grin, brought silence to the commotion with a cracking voice. "With permission... from you all...I must sing!"

While Patiño adjusted the tones of the guitar, the old woman cleared her throat of rumbling phlegm, spat noisily to the floor, wiped her mouth with her sleeve, and tested a voice as harsh as a donkey's bray. The *cante* of María Borrico proved to be all that Chacón had been told, unlike the *cante* of any woman the youth had ever heard. The voice was deep and very *afillá*, as hoarse as that of any man. But it was an aged voice, a voice that betrayed the *cantaora* often in difficult passages.

María Borrico's face contorted with effort, the long white bristles about her chin trembling as she fought to control that broken *voz afillá por seguiriyas*. Chacón listened with reverent rapture to the woman whose *cante* was as respected as that of any man. The gypsies encouraged the old woman: "*Venga* María!...Come on, you can do it!...*Arsa, viva tú!*"

Dice mi compañera	My girlfriend says
que no la quiero;	that I don't love her;
cuando la miro, la miro a la cara,	when I look at her, I look at her face
yo er sentío pierdo.	and go crazy.[1]

The gypsies, emotional with drink and *cante*, responded vociferously and exaggeratedly, crying and ripping their clothes. Even Silverio appeared deeply moved. The great *cantaor* felt at home in that gypsy environment. For too many years he had been away from the pure *cante gitano*, too busy running his cafés and dealing with the eccentricities of performers and the whims of the public. Now, the *cante* threatened to burst from within him.

Chacón could hardly breath as Silverio undid his collar and tested the tones of the guitar. Patiño had not needed to be told where to place the *cejilla* for the man he had accompanied so often. Years of anticipation had not succeeded in preparing Chacón for the moment. When Silverio opened that giant throat, a voice as large as the man himself poured out as if from another age, with the echo of a cathedral:

Soy esgraciaíto	I suffer misfortune
jasta en er andá;	even in my walk;
que los pasitos que p'alante doy,	the steps that I take forward
se me ban p'trás.	carry me backwards.

---

[1] It is not unusual for *cantaores*, male or female, to sing *letras* from the perspective of the opposite sex. This *letra* may also hint at a predilection in María Borrico for lovers of her own gender—not unheard of among *cantaoras* who sing like men.

In that *voz afillá*, in the emotion and the power, in the choice of words and expressions, the *cante* of Silverio showed no hint of the *gachó*:

Qué ducas tan grandes!	What great suffering!
Cáa bes que m'acuerdo	Each time I recall
e los sacais e la bata mía,	the eyes of my mother,
loquito me güerbo.	I go crazy.

The *cantaor* slowly raised a clenched fist, as if seeking something to hold onto, to pull himself out of his grief, or to draw others into sharing his pain:

A mi mayó enemigo	To my greatest enemy,
no le mande Dio	I don't wish God to send
estas fatigas, estas grandes ducas	this suffering, this great anguish
que a mi me mandó.	that he has sent me.

The veins stood out on Silverio's flushed temples, sweat pouring down his cheeks. The gypsies, swept up by the force of the *cante*, participated with grunts, moans, and loud comments, all distinction between *gachó* and *gitano* forgotten. The voice, brutal yet sweet as thick honey, continued in its unforgettably personal style:

Corasón como er mío	Another heart like mine
no lo hay ní lo habrá;	does not exist, nor will it ever;
mientras más ducas y fatigas pasa,	the more pain and suffering it [goes through,]
más contento está.	the more content it is.

El Gordo became delirious, having suffered every note of Silverio's anguish. The others attempted to outdo each other in demonstrations of rapture. El Pata hooked a finger in the collar of his shirt and ripped it open to the waist, sending buttons flying. Wine flowed over heads, bathing faces and chests. Glasses shattered to the floor amid sobs and murmurs. El Mellizo's brother, Mangoli, bit down hard on Juan Dulce's shoulder. Juan barely seemed to notice. Only Curro Dulce sat unmoving, as if stunned. Chacón and others nearby heard him mutter to himself, "*Mare de mi arma, qué es esto?*" [Mother of my soul, what *is* this?]

A plume of white dust billowed up behind the coach as it jounced across the salt flats outside of San Fernando. An early morning sun bathed distant sand dunes in a golden glow. Inside the coach Antonio Chacón, a seventeen-year-old aspiring *cantaor* with a world of dreams ahead of him, sat facing forward. Across from him slumped Silverio Franconetti, a fifty-six-year-old living legend with a world of memories behind him. On the bench seat by Chacón's side, Maestro José Patiño. The three men dozed as the coach headed down the strand toward Cádiz, where Silverio and Patiño would catch a train to Sevilla and Chacón would prepare to return to Jerez. Only the long night and a great deal of wine allowed them to nod off briefly in that lurching coach.

Giving up on sleep, a groggy Silverio asked Chacón, "Your parents sing?"

Antonio replied, "*Qué va!* Not only did they not sing, they didn't want me to. They did everything they could to discourage me. I was supposed to become a shoemaker. But after we moved to the Plaza Orellana when I was nine, and I was surrounded by the forges of the *gitanos*..."

"You too, eh! I was born in Sevilla, near the Plaza Alfalfa, but my family moved to Morón de la Frontera when I was very young. There, I went to school and worked in my brother's tailor shop as an apprentice. But that wasn't for me. By the time I was ten I was spending most of my time in a nearby forge, drinking from that fountain of *cante gitano*. My parents didn't like it, but after my father died, my mother couldn't stop me."

"That is how it was with me. I received my first lessons from *gitanos*...Juan Torre, El Marruro, La Cherna..."

"*Hostias!* Those are good singers. You were lucky to know them, and it shows in your knowledge."

"But I can't sing like they do. I just don't have it in my voice. It's not easy for a *gachó* to have that sound. As much as I love the *cante gitano*, I will never have that sound. I wish I had been born a *gitano!* You are fortunate to have your voice."

"I don't know where I got this voice...I have no *gitano* blood. It is something that is in the hands of God. The Italian side of my family, the Franconettis...you know, my father, Nícolas, was Italian. He came here, joined the Spanish army, and met my mother in Sevilla. The Franconettis are very musical, and my mother's family, the Aguilars, have deep voices, so perhaps I inherited something. I don't know if it is because of my Italian name, but many have tried to convince me to go to Milan to learn opera. But it never interested me. For me it has always been the *cante gitano*. What I have always wanted most is to raise our music to the level of the opera, to give it that same respect and dignity. So I don't know whether my voice is a gift from my Italian ancestors or it is something I learned from my teacher, El Fillo..."

"El Fillo! You really learned from El Fillo?"

"Yes. He came often to Morón when I was a youngster. He was still a young man but a *cantaor ya hecho* [already established as a *cantaor*]. He used to travel *pueblo* to *pueblo*, *taberna* to *taberna*, looking for fiestas where he could earn a living. For some reason he took an interest in me and encouraged me to sing. I used to sit at his feet and listen to him."

"But he was the king of *cantaores*, the greatest in the *cante gitano*."

"Yes, he was a giant, especially in the *seguiriyas*...we called them *playeras* back then...and the *polos* and *cañas*. El Fillo...we called him Curro, because his name was Francisco Ortega Vargas...he was related to the Ortegas of Cádiz, although he came from Puerto Real. El Fillo had a voice that you can't imagine...you had to hear it. His voice was so deep and harsh that many criticized him. Even his teacher, El Planeta, told him he was going down the wrong road. Do you know of La Andonda?"

"No, I haven't heard of her."

"María la Andonda. She was El Fillo's lover. A tough and difficult woman, always looking for trouble. She's getting up in years now, but she still lives in Triana and can sing *por soleá* with any man. We have a *letra por soleá* that says..." And, in that dusty and noisy coach, Silverio half-sang, half-whispered, in a tired and raspy voice:

La Andonda le dijo al Fillo,	La Andonda said to El Fillo,
'Anda y vete, gallo ronco,	'Get out of here, hoarse rooster,
a cantarle a los chiquillos.'	go sing to the children.'

"It took a while for El Fillo's *rajo*, what we now call the *voz afillá*, to become accepted, but now it is the preferred way of singing, especially for *gitanos*. Very few *gaché* can get that sound, but, as you well know, it's not the only way to sing. Look at Curro Durse, for example, or the many fine singers we have in Sevilla who do not have that *rajo*...El Loco Mateo and his sister, or El Chato de la Isla...and how about La

Parrala? Do you know Dolores?"

"No, I don't believe I do."

"Dolores la Parrala...she is married to El Lucena, the guitarist...surely you know of him!"

"Paco Lucena? Yes, of course."

"When Dolores came to Sevilla from Huelva some years ago, she knew nothing but the *fandangos* of her homeland and some little *malagueñas*. She stayed and she learned. I helped her as much as I could and now I have to say that she is my best disciple...the most knowledgeable *cantaora* we have today. She sings everything well, especially the *cantes machunos* [masculine *cantes*]. You have to hear her...and she does not have the *voz afillá*."

Silverio paused a moment in thought and then added, "It's good that Dolores is with El de Lucena...she's not an easy woman. You'll see. She is gifted with an unusual beauty...very attractive...and suggestive. She dominates men just as she dominates the *cante*, plays them like others play at cards. I believe she was with a very rich man in Madrid...some say they were married...but then she ran away with the Lucentino. I think Paco can handle her...he has a strong personality and she has great respect for his talent."

The coach slowed suddenly and Chacón leaned out the window to see what the problem might be. Ahead, a nomadic gypsy caravan struggled to move to the shoulder of the road so that the coach might pass. The motley assemblage of heavily laden donkeys, barking dogs, and a decrepit cart with a tattered hood, fell into disarray. A dozen men, women, and children stood in the dirt, staring impassively at the approaching carriage.

Chacón was about to turn back to his conversation when something familiar caught his eye. It was a figure holding the halter rope of the lead animal. "Stop the coach!" yelled the youth to the driver. With his head out the window, he called out, "Morrongo, is that you?"

The gypsy turned and stared, a puzzled look on his face. For a moment, Chacón thought he was mistaken. The man before him appeared smaller and thinner than the Morrongo he remembered, and his clothes had seen better days. His demeanor seemed fearful rather than fierce, servile rather than commanding. But there could be no mistaking that craggy face with its prominent scar—in spite of an unkempt growth of beard.

"Morrongo, do you remember me? Antonio Chacón...we were

together in the *feria* of Villamartín."

The gypsy remained motionless a moment, then his eyes lit up with recognition. He broke into a broad grin and said, "*Chaval*, I didn't recognize you. Where are your friends, the guitarist and the dancer?"

"They're doing well, back in Jerez."

"What a night we had..." El Morrongo suddenly extended one arm, hand outstretched, and in a parched and broken voice that barely carried to the coach, began to croak, "*Va una partía...*"

Suddenly, the gypsy froze, the rest of his song lodged in his throat. A huge head had appeared in the window of the coach. Silverio, curious and anxious to hear better, had leaned forward and out the window.

El Morrongo looked as if he had seen a ghost. He bowed his head and mumbled out loud, "*Señor Silverio...*" Then he looked again at Chacón and said, "*Chaval*, I knew you would succeed in the *cante*."

"*Sí, hombre*, I have had luck. Here, take this...you were a great help to me."

With that, the *cantaor* withdrew a handful of gold coins from his pocket and, leaning far out the window, placed them in the outstretched hands of El Morrongo.

"*Gracias, quiribó*," said the gypsy. "May *Undebé* [God] bring you much good fortune!"

As the coach began to move again, Chacón let his eyes wander over the rest of the pathetic group of nomads. He recognized Dolores and Rosa, both more gaunt, frail, and dirty than he remembered. The old mother was nowhere to be seen. In the back of the wagon, on a filthy mattress, sat a woman with a swollen belly and a naked child at her breast. *Could it be? Is that Angustias?* Chacón asked himself. *Yes, it had to be her.* The familiar noble features were there, but the youthful vitality had been replaced by worn resignation, her hair hanging limp and dull and the light gone from her eyes. A very thin young man stared dully from the driver's seat of the wagon.

As the coach pulled away, leaving the caravan in its dust, Silverio asked, "Who was that?"

"Just some people who helped me out once...a long time ago!" Chacón remained silent for some time afterward. *Could the gypsies have changed so much in such a short time*, he wondered...*or had they never been what they seemed that night in the mountains of Grazalema?*

Ahead of the coach it was just possible to make out the distant walls of La Puerta de Tierra when Chacon picked up the earlier conversation.

"Maestro, I've heard it said that you were away from Spain for a long time. How could you abandon your singing when it was going so well?"

Silverio remained quiet a moment, as if considering carefully his answer. "Yes, it is true that I left, back in '55. It's also true that I was quite successful with my singing, especially after I began to give concerts in Madrid. You know, in the capital they were surprised by the *cante*. It was something new for them at that time. I didn't wish to abandon my singing career, but circumstances were such that it seemed best to leave for a while. I didn't realize that it would be such a long time before I could return...almost ten years."

Chacon thought back to what he had heard about the mysterious death of El Fillo's brother, but said nothing.

"Let's just say," continued Silverio, "that I had a very good offer to work as a tailor in Montevideo. I saw the possibility of earning a great deal of money and coming back here to do something to elevate the *cante*, to rescue it from its desperate circumstances. It also made my family very happy...they didn't care for the kind of people I was forced to associate with in the world of the *cante*. So I made that long and frightening trip to Argentina. But things didn't go as planned. The tailoring job didn't work out and I was forced to do other things. I worked as a *picador de toros* and eventually joined the army in Uruguay where I rose up through the ranks until I was making good money. Eventually I earned enough to return to Spain in luxury, aboard the steamship *Gravina*. That was in '64. Since then, I have sung when and where I wanted, thanks to God, and here I am today. Unfortunately I have not been able to do all I desired for the *cante*. Some of us have been able to improve our circumstances, but most artists are as bad off as they were thirty years ago."

Silverio paused a moment and then added, "It's hard to help people when they don't want to help themselves. I remember one *cantaor* I hired...Maoliyo, a *gitano* from Triana. He wasn't very good, but I felt sorry for him...he had fallen on hard times and couldn't even feed his wife and six children. The *gitano* was *má salao que las pesetas* [saltier (funnier) than *pesetas*]...he had *gracia* without even realizing it. One night he came in complaining about how tired he was...he had been up all the night before. I asked him what happened. He told me he had run into a friend the previous day, a fisherman, who had given him a string of *guitarras* [guitar-fish] that he couldn't sell because of their reputation for causing intestinal upset and flatulence. The family ate well for the first time in weeks, but a couple of hours after they went to bed, the oldest boy got up and ran outside to the toilet. Soon, the wife began to feel stirrings in her stomach. Then another son began to cry and call to his mother, who had to take him out to join the first boy. That started an unending parade back and forth to the toilet, where the noise was waking the neighbors. Suddenly the *gitana* realized what was happening and shook her husband, saying, 'Manué...wake up! What kind of fish did your friend give you?'

" '*Mujé*...they were *guitarras*, why?'

" '*Guitarras!* [Guitars!] *Pos mira*, get up right now...*porque estamos toós de juerga* [because we're all having a fiesta!]' "

Chacón and Patino had to laugh, in spite of their fatigue.

"But that wasn't what I was going to tell you," continued Silverio. "One night I was drinking with this Maoliyo and he was complaining that he had no money. I asked him what he would do if he had all the money in the world. His mouth began to water as he said, '*Josú, compare* [friend]...if I had that much money we would eat garbanzo stew *every* day in my house!' It's hard to help people who think like that."

"I understand. When I was very young I promised myself that I would not end up like the others, that somehow I would find a way to be successful."

"You are on the right path, Antonio. You have found something special with this new *malagueña*. How did decide to go down that road?"

"As I told you before, I began with the *cante gitano*. But when Fosforito came to Jerez..."

"Fosforito! Fosforito is the reason I came looking for you. That young man just began to work in El Burrero and already he has everyone talking about his *malagueñas*. Within days one of his songs was on everybody's lips. He sings:

Ar campo me ví a llorá,	I go to the countryside to cry,
donde no me vea la gente;	so that people won't see me;
porque me haces pasá	because you make me go through
las fatiguitas de la muerte	the agony of death,
y no te pueo orviá.	and still I can't forget you.

"I don't know where he got that *letra*, but it reminds me of a *caña* I used to sing:

A llorá me salgo ar campo;	I go to the countryside to cry;
jago las pieras llorá	I make the rocks cry
en be las fatiguitas	when they see the pain
con que t'empieso a yamá.	with which I call out your name.

"In any case, there was no café, tavern, or fiesta where they weren't singing this *copla* of Fosforito's. I heard that one day Vicente Vives, one of our popular comic artists, was walking on the Alameda de Hércules [popular promenade] with his head down, lost in thought. A friend asked him, 'What's wrong, *amigo* Vicente?' Vicente looked up and said, 'I was just thinking that, in the old days, a person would cry wherever he suffered some misfortune. But since Fosforito came, everyone goes to the countryside...they have to go to the countryside to cry!'"

Silverio smiled at his joke. Then he became serious once more. "Fosforito is filling El Burrero's café. I can't compete. Manuel and other owners are doing all sorts of things to bring people into their cafés...*cupletistas* [pop singers], orchestras, and even acrobats...can you imagine? *Me cago en la leche!* I have others who sing *por malagueñas*, but not like that Gaditano. I tried to hire El Mellizo, but he wasn't interested. Mellizo spoke highly of you so I came looking for you. Now that I have heard you, I think you can do it. That's why I'm willing to pay you sixty-five *reales* [16.5 *pesetas*], as I told you last night, more than anyone is making."

"Fosforito sings really well. We both drank from the same well...El Mellizo...but he has a lot more experience than I."

"That may be true, but I think you are onto something special."

"I appreciate your confidence in me, *Don* Silverio, and I'll do my best for you. As I told you, I'll come to Sevilla as soon as I complete this last contract for Junquera... I should be there by mid-October."

The coach pulled up in the Plaza San Juan de Dios and deposited the three travelers. Silverio and Patiño headed for the train to take them to Sevilla, while Antonio Chacón prepared to return to Jerez, where he would anxiously count the days until his debut in the Café de Silverio.

Sevilla

Sevilla, 1886

Antonio Chacón stepped into the Café de Silverio on a cool October afternoon. The immense salon rang hollow and strangely silent, its only greeting the acrid odor of stale smoke, stale alcohol, and stale humanity that had thoroughly impregnated every crevice of that empty hall. By the light of day there remained no hint of the excitement and romance of busy café nights. Crude tables and chairs lay scattered about in disarray, some on their sides on the sawdust-covered floor. Dust motes floated in the columns of light entering through the skylight above the fountain.

"How can I help you?"

Startled, Chacón turned and saw a man behind the bar. He replied, "I've been hired to sing…I just got in from Jerez. Is Silverio around?"

"Welcome! I'm Miguel, the bartender here…"

"Antonio Chacón, at your service."

"Silverio is not here. He doesn't usually come in before six."

"I need to find a place to stay. Do you have any suggestions… someplace quiet where I can sleep during the day?"

"I know just the place. Continue down Calle Rosario and turn left on Méndez Núñez. In the second doorway, on the second floor, you'll find the Pensión Sánchez. Ask for Ana María and say Miguel sent you… she'll take good care of you."

"*Gracias* Migué! Do you mind if I look around a little?"

"It's your house."

"Until later, then."

The *cantaor* made his way through the tables and up the stairs to center stage. He gazed out at the room and thought, *a café is not meant to be seen in daylight!* Dust everywhere, especially thick on the huge mirrors. Torn drapes, stains, dirt and signs of wear on everything. Even the famous dance floor had loose boards and holes where pounding heels had splintered the wood and worn through. Yet, as Chacón stood there, thinking that in a few hours he would be singing from that very spot, he felt a twinge of nervousness. *Can I really sing in the Café de Silverio? Can I be the answer to Fosforito that Silverio is seeking?*

To calm his nerves, Chacón left the café, settled into the Pensión Sánchez, and then walked unfamiliar streets until dusk and time to meet with Silverio. When he returned to the café he found the great *cantaor* waiting for him.

"Antonio, I heard you were here. I'm sorry I couldn't get in earlier to meet you."

"*Don* Silverio! I found a place to stay and walked around a little to learn my way through your confusing streets."

"You'll feel at home in no time. Are you ready to begin tonight?"

"At your service, *Don* Silverio...whatever you say."

"*Bien!* Here's how the evening goes. At eight o'clock we have a *comparsa* [singing group] from Cádiz. At nine you go on with the *cuadro*. You will sing first after the dancers have finished. After the *cuadro* we have a group from the academy dancing national dances...you know, castanet dances... *cachuchas*, *jaleos*, *boleros*, *sevillanas*...dances of that sort. It makes a nice change and the customers like the girls. At eleven you go back on with the *cuadro*. After that, you are free to make whatever arrangements you wish for later in the *reservaos*."

Artists began to filter in. Dancers headed for the dressing room. Singers and guitarists gravitated toward the bar. As performance time drew close, Silverio said suddenly, "Here comes Paco...he's going to be playing for you."

Chacón recognized Paco de Lucena immediately, even with the well-groomed mustache he had grown since the Jerezano had last seen him.

"Paco, over here...I want you to meet *Don* Antonio Chacón, the new singer I was telling you about."

The guitarist approached and offered a limp hand. "My pleasure."

"Maestro, do you remember meeting me and my friends in Jerez a few years ago, in the Café del Conde?"

El Lucena studied him carefully, with no hint of recognition.

"I was with my friend Javié...he plays the guitar and you showed him a few tricks..."

"Ah, yes, Javier, now I remember. Do you know that Javier is here in Sevilla, working in the Filarmónico? He's playing very well."

"Yes, I heard he was here, but I haven't had a chance to see him."

"I don't believe you know my wife, Dolores..." The guitarist indicated with a nod of his head the woman who had come in with him and taken a seat by his side. Buxom and matronly in figure, her hair gathered severely into a bun, Dolores la Parrala yielded nothing to the men at the table. Yet there seemed to be something smoldering under her cool and controlled exterior. Chacón found her to be as attractive as Silverio had said.

"I'm pleased to meet you," said Antonio, "Silverio has told me so much about you. I look forward to hearing you sing."

Before the woman could respond, her husband added, "We have just returned from Granada where they loved her..."

"Don't forget Madrid and Paris, Paco," interrupted La Parrala. "Enchanted to meet you *Don* Antonio. I'm sure your singing will be all that people say...I can't wait to hear you!"

Antonio was lost for words. The woman's dark eyes seemed to look right through him and her voice vibrated with invitation. He felt something stir within him. His mind flashed back to Silverio's words: *La Parrala plays men like others play cards*. The *cantaor*'s thoughts were interrupted by a roar from the customers. Eleven men had taken the stage, dressed in brightly colored costumes that could only be described as belonging to Medieval court jesters, with wide-brimmed hats decorated with ribbons, tassels, colored buttons, and bells. They were obviously very popular with the patrons of the café.

"Las Viejas Ricas de Cádiz [The Rich Old Ladies of Cádiz]," yelled Silverio, over the crowd noise and the first strums of guitar and *bandurria* [a mandolin-like instrument] played by some of the men. "They came for the first time last year, to the Filarmónico and people loved them. This year I got them and they have been good for business."

Chacón knew of the famous *comparsas* of Cádiz that enlivened *carnival* each spring. These comic singing groups, with names like "The Pharmacists," "The Modern Doctors," "The Post Cards," or "The Idiots," sang satirical songs making fun of everything. What he didn't know was that the more successful of these groups were beginning to make a name for themselves by performing around Andalucía after *carnival* had finished.

The noise on stage grew as the men beat on percussion instruments made from clay jars, tin kitchen graters, and lengths of split cane. To Chacón's surprise they began to sing a *tango* dedicated to Silverio:

Vinimos sin descansar	We come without rest
a la gran ciudad de Betis	to the great city of Sevilla
tan sólo por saludar	just to honor
a Silverio Franconetti.	Silverio Franconetti.
Desde que este gran talento	Ever since this great talent
del cante se retiró,	retired from the *cante*,
del arte, el sentimiento	the sorrow of this art has
hasta las Indias llegó.	reached even to the Indies.
Qué él y su familia	May he and his family
tengan mucha salud;	have good health;
Dios le dé larga vida	may God give long life
al noble rey del cante andaluz.	to the king of the *cante andaluz.*

Las Viejas Ricas entertained for the better part of an hour before relinquishing the stage to the flamenco *cuadro*. As was the custom, Chacón went on stage with the dancers and other singers. He took a seat beside Paco de Lucena at center stage. La Parrala sat on the other side of her husband.

When the last dancer had returned to her seat, Chacón said to El de Lucena, "*Pónme la guitarra por soleá, al cuatro por medio.*" [Place the *cejilla* for *soleá* on the fourth, in A] Paco adjusted the tuning of his instrument and then began to play *por soleá*. Antonio nervously tuned his voice, tapped the floor with his style-stick and then began with some of the styles of Cádiz he had recently absorbed. Tentative at first, he warmed up with two *letras* in the old dance style of Paquirri el Guanté:

Que bonito estará	How beautiful must be
er ferrocarrí de Cáis	the railroad of Cádiz
con banderas colorás!	with its colored flags!

> *Quiero irme pa Cái,*   I want to go to Cádiz,
> *quitarme de estos biyarros,*   to get away from these wretched
>   [villages]
> *las malas lenguas que hay.*   and their evil tongues.

He thought he heard Silverio say, *"Bien!"*

To Chacón's relief, he found that the guitarist accompanied him flawlessly and he began to gain confidence and relax. *Letras* of El Gordo and El Mellizo followed and soon he was singing *a gusto* [with pleasure]. He concluded to a smattering of applause and cries of *"Bravo!"*

The *cantaor* leaned in toward Paco de Lucena and said, *"Por malagueña,* on the fifth." He hoped the *malagueña* would get the reaction from the audience that he was beginning to expect when he sang.

Paco moved his *cejilla* to the fifth fret on the neck of the guitar and began an elaborate introduction unlike anything Chacón had heard before, filled with crystalline cascades of notes. When the Jerezano began to sing, he was astounded by the way the Lucentino played. Antonio was accustomed to good guitarists. Javier knew him well and always gave him exactly what he needed from the guitar, following his every whim. Patiño had been rock solid and supported the *cante* in the classic style, his playing free of frills and unnecessary adornments; he was the perfect accompanist for a *cantaor* like Enrique el Mellizo. But Paco el de Lucena went beyond all of that. He played the way Chacón sang, filling his accompaniment with elaborate ornamentation. Chacón felt understood. He had an ally in his quest to extract every possible bit of melody from his music. *Cante* and guitar merged to create something new and fresh. Electricity ran through the room and even the most drunken patron could not help but take notice. By the completion of his last *letra,* Chacón had captured the full enthusiasm of the public and they let him know with loud and sustained applause.

It took some time for the room to quiet as La Parrala slid her chair forward slightly and prepared to sing, her guitarist husband by her side. Chacón waited, flush with relief and pride in his apparent success, but also eager to finally hear the *cante* of La Parrala.

"Venga, Dolore!" said Paco as he began to play *por seguiriyas.* When the woman from Huelva began to sing, she proved to be everything Silverio had said. Her *cante* was robust and powerful, with round, warm tones and just enough of the feminine to appeal to her male

audience. Chacón could hear the influence of Silverio, but she had a unique charm of her own:

D'estos malos ratitos	These bad moments
que estoy pasando,	I'm going through
tiene la culpa mi compañerito	are the fault of my boyfriend
por quererlo tanto.	because I love him so much.

Seguiriyas was followed by *soleá*. Chacón quickly saw why La Parrala was the most popular female singer of this *cante*. She had complete control of her artistic faculties and played with the song as she was reputed to play with men, toying with the melodies, teasing and flirting with the audience, always original and surprising as she sang:

Como pajarillo triste,	Like a little sad bird
de rama en rama saltando,	jumping from branch to branch,
así está mi corazón	so is my heart
el día en que no te hallo.	on the day I don't find you.

   Unfortunately, the audience had remained somewhat distracted by the novelty of Antonio Chacón and the room continued to buzz with comments. They had heard La Parrala many times.

   Chacón came down off the stage and headed toward the bar, acknowledging congratulations from some of the customers. As he stood at the bar having a drink, he noticed many customers filing out, leaving the café strangely empty. No one seemed interested in staying for his second performance later in the evening. Concerned, he mentioned it to the bartender. Miguel replied, "I wouldn't worry too much about it. I heard some of the customers say they were going to get their friends."

   And, sure enough, as midnight approached and Chacón prepared to go on stage again, the café began to fill. By the time the Jerezano moved his chair forward to sing, the atmosphere had changed completely from the mood earlier in the evening. The salon had converted into the nave of a church. Chacón sang before a crowd of several hundred and everyone, wealthy or poor, sober or drunk, was captivated by his incomparable art and afraid to breath so as not to miss one detail, not one note of his sublime and emotional style, so unusual and unknown to them. The funereal silence was interrupted only during an occasional *tercio* of *cante* by the voice of the great Silverio, nervous and moved, muttering in a low voice through his tears of emotion, *"Qué bárbaro, qué bárbaro!"* [outrageous, beyond belief!] Chacón's voice had extraordinary melody and his modulations were performed with great facility, equally in the low tones and in the highs that he executed with enchanting sonority. Add to this his personal appearance and his *letras* that fit the *cantes* so well and it was clear that he would soon be at the top in the *cante andaluz*. Nobody moved from his seat until the *cantaor* had finished...[1]

Chacón quickly settled into his new surroundings. He familiarized himself with the narrow twisting streets of Sevilla and located the best restaurants. He often lunched on fresh fish in the Málaga Fishery on the Plaza Campana, or dined in the elegant Café Suizo on nearby Calle de las Sierpes. As a newcomer in the café, he had been accepted and welcomed by most of the other artists, with only the to-be-expected jealousy arising in some of the older singers due to the special treatment he seemed to be receiving.

Chacón found the *cafés cantantes* of Sevilla to be rough places. It seemed that where there were woman and alcohol, trouble wasn't far behind. Silverio's café shared Calle Rosario with a several brothels whose problems often spilled outdoors. Late night crowds in the café tended to be intoxicated and rowdy. Although most grudges were settled outside in the streets, rare were the nights without a fight in the café, often involving waiters, bartenders, and even Silverio himself. Rarer still were the days that Chacón didn't read in the newspaper of some misadventure the night before. Editorials and letters from angry citizens demanded that these dens of gambling, drinking and prostitution be closed down to protect, *"...our husbands, fathers, and sons!"*

One morning he read a tongue-in-cheek account of the previous night: "*Cantaora* assaulted in the Café de Silverio by a dilettante, knife in hand, who had the misfortune of not achieving his intent to give her a good stabbing and was taken by the police to comfortable and secure lodging."

Another day it was: "A drunk in possession of a large knife was jailed after insulting police."

And less than a week later, in the newspaper *El Progreso*: "Fight

---
[1] Adapted from Fernando de Triana, p. 19.

at dawn on Calle Tetuán among clients who had just left the Café de Silverio. Coachman Baldomero killed, another two injured, the rest fled. Public calls for the closing of these establishments..."

One night, as Chacón waited on stage for his turn to sing, a man stood up in front and yelled to the *gitana* dancing in front of him, "Go darling! You move like a snake..."

Scarcely had the word "snake" passed into the smoky atmosphere, when a glass flew through the air, just missing the man. The room went silent. All eyes turned toward a group of gypsies who had risen to their feet, wicked knives visible in their sashes, and had begun to shout: "Wretched good-for-nothing, may you be stung by scorpions...may wasps be born in your eyes!" Another glass flew toward the unfortunate man, who decided his wisest move would be to escape as quickly as possible. He fought his way through the mob, pummeled by blows and insults from every side. One of the gypsies yelled, "*Premía Undebé que oz zargan cuernos y por ellos oz arrastren los ménguez!* [May God cause you to grow horns so that you may be dragged by demons!]" He and his friends followed the man out the door.

It took some time for the café to calm down, but eventually the artists were able to return to the stage and continue. Later, Silverio told Chacón, "I feel for the poor man. You know, the same thing happened to me."

"Really?" replied Chacón, astounded that his idol and mentor could possibly find himself in such a predicament.

"It happened just after I returned from America. I was contracted to sing in a café in Cádiz and all the *gitanos* came to listen to me. They filled the room, and everyone was waiting for me to begin *por polo*. The guitar played and I sang the first *letra* that came to my mind. I intended to sing this..." And with that, Silverio looked around to make sure there were no gypsies within earshot, and then softly sang this *letra*:

Aunque te güerbas culebra	Even if you turn into a snake
y te tires a la mar,	and jump into the sea,
te tengo que perseguir	I have to follow you
hasta mi intento lograr.	until I achieve my goal.

Silverio laughed. "I had sung that *letra* many times in America and didn't think anything of it. But this time I didn't make it past the first line. No sooner had I said 'snake' than everyone in the room was on their feet, yelling furiously. *Gitanas* cried *'Lagarto, lagarto, lagarto!'* Men threw everything they could get their hands on...chairs, bottles, and glasses flew onto the stage. I got out of there as fast as I could and didn't go back. I came here to Sevilla and didn't return to Cádiz until things had time to calm down."

Distressed by the violence that seemed to pervade the flamenco environment and discouraged by the position of his art at the lowest level of society, Chacón renewed his vow to try to elevate the *cante*, to bring it some dignity. He thought: *Why shouldn't I continue the work that Silverio began when he returned from America? His efforts have gone largely unrewarded and most flamenco artists continue to starve and die young. Flamenco continues to exist only in the underbelly of society, among the downtrodden...prostitutes, drunks, gypsies, and misfits. No man would dream of taking his wife or family to listen to* cante.

Chacón began with himself. With his new earnings he spent lavishly to dress himself as a gentleman. Silk three-piece suits, custom made shirts worn with a cravat or bow tie, expensive boots, and—unheard of in a flamenco artist—what the Andalusians called a "mushroom" hat, the fashionable derby so popular throughout Europe and among the Spanish business class. As a final touch, but with some regret and trepidation, he abandoned his *varita de estilo*. He felt the style-stick to be too strongly associated with toreros, gypsy tricksters, and flamenco *cantaores* of the past. In its place he selected a gentleman's walking cane made of polished dark hardwood with an elegantly curved handle and a silver tip.

When Chacón walked out on stage dressed in this manner, more like a banker than an artist, those in the café who had not seen him before were stunned to silence. It became part of his stage persona, his mystique, and prepared the audience for something unexpected. And they weren't disappointed. His appearance, his arrogant demeanor, the totally new style of *cante*, and the playing of Paco de Lucena, all combined to give café-goers a memorable experience. They spread the word and filled the café night after night.

Early one afternoon during his third week in Sevilla, Chacón entered the café to meet Silverio for coffee. He found the *cantaor* in the company of his good friend, Paco el Sevillano. Silverio and Paco had known each other for more than twenty years, ever since Silverio's return from America. El Sevillano had been skeptical about Antonio at first. When he heard that the Jerezano would be paid sixteen *pesetas* rather than the ten that he and other *cantaores* received, he was reported to have said, *"Vamos a ver!"* [We'll have to see about this!] But when Paco, who had been listening nightly to Fosforito in El Burrero, heard the newcomer sing, he had to admit that Silverio had been wise to hire him, no matter what the cost. Chacón, in turn, came to enjoy the company of El Sevillano, a wiry, energetic little man who appeared to be a little older than Silverio. His humor and off-the-cuff ironic observations sparked nightly fiestas in the *reservaos*, and he was a popular performer on the stage of the Café del Burrero where the public always demanded his lively and comical *caracoles*. A highly respected *cantaor*, Paco had sung with Silverio often over the years and was, in fact, the only *cantaor* that Silverio occasionally allowed to sing after him. El Sevillano put it in stronger words: "In the café, age has always been respected. Silverio is good at what he does and I am good at what I do...and I will sing *after* him even if it means I sing to empty seats!"

To sing after Silverio was no small feat. Paco himself had told Chacón that, some years earlier, Silverio had been contracted to sing with Juan Breva and Carito in the Café de la Bolsa in Madrid. The management noticed that many of the customers, who were not yet acquainted with Silverio's *cante*, went home before Silverio's turn to sing, leaving him with only a sparse audience. So they approached the *cantaor* with an offer to have him sing earlier, before the others. The haughty Silverio replied, "Here, take back all the money you have advanced me! He who can sing after me has yet to be born!"

Chacón joined the two men and they chatted over coffee. Suddenly, Silverio, who sat facing the entrance of the café, looked up in surprise and exclaimed, *"Hostias!"*

As he rose to his feet, Silverio muttered, "It's El Burrero...what's he doing here?"

Chacón and El Sevillano watched as a portly man with a full mustache approached. He was in the company of a much taller man, whose silhouette Chacón recognized immediately. It was Fosforito.

"Silverio, *qué hay?"* said the man, fidgeting with the fashionable derby hat he held in his hands.

"Manué...*buenos días*...it's been a long time." Pulling up two more chairs, he added, "Have a seat!"

"What's up?" said the visitor as he shook hands with El Sevillano. Then, indicating his companion, "I believe you already know Fosforito."

El Burrero turned toward the other and presented the tall Gaditano. "Silverio...Francisco Lema."

As Silverio gripped Fosforito's hand, he asked, "Lema, eh? Are you Gallego?"

Fosforito replied, "My grandparents came from Galicia...my name is Lema Ullèt, but I'm pure Gaditano!'

"Well said, *hombre*. Manué, have you met *Don* Antonio Chacón?"

"I've heard a great deal about him, but I haven't had the pleasure."

"Antonio, Manuel Ojeda, the owner of El Burrero."

El Burrero offered a thick hand as he studied the young *cantaor*, who had risen to his feet. His grip was firm and businesslike. "*Don* Antonio, I'm pleased to meet you. In fact, you are the reason for my being here. I've heard much praise for your *cante*."

Silverio spoke. "Whatever you have heard, Manué, cannot begin to describe the *cante* of this Jerezano. What would you like to drink?"

Formalities continued for several minutes. Before he sat down, Fosforito removed a cigarette from his jacket pocket and reached up to one of the highest gas lamps in the room for a light.

Paco el Sevillano's eyebrow shot up in astonishment— to reach that lamp he would have had to stand on someone's shoulders. He said, "Young man, how old are you?"

"Eighteen, why?"

"*Ozú!* When you're twenty-five, you're going to be lighting up from the sun!"

Laughter broke the tension.

"Silverio, I am here on business," said El Burrero. "As you must know, I have been enjoying a great deal of success since Francisco came to sing for me. However, once *Don* Antonio began to sing in your place, my business dropped off. Customers complain that they can't listen to them both. Which is what brings me here...I have a proposal to offer you..."

"I'm listening," said Silverio guardedly.

"If we schedule the two *cantaores* to sing at different times, the public can listen to them both. We will lose customers between their performances, but we can make it up on consumption for each of their two sessions. That way the public is happy, the *cantaores* have a packed house, and we make money. What do you think?"

Silverio thought for a moment, and finding no obvious flaw in the plan, agreed to try it.

After El Burrero had gone, Silverio explained. "Manué has never been in here before...by the way, don't ever call him *burrero* to his face...he doesn't like to be reminded of his days working with burros. As I was saying, he has never been in here. We don't speak. Six years ago we were friends and opened a café together...Paco remembers. It was in the same place as El Burrero, but we called it Café de la Escalera, because of that spiral staircase. That was the old Café del Recreo where I first performed when I came from America. But we couldn't agree on anything. Manué likes the new *cante andaluz* from the Levante [eastern Andalucía], while I prefer the *cante gitano*. He will do anything to bring in customers. I prefer to give the *cante* the dignity it deserves. So, after a year, I left and opened this place. He has never forgiven me."

El Burrero's plan was an instant success. Fosforito sang at ten o'clock and midnight, Chacón at eleven and one. Each evening the streets between the Café del Burrero and Café del Silverio filled with noisy crowds going first one direction and then the other, while debating the merits of each *cantaor*. The cafés were filled to capacity for each performance, with the overflow listening through doorways and windows intentionally left open.

One night, Chacón's curiosity got the better of him and he followed the crowd to El Burrero to listen to Fosforito. Standing in the back of the café, Chacón watched as Maestro Pérez marked the opening *compases* of the *malagueña* and the crowd grew silent in expectation. The silence was broken after Fosoforito's *temple*, as the public, unable to hold back, began commenting on the warm-up and making comparisons with Chacón. In his first *letra*, the popular, "*Ar campo me ví a llorá*," the celebrated *cantaor* seemed to have a throat filled with harmonic bells. He finished the *cante* to a roar of approval and a tremendous ovation. To quiet the crowd, Fosforito did a few small notes of *temple* and then he began his *malagueña grande*. The public listened in religious silence, holding its breath and sweating out the magnificent second-to-last *tercio* with its unusual modulations. It was the crowning moment of the *cante*. Antonio overheard one man say, "*Hombre*, I thought his lungs would burst!" Another added, "I can't stop my tears when he sings." But another came back with, "I still say that Chacón is the more formidable...he amazes me and takes me out of this world.

There is no one like him."

Chacón left the café awed by Fosofrito's talent and charisma. He felt both pride in his friend's accomplishments and a determination to outsing him.

All too quickly Chacón's contracted month with Silverio was coming to an end. In the last week of November, Silverio approached the Jerezano with a new offer.

"*Don* Antonio, I'm very satisfied with your performance here. You have been good for my business. Can you stay longer? I would like to keep you through the summer, until we close for August."

Chacón thought for a moment. He felt flattered, but eight months was a long commitment.

"I'm prepared to pay you twenty *pesetas* a night," continued Silverio, sensing the hesitation in the other, "and I'm going to speak to Dolores about having you sing last. I don't think she will object...people are leaving after you sing so they can go listen to Fosforito."

Twenty pesetas, thought Chacón, *more than anyone is making*. And for him to sing last went against time-honored tradition—seniority and prestige usually determined the order of performance.

"Of course, *Don* Silverio, I'll be glad to stay. Eight months at that salary is a very fair offer."

Chacón was making very good money. In addition to his salary, he was in great demand for after-work fiestas. In fact, he was able to pick and choose, thereby avoiding most of the difficult and degrading *juergas*. Yet the fiestas remained hard work, often requiring the artists to continue through the night, sometimes well into the morning. At the end, the artists were paid according to the whim of the *señorito*, and then they either continued drinking in a nearby tavern or dragged themselves home to bed to get ready to do it all over again.

One night in January a gentleman approached Chacón between performances asking to hire him for a fiesta later in the evening. Antonio remembered the man from a previous fiesta, one in which the pay at the end of the night had not been satisfactory. Without stopping to think, he said impulsively, "I would be happy to oblige...for payment in advance of four *duros* [twenty *pesetas*]."

The *señorito* stepped back, a look of astonishment on his face. "What! That is not customary...and the amount is quite high. If we are not satisfied with the evening, why should we pay? It's just not done!"

"That may be true, but if you wish me to sing for you tonight, that's the way it must be. If that's not satisfactory, I'm sure El Maćaca or one of the others would be happy to accommodate you with the customary arrangement."

"I don't know...it's you we want. Let me talk it over with my friends."

Chacón felt a pang of doubt. *Had he gone too far?* But then he realized that he didn't care if the man accepted his terms or not. He was making good money and there would always be more fiestas.

When the man returned, he said, "We are not completely happy with the arrangement, but we want you. So, let's see how it works out."

The arrangement suited Chacón very well. The money in his pocket put him into a very good mood and he sang well, *a gusto*. In the weeks that followed, he held to his new policy, sometimes succeeding, sometimes not. But, to his surprise, demand for his singing began to increase. As word spread his prestige grew and the wealthy couldn't wait to hire him. He increased his fee to five *duros*—if Juan Breva had been able to earn that, why not Antonio Chacón? And he began to demand payment for his guitarist as well.

Artists came and went in the café. Some rotated through the cafés of Sevilla; others returned home or left to try their luck in Madrid or Málaga. Miguel Macaca, known for his fits of jealousy and frequent fights with his wife, went to prison for taking two shots at a man who made flattering remarks to Enriqueta.

Chacón enjoyed the input of energy that new artists brought to the stage. He always found something to learn from new singers. Sometimes he was surprised. Such was the case the night Silverio approached the *cuadro* as they prepared for the first show of the evening, a stunningly handsome young man by his side. Dark and very slender, the stranger dressed in the garb of the *chulo*—a style of dress from an earlier time. Although he was clearly not gypsy, he wore a short jacket and tight velvet pants of a dark purple color. A *calañés* hat and spats that came almost to his knees completed an outfit generally worn only by the most traditional of gypsies.

"This is Romero," said Silverio "He's the nephew of *Tío* José el Granaíno and he'll be singing with us tonight."

The newcomer flashed a warm smile, his sparkling eyes looking directly into those of each performer as he was introduced.

"He goes by Romero el Tito. He'll be singing for the dance and if he wishes to sing something solo, let him go first, after the dancers have finished. Paco, arrange the guitar with him."

So it was. They went on stage and Romero el Tito sang *cantiñas* for the dancers. One after the other, different styles of *cantiñas*,[2] all sung with *gracia* and an infectious rhythm that had even the seated dancers moving in their chairs. Then, as he began to sing the *cantiñas* known as *caracoles*, Romero leaped from his chair and began to dance. To the surprise of all he danced well, with elegance, brilliance, and a *gracia* that had the public laughing—he wasn't a comic, but his moves were so unexpected and original that the spectators had to laugh. The women in the *cuadro* cheered him on with suggestive and lascivious remarks. His fine figure displayed in tight pants had not gone unnoticed. "*Ole el feo de bonito!*" one of them yelled. [*Ole*, the ugly handsomeness; too pretty for a man.] Romero sang the refrain:

Caracoles!	Snails! [snail seller's cry]
Caracoles!	Snails!
Hermano que ise osté?	What do you say brother?
Qué son mis ojos dos soles;	My eyes are two suns;
vamos viviendo chorré!	let's go on living, children!

The audience gave Romero a tremendous ovation when he finished.

Off stage, Romero el Tito proved to be as cheerful and likable as he was in front of an audience. Between shows everyone seemed to gravitate to him and he never stopped performing, always at the center of a constant fiesta that had singers and dancers laughing non-stop at his songs, jokes, and stories. Chacón interrupted his antics at one point to ask, "Romero, where did you learn all of those wonderful *cantiñas?*"

"*Hombre*, in Cái of course! Those are *cantiñas* of my uncle, José el Granaíno, and some from my *compare* [friend] Paquirri el Guanté..."

"You know Paquirri?"

"Of course! He's my best friend...we were together not long ago in Madrid. That man has rhythm *que no se pué aguantá* [that is too much to bear]."

---

[2]*cantiñas*: a family of bright, festive songs from Cádiz, usually in a major key and with the *compás* of the *soleá*. All *alegrías* are *cantiñas*, but there are many *cantiñas* that are not *alegrías*. Some have names such as *romeras*, *mirabrás*, or *caracoles*, but many are just called *cantiñas*.

Romero glanced around before continuing, "Since Dolores is not here, I can tell you what she did to Juan Breva in Madrid. Those two were competitors, so, to play a dirty trick on Breva, Dolores went to the owner of the Café El Imparcial where Juan was working and talked him into hiring Paquirri. You know, Paquirri plays the guitar for himself just like Breva, and nobody can equal him *por soleá*. So whenever Paquirri sang his *soleares* it caused such a commotion among aficionados that they threw silver coins, hats, caps, and even jackets onto the stage. Breva should have been furious, but you know how he is...he just decided to add more *soleares* to his repertoire!"

Within weeks, Romero el Tito's *cantiñas* had flooded Sevilla. In the café, Romero always began with one favorite *cantiña*:

Romera, ay mi Romera,	Rosemary, ay my Rosemary,
no me cantes más cantares;	don't give me any more of your excuses;
si te cojo junto al jierro,	if I catch you up against the ironwork,
no te salve ni tu mare.	not even your mother can save you.

At first the others in the *cuadro* responded to that *cantiña* with cries of *"Ole las cantiñas del Romero!"* The second week they began to say, *"Ole las cantiñas romeras!"* After the third week, it was just, *"Ole las romeras!"* And *romeras* they remained.

Even Chacón found himself humming or singing Romero's melodies during the day. He found himself particularly attracted to the *caracoles*. It had a melody that he thought he could elaborate and develop into something noteworthy. So he played with it and added more and more ornamentation, treating it much in the same way he had the *malagueña*. He wasn't in a hurry to perform it, but was content to let it develop at a leisurely pace.

On a night only a few weeks after Romero el Tito began to sing in the Café de Silverio, Chacón noticed a man enter the café and come toward the bar. One hand rested on the shoulder of a little girl who seemed to be leading him. It soon became clear that man was blind and being led by his daughter. Chacón was about to dismiss the pair as a couple of beggars when the blind man said to no one in particular, "Is Silverio around?"

Then the *cantaor*'s eyes fell on the girl's clothing. She dressed in the style of the *majo*—the dandy of the Madrid of yesteryear: short jacket, white ruffled shirt buttoned at the neck, tight pants with trim down the sides, decorative knee-high spats over her shoes, and the *calañés* hat.

"He should be here soon," replied the bartender.

"We'll wait." And they stood at one end of the bar, patient and unmoving.

Sometime later, the blind man turned his head toward the entrance and said, "He's here, I can hear him!"

Indeed, Silverio had come in and was speaking with a man near the door. When he finally came closer, he spotted the blind man and said, "Juan, *hombre*, it's been a while! How goes it?"

"*Bien, Don* Silverio...we're defending ourselves. Times are hard for a blind man and his family, but some of my children are beginning to work as artists and that helps."

Silverio greeted Chacón and added, "Antonio, this is Juan Rodríguez, a very good guitarist. You should see him accompany the dance, even though he can't see! Juan, *Don* Antonio Chacón...certainly you've heard of him."

"*Don* Antonio, my pleasure. Yes, who hasn't heard about your singing."

"Antonio," continued Silverio, "Juan is also an excellent teacher. His children all sing, dance, and play the guitar..."

"*Don* Silverio," said Juan, "that is precisely why I am here. This is my daughter, Saluíta...she is the best of them all and ready for the stage..."

Silverio looked down at the stocky little girl with her round gypsy face, estimating her age to be eleven or twelve.

The father continued, "Will you give her a try? She won't disappoint you."

"I don't know, Juan, she's awfully young."

"Just try her...you'll see. She is going to be the next Trinidad Huertas..."

"La Cuenca? She is a phenomenon that will never be repeated." Silverio turned to Chacón, "Antonio, did you ever see Trinidad la Cuenca dance?"

Chacón shook his head.

"She was beautiful and had a good figure, but she dressed and danced as a man. She came from Málaga and created a scandal here with her dancing. They said a woman shouldn't reveal her body in tight pants like that. But she soon won over the public with her *gracia* and powerful footwork. She used to dance the entire bullfight, from the first cape pass to the death of the bull, all done with incomparable *compás*, pure art, and the most intricate footwork. And she was the first to dance the *soleá* of Arcas...she did it as a *zapateado flamenco*... wonderful footwork."

Silverio looked down at the little girl. "*Niña*, can you really dance like La Cuenca?"

Salud returned the huge man's gaze with fearless eyes, her little mouth set in determination, and replied, "Yes, *Señor* Silverio."

"*Bien*, Juan, we'll let her give it a try tonight and see how it goes. Antonio, would you tell the others that Salud Rodríguez, *la niña del ciego* [the daughter of the blind man] will dance first tonight."

And the little girl danced as her father had said. She strutted arrogantly about the stage in her *majo* outfit, fearless in her naiveté and innocence. The audience didn't seem to know what to think at first. But when the first burst of staccato footwork cut through the air amid a cloud of dust rising from the worn floor the crowd grew silent for a moment, then rose to its feet and applauded noisily. More and more footwork, with impeccable rhythm and original and difficult details. Salud danced with the feet of an adult, her youth only amplifying the effect she had on the audience.

When the *cuadro* came down from the stage, Silverio came to the father and said, "*Bien* Juan...the public liked her. She can dance here for a while and we'll see how it works out. I can pay four *pesetas*."

"*Gracias*, *Don* Silverio."

"But, Juan...she has to work on her arms. You can't see it, but she has the defect of forgetting to use her arms. They often just hang by her sides..."

"Of course, *Don* Silverio, that will be corrected immediately, you'll see."

And so it was. Within weeks Salud had corrected her arms and become the darling of Sevilla.

Some dancers, crowd favorites, stayed on in the café for extended periods. But, to keep interest up, Silverio tried to bring in new girls on a regular basis. Chacón was delighted when Rita Ortega brought her younger sister, Carlota, to debut in the Café de Silverio. He immediately recognized the frizzy-haired teenager he had first seen sitting on the stairs of El Águila's *casa de vecinos* in Cádiz. Now sixteen, the young *gitana* had developed into an attractive woman. Her beauty, ripe figure, and youthful innocence combined with her gypsy art and *gracia* to make Carlota Ortega an immediate favorite with the public.

"**Y**ou're really doing that?"

Javier spoke as he and his brother sat with Chacón at a table outside the Café Suizo on Calle de las Sierpes, watching the parade of afternoon strollers.

"Yes...and it's working out well," replied Chacón. "It seems like the more I charge them, the more they want me!"

Antonio Molina shook his head. "I don't think we could ever collect our pay in advance, *tocayo*...they would just ask for someone else."

Chacón didn't know what to say. Antonio was probably right.

"How's Silverio doing?" asked Javier. "I saw in the newspaper that he's still sick."

"He has good days and bad. Some days he is too tired to come down to the café. I don't see him so often these days. How are things at the Filarmónico?"

"Not bad. Patiño can be difficult sometimes, but we manage to get along. Juanero and I have been playing together for so many years that it's easy for us now. Chato is a joy to play for, and our new singer, Fernando el Mezcle, is very good. He's one of the Ortegas from Sanlúcar and excellent in the *cantes* of Cádiz, besides being a great *seguiriyero* [singer of *seguiriyas*]..."

"And the women are phenomenal," chimed in Antonio.

"The Filharmónico is a paradise for my brother. He's chasing everything in a dress...it doesn't matter what they look like!"

"All cats are gray in the dark, *hermano*," replied Antonio with a wide grin. "But the one I really want, *tocayo*, is Juana Antúnez. She's about sixteen now *y está pa comérsela* [and she's pretty enough to eat]. She's dancing in the Burrero and I get over there every chance I get."

Chacón shook his head in amazement. To change the subject, he asked Javier, "Have you seen your old teacher, Paco el Barbero?"

"*Hombre*, of course! He's doing well. His *colmao* [eating and drinking establishment] over on Callejuela de la Plata,[3] off La Campana, is always busy. Usually you can find guitarists hanging out there. Even Patiño stops in from time to time. I go often to play guitar with the

---

[3]Today: *Calle* Martín Villa.

maestro. Although he's retired, Paco continues to study the guitar and still plays well. In fact, he'll be leaving for Madrid soon to play for the opening of a new café. He doesn't want to leave his business, but the owner of the new place is a friend and the money will be good. You should come with me to meet him sometime."

"I'd love to."

"Then you better do it soon...Junquera is sending us back to Jerez at the end of next month. His sister asked for us and Juan can't say no to her."

Antonio Molina made a long face and said, "I'm not ready to leave here yet. Why do we always have to do what Junquera says?"

"We have no choice...if we want to work," answered Javier. "We won't be able to work in the Filharmónico if we leave Junquera, since he does the hiring there."

"We could always go to the Burrero."

"They don't need a guitarist. And if they did, after that what? We have a good situation with Junquera...we are always guaranteed to have work. You can always come back to Sevilla to see Juana."

Antonio shrugged his shoulders.

Silverio and Antonio Chacón sat for lunch at an outdoor table on the Alameda de Hércules. It was the end of April, and Holy Week and the spring fair had just finished. Unusually heavy rains had tried unsuccessfully to spoil the spring festivities and had flooded parts of Triana, but now had left the air crisply clear and the cobbled streets damp and clean. The Alameda, a broad tree-lined promenade that ran some six city blocks north from the end of Calle Amor de Dios, was popular with lunch goers and strollers during the long afternoon *siesta* hours and a center of nightlife in the evenings, especially as the weather warmed. Named for the statue of Hercules atop one of the two tall, slender columns that had been taken from a Roman temple in some earlier century and now formed the entrance to the paved promenade, the Alameda was dotted with kiosk-like cafés, each surrounded by rows of tables and chairs.

There were two areas of Silverio's life in which he spared no expense: He spent lavishly on custom-made clothes and fine dining. Today he had already finished off a large bowl of shellfish soup, a stew of garbanzos and spinach, and *calamares* stuffed with spiced meat. Now he was working enthusiastically on a stew of bull's tails—provided by the recent *corridas* and accompanied by a bottle of wine and several small loaves of crispy aromatic bread from the town of Alcalá de Guadaira, popularly called Alcalá de los Panaderos [Alcalá of the Breadmakers].

Among the crowd of passersby, one man stopped and looked in the direction of the dining *cantaores*. He broke into a smile and called out, "*Don* Silverio!"

Both Silverio and Chacón looked up from their meals to see a slight, well-dressed man coming toward them.

"*Don* Silverio, how fortunate...I've been planning to come to see you."

"Luis, it's been a long time."

"Yes, it *has* been a long time...too long."

"Luis, I'd like you to meet *Don* Antonio Chacón. Antonio, Luis Montoto, a poet and a good aficionado of the *cante*...as well as a good friend."

"*Don* Antonio," said Luis as the two men shook hands, "I have heard a great deal about you, but unfortunately I have been unable to get out much at night, so I haven't been in to listen to you."

Chacón took in the man's scruffy and sparse mustache and goatee and his short undisciplined hair and decided the man had to be a scholar. Silverio was saying, "Luis used to come into the old café, the one I had with Ojeda, along with his friend *Don* Antonio Machado y Álvarez. Remember, Luis, you used to come in almost every day...and even before that, back when I had the summer café here on the Alameda? But I haven't seen either of you for years..."

"Yes, *Don* Silverio, ever since *Don* Antonio went to live in Madrid."

"How is he doing?"

"Well enough. He does some teaching and he has started a society to study Spanish folklore. But there is never enough money...he has a new son."

Turning to Chacón, Silverio explained. "*Don* Antonio is a scholar, very well educated and a marvelous writer. When he wrote, he used the name Demófilo...*qué gracia, no?* And that's what I used to call him...Demófilo. He wrote a book about our *cante*, a collection of flamenco *coplas*...to preserve the best of the old *cante*."

"With much thanks to Silverio," said Luis, addressing Chacón. "This great *cantaor* shared his knowledge and his life's experiences with us...all carefully noted by Demófilo and included in the book."

"That book is a marvel, Antonio. I must show it to you. I have it at home. Why don't you come by tomorrow and take a look at it."

"Which brings me to the reason I wanted to see you, *Don* Silverio. I just received a letter from Demófilo in which he asked me for help in collecting *letras* for a new book. I was hoping I could speak with some of the *cantaores* singing in your café. This book will be different from the first in that it will include *letras* of some of the lighter *cantes*...the *alegrías*, *jaberas*, and others..."

"*Hombre*, I'll give you one of my *letras* of *jaberas* right now. Listen:

Los lamentos de un cautivo	The wails of a captive
no pueden llegar a España,	cannot reach Spain,
porque está la mar por medio	because the sea lies in-between
y se convierten en agua.	and they change into water.

"Exactly what I need, *Don* Silverio. Let me write that down."

"Come in any time you like, Luis. I may not be of much help this time, but there are others who will be able to help you."

"Thank you. This will mean a lot to Demófilo. Let me leave you to your meal now...I'll be in to the café soon. *Don* Antonio, it was a pleasure. I look forward to hearing you sing."

After Luis had departed, Silverio said to Chacón, "Don't forget to come by the house tomorrow...I really want you to take a look at that book."

The following day, a little before noon, Chacón ascended the narrow stairs of Number 30 on the Plaza de la Constitución,[4] just off Calle de las Sierpes near the Cathedral. He had entered the building through the doorway of the Bank of Spain and now he found Silverio's door on the second floor. He knocked. When a young woman opened the door, he said, "*Buenos días*...I'm Antonio Chacón, here to see Silverio." As he spoke he thought, *Silverio has said nothing about having a teenage daughter...maybe this is his housekeeper.*

"*Buenos días, Don* Antonio. I'm María de la Salud...come in, my husband is expecting you."

Silverio's wife! Antonio could hardly believe it. The youthful beauty had taken his breath away with her dark sultry eyes, long black hair,

---

[4]Today: Plaza de San Francisco.

and rounded voluptuous figure. He continued to study her as he followed her down a hall into a small sitting room where he found Silverio ensconced in a comfortable lounging chair.

"Antonio, I'm glad you came. Excuse me for not getting up to greet you...I'm not feeling so well today."

"Relax, maestro."

"You've met my wife, María?"

"Yes, she introduced herself."

"We've been married two years, but I have yet to bring her to the café. I think you can understand why."

"Yes, of course."

"Well, you didn't come here to talk about my wife. Here is the book I was telling you about."

Silverio picked up a small volume from a side table and handed it to Chacón. Antonio studied the elegant cover with its figure of a *bailaora* as he sat back in his chair. The title read, *Colección de Cantes Flamencos: Collected and Annotated by A. Machado y Álvarez (Demófilo)*. It was dated 1881. Antonio leafed through the pages. After a lengthy introduction, he was astounded to see page after page of *letras...soleares* of three lines, hundreds of them...*soleariyas*, *soleares* of four lines, *seguiriyas*, *cañas* and *polos*, *martinetes*, *tonás* and *livianas*, *deblas*, and *peteneras*. It was too much to take in all at once. Then, surprise of surprises, there before him was a photo of Silverio, his biography, and many of his favorite *letras*. Chacón's examination of the book was interrupted when a folded paper fell from the back cover. He handed the brown and brittle newsprint to Silverio, who opened it, looked at it a moment, smiled, and handed it back.

"Look at that, Antonio, it is the announcement of my first performance here in Sevilla when I came back from America. I forgot I had it."

Chacon read:

El Porvenir, March 25, 1865: Salón del Recreo, located on Plaza Campana, Calle Tarifa No. 1. Tonight there will be an extraordinary rehearsal of national dances, that is, castanet dances, involving eight good couples, being assisted by the famous cantador *Silverio, who recently arrived from Cádiz, José Ordóñez, known as Juraco, and by some* jitanas *who will do the* jaleos. *It begins at eight o'clock.*

"That was when I first came back here from Cádiz, after the snake incident. The night before that, I surprised the *gitanos* of Triana when I pretended to be a South American who wanted to sing...there in the Venta Laureano."

Chacón remembered the story his *Tío* Juan had told him so many times.

"It was around that time, or maybe when I came back the following year, that I began to spend time in Triana. A number of good *cantaores* used to get together to sing...that's when we began to sing the new *soleares*. But we can talk about that some other time. What do you think of the book?"

"I haven't been able to read any of it yet, but it seems so strange to see flamenco *cantes* written down on paper. And, is that really your biography?"

"Yes. Demófilo asked me so many questions about my life, but I didn't think he would really put it all into his book. And if you read carefully, you will see that he criticizes me, accuses me of *agachonando* the *cante* [making the *cante gitano* into something *gachó*]. He believes that we are destroying the *cante gitano* by elevating it, by taking it out of the local tavern and presenting it on the stage of the café or theater. When I look at the miserable lives of most *cantaores gitanos*, I can't help but feel pride in the little I have been able to do to make their lives better. But I also see that he may be right. You know, the *cante* used to be something very personal. The old *letras* lacked formal structure or theatrical value. They were direct cries from the soul, nothing more. We sang of events in our lives, of our families, of our suffering and our love. But we can't sing of those things in the café. The public is not interested in what our brother or sister did on a particular day. In the café, we must sing of those experiences that are shared by all...our mothers and our romances...or our death. I can't sing this *seguiriya* anymore:

Audiencia de Sevilla,	Court of Sevilla,
tener caridá;	be charitable;
qué mi amigo Bastián Quintana	let my friend Bastián Quintana
salga en libertá!	go free!

So we are not free to sing what we feel at a particular moment...and we are not free to sing when we feel the need...we must sing on demand.

So what are we to do? The situation before was not acceptable, and the situation now is becoming unacceptable!"

Chacón had no answer. He had not given much thought to those things. Now, respecting Silverio's need for rest and the approaching lunch hour, he excused himself, saying, "*Don* Silverio, I really must be going. May I borrow this book for a few days?"

"Of course. Keep it as long as you wish. I'll see you in a couple of days...I'm beginning to feel better."

Chacón said goodbye to María and went directly to his favorite table on nearby Calle de las Sierpes. Over lunch, he buried himself in Demófilo's book, devouring every word—or at least every word he could understand. Having left school at such a young age, his reading ability was not up to Demófilo's scholarly writing. Fortunately, he had developed the habit of reading the newspaper each day, so his skill had been improving. With patience and skipping words he didn't know, he painstakingly made his way through Silverio's story. He was astounded to see in print many of the details that he had heard from the mouth of the *cantaor*. After three pages dealing with Silverio's life, the author began his criticism of the *cantaor*'s attempt to elevate the *cante gitano*. Chacón read:

> *In the taverns, in the reunions of families and friends, the* cantaores *were true kings, honored always, and even though they were paid on occasion, they were always listened to with religious silence—pity the poor man who dared to interrupt them. In the cafés, on the other hand, the public commands and is the true king. Since the majority of the public are neither intelligent nor accustomed to distinguishing the good from the bad and, in general, they do not participate in the profoundly sad emotion that dominates the* gitano *when he sings, the* cantaores *[in the cafés] start* agachonando *the* cante, *motivated more by self-interest than by their art. They must always be accommodating the tastes of the public who pays, a public made up of an infinite number of individuals who, for the two* reales *they pay for their coffee or glass of wine, feel they have a perfect right to applaud or jeer, according to their mood.*
>
> *The cafés will completely kill the* cante gitano *in the not-too-distant future, in spite of the gigantic effort made by the famous* cantaor *of Sevilla to lift it out of the dark sphere where it previously resided and never should have left if it wished to remain pure and genuine. When the* cante gitano *left the tavern for the café, it became some*

thing Andalusian, changing into what everyone today calls "flamenco," a mixture of gitano *and Andalusian elements.*

Demófilo went on to write that Silverio had put himself into a position where he was now forced into putting up a last defense of the *cante gitano* in his café on Calle Rosario. He also lamented that it had come to the point where a man learns no more than a few warbles and then he wants to go up on stage to sing for a *duro*.

Chacón sat back from the book and tried to digest what he had read. Perhaps it was true that the *cante gitano* would be lost if it were taken out of its natural environment. The creative miracle of the *cante*, its sensitivity, profundity, and beauty, often came out of miserable human beings who were practically incapable of holding an intelligent conversation and who were filled with petty hatreds and prejudices. But, at the same time, many gypsy artists led miserable lives and often died young, of tuberculosis, syphilis, alcoholism, or violence. It didn't seem right that they should be left to their often tragic existences just so that their suffering might provide substance for their song. And Chacón had no doubts about his intention to avoid that kind of life.

The *cantaor* turned his attention to the *letras* collected by Demófilo. He still could not believe that it was possible to write down authentic flamenco *cante*. When he tried to read, he ran into trouble right away. Under the title, *Soleares de Tres Versos* [*Soleares* of Three Lines], the first verse read:

> *Anda, que ya biene er día;*
> *si esta flamenca no ispierta,*
> *ba a sé la perdisión mía.*

He found he didn't know some of the words...words such as *biene, ispierta, ba a sé*. These were not words he had learned in school, nor were they words he had read in the newspapers. Frustrated, he said the words he knew out loud. After several attempts, he added the words he didn't know, trying to approximate their sound. Suddenly he heard them. When he spoke them, they took on the familiar sound of his speech. He had found the secret. If he spoke the *letra*, it made sense. This *letra* should have read:

Anda, que ya viene el día;   Come on, daylight is coming;
si esta flamenca no despierta,   if this girl doesn't wake up,
va a ser la perdición mía.   it will be my downfall.

Thrilled by his discovery, Antonio struggled through several more verses. Then he paid his bill and hurried back to his *pensión* room. Forgoing his usual afternoon nap, he buried himself in Demófilo's collection of verses. Gradually the reading became easier. Now he was stunned to find that the collection contained dozens of *letras* that he had learned from their creators. There were *letras* from Silverio, El Mellizo, Curro Dulce, Paquirri el Guanté, Salvaoriyo, and so many others. As he read through them he found it unsettling. He had spent years traveling the back roads of Andalucía, seeking out *cantaores* and begging them to teach him these songs. One by one he had learned these jewels of personal expression, had memorized them and perfected them. Now, here they were, written down for all to see, to hold in their hands without effort. Of course, it was only the lyrics. Without the song, the music, the words were meaningless. But still...he found it unsettling.

Over the next several days, Chacón spent every spare minute in his room, reading and copying *letras* onto paper, *letras* that would fuel his future creativity. As he read and wrote, something beyond the easy accessibility of the verses bothered him, ate away at him. It wasn't until the third day that he suddenly realized what was disturbing him. *If these* letras *were so difficult for him to understand, even when written down on paper before him, how could the public be expected to understand them when distorted in song by the* cantaor?

Demófilo had filled as much as half of each page with footnotes explaining the *letras*. What chance did the average listener have of understanding them? On top of that, the language of the *cante* seemed to come from the lowest levels of society, the jargon of the poor and uneducated, of *gitanos* and thieves. How could he, Antonio Chacón, expect to elevate the *cante* and give it dignity if it were to be forever unintelligible and associated with degenerate lifestyles?

Chacón made a decision. From that point on, he would sing in correct Castilian Spanish. If Silverio sang:

Qué ducas tan grandes!
Cáa bes que m'acuerdo
é los sacais é la bata mía,
loquito me güerbo.

SEVILLA

Then he, Antonio Chacón, would sing:

Qué penas tan grandes!	What great suffering!
Cada vez que me acuerdo	Each time I remember
de los ojos de mi madre	the eyes of my mother,
loquito me vuelvo.	I go crazy.

Where another would sing:

Toma gachí estas dos jaras;
díñasela'r libanó
pa que ponga en los papires
de que no abiyelo yo.

He would sing:

Toma mujer estas dos onzas;	Woman, take these two gold coins;
dáselas al escribano	give them to the clerk
para que ponga en los papeles	so he can write in his papers
de que no las tengo yo.	that I don't have them.

Chacón felt exhilarated by this decision. At the same time he realized that he could not commit the heresy of changing the *letras* of the masters. He would continue to sing these *letras* the way he had learned them, pronouncing the words as clearly as possible. But everything he created in the future would be sung in his best Castilian Spanish.

A few days later, Silverio sent for Chacón. When the Jerezano arrived at the café, he found Silverio and Paco el Sevillano waiting for him.

"Paco...how's it going? Maestro, I'm glad to see you're feeling better. What's up?"

"*Mira*, Antonio, I see that there's a lot of smoke over Triana today. That means they're firing the pottery and maybe the potters will have some time off. I'd like you to meet Ramón... Ramón el Ollero [the pot-maker]. I think you'll like how that man sings *por soleá*. What do you say?"

"Why not...let's go!"

Silverio hailed a carriage. The three men chatted to the leisurely rhythm and hollow echo of horse's hooves on cobblestone as the carriage made its way through the narrow streets.

"Silverio, you know Bartólome, that guy who comes into the café sometimes?" El Sevillano was in fine form this day, full of witticisms and bizarre observations.

"Which Bartólome?"

"The one who always has his wife with him." Turning to Chacón, Paco explained, "There is this guy who never goes anywhere without his wife. So, the other day I finally asked him why he takes his wife with him everywhere...and you know what he said?"

The others waited.

"He said to me, 'I have to...my wife is so ugly I can't stand to kiss her goodbye!'"

Chacón and Silverio laughed until tears rolled down their cheeks.

When he had regained his composure, Silverio said, "Antonio, you know, before I went to America, we had no *soleares*. We had the *jaleos*...very lively, for dancing. One of the best singers of *jaleos* was a woman named Soledad, and when I returned everyone was singing *por Soledades*. We began to call these *cantes* "*soleá jaleo*" or "*soleaes*." Paquirri el Guanté was excellent in the *soleá jaleo*, as was El Fillo's woman, La Andonda. But most of us preferred to sing *polos*. Well, like I was telling you the other day, when I came back to Sevilla I began to get together with *cantaores* in Triana. We met in taverns on Calle Castilla, next to the ceramic factory, or in Casa de Joaquina de la Vega over near the Plaza Chapina...Joaquina's brother was an excellent guitarist. Paquirri was living in Triana, as was La Andonda. Enrique el Gordo Viejo was here, too. Paco, you remember...you were with us often."

"Like it was yesterday, *compare*. And don't forget Lorente."

"Yes, José was often with us. There were many good singers here at that time. Merced la Serneta was here for a while..."

"La Serneta?" said Chacón. "I used to hear about her in Jerez...all the old men speak of her. I believe she was from Santiago."

"Yes, that's her. She grew up in the forges there and sang all the old *cantes* well. But just before I came back from America, a wealthy *señorito* took her to Utrera...she was still a young girl...and there she has stayed."

"I believe she was a Fernández, the family of Los Serna..."

"Yes, she is Fernández Vargas," added El Sevillano, "but she told me her father named her after a lively little bird, *la serneta*. And what a beauty she was in her youth. We all fell in love with her...it was impossible to resist her. Eyes like almonds, dark pools in which to drown yourself. Long lashes and perfectly shaped brows..."

"And a small mouth with lips like caramels," added Silverio.

"*Ozú, compare*," said El Sevillano, "I'm too old to be thinking the thoughts I'm thinking now! Her face had the beauty of the Virgin Mary. Antonio, if you want to know the extraordinary beauty of Mercedes la Serneta, go to the Chapel of San Román and look at the statue of The Virgin of the *Gitanos*."

"That's true, *compare*, but it was her singing that made us all want her. La Serneta came to Triana while I was gone. She was a good friend of La Andonda and was here to help her after El Fillo died in '62 of lung disease. María la Andonda was one of the best in singing the old *soleá jaleo* and Mercedes learned from her.

"As I was saying, when I came back to Sevilla, I went often to Triana and we would sing all night. Mostly we sang por *seguiriyas*, *cañas*, and *polos*...and *por soledades*. Then, one night when we were singing *por soledades*, someone...I think it was El Gordo, although it could have been Paquirri...put in a *letra* of *polo*. It had the melody and *letra* of the *polo*, but the *aire* [air; mood] of the *soleá*. It came out beautifully. It was genius. We all began to try it, using different styles of *polo*. We had to slow the *cante* a little and give it a different *aire*. It became more profound and soon we were looking for the most tragic *letras* we could find to go with that mood. Before long we forgot about singing *polos*...all we wanted was the *soleá apolá* [*soleá* in the style of *polo*].

"Ramón, the pot-maker I want you to meet, was one of the best. Soon he began creating his own melodies and over the years other ceramic makers copied him and now they have the *soleá* of the *alfareros* [ceramic makers] that is unlike any other *soleá*...very simple, with much melody and not much rhythm. I think you will like them. You have to hear some of the women singing that style...La Gómez is a follower of Ramón and one of the best *por soleá*, and La Cuende is her competitor.

"The other who created a completely personal style of these *soleares* was La Serneta. Hers were the most ardent and passionate of all. She was irresistible when she sang:

Yo nunca mi ley farté;
qué te tengo tan presente,
como la primera vé.

I was always true to my word;
I'm still as true to you
as I was the first time.

Siendo que soy tuya,
qué caenita me has echao
que me tienes tan segura?

You say that I am yours,
what chain have you tied me with
that you feel you own me?

"When we began to sing the *soleá apolá*, both La Andonda and La Serneta were superb in combining the new style with the old. Mercedes...we called her Mercé...had the gift of creative genius in her *cantes*, and her voice had incomparable sweetness, yet could be full and virile when she desired. I can't do justice to her *cante*, but listen to these *letras*:

Me acuerdo de cuando puse
sobre tu cara la mía,
y, suspirando, te dije,
'Serrano, ya estoy perdía!'

I remember when I placed
my face on yours,
and, sighing, I said to you,
'Man of the mountains, I'm lost!'

Presumas que eres la ciencia,
y yo no lo entiendo así,
porque sabiendo tú tanto
no me has entendío tú a mí.

You pretend to know so much,
but I don't see it that way,
because, knowing so much,
you haven't understood me.

"It gave you shivers to listen to her," said El Sevillano.

Enthralled by the *cante* of Mercedes la Serneta, Chacón asked, "How can I listen to her...where is she now?"

"She's getting up in years now, and she almost never leaves her home in Utrera. You would have to go there to listen to her, but it would be worth the trouble...she's a true specialist in the *soleares* and has created a very pure *cante* that is influencing everyone.

"*En fin* [In summary], over the next ten years or so, this new *cante por soleá* became so popular that it spread everywhere. Paquirri took them to Madrid and, together with El Gordo, to Cádiz. Paco la Luz was one of the first to sing them in Jerez. Even Juan Breva learned them, from La Serneta, and took them back to Málaga. And of course, in Utrera, all they want to sing now are the *soleares* of Mercé la Serneta."

The carriage descended down off the bridge into the Plaza Altozano in Triana. A gang of gypsy ragamuffins, cigarettes in their mouths and curses on their lips, sauntered leisurally across the street in front of the vehicle, causing it to slow. Chacón recalled that day, two years earlier, when he and the Molina brothers had crossed this same bridge to look for lodging. It seemed so long ago. A right turn at the first corner and a moment later the three men stepped down from the carriage in front of a building with an ornate tile façade. Clouds of black smoke had turned the day into gray dusk and a steady mist of white ash fell like snow.

Silverio led the way into the building, brushing the ash from his jacket. Inside, the shop displayed endless ceramic objects, among them decorated tiles, earthenware pots, shaving bowls, chamber pots, cups and plates.

"*Señora*, is Ramón around?" asked Silverio.

"I think he is in the back working with the fire. Go on in."

The men passed through a small doorway and entered a gray labyrinth occupying the inside of the largest city block in Triana. What from the outside appeared to be streets of homes and shops was actually only the outer skin of an immense series of ceramic factories. Inside, a skeleton of unfinished wood beams, ceiling supports, and room dividers created a seemingly endless maze of rooms and half-rooms, all interconnected. Gray clay and clay dust coated everything. The three men made their way past unattended potter's wheels, glazing wheels with pots of dull glaze scattered about, and endless wooden forms and tools. They passed a row of ladder-back chairs facing a slanted wall as if waiting to punish delinquent students. A few tiles leaning against the wall next to pots of glaze and brushes revealed the true purpose—a work area for painting tile. In spite of the cool weather outside, the air was stifling with an oppressive heat and the dank smell of wet clay.

Silverio was about to call out for Ramón when they spotted a man using bricks and mortar to seal the door to a stone-lined room. Chacón could see past the man into the room, where raw pottery was packed tightly from floor to ceiling. The man turned and grinned at the visitors. "*El empañetao*," he said, "to seal the oven for the firing."

"Is Ramón around?"

"He's firing the next oven…up further."

"*Gracias*."

Silverio led the way through more rooms, until they passed another kiln and heard the thud of wood hitting wood. Just beyond the kiln, the floor sloped downward to a room underneath the oven. Intense heat hit them just as they spotted a man at the door of the lower room, throwing logs of wood into an inferno.

"Ramón!" yelled Silverio, when the man paused between logs.

The man turned and grinned. "Silverio, Paco...give me a few minutes."

He threw more wood into the fire, and finally satisfied, turned and approached the visitors. "Let's get out of here...I need a break from this heat."

Ramón el Ollero was a ruggedly handsome man, appearing to be in his fifties, with receding black hair and several days' growth of stubble. Shirtless, his muscular body dripped with sweat and was covered with streaks of black carbon and gray chalk. He led the others to a small room where he found his shirt and jacket. After wiping himself down, he dressed and led his visitors out a side door onto Calle Alfarería. The cool air hit with a refreshing shock. Chacón felt that he could breath again. Finally, Silverio was able to introduce the Jerezano to El Ollero.

"Ramón, I'd like to present *Don* Antonio Chacón, from Jerez. He's currently singing for me."

Ramón looked at Antonio without speaking, taking in the clothes and the bearing of a *señorito*. Then, offering his hand, he said, "*Don* Antonio, eh! *Hombre*, how can you sing dressed like that?"

Chacón looked directly into the Ramón's eyes and replied," My singing pays me well enough to dress like this!"

The other paused a moment, then laughed and said, "Let's go get a drink."

In a small tavern, made smaller by Silverio's bulk, the men chatted over glasses of sherry. Ramón explained that he would have to return to check the fires and keep an eye on the pottery through a hole in the kiln. After one day of firing they would let the pottery cool for another day before a team of unloaders would arrive to empty the kilns. About half of the pots would be broken and lost. Then everybody would go back to work glazing and starting a new load of ceramics.

"How many kilns do you have?" asked Chacón.

"We have five here, but there are at least sixty around Triana."

"*Mira*, Ramón," said Silverio, "I've been telling Antonio about the old days, when we were beginning to sing *por soleá*. And how, here in the *alfarería*, you have created a *soleá* different from any other."

"Here in the *alfarería* we sing *por soleá* better than anyone. Over there in the *la cava de los gitanos* they sing the best *por seguiriyas* and *martinetes*, but they can't sing *por soleá* the way we do."

"Why do you say *cava?*" asked Chacón.

"*La cava?* We say *la cava* [the trench] because of Calle Cava Nueva,[5] the street that encircles Triana. They say that the *cava* was once a moat used to defend the castle.[6] It's no longer there, but we still say *cava*. On the other side of Calle San Jacinto, the street that divides Triana, the *gitanos* have their forges on Calle Cava Nueva, so we say *cava de los gitanos*. On this side we say *cava de los civiles*, because the Guardia Civil has its headquarters here."

"And how are your *soleares* different from those of the *gitanos?*"

El Ollero looked at Antonio for a moment, as if puzzled that anyone could ask such a question. "A *gitano* sings like this." And he sang a *letra* similar to what one would hear from El Mellizo, El Gordo, or Silverio. Then he said, "This is the way the *soleá* should sound."

Ramón didn't bother to rap out rhythm. Glass in hand, he turned and sang directly into Chacón's face. In an agreeable voice, deep and powerful but free of *rajo*, he sang a *soleá* unlike anything Chacón had ever heard:

Capilla del Carmen;	Chapel of El Carmen;
aunque vayas tú y te metas	even if you go and enter
en la Capilla del Carmen,	the Chapel of El Carmen,
tú de mis uñas no te escapas.	you won't escape my grasp.
M'has hecho un agravio mu grande.	You have done me a great wrong.
Aunque tu vayas y te metas	Even if you go and enter
en la Capilla del Carmen.	the Chapel of Carmen.

After singing the first three lines, Ramón sang the rest of the *cante* in one long and potent burst, without stopping for a breath. It was an amazing display of lungpower. Then El Ollero changed to a simpler style:

Qué me s'importaría a mí	What difference would it make to me
qu'haya tan buenos doctore,	that there are such good doctors,
si me tengo que morí?	if I have to die?

---

[5]Today: Pagés del Corro.

[6]Castle of the Inquisition; the food market of Triana is located in its ruins near the bridge.

The beautiful melodies soared with little emphasis on rhythm. It struck Chacón immediately that this *soleá* could be compared to the *soleares gitanas* of Silverio or El Mellizo as his own *malagueñas* compared to those of Juan Breva. Rhythm had been sacrificed to permit the *cantaor* freedom in developing his melodies and expressing his feelings. This *soleá* held a tremendous appeal for Chacón. He could imagine molding and elaborating it as he had the *malagueñas*. He knew he had to learn this style, but he also sensed he wouldn't be learning it from Ramón el Ollero.

Letra after *letra* poured forth from the pot-maker, *letras* filled with poetic sentiment. It seemed that once started, a floodgate opened that would be difficult to stem. Then, as abruptly as he had begun, he stopped, saying, "I have to get back to the fires."

As the three *cantaores* said goodbye to Ramón and turned to go, the *alfarero* grabbed Silverio by the sleeve and said something to him. Moments later, as the trio turned the corner and strolled toward the Plaza Altozano to hail a carriage, Silverio revealed Ramón's parting words. "The pot-maker said to me, *'Deja que güelva el señoritín este, que se ba a quear jecho un cigarro de liaillo!'* [Let that wannabe *señorito* come back here to sing and he'll come apart like a poorly rolled cigar!]" Silverio laughed. "The *cantaores* here in la *alfarería* are very proud and possessive of their *cante*. They don't want to admit that anyone can outsing them."

Chacón smiled smugly to himself as he looked ahead, across Calle San Jacinto, to the side of Triana he had never dared enter—*la cava de los gitanos*. Smoke rose in narrow columns across the horizon, smoke from dozens of forges, contrasting with the thick clouds belching from the kilns in the *alfarería* behind him. "Is the barrio of the *gitanos* really a dangerous place for us *gaché?*" he asked.

"*Hombre*, it's not like that," answered Silverio. "The *gitanos* and the *gaché* get along well here. There are even ceramic factories over there and some forges here on this side…"

"But that doesn't mean that there aren't some bad types…you have to watch yourself," added El Sevillano. "And there are *gitanos* over there who will have nothing to do with the *gaché*. They have their language and their customs. A *gitano* there will tell you proudly, 'My woman has never crossed the iron bridge of Isabel the Second into Sevilla.' Some of them won't even sing for us."

"It's true, Antonio. Blacksmith families like the Caganchos and the Pelaos refuse to sing in the presence of the *gaché*. I have been fortunate to hear them on occasion and it sends shivers up my spine just remembering. Their's is a hard *cante...por seguiriyas* and *martinetes...mu corto*, very short, brusque, and powerful. It is not a *cante* for the cafés, for the public. But for us *cantaores* there is none better."

"Silverio is the only one who has heard the father, Tío Antonio Cagancho...he is the most secretive and brags that he has never left Triana. How did his *seguiriya* go, *compare?*"

Silverio thought for a moment and then said, "It has been a while, but it was something like this. He sang under his breath:

No pierdas la esperanza	Don't lose hope,
que aunque el pocito era jondo	because, even if the well is deep,
la soguita alcanza.	the rope will reach.

Just as Silverio had said, it was a hard and stark *cante*, gripping the listener with brutal honesty.

"*Caramba*, what a *cante!*" said Chacón. I wish I could hear the *gitano*."

"It is unlikely. Tío Antonio is getting up in years and unlikely to change his ways. But his son Manuel is a little less closed. What a *gitano*...dark copper skin, bulging eyes, kind of frightening, but his looks are deceiving...if you know him, *e mú simpático* [he's very likeable]..."

"They are called Cagancho, but their family name is Rodríguez..." added El Sevillano.

"Tell Antonio the reason."

"*Mira*," said Paco, "they are called Cagancho because *ca gancho* [each hook] they make in their forge is perfect, a work of art."

Silverio hailed a carriage driver who had just deposited some patrons in the Plaza Altozano. Moments later the three *cantaores* were seated in the carriage and headed back across the bridge.

"How can I listen to the Caganchos?" asked Chacón, excited by this taste of pure *cante gitano*."

"*Hostias*...that's not easy, Antonio!" said Silverio, still breathing heavily from the effort of getting up into the carriage. "You can't just go over to their *fragua* on Calle Monte María Niño[7] and ask them to sing."

---

[7]Today: Calle Zorilla; Calles Monte Pirolo (today: Calle Rosario Vega) and Monte María Niño were literally "*montes*" [mountains] of accumulated trash that were covered over to become streets and gypsy residences.

"Here's what we used to do...to be able to listen to them," said El Sevillano. "When they got together to sing, word often spread quickly through Sevilla and we aficionados hurried across the bridge. The *gitanos* used to go to Casa Rufina, down at the end of Calle Pureza. Manuel and Rufina have a small place there, to sell food and drinks. But, in the back, they built some small rooms out of wood. And that is where the *gitanos* gathered to sing...the Caganchos, the Vargas, the Pelaos... And we aficionados used to crowd into the store and listen to the *cante* coming through the walls from the back. And what *cante* it was. I remember Manuel Cagancho used to sing:

Reniego de mi sino,	I renounce my fate,
como reniego de la horita, mare,	just as I renounce the hour, mother,
en que la he conocío.	that I met her.

"Of course, I can't sing it like Manuel does. He repeats that first line and then, after a momentary pause, he sings the second and third in one tremendous effort, without stopping for a breath. And all of it absolutely without adornment of any sort, other than a difficult and subtle *melisma* [singing of an extended melody on a single syllable of lyric].

"When Manuel forced those notes harder and harder to crown the *cante*, he created such a sense of tragedy that the other *gitanos*, as well as some of the *gachés* listening from outside, would express their rapture by ripping at their clothes and throwing into the air all the glassware within reach. No one could listen to that majestic and brutal *cante* without trembling and suffering a shock to the nerves that could only be calmed by strong drink...and lots of it!"

"*Compare*, that was more than fifteen years ago," interrupted Silverio. "I haven't been over there in years. I don't even know if Casa Rufina is still there."

"Me either. Do you remember Fernandillo?"

"Which Fernandillo?"

"*El de Triana* [he of Triana][8]...the one who has sung in your place a few times."

"Yes, of course, that *chaval* from Triana...a good singer."

---

[8]Fernando el de Triana: *cantaor*, impresario, and author of a book (1935) of artist's biographies that is the foundation of our knowledge of the flamenco environment in Sevilla during the last twenty years of the 1800s.

"Antonio, Fernando is not *gitano*, but he grew up among them here in Triana. He even looks *gitano* and, as he says, he 'favors their ways.' He sings a *martinete* that says:

Aunque mires mi color moreno,	Although you see my dark skin,
no soy gitano, no;	I am not gypsy, no;
me he criaíto entre ellos	I was raised among them
y me tira la inclinación.	and am inclined toward their ways.

"He told me of a time when, as a child, he was with the *gitanos* in the *camarote*...that's what they call the backroom in Casa Rufina...and when he came out he found the famous Captain General Sánchez Mira in front, listening to the *cante*."

"Antonio," said Silverio, "General Sánchez Mira is a good aficionado of the *cante*..."

"I served under him in the military," added Paco, "and he often called me to sing for him. As I was saying, Fernando told me that the general said to him, "Listen, boy, when you go back in there, do me a favor. Ask Juan Pelao on behalf of General Sánchez Mira, if he would please, if he can, sing again the second *martinete* that he just sang.'"

"You have to know this Juan Pelao," said Silverio. "His rough appearance made outsiders uneasy...his skin so black that many called him *El Negrito*. People asked, 'How can so much melody come out of such a brutish gypsy?' More than any other, he wanted nothing to do with the *gaché*. And he would never accept payment for his *cante*...not from anyone. He used to say that taking money for his singing would be like a woman taking money for her body."

El Sevillano was anxious to continue his tale. "So Fernandillo took the message from the general back into the *camarote*. The *gitanos* held a conference and finally decided that, since the one asking was such a good aficionado of the *cante*, they would honor his request. Juan Pelao, the giant of the *martinetes*, sang there in the *camarote*, without guitar:

Esgraciaíto aquer que come	Unfortunate is he who eats
er pan por manita ajena,	bread from a stranger's hand,
siempre mirando a la cara	always looking at his face
si la ponen mala o güena.	to see if he approves or disapproves.

Just hearing this *letra* sent Chacón's mind into a spin. In an instant he flashed back ten years to the blacksmith shop of José Cruz, when as a nine-year-old boy he first heard that verse sung by Juan Torre. So long ago, but the memory as fresh as if it had occurred the day before. Was it really possible that he had been through so much: El Torre, Joaquin la Cherna, El Marrurro, and others in Jerez, listening to many singers during his journey through Andalucía, lessons with Sarvaoriyo, long nights in the cafés of Jerez, in Cádiz with Paquiro, El Gordo, Curro Durse, Juan Durse, Fosforito, and El Mellizo...Sevilla and Silverio, and all the other *cantaores* who had influenced him in the cafés...

"Antonio, are you listening?" El Sevillano brought Chacón back to the moment.

"Yes, of course. Forgive me, I was thinking of something. What were you saying about El Pelao?"

"Juan's singing was so extraordinary that night that his friends proclaimed him king of the *cante por martinetes*, and the ecstatic general, in a grand gesture, tried to send a monetary gift back to the *camarote*. El Pelao refused to accept it. But the following day, the general sent an orderly to the home of the gypsy with an envelope containing one hundred *pesetas* and a note saying 'A gift from General Sánchez Mira for the king of the *cante por martinetes*.' The *cantaor* refused the gift at first, but when his wife gave him an angry look and said impatiently, 'Take it, Juan Pelao, we don't even have anything to eat today,' he relented. That is how it is with these giants of the *cante gitano*."

In May, Antonio turned eighteen. Eighteen years old and he found himself at the top of the ranks of flamenco artists in Sevilla, catered to and sought after by other flamencos, businessmen, toreros, and civic leaders. Even the other artists had given up their right to seniority and agreed to sing before the young phenomenon. He never lacked for invitations to dine or drink. On nights when a private fiesta did not fall his way after work, he often went with other artists to some tavern or café and paid them to continue singing and drinking through the night. In his heart, Chacón would always remain a true aficionado of the *cante*, and nothing gave him greater pleasure than listening to others. Whenever possible, he visited other cafés to listen to his favorite singers. In the Filarmónico it was El Chato de Jerez with his *seguiriyas* and La

Bocanegra with her *malagueñas*. Chacón never forgot the effect La Bocanegra had on him in El Burrero two years earlier. Not a particularly attractive woman, heavy-set with pale skin, porcine features, and frizzy hair, she nevertheless sang divinely. Being from Málaga, she sang the *cantes* of El Canario with more authenticity and skill than most. Chacón felt he learned something every time he listened to her.

But it was in the Café del Burrero that Chacón spent most of his free moments. He found himself irresistibly drawn to the Burrero by Manuel Ojeda's fascination with *cantes* and *cantaores* from the *Levante* [the eastern half of Andalucía]—from Málaga, Granada, the mining regions of Almería, and the eastern seaport of Cartagena. In each of these areas the local *fandangos*, danced in mountain villages on fiesta days, had followed the path of the *malagueña* and evolved into more rhythmically relaxed and emotionally intense *cantes*. *Cantaores* had more freedom to improvise the six *tercios* of each *letra*, the guitarist holding back and following the singer's lead in his accompaniment.

Singers tended to travel between Granada, La Unión and Cartagena in the province of Murcia, and eventually try their luck in Málaga. They brought their *granaínas*, *cartageneras*, and *malagueñas* to the city of Málaga, where they influenced and learned from each other. All of these *cantes* shared a similar structure, differing primarily in their melodies.

Ojeda had told Chacón, "I realized a number of years ago that these *cantes* from the *Levante* would be a novelty in Sevilla, where the public was accustomed to the *cante gitano*...the *soleá* and the *seguiriyas*. I was right and now everyone else tries to follow my lead, but I will always have the best of these artists because of my connections in Málaga."

On a night when Chacón had been able to escape from the Café de Silverio between performances, he sat at a back table in El Burrero with Ojeda. The two men were listening to *malagueñas* from the throat of Juan Trujillo "El Perote," a slender and handsome man seated by the side of Maestro Pérez on the Burrero stage.

"What do you think of El Perote, Antonio?" asked Manuel.

"He fascinates me, *Don* Manuel," replied Chacón. "I never had the good fortune to hear the other *perote* [person from Álora, in the mountains above Málaga], El Canario, so it gives me great pleasure to listen to this pure *cante malagueño*."

"The two of them don't sing the same, but this Juan el Perote sings a *malagueña* as pure as is possible. I was lucky to have him come along so soon after Fosforito left. I tried another guy, Manolito Reina...called himself El Canario Chico and imitated the *cante* of El Canario, more or less. I believe he came from around here...he definitely wasn't from Málaga. But he really wasn't ready...he had a nice voice and passion for the *cante*, but he hadn't yet become a true *cantaor*. I think his friends encouraged him and pushed him to come here from his pueblo. In any case, he got off to a bad start. One night he had just begun to sing:

Yo he visto a un niño llorá	I have seen a child crying
en la puerta de un camposanto...	in the entrance to a cemetery...

"...when, suddenly, from behind him, Paco el Sevillano said in a voice loud enough for the public to hear, 'I saw another one crying in the door of a *fonda!*' The *cuadro* broke up laughing, and Manolo became so flustered he forgot the rest of the *letra*. He was never the same after that. In fact, I heard that he has become obsessed with accompanying his *cante* on piano...but he doesn't know how to play the piano. A real case!"

The two men were quiet for a while, listening to El Perote. Then Manuel Ojeda said, "Even Juan caused some problems when he first got here. With his good looks he could have the choice of the women, and it wasn't long before he began an affair with one of them. Unfortunately, he chose the wrong one...Carmelita Pérez...the young girl you see there in the last chair. She's Maestro Pérez' daughter, and her father didn't like it. There was some friction for a while and I thought that the father would insist that I let Juan go, but then El Perote asked Carmelita to marry him and that seemed to satisfy everyone."

A short while later, as Chacón prepared to return to work, Ojeda said to him, "*Don* Antonio, when are you going to come to work for me?"

The Jerezano replied, "You know I'm contracted with Silverio through the summer. After that we'll see."

"You know, it's not good to stay in one place too long. Your friend Fosforito moved on after six months here. And whatever Silverio is paying you, I'll pay you more."

"That's very generous *Don* Manuel. Let's see what happens in the fall."

"Antonio, I'm afraid I'm not going to be able to open up in September."

"Why not, *Don* Silverio? What's going on?"

"Some people from the city were in the other day, and they told me they're taking my permit until I put a fire hydrant in the patio...near the stage. I can't get workers in here until September and I don't know how long it will take. So I don't know what to tell you...I'm sure you can find work."

"Don't worry about it," replied Chacón. "I want to stay here in Sevilla, so I'll ask around and see what I can find until you open again."

Of course, Chacón knew exactly where he would look and within days he had arranged with Manuel Ojeda to sing in the Café del Burrero in the fall. The Burrero had come under even greater censure than Silverio's café, with orders to put in water, make safety repairs, and come up with a fire escape from the second floor café. However, Ojeda assured Chacón that with some cosmetic repairs, a few bribes, and paying some fines, he would be able to remain open.

At the end of July, Sevilla shut down. Most *cafés cantantes* would remain closed for the next month. With no work in the oppressive heat of August, Chacón returned to Jerez, where he reunited with Javier and Antonio Molina. But, by mid-month, bored and suffering from the heat in an unusually hot summer, he decided to escape to the coast. At first he intended to go to Cádiz, but then, on sudden impulse, he chose Málaga. He had never been to the homeland of the *malagueñas*, and Paco el Sevillano had once told him, "If you are ever in Málaga, go to the Café del Sevillano, or as some call it now, Café de las Siete Revueltas, and speak to my son, Bernardo. I used to own the place, but Bernardo runs it now. Tell him I sent you, and I'm sure he'll give you work."

The Pope of the *Cante*

Antonio Chacón took a train to Málaga, a white coastal town clustered about the base of the Alcazaba—its ancient castle—and El Gibralfaro, the fortified hill that commands a view of the city and the harbor. El Gibralfaro crawled with gypsies who lived in caves dug into the crumbling walls of the fortress, their children running naked in the filth of human habitation. At the base of the Alcazaba, low buildings, cheap bars, and the ragged canvas shelters of wandering *canastero* gypsies bordered the broad Plaza de Santa María. But further down, in the city, which ran along the Guadalmedina River to where it spilled into the azure Mediterranean Sea, the aristocracy rode up and down wide palm-lined avenues through the commercial district.

A carriage delivered Chacón to the Café de las Siete Revueltas, a modest café in a two-story building located on the corner of a street of the same name. Later, Antonio, looking for a shortcut to his hotel, would make the mistake of continuing up this Street of the Seven Turns. After the second turn he had found himself surrounded by middle-class brothels. By the fourth turn the street had turned dark and foul smelling, with women's sunken and pallid faces staring at him from open doorways and offering their services for a *peseta*. In that slum, the denizens lived mostly outdoors amid dirty children, dogs and the pervasive odor of filth, hot rancid olive oil, and stale fish. Chacón had dared go no further and hastened back in the direction he had come.

Entering Café de las Siete Revueltas through a nondescript small doorway, Chacón found himself between a small room on the left and a larger salon on the right that had balconies on three sides almost overhanging a rather plain stage. Bernardo, the owner, delighted to hear from his father, contracted the Jerezano immediately for the salary of five *duros* [twenty-five *pesetas*] a day. He said, "Your reputation precedes you *Don* Antonio...although I didn't expect you to be so young. I'm thrilled to have you here. Maybe you can offer some competition to a young singer who has become somewhat of a sensation over in the Café Espana."

"And who might that be *Don* Bernardo?"

"A young girl named Trinidad...Trinidad Navarro. They call her La Trini and she's packing them in to listen to her *malagueñas*. I have heard that you have some talent in that particular *cante* as well...in spite of not being from here. If so, you will be continuing a tradition of excellent *malagueña* singers who have sung on this stage, including Juan Breva, El Canario, and El Perote."

"I hope I won't disappoint you, *Don* Bernardo."

Antonio Chacón's *malagueñas* did not disappoint, but astonished the villagers and sailors who filled the Café Siete Revueltas each night. In place of the usual local variations of small-town *malagueñas*, they heard a majestic and solemn *cante* filled with musicality and emotion, and delivered with remarkable vocal skill. In a very short time Chacón won over the Malagueños and became the talk of the town. He had brought the city a *malagueña* that filled its citizens with pride. They quickly forgot that the *cante* came to them from an outsider and began to debate the relative merits of his *malagueñas* and those of their *paisana*, La Trini.

At the first opportunity, Chacón went to listen to Málaga's newest singing phenomenon. Café España occupied a two-story building on Calle Compañía near the main plaza. Inside, the salon proved to be luxurious beyond anything Chacón had seen in Sevilla, with an elegant stairway leading to upstairs *reservaos*. Scanning the room, Chacón saw nobody who might be the acclaimed *malagueña* singer. The singers on stage were all men. Then, after the *cuadro* had finished, he was surprised to see a young girl get up from a table and make her way to the stage. Chacón couldn't believe his eyes. The young woman, still a girl really, was as out of place in that environment as he had been making shoes in his father's *zapatería*. She was not one of the hardened *cantaoras* who smoked, drank, and cursed, the equal of any man. She was not like the women of *la vida alegre* [the merry life] who enticed men on Calle Rosario as they came and went from the Café de Silverio, or in the many brothels east of the Alameda in one of Spain's largest red-light districts. And she was certainly not like the more cultured women who entertained men in discreet high-class houses west of the Alameda, houses where Antonio had been a guest on several occasions—usually hired by wealthy clients to provide entertainment. On one early visit, he had been goaded into partaking of the women's services. His guitarist had said, "What are you afraid of Antonio? Disease? I have every disease these girls can give you, but they can't kill me...I thrive on them, they stimulate me. Here, feel my pulse...see, I'm in good health!"

No, the girl who went out on the stage of the Café España was unlike any woman Chacón had encountered in his daily life. Taking her seat demurely beside the guitarist, La Trini—it had to be she—appeared to be a young debutant, the pampered daughter of a well-to-do family. Chacón couldn't take his eyes off her. She had the face of an innocent: pale skin, a small mouth with full, perpetually smiling rosy lips and dimples, a small, upturned nose, large eyes with finely shaped lids, long lashes, and soft, natural brows. Her light brown hair was swept back gracefully off her face and gathered in back, a red carnation perched saucily on top of her head. Dangling silver earrings and a matching choker necklace with a pendant framed her face, while elegant lace set off her slender figure.

Then she began to sing. Demureness vanished, replaced by a dazzling vivaciousness. Her sound was as clean and pure as the girl herself. She manipulated her agile and flexible voice with ease as she sang:

Yo recuerdo que una vez	I recall that once upon a time
fuiste tú, paloma mía,	it was you, my pigeon,
quien dejaste mi querer	who rejected my love
por unas hablaurías	because of the false words
que te contó otra mujer.	told to you by another woman.

La Trini held Chacón spellbound. He thought: *If angels were to sing flamenco they would sound like this.* The word that came to mind was "tenderness." She sang with a feminine tenderness that belied her age. But certainly she couldn't understand the words she sang—she couldn't have experienced the suffering expressed in her *letras*. She sang with the facile ease of one whose heart had yet to cry. For Chacón, the lack of heartfelt pain in her sentiment was overshadowed by the originality and difficulty of her melodies. The audience went crazy listening to her.

When La Trini had finished, Chacón moved to intercept her as she descended from the stage. Hat in hand, he said, "Excuse me..."

La Trini turned briefly toward the sound of the voice and then dismissed the young man as just one more *señorito* looking for a date.

"*Señorita*, may I speak with you for a moment, please ...about your singing?"

Something in his voice, the urgency perhaps, stopped the girl and she turned back to him once more. "Yes?"

Her eyes were like dark amber honey, beckoning, threatening to pull him in and drown him in their depths.

"My name is Antonio Chacón, at your service. I have just come from Sevilla, where I've been singing in the Café de Silverio..."

A look of surprise came over Trini's face. His name meant nothing to her. The young man—she guessed him to be about her age—well-dressed in the manner of a successful businessman, seemed as unlikely as she to be a singer of *cante flamenco*. But there was no hint of jest in the intense expression on his face.

"Your *malagueñas* are remarkable, *señorita*..."

"Trinidá, please."

"Trinidá!" The name tasted sensuous on his tongue. "Trinidá...you know there are three essentials for singing the *cante* well..."

"Oh?"

"Yes. They are voice, voice...and voice. And you have all three."

"You are very kind."

"No, I'm very serious. I have sung with the best, with Enrique el Mellizo, Silverio, Paco el Sevillano, and with some of your countrymen...and I can see that you have a gift. You are going to be somebody..."

Chacón was interrupted by the arrival of a darkly handsome young man who came up behind La Trini and placed one hand affectionately on her shoulder. Antonio's heart sank when he saw the look of adoration that came over the girl's face and the warmth of her smile as she turned to greet the man. Over her shoulder she said, "Thank you for the kind words, Antonio...perhaps I will get to hear you sing one day."

All Chacón could manage to say was, "My pleasure...I'm singing in the Café Siete Revueltas..." And she was gone.

Chacón couldn't bring himself to visit the Café España again, but he took advantage of his stay in Málaga to listen to *malagueñas* at every opportunity. In his free moments he strayed across the river into the gypsy barrios of Perchel and Trinidad. There, in small taverns, he played the part of a wealthy *señorito* and listened to *cante*. He put money into the pockets of impoverished gypsies, seldom letting on that he could sing. Bad singing, broken voices, and occasional sparks of genius—it didn't matter to him. He loved to listen to all *cante*. He could find inspiration in unexpected places.

On Chacón's third night in Málaga, a man approached him after he had sung and said, "Well done, *Don* Antonio. I'm very interested in having you sing in my place."

"But, *hombre*, I'm contracted to sing here."

"That doesn't matter. You can sing in my place earlier, before you come here."

Chacón thought for a moment. The idea of singing extra hours, and during the early evening did not appeal to him. "I don't know..."

"Before you answer, why don't you come to see my place...see what you think and then give me your decision."

Not wanting to shut doors without good reason, and having nothing better to do the following afternoon, Chacón agreed to meet with the man.

Café Universal dominated a corner on Calle Granada, a short, broad street in the town center. As soon as Chacón entered, he could sense it was not a place for *cante flamenco*. It resembled *casinos* he had worked in, but was more elegant, with polished wood trim and marble tables—the sort of place that would be frequented by select groups of bureaucrats, intellectuals, artists, and military officers. When the owner greeted him, Chacón said immediately, "You have a marvelous place here, but I really can't sing under these conditions."

"I'll pay you double what Bernardo is paying you."

"*Hombre*, that's very generous, but..."

"One hundred and ten *pesetas* a day..."

"A hundred and ten a day?"

"A hundred and ten."

"In that case...when should I start?"

"How about this evening?"

So Antonio Chacón began each evening in the Café Universal, singing two sessions of two *cantes* each with the guitar of local player Enrique el Negrete, and then rushed immediately to the Café Siete Revueltas for two sessions. At the end of the night, if there were no private fiesta, he went with local artists to the small *ventorros* [rustic taverns] in La Caleta, a barrio along the beach on the eastern outskirts of the city.

One night, El Negrete took him to the Ventorrillo of El Zocato where they found El Zocato and another guitarist, a gypsy who went by the name of Romerillo, with some local singers. Negrete introduced the tavern owner as his teacher and one of the most popular guitarists in Málaga. No one knew what to think of Chacón at first, but before long they were drinking like old friends and eating fried fish. When the singing began, it continued until sun-up, echoes of *cante* floating across the beach on a salty breeze to the accompaniment of the gentle crashing of waves on the shore.

Somehow the press learned of Chacón's salary in the Universal and a series of articles and editorials appeared expressing indignation at the amount being paid to a *cantaor flamenco*. The negative press only added to the guilt Antonio had begun to feel for not fulfilling his commitment to Manuel Ojeda—his promise to sing in the Café del Burrero. So, in the middle of September he returned to Sevilla.

Chacón had spent so much time in the Café del Burrero as a customer that he immediately felt at home there. Silverio was unique in referring to his artists as *maestros* and *profesores* and addressing them as *Don*. It was not a custom adhered to by others in the world of flamenco. But the *Don* followed Chacón to the Burrero: his manner and reputation seemed to demand it.

Two singers in the Café del Burrero had a profound effect on Chacón. Concha la Peñaranda had first impressed Antonio when he visited Sevilla two years earlier. Now he had the opportunity to hear her every night. The woman, now in her mid-thirties, lived under the weight of a *copla* widely circulated about her:

Concha la Peñaranda,	Concha la Peñaranda,
la que canta en el café,	the one who sings in the café,
ha perdido la vergüenza,	has lost her sense of shame,
siendo mujer de bien.	when she had been so good.

Chacón didn't believe a woman should be judged for working in a café. As he told the Molinas one afternoon, "I don't believe a woman is bad just because she sings or dances on stage. A woman is good or bad no matter where she is...she is whatever she wants to be."

Antonio Molina had added, "A woman is like a vineyard. Why put a guard to watch over her? The good ones can guard themselves. The bad ones...there is no one who can possibly guard them!"

"Who are we to judge? Even the bad ones once had mothers...just like us..."

"Like the *letra* says," added Chacón:

A la mujé de la vía,	A women in the "life"
no la trate con desdén;	should not be treated with scorn;
qué ante de ser mujé mala,	before turning bad,
ha sío mujé de bien.	she was a good woman.

Concha la Peñaranda had come to El Burrero in 1884 and triumphed with a *cante* foreign to Sevilla. Because she had come from Cartagena, in the eastern province of Murcia, people called her "La Cartagenera." And her *cantes*, based on the *malagueñas*, but filled with the plaintive tones of the mining regions of the Levante, came to be called *cartageneras*. Concha sang with a clear, clean voice, skillfully used, with good taste and *gracia*. Her tremendous popularity had assured that her contract with the café would be extended indefinitely. Chacón found in the *cartageneras* a *cante* with much appeal, a *cante* suited to the same sort of treatment he had given to the *malagueñas*.

But the most exciting revelation was another singer of *cartageneras* who came to sing in the Burrero that fall. África Vázquez, originally from Granada, had been discovered by Manuel Ojeda in Málaga after years of singing all over the Levante. A gifted singer with a beautiful and agreeable voice that came from "the throat of a nightingale," África delivered her songs in a delicate style and with intense emotion. Chacón studied her *cartageneras* with great interest, but it was a different *cante*, again related to the *malagueñas*, that captured his imagination. África had brought with her, from Granada, the *granaínas*:

En la Torre de la Vela	In the Tower of La Vela,[1]
una campana de plata;	a silver bell;
cuando sus metales suenan,	when its metals sound,
dicen, 'Viva Graná!'	they say, 'Long live Granada!'

---

[1] The Torre de la Vela is a tower in the Alhambra.

> *Viva Graná, que es mi tierra;* Long live my land, Granada;
> *viva El Puente de Genil,* long live the Genil Bridge,
> *La Virgen de las Angustias,* La Virgen de las Angustias[2]
> *La Alhambra y El Albaicín.* the Alhambra and the Albaicín.

The *granaínas* excited Chacón. Here was a *cante* ripe for development in his style. He went to work immediately.

When Silverio finally completed the required improvements to his café in late October, he found himself faced with a new problem. He had lost a number of his most popular artists, those who could be counted on to attract the public. Chacón was singing in El Burrero. The ever-popular singing group, Las Viejas Ricas, had moved on to the Salón Filarmónico. Paco de Lucena and La Parrala had gone to Málaga. Miguel Macaca was in jail. Many singers and dancers, including La Macarrona, were trying their luck in Madrid where the *cafés cantantes* were flourishing in an environment relatively free of government restrictions.

Construction costs in the café had been high and Silverio needed to open immediately. In desperation, he made a difficult decision. He had no choice but to come out of retirement. He announced in the newspaper that for two weeks he would sing nightly in the café.

His plan worked. The café filled every night. For the man on the street it was a unique opportunity to hear this living legend. Other artists, including Chacón, slipped in between their performances to listen to the maestro. The press reported that, "even the marble columns shook with the power of Silverio's mighty voice."

One night in the middle of those two weeks, Paco el Sevillano came to Chacón with a glint in his eye. "Guess what, Antonio!"

"What?"

"You won't believe it."

"*Hombre*, what?"

"Last night, after we finished here, I went over to Silverio's place. We were having some drinks and who should come in but General Sánchez Mira...the captain general here in Sevilla. With him were a retired chief of the *Guardia Civil* and the governor of the city. They said, 'Listen, Franconetti...we've come in to listen to you...let's get a room!'

---

[2] La Virgen de las Angustias is the patron saint of Granada.

"And you won't believe what Silverio said to them. He says, '*Pues*, this is your house, and you have me at your disposal, but in this moment it is impossible, because, for these two weeks I have announced that I will sing for the public. Therefore I owe the public, and if I let them down I will lose prestige. So when I have fulfilled my commitment for these two weeks that I have promised, then your honors can count on me for whatever you wish. But, for the moment, you have come in too late. To hear Silverio you must come at the designated hour.'

"The few of us who were left in the café at that late hour held our breaths. No artist says those things to such important people. A few years ago we would have found ourselves in jail. But, they just said, '*Bueno*, I guess there's nothing to be done. We'll come back.' Only Silverio could get away with that."

When it came to Silverio, nothing surprised Chacón.

By the beginning of November, Chacón had fulfilled his initial contract with Ojeda. While he was considering whether to continue in El Burrero or return to help out Silverio, an offer came from Málaga. It came from the queen of cafés, the legendary Café de Chinitas, and for the impressive salary of forty *pesetas* a day. To make the offer even more irresistible, the contract was timed to coincide with Juan Breva's return to Málaga after a three-year absence.

A narrow, dark, and malodorous alley, popularly known as Pasaje de Chinitas, branched off from Málaga's main town square and led to a tiny plaza formed by the junction of four buildings. The entrance to Café de Chinitas was through a doorway off that plaza, set into the corner of one of the buildings. Inside, the café had the appearance of an opera house, with two tiers of box-seat balconies rising up vertically around the circular walls. The patrons in these boxes had a close and intimate view of the circular stage that protruded from a back wall draped in colorful shawls. Tall arched columns supported the high ceiling and skylight, complementing the arches framing each balcony box.

On a November night in 1887, the night of Antonio Chacón's debut in the Café de Chinitas, the salon began to fill early in the evening. They had come from nearby towns, from Marbella, Estepona, Vélez, and Torre del Mar. They came because Juan Breva, *their* Juan Breva, the nightingale of Vélez and the king of the *malagueñas*, would be singing. Those who had not heard Chacón asked, "Who is this young man from Jerez who has come from El Burrero in Sevilla? He must not be much, because we haven't heard his name." Others responded with, "They say that in spite of his youth, he's already an artist who can hold his own."

Those who had heard the *cantaor* during his visit a few months earlier eagerly anticipated the competition between the maestro, Juan Breva, and the newcomer. They asked, "What will Breva say when he hears the Jerezano?" Or, "Will the young man be able to sing in front of a giant like Juan Breva?"

The ground floor of the café, with its marble-topped tables and crude wicker chairs, quickly filled to capacity. When no room remained in the salon to squeeze in even a needle, latecomers had to stand in the doorway and the passageway outside. Never before had such a thing been seen in Málaga.

A tremendous *cuadro* had been assembled for Breva's return. Joining local *bailaoras*, several dancers had been brought in from Sevilla, among them Carlota and Rita Ortega. Paco el Águila, the guitarist who had competed with Paco de Lucena when he first came to Málaga as a youth, was in charge of the *cuadro*. Another Malagueño, the veteran guitarist Maestro Onjana, played primarily for singers *p'alante*. And Paco de Lucena was there to reunite with both El Águila and his old friend, Juan Breva. The featured singers were La Parrala, Chacón, and Breva.

In truth, the *cuadro* was only a prelude to the performance of Juan Breva and his confrontation with Antonio Chacón. The audience waited politely but restlessly through the dances and even the *cante* of La Parrala.

At last the anticipated moment arrived. Chacón stood and moved to the front of the stage in the dim light of feeble candle lanterns, his manner eloquent and self-assured. He acknowledged the public, smiled, and with a grand gesture sat down beside Paco de Lucena. Applause cut through the dense, smoky atmosphere.

"*Por soleá*," he said softly, and he began to tap the rhythm with his cane. The guitar wove its spell and Chacón sang. The audience listened in absolute silence. The *cante* was familiar but also new to their ears. When he finished, the applause and cheering resounded through the Pasaje de Chinitas and beyond to the street.

But this was not the *cante* they had come to hear. "*Otro...otro, muchacho* [Another...another, young man]!" "*Por malagueñas*, sing *por malagueñas!"*

"*Señores*," said Chacón when the crowd had quieted sufficiently, "I would like to dedicate this *cante* to the maestro, to Juan Breva...the great artist who created this *cante por malagueñas*. And I want everyone here to know that I have no intention of creating a competition. My only wish is to offer a show of respect and affection by singing my *malagueña*...something *he* has asked me to do, here by his side, in his homeland."

The audience, moved by the dignified display of modesty and tribute, showed its appreciation. "*Olé* for good young men with heart and a sense of decency!" "*Viva Jerez!*"

Chacón leaned toward his guitarist and whispered, "My voice is extraordinary tonight... *súbele medio tono y pónmela en el seis* [go up a half tone and put the *cejilla* on the sixth]." Again the magic of Lucena's guitar, and then that voice, filled with emotion and sweetness, the words pronounced in perfect Castilian Spanish: "*Yo entré en el jardín de Venus...*" followed by "*Yo te quise con locura...*"

Chacón's *malagueñas* were not the simple emotional style of Fosforito, or the classic style of El Canario or El Perote, or the light and *gracia*-filled *fandanguillo* of Juan Breva. This was something completely new, a *cante* with grandeur, a display of virtuosity. It was a difficult *cante* that Chacón made look easy—something that would mislead future imitators who more often than not were to drown in their efforts. The public listened in reverent silence to each *letra* until the *cantaor* reached the climactic fifth *tercio*. At that point they could no longer control themselves and broke into a tremendous applause that all but drowned out the final concluding line. There could be no doubt: the Jerezano had planted his flag in the soil of Málaga.

The crowd demanded *letra* after *letra*, until, with respect for Juan Breva who had yet to sing, the *cantaor* excused himself and retreated with Paco de Lucena to the back of the stage.

Juan Breva, singing last due to seniority and prestige, walked slowly to the front of the stage with serene majesty. Guitar in hand, he took the seat vacated by Chacón. He wore an expensive suit, and large rings sparkled on his thick fingers—his years of labor had not been without reward. Such was his presence that, as he raised his guitar into playing position, his crude wooden chair seemed to change by magic into a magnificent throne.

Breva warmed-up by singing *por peteneras*. His broad hands

dwarfed the guitar, covering the bridge and strings, but his graceful thumb and tapered fingertips caressed the strings with surprising delicacy. The public listened respectfully to this bear of a man who sang incongruously in what some called *una voz de niño* [the voice of a child], a high-pitched, lilting voice with great sensitivity and musicality. They cheered their idol, but this wasn't what they had come to hear. No sooner had he finished than they began to chant, *"Por malagueñas... por malagueñas!"*

Breva signaled Maestro Onjana to join him, and while the veteran guitarist seated himself the *cantaor* addressed the room. "*Señores*...fellow Malagueños, I am honored to be here with you in my homeland, which is Málaga and Vélez. With all my heart I dedicate to you our *cante*, our *malagueñas*."

And he sang. With the guitar of Maestro Onjana supporting him, he sang his legendary *malagueñas*, the *cante* flowing with the rhythm of mountain fiestas and the rolling pulse of Mediterranean waves. It was a *malagueña* of the people—*his* people. And the people demanded more and more. The competition had been forgotten. Chacón had been forgotten. Finally, when it seemed there could be nothing left to sing, the *cantaor* revealed his noble character by improvising the following *copla*:

En El Café de Chinitas,	In the Café de Chinitas,
cantó una copla Chacón,	Chacón sang a *copla*,
y le contestó Juan Breva,	and Juan Breva answered,
"Cantas tú mejor que yo	"You sing better than I
esa malagueña nueva."	that new *malagueña*."

In early 1888, Chacón returned to Sevilla and the Café de Silverio. For the rest of that year he would alternate between Silverio's café and El Burrero. As his reputation grew, he began to receive more and more offers to sing in different cities throughout Andalucía. That summer he sang in the Café de Martín in Algeciras, a white Moorish town with flat-roofed buildings, located across the bay from the Rock of Gibraltar. The contract was for fifteen hundred *pesetas*. By that time, he had grown a thick mustache, waxed and curled upward slightly at the edges of his mouth—contrasting with his close-cropped hair that had receded well back off his forehead. A hint of a double chin provided evidence of the success he had achieved, and his formal and meticulous manner of dress continued to attract attention and surprise aficionados.

The novelty of the year for Chacón was the appearance of Pepa de Oro in the Café de Silverio. Looking every bit the *gitana de pura cepa* [pure gypsy], although she had not a drop of gypsy blood, this cigar-smoking *bailaora* took over the stage with her beauty, her arrogance and her *gracia*. Aggressive and talkative to the extreme, she dominated the stage and had her audiences in her hands even before she began to sing or dance. She often came in accompanied by her famous father, the torero Paco de Oro, who coached her and pushed her hard. Part of her talent had been inherited from her mother, the *cantaora* La Bizca. Original in everything she did, from her multicolored striped stockings and plaid dresses to her feisty performing style, she was best known for singing and dancing the Argentinean *milonga* in a lively *tango* rhythm. Pepa had spent time in America with her father and sister, and later toured Argentina under contract to Juan Junquera. She brought an authentic South American flavor to the cafés of Andalucía and Madrid. And Antonio Chacón added one more *cante*, the *milonga*, to his ever-growing repertoire.

Manuel Ojeda had been gradually losing his battle with the city over the safety of his café. He could no longer procrastinate and bribe his way out of infractions and threats to pull his permit. The café was beyond repair, forcing him to relocate. The new building, at Calle de las Sierpes, Number 11, just off the Plaza Campana, had doors opening to streets on either side. One of them, narrow Calle de la Pasion,[3] was little more than an alley and appropriately named for its many brothels, clandestine card games, and the almost nightly brawls associated with each.

The new Salón Cantante de Manuel Ojeda, popularly known as Café del Burrero, had a huge stage, set back into the wall, and a balcony that ran around three sides of the salon. Chacón helped to inaugurate it in the fall of 1888. Most of the familiar cast was there to support him, including Concha la Carbonera, La Escribana, Fernanda and Juana Antúnez, Paco el Sevillano, and Maestro Pérez. Manuel Ojeda would do practically anything to make money. Along with gambling, he made sure there were always plenty of women, some as young as fifteen, available to his customers. One night, the celebrated torero Frascuelo

---

[3]Today: Calle Vargas Campos.

paid to have the doors locked so that he could have the place to himself to listen to Chacón. On another occasion a young bull was brought in for a bullfight on the stage. Customers had to be prepared to flee when fights broke out, to escape before the police could arrive and begin making indiscriminate arrests.

Chacón had established a warm friendship with the Antúnez sisters. He very much enjoyed watching both of them dance, although they were quite different stylistically. In conversation, Fernanda once said to him, "*Mira* Antonio, Juana and I come from the same roots, but the fruits have different flavors. By that I mean that we had the same apprenticeship, but in the hour of revealing our feelings, we do it differently. I dance as our mother danced at home in Santiago, the old way of our family and other families of Jerez. Juana has adopted the new posture of La Mejorana."

Paco el Sevillano continued to be an almost constant source of entertainment for Chacón. When the guitarist Juan el Jorobao [the Hunchback], whose hunched body and humped shoulder did nothing to impede his dexterity on the guitar, came in late one night, Chacón heard El Sevillano say, "Juan, what happened? Did you stop somewhere for a drink?"

El Jorobao answered, "No, I came straight from home."

"You came *straight* from home? *Pos, camaraíta* [comrade]...it seems to me that you have changed a great deal since you got here!"

On another occasion Chacón and Paco were having lunch with Antonio "El Mochuelo" [The Owl], a new *cantaor* in the Burrero. Barely twenty years old, El Mochuelo had been hired previously by Silverio to sing for Enriqueta Macaca while her husband was in jail. Now he had moved to the Burrero. When asked where he was from, El Mochuelo, a lively little man with the mannerisms of a country hick, had replied, *"Yo...de donde iba yo a sé, cristiano?...de Sebiya, ná má!"* ["Me? Where *could* I be from, Christian? From Sevilla, where else?"]

Paco asked him, "Why are you called Mochuelo?"

The young *cantaor* explained, "With so many *canarios* [canaries] singing today, my friends thought an owl would be something different."

The name, in fact, suited El Mochuelo well. Short and stocky, with big eyes and hair combed straight back, his face was pockmarked and always flushed, as if he had just eaten a big meal. He always ordered fish-head soup and then made a point of how much he liked *las cabezas* [the heads]. El Sevillano, tired of hearing about *las cabezas*, said,

"*Hombre*, you really like *las cabezas?*"

"Of course...what's not to like?"

"Well, you may like Las Cabezas...but I prefer Utrera!" [Las Cabezas and Utrera are two towns near Sevilla.]

Aficionados among the aristocracy in Sevilla had remained cool toward Chacón. They found him aloof and felt he dressed above his station. The "*Don*" so often attached to his name did nothing to allay their suspicions of pretentiousness. So it came as somewhat of a surprise when a well-dressed man came into the Burrero late one night and said to Chacón, "*Don* Antonio, I represent the Marquis de Villalba, who requests your services this evening in his home."

"I would be honored. Is His Honor aware that it is my policy to collect my fee before I sing?"

"Tell me the amount and I will take care of it right now."

Given the status of the client and the need to go to the man's home, Chacón inflated his usual fee substantially. The representative heard the amount without blinking and paid on the spot. He waited through the *cantaor*'s last performance and then led him to a waiting carriage for the short trip to the marquis' home on Avenida de la Constitución— the major thoroughfare running from the government buildings and the Plaza de San Fernando past the Cathedral and south to the Puerta de Jerez. Stately three and four-story homes lined the avenue, and the carriage deposited Chacón, the guitarist Juan el Jorobao, and their escort in front of one of them.

Up a flight of stairs to a tall, heavy wooden door adorned by a family crest, and then they stepped into a world of luxury heretofore unknown to Chacón. High ceilings, dark exotic woods, heavy, lush drapes, oriental rugs, and ornate furniture in the French style. The marquis and his guests had gathered in the sitting room. Even before Chacón could be introduced, one familiar figure rose to acknowledge him. It was Ramón el Ollero. The first words out of the pot-maker's mouth were, "Ah, *el señoritín* from Jerez, here to show us Sevillanos how to sing!"

"Ramón, I'm glad to see you could get away from your pots long enough to honor us with your presence."

The dignitaries smiled and nodded as they were introduced to the new arrivals, oblivious to the tension that had just charged the air in the room. The marquis said, "I see that our two *cantadores* know each other...but then I guess that is only natural with these people. What would you have to drink, gentlemen? We have cognac, port, and a fine *jerez* [sherry] from the González Byass vineyard...a personal gift from *Don* Manuel, himself."

As he drank, Chacón studied the five men in the room. All were dressed in expensive suits. Two were accompanied by attractive women and, judging by the doting attention the women were receiving, they were almost certainly not wives. No, these women had to be *queridas* [mistresses] or *entretenidas* [paid girlfriends].

The flamencos were forgotten as the others made small talk. El Jorobao retreated uncomfortably to a corner and began to tune his guitar. Chacón and Ramón waited patiently, without speaking to each other. At last, the marquis turned to Chacón and said, *"Don* Antonio, we're ready for some music. Would you care to give us a taste of *cante?"*

Chacón, accustomed to singing last, balked for a moment at the idea of singing before El Ollero. But he realized that the pride of the older Ramón would almost certainly result in an unpleasant scene if he refused, so he smiled and said, "It will be my pleasure, *Señor* Marquis." Then, addressing his guitarist, he said," Juan, put it on the fifth, *por medio* [in A]."

To warm up the atmosphere, Antonio sang a string of light *soleares*, those of Paquirri el Guanté and others in a similar vein. This first *cante* of the evening, in the pleasant voice of the Jerezano, captured the complete attention of all in the room. The smug look on Ramón's face, said that he must be thinking: *The Jerezano has a good voice, but if that's all he has to offer, I will have no competition here tonight.*

When Chacón had finished, El Ollero said to the guitarist, "Continue *por soleá*, but on the sixth, *por arriba* [in E]" And then he showed why he was so respected in his specialty. His potent voice filled the room with creative melodies and moving poetry. The dignitaries forgot their drinks, completely captivated by the sound emanating from the contorted features of the *cantaor* from Triana. Once started, El Ollero couldn't be stopped, and he sang on longer perhaps than he should have. The women lost interest long before he had finished.

The spectators had heard enough of the *soleá*. They were ready for a something different, perhaps some popular songs. But Chacón dashed their hopes when he said, "Juan, continue *por allí* [there, in the same style]."

The guitarist reached for the *cejilla*, to put it back on the fifth for Chacón, but the singer stopped him. "No, Juan, leave it there, *por arriba*, in Ramón's tones."

El Ollero raised an eyebrow. The Jerezano would be singing two whole tones lower than his accustomed pitch. He would be at a severe disadvantage.

Now, singing a full two tones out of his comfort zone, Chacón went for the kill. He didn't attempt the melodic style of Triana, a style he had been slowly learning from followers of El Ollero, from the Cuende sisters and La Gómez. Instead, he sang the *cante gitano*—the *soleares* of Enrique el Mellizo and the Jerez and Sevilla styles of Paco la Luz. But his innate musicality gave these *cantes* new breadth and grandeur. He exploited fully his three vocal ranges: From the belly came resonance and earthy emotion. Shifting to a natural voice he gained power and a rich timbre. And, to show off his flexible voice he could go into an agile falsetto. The transitions from one voice to another were smooth and undetectable.

The spectators listened with renewed interest and applauded enthusiastically after each *letra*. El Ollero felt his confidence crumble. This wasn't what he had expected. When the Chacón brought his *cante* to a close, the marquis chose that moment to show off his knowledge. He said, "*Tocador* [guitarist], please play *por martinetes*...I would like to hear these two *cantadores* compete in the *martinetes*."

El Jorobao looked over at Chacón, clearly perplexed. He didn't know what to do. The *martinetes* were never sung with guitar accompaniment. They were sung in free rhythm or to the steady beat of hammer on anvil. But to show up the marquis in front of his friends would be unthinkable.

Chacón broke the awkward silence. "*Señor* Marquis, I have an idea. With your permission, and if Ramón is willing, we will do something quite difficult. We will compete in the *martinete*, but we will do it *a palo seco* [a capella], without the guitar. In that way you will be better able to judge our *cante*." He looked at Ramón, who acknowledged the clever trick with a nod.

The marquis said, "Brilliant Chacón, brilliant! *Vamos*, I'm anxious to hear it!"

So the two *cantaores* alternated in the *martinetes*. Chacón, with his extensive knowledge of this *cante*, had a clear advantage. When he had finished, the marquis said, *"Bueno hombre, muy bien!"* But how is it possible for you to sing like that and you are not a gypsy?"

Chacón thought for a moment before answering, "*Señor Marqués*, do you believe that human beings can have their hearts in different places? No, *hombre*, of course not...the heart is always in the same place. Whether a man is white, black, Madrileño or Catalán, everyone has his heart in the same place when it comes to performing an art."

Before the marquis could respond, another of the men said, "Remarkable Chacón! I'm a trained singer and I find it amazing that you are able to divide a tone into four parts. Have you ever thought of studying opera? I might be able to help finance your studies in Milan."

"That's very kind and generous, but I am completely dedicated to our *cante*."

"That's a shame...you would make a fine tenor."

The gathering broke up early, at close to four in the morning. The women were bored, and some of the men had businesses to attend to the following day, or women to tend to that night. As the three artists stepped into the street, El Ollero made a grand show of placing a twenty-five-*peseta* note, unmistakable in its gold color and prominent portrait of Francisco de Goya, into his pocket, saying, "Good singing is always well-rewarded."

Without blinking, Chacón retorted, "I'm always paid *before* I sing!" And he turned toward home, leaving the surprised Ramón standing in the street with his mouth open.

Early on a November morning Chacón was awakened abruptly by a series of jolts. At first he thought someone was shaking him out of bed, but when he had awakened fully and his mind had cleared he felt the room tremble. He had been through earthquakes before. This one seemed substantial. He dressed and went out. Concerned Sevillanos filled the streets, chattering nonstop about the damage they had sustained in their homes. As the morning wore on it became clear that there had been significant damage done around the city. The dome of the Cathedral had collapsed, littering the ground inside and out with crumpled masonry.

When Chacón arrived at Silverio's cafe, he found his mentor appraising damage to the building.

"How does it look, maestro?"

"There is some damage that would need to be repaired, some cracks. I don't know how bad it is. You know, this might be the end of the café. The city has passed some new statutes that are going to make it very difficult for cafés like mine to stay open. Now, neighbors can make official complaints for noise or immoral behavior, and if there are enough of them, we lose our license. I have had enough. I plan to close at the end of this month."

"What will you do then?"

"I'm thinking of looking elsewhere, perhaps in Madrid, where conditions are better for operating a café."

Chacón couldn't imagine Sevilla without Silverio.

Soon after the holiday season, Silverio left for Badajoz. He planned to open a café there and told Chacón he would send for him when he got established. A little more than two months later, he was back in Sevilla. The government in Badajoz had fined him and closed him down for moral infractions.

To keep busy Silverio gave a few concerts, one in Córdoba, in a rented church. Finally, fed up and frustrated, he told Chacón, " I'm going to Madrid. I hope conditions there will better for opening a café."

Before the two *cantaores* parted, Silverio grew quiet for a moment and then said, "Antonio, take good care of the *cante*...it's in your hands now."

Chacón didn't understand the full significance of Silverio's words, but assumed that the great man meant he wouldn't be singing in public anymore. All he could think to say was, "Of course, maestro. You can count on me."

In late May, Chacón was contracted to sing for three days in the newly constructed Teatro Eslava in Jerez. It would be his debut as an established artist in his hometown. He asked Javier to play for him. The performances were a tremendous success. The audiences wouldn't let him go, pleading for encore after encore. After the first night, Javier said to him, "I can't believe how much you've changed. Your singing just keeps getting better and better...and you are singing things I have never heard before."

"I appreciate that, Javié. You know, I couldn't have done it without you and Antonio. Together we built the foundation for everything I am doing now."

"I hope my playing is satisfactory for your new *cantes*..."

"*Hombre*, your playing still inspires me...you know me so well. There is no guitarist I would put before you."

Over drinks on the second day, Chacón and the Molinas caught up with what each had been doing the previous year. Chacón recounted his days in Málaga and Algeciras.

Javier said, "We were in Algeciras, too. It was during another trip like the one we did with you. Junquera's sister closed the Vera Cruz, so we took a singer with us...a so-so singer named El Águila...and went all along the coast. From Chiclana we went to Conil and Vejer, where my family was living at that time...my father was captain of the field crew in a vineyard there. Then we continued along the coast, walking from town to town and giving concerts in *casinos* and working in *cafés cantantes*. In Algeciras, we worked for two weeks in a café at a fixed salary. The same in La Linea. Then we worked our way back to Vejer to stay with my family. When my father's job ended, my family moved to Chiclana, where we stayed and worked for a long while in a café...with very good artists. Then, one day, my father took off in a *manola* [two-wheeled carriage] for La Isla and caught a train to Cádiz to visit his sister. We haven't heard from him since. So we brought my mother back here to Jerez. Since then, we've been working in various cafés...although many have closed...and I have my guitar students."

As Javier talked, Chacón thought to himself, *They haven't changed. They're still where we were almost five years ago...living from desperate job to desperate job!*

"Why don't you come with me to Madrid?" he said.

"We can't leave here now. We have work. I have my students. And I have patrons who call me frequently for fiestas. In a new city, I would have to start all over."

Chacón shrugged. What could he do?

On the morning after the third night's performance, Javier found Chacón and told him with an anguished expression on his face. "Antonio, I just heard that Silverio is dead."

"No!"

"Yes, unfortunately it's true. He died yesterday, just after he returned to Sevilla from Madrid"

Chacón was on the first available train to Sevilla.

Sevilla, May 31, 1889

Chacón went directly from the train station to Silverio's home to pay respects. On approaching the building the reality of death hit him when he saw the balcony on the second floor. All of the flowerpots were gone from what had always been the most colorful balcony in the building. It was the second time in his life that flowerpots had given body to his grief, confirming the devastating finality of his loss. In addition, the barrier along the bottom of the balcony ironwork, the barrier that prevented men from looking up at women's ankles, had been raised to the top of the railing, indicating that there would be no woman going out onto that balcony.

Silverio's door was propped halfway open, as it would remain until the burial. Just inside, on a small table draped in black, a tray received sympathy cards, and next to it a sheet of paper awaited visitor's signatures. Chacón found Silverio's wife surrounded by friends and family, her beautiful face swollen and red. She had not yet dressed in black—to dress in mourning too soon implied that you had been preparing for the death.

"Thank you for coming Antonio," she said between sobs.

"I'm so sorry, María. This has been a great shock. To me he was more than a friend...he was like a father."

"He was very fond of you and always spoke highly of you."

"May I see him...to say goodbye?"

"Certainly. He's in the bedroom, the first door in the hall."

Antonio took a deep breath to compose himself and stepped into the bedroom. Silverio lay on a draped platform made from planks supported by two tables. He appeared to be sleeping, dressed in his best suit. The suit had almost certainly been cut away in the back, both for convenience in dressing the body and to prevent theft of the clothes by the burial workers before they closed the casket. A candle burned at each corner of the platform and a crucifix stood at Silverio's head. Flowers had been placed around the platform on the floor.

Chacón stood there a while, trying to grasp the reality of Silverio's passing. Then he mumbled, "Maestro...thank you for all you have done for me, for guiding me on the path of the *cante* since my childhood. I promise to fulfill your dreams for the *cante*, and to always hold it to your high standard. *Vaya con Dios*, maestro!"

He left María in the care of family and friends who had spent the night in vigil over the body. Neighbors were there to serve coffee and brandy, and they would also do the cooking for the next few days so that the house wouldn't smell like a kitchen.

No sooner had Chacón stepped into the street than he felt the emptiness of Sevilla without Silverio Franconetti. "I can't stay here," he said out loud.

An uncharacteristically somber Paco el Sevillano filled Antonio in on what had happened: "The maestro returned from Madrid yesterday morning, seemingly in good health. In the afternoon he went to the Plaza de San Fernando[4] to chat with friends. Suddenly he said he didn't feel well, and his friends had to help him home. He went to bed and died shortly afterward...around eight o'clock. It was his heart...you remember how he was often too tired to leave his house? Within a couple of hours we all knew what had happened. Many of us didn't go to work...we just couldn't."

Chacón's thoughts flashed back to Salvaoriyo's ominous warning about the devastating effects of the *cante por seguiriyas* on the nerves, lungs and heart.

That afternoon a small crowd gathered in the Plaza de la Constitución in front of Silverio's building. The immense coffin, specially built to accommodate Silverio's bulk, would not fit through the stairway, so a music company with expertise in moving pianos was brought in to lower the coffin from the balcony. Once on the ground, the coffin was hoisted onto the shoulders of La Viejas Ricas, paying homage to their friend and benefactor. Silverio's body was carried several blocks to the burial company, where it was loaded onto a hearse to be drawn by four horses draped in black trappings with black plumes on their heads.

When the procession was ready, it began its slow journey through the streets of Sevilla, led by two choirboys holding tall candlesticks and a clergyman dressed in black with a silver cross hanging from his neck. After the coffin came family and friends, but only men. Women remained behind in the house, crying and praying. Crowds gathered along the streets to watch. Whether they knew Silverio or not, all removed their hats in respect as the coffin passed.

At the last remaining vestige of city wall in the Barrio de la Macarena, the hearse stopped under the arched gateway. Since the San Fernando Cemetery was located a considerable distance from the city, the procession came to an end at that point. The clergy departed and family members lined up to receive mourners, who bowed their heads and passed by without speaking. Mourners returned on foot to the city,

---

[4]Today: Plaza Nueva.

while the family and close friends mounted hired carriages for the ride to the cemetery. Silverio was buried in a simple grave in the Catholic cemetery of San Fernando.

Chacón rode back to town with Silverio's two nephews, owners of a tailor shop on Calle Tetuán. Men in the two families would return immediately to Silverio's home to rearrange the furniture and remove all photographs from the walls. It was hoped that the deceased's ghost would not recognize anything familiar and therefore not return to live in the home.

As Chacón walked the short distance from Plaza de la Constitución to his *pensión* he recalled Silverio's words to him in one of their last conversations. He had said, "Antonio, you are not like the others. There are many who learn a few *malagueñas* and think they are ready to go on stage. Even the great *malagueña* singers like El Canario or El Perote sing little more than that one *cante*. You carry in your blood the hot breath of the forges, where the *cante* is hammered out on the anvil. You have brought all your knowledge of the *cante gitano* to your creativity in the *cante andaluz*. Only Enrique el Mellizo comes close to your preparation in the *cante* and I believe you are even more complete than he. You have swooped down on the *malagueñas* from the heights of the *seguiriyas* like an eagle falls on its prey from its perch on the cliffs. You are a nightingale with the vigor, the talons, and the valor of a sparrow hawk."

Antonio felt the weight of responsibility. Barely twenty years old, he had already been ordained by the three giants of the *cante*: Juan Breva, creator of the *malagueña*, had given him his blessing and acknowledged his supremacy in the new *malagueña*. Silverio Franconetti, king of *cantaores*, had proclaimed him his successor. And Enrique el Mellizo, the great innovator and teacher of the *cantes* of Cádiz, had anointed him Pope of the *Cante*.

Three days later Chacón returned to his room to find a framed photograph of Silverio sitting on his dresser—the same photo that had been included in Demófilo's book. A note said, *María wanted you to have this.*

Four days later, *Don* Antonio Chacón sat staring blankly out the window of a train headed for Madrid.

Epilogue

Antonio Chacón reigned as the divo of flamenco for forty years, until several years before his death in 1929. In his last years, when he had to sing in a thin, high-pitched falsetto, he was booed even in his hometown of Jerez—a victim of a phenomenon of his own making. His many innovations in the *cante* had been carried to such extremes that he was considered to be old-fashioned by the younger generation.

Just as Silverio before him had carried out the noble idea of elevating the *cante gitano* and giving it the dignity and recognition he thought it deserved, only to see it degenerate into commercial *cante flamenco*, so Chacón had fought to elevate the *cante flamenco* and give it respect in society, only to see his efforts lead to the decadent period of the *ópera flamenca* in which the *cante gitano* was ignored and much of it lost.

Without Antonio Chacón, flamenco would be very different from what is today. He single-handedly created the modern forms of the *fandango* family as we know them, including the *malagueñas*, *cartageneras*, *murcianas*, *mineras*, *granaínas*, and *media granaína*. Many of these creations had their roots in the period covered in this book, but some of them were not fully developed until the years immediately afterward. He elaborated the *granaína* to such an extent that it became almost unrecognizable, so he invented a new name for it, calling it *media granaína*. His *letras* for this *cante* were so beautiful that I am including a couple of them here. The second one often caused a scandal when he sang it in public.

Rosa, si no te cojí,
fue porque no me dió gana;
al pie de un rosal dormí
y rosa tuve por cama,
de cabecera un jazmín.

Rosa, if I didn't catch you,
it was because I didn't want to;
I slept under a rosebush
and I had roses for a bed,
and jasmine for a headboard.

Llevas una cruz al cuello,
engarzá en oro y marfil;
déjame que muera en ella
y crucificarme allí.

You wear a cross around your neck,
inlaid with gold and ivory;
let me die on it
and crucify myself there.

Through his recordings, Chacón popularized some *cantes* that might have been forgotten, including the *caracoles*, *mirabrás*, and *milonga*. He gave the *tientos* their modern style and created the name. He was the most encyclopedic *cantaor* in flamenco history. Although his voice was not ideal for the *cante gitano*, his unequaled knowledge of the gypsy styles preserved many of them through his recordings and the *cantaores* who learned from him. His versions of the *serranas*, *polo*, *caña*, and certain styles of the *soleá* are primarily the ones we know today. He astounded gypsies by singing *por seguiriyas* for hours, pulling endless styles from his prodigious memory. The great gypsy guitarist Ramon Montoya said of him that he was capable of beginning to sing at eight o'clock one night and continuing to sing until eight the following night with the same enthusiasm and ability. The gypsy *cantaora* La Niña de los Peines said that when he sang at half-voice, without effort, he could be heard better than any shouter.

Chacón succeeded in elevating the *cante*. He was equally at home among gypsy artists or aristocrats, in taverns or palaces. Silverio had taken the *cante* from the tavern to the café. Chacón took it from the café to the theater. The *cante* finally received the respect it deserved... but in the process a great deal was lost.

Chacón carried Silverio's picture with him throughout his life. On his deathbed his instructions to his wife Anita were to put the photo in his coffin with him. But, instead, Anita gave it to a close friend who begged her for it.

Javier Molina eventually went to Madrid where he amazed guitarists with his solo playing and accompanied many of the great artists of the first half of the twentieth century. He would become the father of what we today call the Jerez school or style of guitar playing. He lived until 1956.

Antonio Molina faded from the historical record and it is assumed that he died young.

Appendix A

A Historical Flamenco Novel?

The history of flamenco is largely recorded in legend, anecdote, and fragments of song passed from generation to generation. Flamenco has traditionally been an underground art form, an emotional expression for poverty-stricken and oppressed people—gypsies, laborers, drunks, prostitutes, and criminals. Largely illiterate, these people could not be expected to record details of their lives for posterity.

With the appearance of the *café cantante* in the second half of the nineteenth century, certain segments of the upper classes began to view flamenco as a source of entertainment, as part of a nightlife that included drinking, gambling, and available women. The music began to attract the attention of intellectuals, particularly foreigners, and made its presence felt in classical compositions, opera, *zarzuelas* [Spanish light opera], and literature. But the well-deserved unsavory reputation of the music and its association with a lifestyle that was generally perceived as degenerate and worthless continued to discourage interest by the press or by those writers who could have recorded factual information for the historical record.

By 1920, flamenco had entered a new phase, passing from the cafés and taverns to the theater. The gypsy element was suppressed and, with the addition of orchestral accompaniment, stage decoration, and ballet choreography, the music became more acceptable to the Spanish public. This type of "flamenco" was exported around the world by such touring companies as those of La Argentina, La Argentinita, Carmen Amaya, Pilar López, and José Greco. The press took more interest in this stylized and sanitized *ópera flamenca*, but still there was little effort put into recording events for history. It was not until the 1950s that a resurgence of interest in the old gypsy styles initiated the start of intensive investigation into flamenco's past. Flamencologists began a period of exhaustive searches through church records, seeking birth dates and family backgrounds of shadowy historical figures whose birthplaces and even real names were often unknown. They went methodically through old periodicals hoping to uncover any mention, however brief, of flamenco events and personalities. And they built a body of knowledge based upon fragmentary information gleaned from the fading and nostalgic memories of veteran flamenco artists who had been active at the turn of the twentieth century. By 1990, the last of those artists had died, more or less closing the book on that epoch.

Beginning in the early 1960s, a flood of books and journals began to reveal the results of this ongoing research. Unfortunately, the majority of these publications have not been accessible to the English-speaking aficionado. They have been written in Spanish and they have generally not been available on a wide scale, even within Spain. Many books have been privately printed in small numbers and have vanished immediately into private collections. It has not been uncommon for an institution such as a bank to fund a publication, distribute it to a small number of customers, and then allow it to pass into oblivion. There is, however, an attempt being made today to reprint some of these works and make them available through universities, research centers, and in conjunction with special flamenco events.

Even when published material is available, there is often a frustrating lack of agreement among authors. Hardly a single historical or biographical fact is not disputed somewhere in print, with opposing views supported only by conjecture and shaky evidence. When not disagreeing, authors have freely borrowed from one another. Information passes from book to book, changing slightly with each appearance, until what was originally a minor conjecture becomes a fully accepted "fact."

Investigators have tended to focus on specialized areas of interest and there has been little attempt to integrate existing knowledge. The few comprehensive compilations of information are worth mentioning: One of the first, and the only one to be published in English, is Donn Pohren's *Lives and Legends of Flamenco* (1964, 1968). Borrowing heavily from the earlier works of Guillermo Núñez del Prado (1904) and Fernando de Triana (1935), Pohren compiled biographies of flamenco personalities based upon what was known at the time. It was a valuable pioneering effort, but viewed today the work is quite out-of-date—incomplete and inaccurate. Published about the same time, *Mundo y Formas del Cante Flamenco* (1963), by Antonio Molina and the gypsy *cantaor* Antonio Mairena, is a highly subjective and biased account organized around the analysis of the different song forms. Felix Grande, in his two-volume *Memoria del Flamenco* (1979), makes contributions in the area of flamenco pre-history (Arabic influences and gypsy history), but, in general, concerns himself more with the social conditions that helped to mold flamenco rather than attempting a complete picture of flamenco's history. Perhaps the best historical account is Angel Alvarez Caballero's *Historia del Flamenco* (1981), which attempts to present all available information and opinion about highly contested subjects. Unfortunately, he leaves many controversies unresolved.

The most accurate and prolific flamencologist to date has been José Blas Vega. He has attempted to remove as much conjecture as possible from his work and to document his conclusions wherever possible. His books, *Vida y Cante de Don Antonio Chacón* (1986) and *Silverio: Rey de los Cantaores* (1995) are masterpieces of detective work. Yet, even these important contributions have errors and omissions and leave the reader unsatisfied, without a concrete feeling for the kind of men Antonio Chacón and Silverio might have been. In 1988, with Manuel Ríos Ruiz, Blas Vega published his monumental *Diccionario Enciclopédico Ilustrado del Flamenco*, in which he attempted to bring together all existing information on flamenco. As important as this work is, it has some serious shortcomings. In his obsession with accuracy, Blas Vega omits much undocumented material. The reader therefore misses out on a great deal of information that *might* be accurate. This is particularly true with dates of birth and death, where an approximation would be preferable to nothing at all. In addition, in what appears to be a reaction to the ongoing controversy over how much credit gypsies should receive for their role in the evolution of flamenco, the authors refuse to indicate whether an artist is gypsy or non-gypsy—perhaps the single most important fact we can know about a flamenco artist. Blas Vega's subsequent books, *Los Cafés Cantantes de Sevilla* and *Los Cafés Cantantes de Madrid* have helped to make my book possible.

In order to understand my approach to writing this book, it is necessary to be familiar with the nature of the flamenco historical record. Except for a few documented facts, i.e. birth and death dates, dates of performances taken from programs or newspapers, and certain kinds of information taken from early recordings, flamenco history is based upon highly colored second or third-hand accounts. Very little of what is generally accepted today can be verified. Witnesses to events do not always recall them accurately, and the past tends to take on an aura of heightened magnitude—the good becomes better, the bad worse. Death tends to canonize individuals and give them mythological proportions. Even newspaper accounts will be biased by the reporter's prejudices or ignorance.

Imagine the participant in a flamenco gathering who, many years later, describes to his son what he experienced in that drunken and emotional moment, his recollections further distorted by the passage of time. Half a century later the son tells his version of the story, exaggerating his father's role, to a newspaper reporter who sensationalizes it for the public. A flamenco historian uncovers the news article and publishes the story in a book, from where it is borrowed by other flamencologists and passed on in altered forms until it becomes established as fact. That kind of information is the basis of much of flamenco's history.

Given that we cannot distinguish between real facts and distorted or inaccurate "facts," I have chosen not to discriminate between fact and legend. Since we cannot know exactly what happened on a particular occasion, we have no choice but to accept what we are told *unless* it is in disagreement with other sources, common sense, or a well-documented fact. It may not be so important to know *exactly* what happened if we can get a feel for the times and the music through what old-time flamencos tell us happened.

How can one write a fictionalized history? How will the reader distinguish between material that is pure fiction and that which has some historical basis? First, only the central figures in this novel are filled out with fictional material. All of the information about flamenco, its structure, philosophy, and historical dates, places, and events, are as accurate as current knowledge will permit. All historical personalities other than the central characters are described using only documented information (faulty as that might be). Sources and references for each chapter are given in Appendix B, where I also carefully delineate the fictional elements in the writing.

Much of the dialogue is either taken directly from historical records or expanded from brief fragments. In reality, these documented conversations have little more basis in fact than those that I have invented. In most cases they were fabricated by someone else, perhaps even the person who was involved in the original conversation. When an old man reproduces a conversation he claims to have had as a child, he invents almost as much as would an outsider. Except where a conversation was recorded firsthand (which never happened in early flamenco history), we must view all historical dialogue, no matter how well-documented, not as fact, but as an interesting possibility and an approximation of what could have been said.

No historical figure can be accurately recreated on paper. No matter how skilled the author, each reader creates his own reality and fashions characters that are unique to his experience and unlike those in the minds of other readers. So, when I portray Antonio Chacón, I do not claim to give you the definitive Chacón, but rather a Chacón who is consistent with what is known of him. I attempt to extrapolate from documented information in order to fill out the character and move the story along in a plausible manner, but I have avoided over-developing characters through pure, undocumented invention. It seemed preferable to me to leave these personalities somewhat shallow and dimensionless in certain areas rather than conjure up qualities, thoughts, or actions that have no documented basis.

It has been my intention, using whatever means necessary, to present a flamenco history that not only compiles the facts of flamenco's development and the lives of its proponents, but leaves the reader with a feeling for the people and the times that were crucial in its evolution. Only with an understanding of the factors that forged flamenco, the contexts that created its forms and conventions, can the aficionado truly appreciate the music. I have freely invented situations, events, and characters where necessary to advance the story or convey information. These fictional fabrications are indicated in Appendix B and are always based upon real possibilities, with all elements being historically authentic.

This book contains a great deal of Spanish language. There are a number of reasons for this. A few words are thrown in for flavor, but I have tried to minimize this type of usage. Many Spanish words have been assimilated into English, so I do not even italicize such words as gazpacho, pueblo, matador, chorizo, etc. Words that are an integral part of flamenco—the names of song styles, the names for guitarists, singers, and dancers, etc.—are too important to be left out. Any aficionado should know these words. Some words have no English equivalent: using "non-gypsy" to refer to those who are not gypsies is awkward, so I have used the old Spanish word "*gachó*."

Often I include a long phrase in Spanish, followed immediately by its translation. I assume that many of my readers will speak Spanish on some level. They will enjoy the subtleties that are hard to translate, while the non-Spanish speaker will not miss out on the essential meaning. This is especially true with the *letras* of the *cante*—the lyrics of the songs. These concise gems of folk philosophy tell us so much through the use of language. I have translated them for meaning rather than attempting to preserve the poetic structure (rhyming, length of lines, etc.), but often there remain elusive nuances that defy translation. Some authors who have opted for poetic structure over meaning often end up with comical results (see works by George Borrow or Walter Starkie). Since the English rendering distorts the structure of the verse, even English-speaking readers might want to refer to the original Spanish.

Not only do the songs suffer in translation, but they also lose a great deal when they are not sung. Flamencologist Felix Grande put it well: "One cannot conceive of a single verse of *cante flamenco* that was written to be recited and, likewise, there is no flamenco verse, no matter how overwhelming its poetic strength, that does not grow in expression, in violence or tenderness, in the very instant of being interpreted by a *cantaor* [singer] in a fortunate moment." (*Memoria del Flamenco*, pp.387-388)

Much of the Spanish in the verses and dialogue is written in the colorful Andalusian dialect, since it is an integral part of flamenco. Some of the common characteristics are the use of *r* in place of *l* (*er* for *el*; *argo* for *algo*), *g* in place of *b* (*güeno* for *bueno*), *j* for *h* (*jondo* rather than *hondo*), *y* for *ll* (*Salvaoriyo* for *Salvaorillo*), the omission of letters *s*, *d*, and final *r* in many cases (*mare* for *madre*, *Cái* for *Cádiz*, *cantaó* for *cantaor*), and reversal of letters (*probe* for *pobre* and *naide* for *nadie*).

Usage varies greatly according to locale and social class and is inconsistent even with each individual. Therefore you will find a great deal of variation in the Spanish used in this book, with such practices as omitting the final *s* in one word and including it in another in the same sentence. These things are decided by the flow of the sentence and the need for comprehension.

It is my hope that this book can be read on different levels. The native Spanish-speaking aficionado will enjoy the subtle nuances of the verses and the colorful jargon of the flamencos. The non-native Spanish speaker will be exposed to an unfamiliar use of the language. Knowledgeable aficionados will be able to follow the technical intricacies of this flamenco odyssey, while the layman will, hopefully, enjoy the story and gain an appreciation for the complexity of the flamenco art.

A final word about the gypsy language, *caló*. This language, a mixture of Spanish, *Romaní* (the Sanskrit based language of European gypsies), and *germanía* (criminal and delinquent slang), was practically lost by the middle of the twentieth century. It was preserved primarily in the early writings of foreigners such as George Borrow until—much too late—Spaniards began to take an interest. I have used a sprinkling of the *caló* that was typical of late 1800s in those situations where I wanted to emphasize the distinction between gypsies and non-gypsies. Some of these words have passed into today's standard Spanish (*parné, chaval, sandunga, ducas,* etc.).

Because I wrote in English, I had to modify some Spanish rules. I could not place inverted exclamation or question marks at the beginning of sentences. And I have capitalized some words, such as Sevillano (a resident of Sevilla), that would not be capitalized in Spanish.

Appendix B

Fact or Fiction?

For those readers who wish to treat this work as a biography rather than a novel, I include here the sources of my information and attempt to separate as much as possible the fact from the fiction.

Chapter One— Chacón

The scant information available on the early life of Antonio Chacón comes from three sources. José Blas Vega discovered Chacón's birth certificate after an exhaustive search of church records, thereby supplying his birth date, the names of his parents, and the suppressed fact that he had been adopted. Blas Vega also quotes from several interviews (*Vida y Cante de Don Antonio Chacón*, pp.11-13) in which the singer gives a sketchy outline of his early life, including his occupation, relationship with his father, school, and his desire to sing. From the memoirs of Javier Molina (*Javier Molina, Jerezano y Tocaor*, by Augusto Butler) we learn the address of Chacón's childhood home (still in use today).

All places described are factual and all information about flamenco and flamenco personalities are documented in accounts from the period or by oral tradition. However, much of the dialogue and the details of Chacón's daily life are fictionalized. Chacón must not have had close ties with his family, for they appear to have played little role in his life after he left home. That he never mentioned brothers or sisters, and the fact that he was adopted, led me to the conclusion that he was an only child.

The *taberna* and blacksmith scenes are fictional. The meeting with Juan Torre and the baptism of Manuel Torre are undocumented. Chacón never mentioned knowing the Torre family in his youth. But given the proximity of their homes and the fame of the *cantaores* who frequented the Torre patio (Marrurro, La Cherna, Torre), it seems unlikely that Chacón was not acquainted with the family. The Torre home, now in ruins, is marked with a commemorative plaque.

All song verses given throughout this book are attributed to the indicated *cantaores* by oral tradition or documented by actual recordings. There are several ways to spell *seguiriyas* (the modern spelling is *siguiriyas*). In the 1870s the word was relatively new. Only a decade or so earlier this *cante* was called *playeras*. The most common name for the song became *seguidillas gitanas*, the "*gitanas*" needed to distinguish it from the *seguidillas*, an unrelated festive folk music (*sevillanas* being one example). *Seguiriyas* is nothing more than the Andalusian deformation of *seguidillas*. During this early period *cantaores* often called these songs *cantes de sentimiento* [songs of feeling] or *tóo lo jondo* [maximum profundity].

Some words used here are from the Sanskrit-based gypsy language, *caló*. *Currandó*, for example, is gypsy for *martillo*, or hammer. I use the gypsy word *gachó* for "non-gypsy" because there is no equivalent word in English. The word *payo* (*paillo*), also gypsy language for "non-gypsy," appears to be more recent.

Chapter Two—Javier

Chacón described in some detail his experiences in the *tonelería* (Juan de la Plata, *Flamencos de Jerez*, p.45). But the most valuable document dealing with this period in Chacón's life is Javier Molina's memoir, *Javier Molina, Jerezano y Tocaor*, published by Augusto Butler in 1963. Through Javier we learn of the Chacón family's move to Plaza Orellana, the boy's obsession with *cante*, his problems with his father, and his first earnings from singing in a *dicho* celebration.

The story of Silverio's return to Spain is based on the version told by the poet Manuel Machado—son of Antonio Machado y Álvarez, Silverio's biographer. I added some details told to me by Manuel Oliver, the oldest surviving *cantaor* of the Triana school of *cante* (Manuel died in 1989).

The meeting between Javier and Chacón, as well as events in the Molina home (still in existence and marked with a plaque), are fictionalized accounts. The mating dance of the chickens has been described in print and can be seen performed by old gypsies of Triana on video. The discussion about guitar playing is fiction, but all facts presented are documented. The guitar solos played by Arcas and Paco el Barbero are taken from actual programs and newspaper accounts (*Antonio de Torres: Guitarmaker—His life and Work*, by José L. Romanillos; *La Guitarra: Historia, Estudios y Aportaciones al Arte Flamenco*, by Manuel Cano, p.87).

According to biographer Augusto Butler, Javier was elusive when it came to identifying his teachers. He mentions Patiño, Paco el Barbero, and Paco de Lucena, the latter two being the only two soloists of the time after the death of Arcas in 1882. Given Javier's early predilection for solo playing, these would certainly be his major influences.

There is a reference to the Café de Silverio on page 4. According to Blas Vega in his book, *Los Cafés Cantantes de Sevilla*, this would be the Salón Recreo, directed by Silverio. In 1880 Silverio and Manuel Ojeda Rodríguez "El Burrero" would open the Café de la Escalerilla, usually referred to as the Café de Silverio. In fact, any café operated by Silverio became popularly known as the Café de Silverio—creating some confusion from a historical perspective. In 1881, Silverio would open his own café.

Chapter Three—Breva

Information about Juan Breva comes primarily from generally accepted accounts compiled by Miguel Berjillos in his book, *Vida de Juan Breva*; Gonzalo Rojo Guerrero in *Cantaores Malagueños*; Fernando de Triana in *Arte y Artistas*; and José Blas Vega and Manuel Ríos Ruiz in their *Diccionario Enciclopédico del Flamenco*.

It has not been shown that Breva sang in Jerez or that he met Chacón at that time. But Breva sang throughout Andalucía in that year and it is unlikely that he missed Jerez or that Chacón did not hear him sing. The essential facts about Breva's performances in 1882 have been documented by actual programs and newspaper accounts from a concert given in Lucena (Córdoba) in that year (Berjillos; Blas Vega-Ríos Ruiz). There is also an amazing photo of Breva and Paco de Lucena playing guitar together (see: Rojo Guerrero).

Stories about Paco de Lucena are taken verbatim from accounts by Fernando de Triana, longtime friend of the guitarist. Supplementary material comes from Berjillos, Manuel Cano, and Blas Vega/Ríos Ruiz. Lucena's repertoire is taken from a solo concert given in Córdoba in 1879, in which he also played *guajiras, seguiriyas,* and *malagueñas* (Cano, p.89). Descriptions of Lucena's appearance and his guitar are based on photographs. Paco de Lucena never recorded, but there are recordings of Ramón Montoya, early in his career, playing with Juan Breva and imitating the style of Lucena. Paco de Lucena's lecture to Javier on *compás* is paraphrased from conversations with Pericón de Cádiz (Ortiz Nuevo, pp.269-70).

Chapter Four—Fosforito

Information about Fosforito is sketchy and comes primarily from two sources: Fernando de Triana in *Arte y Artistas Flamencos*, and an interview with the *cantaor* in 1931 (partially reproduced by Blas Vega in *Vida y Cante de Antonio Chacón*, p.27). I have paraphrased Fosforito's comments in that interview for his description of learning from El Mellizo. Angel Álvarez Caballero, in *Historia del Cante Flamenco*, p.148, describes Fosforito's debut and subsequent performances in Junquera's café, El Palenque. As is so often the case in flamenco studies, no source is given for that information. Other artists performing in El Palenque with Fosforito are taken from newspaper accounts of performances in Jerez during that period (Gerhard Steingress, *Los Cafés Cantantes de Jerez*). There is only one existing photo of Fosforito—in his later years.

The life and personality of Enrique el Mellizo come largely from those who knew him: Aurelio Sellés and Pericón de Cádiz (*Aurelio: Su Cante, Su Vida* by Manuel Moreno Delgado; *Conversaciones Flamencas con Aurelio de Cádiz* by José Blas Vega; *Las Mil y Una Historias de Pericón de Cádiz* by José Luis Ortiz Nuevo). Fernando Quiñones gives additional material in his excellent work, *De Cádiz y Sus Cantes*.

The account of Chacón's unsuccessful debut in the Vera Cruz is taken directly from Javier Molina's memoirs (Butler).

Chacón's encounters with the Torre family are fictional, although all information about the family is documented or at least widely accepted. Major sources are: *La Sevilla de Manuel Torre* by Manuel Ríos Ruiz and *Historia del Cante Flamenco* by Angel Alvarez Caballero. The few available facts about Joaquín La Cherna and El Marrurro have been gathered by Juan de la Plata in *Flamencos de Jerez* and Manuel Ríos Ruiz in *De Cantes y Cantaores de Jerez*. There is some controversy concerning the correct spelling of "La Cherna." This is the older spelling, but, due to the common occurrence of the name "Serna" in Jerez, many feel that Cherna is a local deformation of Serna. I have two reasons for preferring Cherna. First, Serna is most often associated with men and we see it as "El Serna" or "El Sernita." The feminine "La Cherna" hints that it may be a different word, although it is possible that the name came from Joaquín's mother. In either case, the pronunciation was "Cherna" so I have decided to go with that.

El Señor Manuel Molina was the subject of a chapter in Núñez de Prado's sometimes fanciful *Cantaores Andaluces*, published in 1904.

The three boys' conversation about their intended journey is fictionalized, but the enthusiasm and the exaggerated concept of "touring the nation" come directly from Javier's account.

Chapter Five—*Los Artistas*

The journey of Chacón and the Molinas is based upon Javier's extensive description (Butler). I have used this phase of Chacón's life to describe the Andalucía of that period and the problems that would arise for a young performer. Descriptions of travel, the scenery, and the small town atmosphere of the late 1800s come from a great many adventure-travelogue books that were very popular around the end of that century.

Javier, in his account, mentions briefly traveling to Arcos, staying in the Posada de las Cuevas, and continuing on to Villalengua del Rosario. The story of the drunk who wanted his money back was described in detail by Javier in a magazine account quoted by Blas Vega in *Vida y Cante de Antonio Chacón* (p.19). The incident actually took place in the town of Facinas, far off the route of the journey described by Javier. Blas Vega incorrectly surmises that the incident must have occurred early in the trip. In fact, Javier gives another version of this event in his memoirs (pp.40-41), stating that it happened during a later trip, one in which Chacón was not present. I included it in Arcos because it is so typical of the sort of thing an artist would encounter.

Javier describes how they traveled, the meals, the wearing of *alpargatas*, changing clothes to enter towns, and how happy they were. The meeting with El Morrongo is fiction.

The *rondeñas* sung in the *posada* are those sung by Rafael Romero on the record anthology, *Archivo del Cante Flamenco* (Everest 3366/5).

Chapter Six—The Gypsies

All interactions of Chacón and the Molinas with the gypsy family, Los Morrongo, are purely fictional, as are the individual gypsies themselves. The life of the nomadic gypsies as portrayed here may appear somewhat exaggerated due the fact that one family is asked to demonstrate a great deal of gypsy lore in a brief period of time. But every incident is typical of early gypsies, no matter how exaggerated or incredible it might seem. Many of their customs are still seen in relatively modern times and many of the types of events described here have been verified in person by the author. The following references have been particularly helpful:

Rafael Lafuente wrote in *Los Gitanos, El Flamenco, y Los Flamencos* of his travels with a gypsy family in the mid-1900s, giving an accurately flavored account. José Carlos de la Luna is probably the most quoted authority on the *gitanos*, having described their lifestyles and customs in the early 1900s in his *Gitanos de la Bética*. Walter Starkie, knowledgeable flamenco aficionado and student of gypsy lore, published several highly entertaining books in the 1920s and '30s about his adventures with the gypsies of Spain.

The earliest serious portrayal of *gitanos* and an invaluable account of their language are found in George Borrow's *The Bible in Spain* (1842) and *The Zincali: An Account of the Gypsies of Spain* (1841). Finally, Bertha Quintana shed light on gypsy philosophy in her study of the modern gypsies of the Sacromonte in Granada, *Qué Gitano! Gypsies of Southern Spain* (1972).

The *serranas* sung by El Morrongo are all traditional, dating from the mid-1800s. I have taken many of them from a collection titled *Cantes Flamencos*, by Antonio Machado y Álvarez. The form of the *cante*, as sung by El Morrongo, is based on a recorded version sung by Pepe el de la Matrona (Pepe de la Matrona: *Tesoros del Flamenco Antiguo*, Hispavox, Madrid). Pepe, who died in 1980 at age 93, gives us a rare example of how the *serranas* might have been sung at the turn of the century. Due to the length of this *cante* it could not be recorded in the early years of the recording industry.

Chaper Seven—The *Feria*

Javier Molina described the boys' travels to Grazalema, where they worked in a café and Antonio was given a pair of boots. He mentions, in passing, working in a café in Algodonales and going to Puerto Serrano ("I don't remember what we did there.") However, he goes into great detail about events in Villamartín: working in the *feria*, El Puli, the adventure with *Don* José Gonzalo, the fight with El Quico, and Antonio going to jail. All descriptions of paper money (as in the note El Quico was supposed to change) in this book are taken from the *Standard Catalogue of World Money* (George Cuhaj, editor, Krause Publications, Iola WI, 2006). Anecdotes involving the *feria* and gypsy livestock traders are adapted from José Carlos de la Luna, *Gitanos de la Bética*, Más y Prat, *La Tierra de María Santísima*, and especially, F.M. Pabanó, *Historia y Costumbres de los Gitanos* (published in 1914, but based on earlier works).

Chapter Eight—*El Café de Silverio*

The story of Arturo and Esperanza in the Café de Silverio is adapted from an account by the *costumbrista* [novelist who writes descriptive period pieces] Benito Más y Prat (*La Tierra de María Santísima*, 1889. pp.58-64). Chacón and his friends were, of course, not present in the original version, nor was Juana la Macarrona mentioned by name (Más y Prat clearly did not use the real names of any of the performers). This work gives us the best available description of this famous café. It has been supplemented from other sources made available by Blas Vega in his *Los Cafés Cantantes de Sevilla* (p. 35). The dance of La Macarrona is taken from Fernando de Triana and a description by Pablillos de Valladolid (Blas Vega, *Diccionario Enciclopédico Ilustrado del Flamenco*, p.434).

Chapter Nine—Salvaoriyo

Javier's account of the journey with Chacón continues. I have stayed as much as possible with the simplicity of the original version in describing the journey. Keep in mind that, where Javier might use one or two sentences to describe an event, I use supplemental material to fill out the story at length. Javier tells of taking the mail coach from the Parador de Patrocinio with the *quincallero* and the load of dried cod, and the overnight stops in Santa Olalla and Fuente de Cantos, where they had to arise before dawn. The events in Zafra, except for the gypsies and events of the *feria*, are paraphrased from Javier's description. The verses of *tangos extremeños* sung in the *feria* date from this period, although they have been used in some modern *tangos*. Javier's version of the return to Sevilla includes the meeting with Manuel Mejías, the fall from the burro on the way to Guadalcanal, and brief mention of the other pueblos. The trip to Huelva is essentially in the words of Javier, including the details of the incident in the train station of Beas, where I have only filled out the dialogue slightly.

In Huelva, Javier tells of buying new clothes, of Salvaoriyo's interest in teaching Chacón (specifically mentioning *soleares*, *siguiriyas*, *la caña*, and *el polo*), his lack of generosity with money, and his advising the boys to go to Isla Cristina. Information about Salvaoriyo is sparse. Javier tells us he was "...somewhat older than we were..." (p.28). Butler adds that he was a great *siguiriyero*, that he retired young and went to Huelva, where, "...it is supposed that he lived out his days," and that Chacón considered him to be one of his best teachers (p.83). Other sources (Álvarez Caballero, Blas Vega-Ríos Ruiz) state that Salvaoriyo had gone to Cuba, where his son was born in 1872. Most of what is known of Salvaoriyo's personality comes from Guillermo Núñez del Prado (*Cantaores Andaluces*, 1904). Unfortunately, this collection of biographies of *cantaores* of the nineteenth century is not as valuable as it should be, for Núñez del Prado placed little emphasis on factual information—birth and death dates or times and places of performances. Instead, the author reflected upon the inner motivations of the singers and wrote poetically and symbolically of the qualities that produced their art. What little biographical information he included is often sensational in nature and sometimes in conflict with other accounts. He devotes many pages to Salvaoriyo's dark past and great sadness.

All other descriptions of Salvaoriyo as presented here, including the details of the lessons, are fiction. There is no evidence that the *cantaor* became a fish vendor.

The portrayals of El Fillo and El Nitri are pieced together from diverse sources and attempt to resolve the often conflicting accounts that have been passed down by oral tradition. There are few documented facts about these two early *cantaores*. There is a lack of agreement concerning the date of El Fillo's death. Some sources state that he died in Sevilla in 1878, while oral tradition has it that he was dead when Silverio returned from America in 1864. In the years between 1864 and 1878 there is no mention, documented or oral, of El Fillo still being alive—he is always referred to as ancient history. In either case, it seems certain that Silverio had no contact with him during that time.

The date of El Nitri's death is based on a eulogy found in *La Ilustración Ibérica* of July 6, 1884, which says that he was "*muy bebedor y juergista* [very much a drinker and party lover]." If we can trust the authenticity of his birth certificate, that would make him thirty-four when he died. Concerning the presentation of the *Llave de Oro del Cante Flamenco*, there are different versions. The one I have chosen is taken from Antonio Mairena's *Confesiones* and was told to Mairena by the ninety-year-old daughter of one of the participants. A more far-fetched version, reported by José Luis Pantoja Antúnez (*Evocación de las Grandes Figuras del Flamenco*, p.63) has a silver key being presented in 1868, in Málaga's Café Sin Techo, by some well-known aficionados and the legendary *cantaor* El Planeta (flamenco's first known *cantaor* and supposed teacher of El Fillo). Considering Nitri's birthdate in 1850 and some other recent findings, it is likely that the the presentation took place after the 1860s— perhaps the early 1870s. The photograph, perhaps the most unusual aspect of the event, shows a young and very well dressed El Nitri holding a large key.

Silverio's views on the *cante* came from two sources: Fernando de Triana tells us about Silverio dismissing the aficionado for singing too fast (p.122). And Cano (p.80) describes Silverio's aversion to the use of diminutive terms such as *maresita*.

The story about Silverio and Enrique Ortega has another version, widely repeated by modern writers (Blas Vega, Alvarez Caballero), in which Silverio goes to Cádiz, finds Enrique not home, and sings his tearjerking *seguiriyas* when he misses his friend while passing through Puerta Tierra. Pretty silly if you try to imagine it. The date of Enrique's death is not known, but it would seem likely that his death inspired Silverio's *letra* (as in the version given by Fernando Quiñones in *De Cádiz y sus Cantes*, p.126).

The account of the stay in Isla Cristina is almost entirely paraphrased from the facts given by Javier, including the trip in the *pareja*, cleaning up and lunch on the dock, working conditions, staying with the Rojas Family, performing in neighboring towns, and the return to Jerez. The story of the lessons in *serranas* is fiction, as is the presentation of Silverio's *vara*. However, Chacón did study *serranas* with Salvaoriyo. Javier mentioned that Chacón also learned *caña* and *polo* from Salvaoriyo at that time, but I decided to put those lessons into a later chapter to avoid burdening the reader with too much technical information at one time.

The thoughts of the boys on returning home are also undocumented.

Chapter Ten — María

Chacón's activities upon returning to Jerez in 1885 are only briefly documented. Blas Vega (p.19) tells us that Chacón worked for Tomasa in a café in Jerez, earning four *pesetas*. Javier (Butler, p.39) affirms that this café was the Vera Cruz. Javier also mentions the successful three-week contract in Medina Sidonia. Performers in the Vera Cruz are not documented, but those featured in this account were popular artists in Jerez at that time (Steingress, *Los Cafés Cantantes de Jerez*). Chacón's experiences in the Vera Cruz are based on conjecture; the account of the fiestas in the *cuartos* is a composite of typical events taken from a wide variety of sources.

There are very few documented references to Chacón's family. Blas Vega implies that Chacón cared for his mother throughout her life, so we can assume that the father died sometime during the early part of his son's career. There is no evidence that he was the victim of cholera, but the epidemic of 1885 and the death of Alfonso XII were historical events.

Regarding Chacón's first girlfriend, we have only a brief, unreferenced mention by Blas Vega of the "...love of his first *novia*, whose family had a *tahona* [bakery] on Calle Campana. The courtship would end when he went to Sevilla." (Blas Vega, p.19)

Chapter Eleven— El Canario

The entire episode of Chacón in Sevilla is based upon one statement made by the *cantaor* in an interview, in which he says he returned to Jerez immediately because "... Sevilla frightened me, it was so big..." (Blas Vega, p.19). I have used this opportunity to introduce the flamenco environment of Sevilla in the mid-1880s and to treat the controversial subject of the death of El Canario. All artists featured here are documented as to the place and style of performance (primarily in Fernando de Triana's *Arte y Artistas Flamencos*, with supplementary material from other sources). Physical descriptions are taken from photographs. The account of El Chato de Jerez is based largely upon a description by Núñez de Prado (pp.225-233). The dancing of El Pintor, Lamparilla, and Juana and Fernanda Antúnez is taken from the descriptions by Fernando de Triana, including the account of Maestro Pérez dancing with Fernanda. However, the specifics of Fernanda's *baile* are my interpretation of what Fernando de Triana might have meant when he wrote, "... an extraordinary *bailadora* who needed extraordinary *cante* for her dance." (p.58) We also get a feel for this woman's *baile* from her photographs.

We have to wonder exactly what was meant by "*falsetas*" with regard to the dance (as used here in conjunction with Lamparilla). The word meant "guitar melodies" as it does today, but how did it apply to dance 120 years ago? Fernando de Triana writes of Lamparilla: "He never missed a single detail in his very difficult *escobillas*, nor in the infinite *falsetas* and *desplantes* he executed." (p.142). Guitarist Rafael Marín sheds some light on this matter in his 1902 guitar instruction book when he writes: "[the dancer gives a signal]...when he wishes to enter the *falseta* and then the accompanist begins a variation that he plays as many times as the dancer wishes, or connects it to a second variation, and so on..." He adds that, during the *falseta*, the movements of the dancer's body are very varied and could go on at great length. So it appears that the meaning of the word was identical to the way it is used today, that is, the dancer interprets melodies played on the guitar.

The *malagueña* sung by La Bocanegra, "*Por las trenzas de tu pelo*," has been attributed to different sources, in particular, the *cantaor* from Huelva, José Pérez de Guzmán (M. Yerga Lanchero, *Candil*, Jan-Feb 1991, p.636). However, since it is invariably sung in connection with El Canario (among many examples, see: *Enrique Morente: Cantes Antiguos del Flamenco*, Hispavox S 20.049, 1978), I have chosen to include it here.

There has been much conjecture, mostly erroneous, concerning the life and death of El Canario. There can be no denying his contribution to flamenco and the creation of the new *malagueña*, but the exact nature of his contribution has not been clear. There are different accounts of his death. José María de Mena tells us in *La Sevilla Que Se Nos Fué* (p.278) that El Canario performed with Chacón in the Café de Silverio. One night, after performing, he went to Triana to see his girlfriend, La Rubia de Málaga. On the bridge to Triana, a gypsy assassin, paid by one who was in love with La Rubia, stabbed the *cantaor* to death. When the news was brought back to Chacón, he went out on stage and improvised this *copla*:

El Canario ya no canta;	El Canario no longer sings;
El Canario se calló;	El Canario has been stilled;
que en el Puente de Triana,	on the bridge to Triana,
un gitano lo mató.	a gypsy killed him.

Some authors write that El Canario imitated the *cante* of Chacón, others that Chacón learned from El Canario. It was José Blas Vega who uncovered the facts about El Canario's death, specifically in two articles that appeared in newspapers of the time (Blas Vega, *Los Cafés Cantantes de Sevilla*, p.44). If El Canario was killed in August of 1885, then it is clear that Chacón never heard him sing. It is equally clear that Chacón must have learned the *malagueñas* of El Canario from others, from La Rubia, La Bocanegra, and perhaps even El Mellizo, and that El Canario was not influenced by Chacón.

The version of El Canario's death that I have presented here was compiled from the following sources: The *nevería* "El Chino" is described by Blas Vega (*Cafés Cantantes de Sevilla*) as being situated by the Triana bridge and suggested as the site of the death. The newspapers reported that the café was located next to the bridge so I have accepted El Chino as the murder site. Fernando de Triana also described this café as belonging to El Burrero. The story of Canario's arrival in Sevilla and eventual artistic success is told by Fernando de Triana, who was fifteen years old at the time (p.28). The events leading up to the murder are taken from Núñez de Prado (p.12). The specifics of the final argument and the fight, including all of the dialogue between El Canario and the father of La Rubia, are given by Pepe el de la Matrona as he heard them in his youth (Ortiz Nuevo, p.208). Matrona is also the only source of La Rubia's family name, Colomer.

The creation of Chacón's *letra*, "*La campana triste*," is a fictionalized version of how such a *letra* might have been composed. This *letra* was one of Chacón's first and, according to his own words, he sang it a couple of months later in Cádiz, not knowing the words or the music very well. This and much of the information we have about Chacón's early life comes from an interview with him by Galerín: "*Un rata de charla con Antonio Chacón*" (*El Liberal*, Sevilla, July 9, 1922). Blas Vega reproduces the contents of the interview throughout his study of Chacón's life.

Chapter Twelve—El Mellizo

The fiesta in La Rondeña and the success of Chacón that night are generally accepted as fact, although I have been unable to discover the original sources of some of this information. Chacón confirms the presence of El Mellizo and Joaquin La Cherna, "...who were the best artists of those times..." (Blas Vega, p.21). Blas Vega reproduces the newspaper article describing the bullfight (p.20). Details of the style of *toreo* of Manuel Hermosilla, as well as the anecdote about Hermosilla in Málaga, are from the encyclopedic *Los Toros* by Cossío (p.325). Cossío also confirms the presence of Mellizo in the *cuadrilla* of Hermosilla with an 1879 poster from Málaga, in which Enrique is listed as *puntillero* (p.179). The description of El Mellizo is from the only known photograph of the *cantaor*. The guitarist "El Lolo" was performing in Jerez in the 1880s (Steingress).

The specific events of the fiesta as portrayed here are fiction. The story of the *gitana* in the church was told by Pericón de Cádiz in *Las Mil y Una Historias de Pericón de Cádiz* (Ortiz Nuevo, p.182). Pericón (1901-1980) was a close friend of one of El Mellizo's sons. The enthusiasm of El Mellizo for the *cante* of Chacón and his declaration of Chacón as the future "Pope of the *cante*" are taken from popular accounts of the event (Alvarez Caballero, p.146).

The *malagueñas* of El Mellizo as sung here were pieced together from a variety of sources. Pericón de Cádiz described the *salida del perdón* (Ortiz Nuevo, p.236). The first *letra*, "*De la pena*," can be heard sung by Aurelio Sellés (1887-1974), the only disciple of El Mellizo to record in modern times (*Aurelio Sellés " El de Cádiz"*; Hispavox 730 40 3107 4; 1962, 1986). The second *letra*, "*Se la llevó Dios*," is quoted by Pericón in connection with "*El perdón*." Many authorities cite the influence of the Gregorian chant in the *malagueña* of El Mellizo. The most explicit documentation of this influence is given by García Chicón (*Estoicismo de la Malagueña*, p.68), when he says that experts have confirmed a relationship between Mellizo and the simple Mass for the dead ("*misa de difuntos*").

It is difficult to be certain about the placement of the *cejilla* for Chacón's *cante*. We cannot be certain of the speed at which early recorded cylinders and disks revolved; modern releases of these recordings always sound speeded-up and high-pitched, similar to the jerky, speeded-up appearance of early silent films. However, it appears that Chacón sang *por medio* (*soleares, seguiriyas*) in the early years with the *cejilla* on the fourth fret (possibly one fret higher or lower). Toward the end of his life, using a falsetto voice, he sang much higher, on the sixth and seventh frets.

Chapter Thirteen—Patiño

The invitation to sing in Cádiz is taken directly from Javier's memoirs and other popular accounts. Description of the Velada de los Angeles is taken from Aurelia Sellés, from a chapter note by Butler, and from period references cited by Blas Vega (*Chacón*, pp.23-26). At the time Chacón first went to Cádiz, there was still a wall enclosing the city, with gateways opening onto a surrounding outer strip of land and the seawalls. All of those walls, except the section across the land at Puerta de Tierra, the entrance to the city, were demolished toward the beginning of the 1900s. The Alameda de Peregil was eventually renamed Las Delicias and today is the site of Parque Genovés.

The café where Chacón made his debut in Cádiz is unknown, but it was certainly one of the many constructed on the Alameda for the Velada. The facts of this event are sketchy. What little is known of Patiño has been compiled by Quiñones (*De Cádiz y Sus Cantes*, p.157) and Blas Vega-Ríos Ruiz (*Dicionario Enciclopédico Ilustrado del Flamenco*). Oral legend tells us that he was adamant about the proper role of the guitarist as accompanist and proud of his part in developing modern accompaniment. Fernando de Triana (p.245) quotes Patiño as saying the guitar is *"pa acompañá ar cantaó* [for accompanying the *cantaor*]." Pericón de Cádiz said that Patiño played a tiny guitar, implying that the guitarist preferred an instrument typical of those played in his youth. Aurelio Sellés knew Patiño as a very old man, with his cape and tiny *"guitarillo."* From the known information, I have developed a picture of Patiño as an artist clinging to his past, to what he knew best. This has been typical of flamenco guitarists of all epochs. A young revolutionary becomes more conservative in middle age and a traditionalist in old age, when he can no longer keep up with new trends. Many of the comments I have put in the mouth of Patiño are those of other guitarists with similar viewpoints. Both Patiño and Paquirri el Guanté are credited with the invention of the *cejilla*. I have chosen to give credit to both of them. Patiño's story of Silverio's return to Cádiz is taken from Quiñones (p.53).

We arrive now at a serious conflict between oral legend and logic, between documented sources and common sense. Javier Molina (Butler, p.37) tells us that Chacón went to Cádiz to sing with the "great maestro and composer of *cante flamenco* and *malagueñas*, Enrique el Mellizo." From the reminiscences of Chacón (Galerín, in Blas Vega, p.27) we learn further details: Chacón says El Mellizo was earning eighty *pesetas* a night. This was in a time when most sources say that ten *pesetas* was tops (Fernando de Triana, p.19) and when the most celebrated of all *cantaores*, Juan Breva, earned the extraordinary amount of twenty-five *pesetas* in each place he performed. Chacón tells of appearing on stage with Patiño when El Mellizo came in with various intelligent aficionados and Enrique Ortega. The dialogue between Chacón and Patiño is taken, without change or addition, from Chacón's description.

According to Chacón's account, following the singing of the *malagueña*, "*De aquella campana triste*," which, by Chacón's own admission he "didn't know well," the public applauded to such an extent that he and El Mellizo began a nightly competition in the café. El Mellizo went out on stage with the guitarist Maestro Tapia to sing *seguiriyas* and then Chacón with Patiño to sing *malagueñas*. In the breaks between, aficionados argued about who was better, and then the *cantaores* went on stage to do it again. There are so many implausibilities in this account that we must conclude that it represents the inflated and erroneous recollections of a pompous old man.

We are told that Chacón became so frightened when Mellizo came in with some aficionados that he was he unable to sing *por seguiriyas*. Then we are expected to believe that a nervous young singer performed a *cante* that he didn't know well, the *malagueñas*, so successfully that the audience went wild, and that very night he began to compete with one of the most esteemed *cantaores* of his time, El Mellizo. Not only was Mellizo highly regarded for his *seguiriyas*, but he was known as a singer of *malagueñas*. How then did Chacón, who didn't know the *cante* well, compete so successfully that the aficionados debated about who was better? And on El Mellizo's home turf? In addition, Chacón claims that he sang *after* El Mellizo; in those times it would have been unthinkable for a renowned *cantaor* to sing before a young unknown. Considering that El Mellizo was already singing in another café during the Velada, at a very high salary, it is a real stretch to imagine that he would leave his job to compete with a young newcomer. It is likely that Chacón confused different events and colored his account with the biases and experiences of a lifetime. I have chosen what I feel is the most logical and interesting of possibilities—that the anecdote of the *malagueñas* happened and that Chacón did not compete with El Mellizo at that time.

The *malagueña*, "*En la tumba de mi mare*," is said by Blas Vega to be in the same style as "*De aquella campana triste.*" According to Fernando de Triana, Chacón would sing this *letra* a few months later in Sevilla, so we can assume that it was created sometime during this period. It would be one of his favorites throughout his life. Chacón says of the night he first sang a *malagueña* in the café, "Since that night I fell in love with the *malagueña* and began to add to and subtract from my crop. Those applauses led me to create various styles of *malagueñas*." (Blas Vega, *Chacón*, p.27).

Patiño's story of Silverio's return to Cádiz in 1864 is widely repeated and may be based upon the simpler version by Demófilo (1881) as told to him by Silverio. Demófilo quotes María Borrico as saying, *"Cómo quieres que cante si ese gachó de las barbas me ha estemplao?"* (p.181)

The most important school of guitar during this period was that of Patiño and his disciples. Paco el Barbero, Habichuela, and El Pollo de Cádiz, are documented to have been students of Patiño. Various posters and programs show that Patiño and El Barbero played together in Jerez in 1867 (Steingress), Madrid in 1873 (Blas Vega-Ríos Ruiz, p.574), and again in the Teatro Principal of Jerez in 1878 (Steingress). Paco de Lucena is often cited as being a student of Patiño, but his friend and biographer, Fernando de Triana, makes no mention of it. Lucena's dispute with Patiño over the tones of *la caña* is widely repeated, but with little detail and is undocumented.

Chapter Fourteen—Curro Dulce

Surprisingly little is known of Curro Dulce, especially considering the widespread influence of his *cante*. Chacón would come to prefer his *seguiriyas* and sing them throughout his life. It is not even clear if Curro was gypsy. In the gypsy barrios of Cádiz, as in Jerez, everyone was considered to be gypsy whether they were or not. However, several factors seem to indicate that Curro Dulce was indeed a gypsy: First, his disdainful remarks about *gachó* singing. Second, the extensive intermarriage of his family with other gypsy families of Cádiz. And finally, Aurelio Sellés, the source of much that we know about early flamenco in Cádiz, never says otherwise. Aurelio was born in 1887, so he didn't personally witness the flamenco scene before about 1900. But he was the youngest of twenty-two children and his oldest brother, Chele Fateta (born in 1860), was a close friend of Curro Dulce.

I have estimated Curro's age in the following way. There is a newspaper article that announces a performance in Jerez by Curro Dulce and his son, Juan Fernández *"El hijo de Curro Dulce,"* in 1867 (Steingress). If we assume Juan's age to have been twenty at that time and Curro's as forty (twenty at the birth of his son), that would make Curro about sixty in 1886. Of course, Juan could have been younger and Curro could have had his son at an earlier age, but that still gives a likely age of at least fifty-five. It is also possible that they were both older, but I still think it is safe to give Curro Dulce's age in 1886 as being between sixty and seventy-five. This age range is supported by the fact that Curro's daughter, Rufina, was married to El Águila, who was in his mid-thirties at this time. One last confirmation comes from the fact that Curro's two sons partnered the daughters of El Viejo de la Isla in a performance with Silverio in 1865, suggesting a birth date for Curro somewhere between 1815 and 1825.

The stories of Paquiro Ortega and Chacón visiting the gypsies of the Barrio de Santa María are fiction. Paquiro has not been documented as being a friend of Chacón, but he did perform in Jerez in the early 1880s and they could have been acquainted. His personality, as an "inimitable buffoon" has been well documented by Blas Vega (*Diccionario*, p.568) and others. The people and places described in this chapter are historically accurate, but Chacón never gave any details about his time in Cádiz. We know that he favored the *cantes* of Cádiz, especially those of Curro Dulce, but he never revealed how or where he learned them. I have created a scenario to introduce some of the important influences on Chacón and to give a little feel for the flamenco of Cádiz. Information about the flamencos of Cádiz comes from a wide variety of sources; among the more important: Blas Vega's *Diccionario Enciclopédico* and *Conversaciones con Aurelio Sellés*, Fernando de Triana's *Arte y Artistas Flamencos*, Quiñones' *De Cádiz y Sus Cantes*, Ortiz Nuevo's *Las Mil y Una Historias de Pericón* [henceforth to be referred to as "*Pericón*"], and Manuel Moreno Delgado's *Aurelio: Su Cante, Su Vida*.

The inspiration for the fiesta in the tavern comes from an anecdote by Aurelio Sellés (Moreno Delgado, p.42). The comments of Silverio and Curro Dulce about each other are from Aurelio Sellés (Blas Vega, p.35). The story of Quiqui and the debt is from *Pericón*. Descriptions of La Mejorana come from Aurelio and Fernando de Triana. The innovation of the raised arms is from Quiñones, and her performance in Sevilla is taken almost verbatim from Fernando de Triana. The story of Rita Ortega is widely known, but I have supplemented it with information from a newspaper article (*Sur*, November 26, 1984). More information on her husband, El Guarriro, comes from Carlos de la Luna (pp.108 and 117).

The *letras* of *alegrías* are those attributed by Aurelio Sellés. The *soleares* are from the 1881 collection by Machado y Álvarez [henceforth to be referred to as "Demófilo"]. Demófilo confirms that the *seguiriyas* "*Dices que duermes sola*" of Manuel Molina and the *seguiriya* of *los campanilleros* were created by Curro Dulce. El Gordo Ortega was known for his *seguiriyas* and *soleares*, but none of his *letras* have survived or been documented. Those that he sings in this chapter were collected by Demófilo from this period.

The meeting with Juan Fernández (Curro Dulce's son) is pure fiction. Chacón never mentions learning from Curro Dulce, although he favored the man's *cante*. Given Curro's antipathy toward non-gypsies, it is unlikely that he would have taught Chacón. So we have to assume that Chacón learned Curro's *cante* from others and perhaps by listening in fiestas.

Chapter Fifteen—Juan Junquera

El Mellizo's home was located on the corner of Calles Botica and Miraflor (different name today). Mellizo's story of the trunk filled with flamenco sheet music was told to Pericón by the singer's son, Enrique, who said he heard it from his father (Ortiz Nuevo, *Pericón*, p.20). The *malagueñas* of El Mellizo: "*De quererte toa mi vía*" and "*Loco y no sentir*" can be heard sung by Antonio Mairena on the record *Antonio Mairena* (Gramusic GM-470, 1976). I have no other confirmation of the authenticity of the *letras*, but they are very similar to others by El Mellizo.

Chacón's *malagueña*, "*La flor que amaba*," can be heard sung by El Lebrijano on *El Lebrijano con la colaboracion especial de Paco de Lucia* (Polydor 24 85 18 S; 1970). That *letra* is confirmed as being original to Chacón by Garcia Chicón (p.175). The *malagueña grande*, "*Que te quise con locura*," was recorded often by Chacón. It can also be heard in a faithful version by Enrique Morente on *Cantes Antiguos del Flamenco* (Hispavox S.20.049; 1978).

The story of the *carne de bragueta* is from *Pericón* (p.87). In his biography of Chacón, Blas Vega reproduces an interview with Fosforito in which the *cantaor* describes his studies with El Mellizo and meeting Chacón there (p.27).

I can find no evidence that Fosforito ever recorded, which is strange considering that his popularity as a singer lasted well into the second decade of the 1900s, when just about everyone was recording. His style was apparently so unique that few attempted to imitate him and, thus, we don't really know how he sang and must depend upon descriptions of his singing by Fernando de Triana, Núñez de Prado and others. It is not known how accurate are the versions of his *malagueñas* recorded by two singers from Álora—Ángel de Álora (*Archivo del Cante Flamenco*) and Diego el Perote (*Magna Antologia del Cante Flamenco*).

Fernando de Triana describes Fosforito as a typical Gaditano, jovial and quick to enjoy a joke, but deadly serious when it came to the *cante*. Núñez de Prado plays up the *cantaor*'s inner sadness.

My descriptions of Cádiz are based upon photos of the period. The story of the *pupileros* is from *Pericón* (p.94). The names of the cafés used here are from Quiñones. The account of Chacón and El Mellizo in the Café de la Paz is fiction, but is based upon Chacón's description of his competition with El Mellizo. The reconciliation with Juan Junquera is likewise fictionalized, but certainly plausible according to Blas Vega's statement that Junquera went to Cádiz to hire Chacón for the *feria* in Utrera (*Chacón*, p.28). The nature of their conversation is based on the rancor with which Chacón recalled, even years later, his initial rejection by the impresario.

Chapter Sixteen—Silverio

As with other artists of this period, little documented information exists dealing with the life of Silverio Franconetti. In published book-length biographies of both Silverio and Chacón, the actual facts of their lives could easily be boiled down to several pages. Demófilo's biography of Silverio consists of three short pages. That's it! Then we have scattered of bits of information placing him here or there on such-and-such a date. In the biographies of both Silverio and Chacón written by José Blas Vega, the books are filled out with conjecture, long dissertations on side issues, poems and impressions by various writers, and analysis of their *cante*.

We have three dates for Silverio's birth. His death certificate places his birth in 1829. Silverio told Demófilo that he was born June 10, 1831. His second marriage certificate gives the date as 1834. This last date was probably an exaggeration by Silverio due to the fact that he was marrying a nineteen-year-old woman. I have chosen to accept the 1831 birth date, making Silverio fifty-five years old when Chacón began to work for him.

There is only one known photograph of Silverio, and a questionable one at that: someone inked in his hair. Could he have been bald? We'll never know. Why there should be only one existing photograph of such a celebrated personality is quite odd, considering that others, including Juan Breva and Paco de Lucena were photographed quite often. But it is also true that there are no known photos of Chacón from this period, although there is at least one from slightly later, when he returned to Sevilla after his first trip to Madrid.

Chacón's appearance in the Café Filarmónico in Sevilla and the events that took place there are given by Blas Vega (*Chacón*, p.28) without any documentation. It is not clear whether Junquera was in charge of hiring for the Filarmónico at that time, but he would be doing so very soon afterward. The same is true for the presence of José Patiño. Javier places him there a couple of months later. The description of the Café Filarmónico is given by Pepe Matrona (Ortiz Nuevo).

I have not been able to locate documentation for the dinner to honor María Borrico. It is a widely accepted bit of flamenco legend, including the presence of Silverio, and I believe that Chacón commented about it later in life. Javier Molina writes that Silverio went to Cádiz looking to hire Chacón, who had made a name for himself there.

El Viejo de la Isla's famous quote about not doing complicated things with the *cante*, as well as his *letras*, are described by Blas Vega (*Diccionario*) and Aurelio de Cádiz (Blas Vega). Curro Dulce's letra "*Los méicos*" is quoted in Quiñones. The only *letra* known from María Borrico is this famous *seguiriyas* used to close the *serranas*. All *letras* sung by Silverio here are those attributed to him by Demófilo.

The trip back to Cádiz in the carriage is fiction. We do not know Chacón's whereabouts during the next couple of months. Silverio's biography is taken from Demófilo. The fact that La Andonda lived in Triana, as well as the *letra* about her and El Fillo, come from Demófilo. Núñez de Prado describes her personality. La Parrala was a close friend of Fernando de Triana, who describes her prodigious singing ability. Núñez de Prado dwells on her personality.

Fosforito's letra, "*Ar campo me ví a llorá*," and the accompanying anecdote are taken from Fernando de Triana in his chapter on Fosforito.

Chapter Seventeen—Sevilla

We really have very little documentation dealing with Chacón's first three years in Sevilla. Fernando de Triana and Javier Molina place his debut in 1886 and Fernando describes one of his performances. That's about it! Therefore, my description of this period is largely fiction. We can be fairly certain of the influences on Chacón during this critical time in his development, and with a little detective work and imagination we can create a possible scenario. The artists who performed in Sevilla between 1881 and 1889 are brought to us primarily by Fernando de Triana—writing some forty years later. For the most part, we don't have specific dates for performances of these artists, but it really is not so important whether an artist performed in the Café de Silverio in 1884 or 1887. I have tried to bring the reader just a few of the more important or interesting artists and those who played a significant role in the development of Antonio Chacón.

We know that Chacón went to Sevilla after the Verbena of August

1886. Blas Vega places his arrival in late October. Fernando de Triana gives us a description of his performance in the Café de Silverio, as well as Fosforito's performance in El Burrero and the information about Chacón and Fosforito alternating performances. Javier Molina tells of working in the Café Filarmónico with his brother and Patiño, El Chato de Jerez, and El Mezcle.

Newspaper announcements establish the presence of Las Viejas Ricas de Cádiz in the Café de Silverio in 1886. La Parrala's *seguiriyas* came from Ricardo Molina's *Cantes Flamencos*. Her *soleá* is from Núñez del Prado.

Chacón sang *malagueña* with the *cejilla* on different frets, ranging from the fourth to the sixth. His choice of pitch may have varied depending on which *letras* he planned to sing, or it may be something that changed in different periods of his life.

The newspaper articles describing crimes in Sevilla were discovered by Blas Vega and reproduced in his book on Silverio. They come from various dates, but I have condensed them to one time period here. The story of the man who yelled "snake" is adapted from an article by Ramón del Valle Inclán in the Mexican newspaper, *El Universal* (June 11, 1892) and was reproduced by Blas Vega in his *Cafés de Madrid*. The anecdote about Silverio singing *"Aunque te güerbas culebra..."* was told by Rodríguez Marín in 1910 (see: Blas Vega, *Silverio*, p.23). The *letra* itself is included in Demófilo's collection and attributed to Silverio (p.144). In both of these snake stories, the authors elaborated fantasies based on fragments of fact. I have taken the basic facts and tried to integrate them into a more realistic scenario.

Paco el Sevillano is well-described by Fernando de Triana, including the anecdotes about Silverio singing last and Fosforito lighting up from a gas lamp. Blas Vega gives some additional information about this renowned *cantaor*. The split-up and bad feelings between Silverio and Manuel Ojeda are described by Demófilo. The agreement to have Chacón and Fosforito alternate was reported by Fernando de Triana. However, the scene describing the meeting is fiction.

Chacón's eight-month contract extension and the raise to twenty *pesetas* were reported by Fernando de Triana. Chacón is generally considered to be the first to demand an agreed-upon fee before performing in fiestas. My account of his first time is fiction.

Pepe de la Matrona tells of Miguel Macaca going to jail (Ortiz Nuevo, p.207). Romero el Tito is usually relegated to a footnote in flamenco studies. Very little is known of him. The basic facts come from Fernando de Triana and Blas Vega (*Diccionario*), but I have been able to fill out the picture a little by making connections to other information. The story of Paquirri, La Parrala, and Juan Breva in Madrid, is reported by Blas Vega (*Cafés Cantantes de Madrid*, p.129). The *caracoles* sung by Romero are the lyrics to the original popular song discovered by Blas Vega (*Diccionario*; under *caracoles*). The *romeras* are traditional. Some attribute the name of this *cante* to Romero, others say it came from the *letra*. We find the same lack of information about Salud Rodríguez and La Cuenca. Fernando de Triana is the main source of information and, fortunately, he supplies a good photo of each.

The conversation between Chacón and the Molinas is fiction, but all the essential facts about Paco el Barbero come from Fernando de Triana.

All facts about Demófilo, including the letter to Luis Montoto requesting information for a new book, are taken from his biography by Daniel Pineda Novo. However, the entire scenario involving Chacón, Silverio, and Demófilo's book, is fiction. Chacón came to many of the conclusions described here, but over the duration of his life—we don't have dates. It is generally accepted that Chacón decided early on in his career to sing using correct Spanish. Silverio's *jaberas* were listed by Fernando de Triana. Chacón's visit to Silverio's home is, of course, fiction. Maria's age (twenty-one at the time of Chacón's visit) and the date of her marriage are verified by marriage documents (Blas Vega, p.61). Silverio's jealousy is described by Núñez de Prado and Pepe de la Matrona. Blas Vega tells us that Silverio spent extravagantly on food and clothes (*Silverio*, p.62).

The development of the *soleá* from the *jaleos* and *polos* is largely a matter of conjecture. It is generally accepted that the *soleares* were based on the old danceable *jaleos* and took on their more profound form in Triana during the 1860s. Blas Vega, who has written often on this subject, feels that Silverio was involved in this conversion. It is true that we find no reports of Silverio singing *soleares* before 1865, but by the end of the decade he was including this *cante* in his performances. I have pieced together the story of the first *soleares* from many fragments of fact and oral legend.

Mercedes la Serneta is another of these enigmas so common to flamenco history. Her *soleares* are prominent in the modern repertoire and were favored by Chacón in his recordings, but little is known of her life. Her birth date is given variously as 1834, 1837, and 1840 (this latter from her family on the occasion of her death). Many attribute her name "La Serneta" to her family, and it is true that in Jerez the family name Fernández is often associated with the nicknames Serna or Sernita. However, in an interview toward the end of her life, Mercedes said she was named for a small bird. Because La Serneta did not perform in public, she left no public record. She lived most of her life in Utrera and performed primarily in private fiestas. It is generally accepted that she spent some time in Triana and sang in the style of La Andonda. Fernando de Triana gave us a description of Mercedes, praising her beauty and singing. It is not clear when he knew her, but it may have been in her later years. Núñez de Prado wrote a chapter about her. Chacon knew her later, toward the end of the 1800s.

Virtually nothing has been documented about Ramón de Triana "*El Ollero.*" He lives on in oral tradition as the legendary creator of a school of singing that specialized in the *soleá de Triana*. The examples of his *letras* given here are the only two I have been able to locate. We can't even be absolutely certain of his occupation. He is said to have been a ceramic worker, but his nickname "*El Ollero*" means pot-maker, not ceramic-maker [*alfarero*]. It's possible that he specialized in making large pots out of coarse red clay rather than the more delicate ceramics made of fine gray clay. Blas Vega gives us his belligerent comment about Chacón "coming apart like a poorly rolled cigar" (*Chacón*, p.39), but does not reveal his source. I had the great fortune of playing guitar for Manuel Oliver, the last surviving creator of the Triana style of *soleá*, just before his death. The traditional singers of this style prided themselves on the poetry of their lyrics and the beauty of their melodies, but had little regard for rhythm. To play for them, a guitarist had to be flexible and have a relaxed approach in his accompaniment. Young singers today have restored the proper rhythm to these *soleares*. The old-timers had great pride in their singing ability, and their neighborhood in Triana came to be known as El Zurraque. Manuel Oliver explained to me that the name came from the verb *zurrar*, which means, "to thrash," and arose from the belief that the Trianeros would soundly thrash any outsiders who came to challenge them in singing *por soleares*.

Information on the Caganchos and Pelaos comes primarily from Fernando de Triana, Antonio Mairena (Molina and Mairena), and Torcuato Pérez de Guzmán in his excellent book, *Los Gitanos Herreros de Sevilla*. The *cante* of these secretive gypsies comes to us through Tomás Pavón, brother of the great *cantaora* La Niña de los Peines and a nephew of Juan Pelao's brother. Subsequent versions have been sung by Antonio Mairena and others. The story of Sánchez Mira is taken verbatim from Fernando de Triana.

We learn the details about Juan el Perote from Fernando de Triana, Blas Vega (*Diccionario*), and Núñez de Prado. It was Núñez de Prado who suggested that Canario Chico was not a legitimate *cantaor*. Pepe

FACT OR FICTION? 383

Matrona tells of Canario Chico attempting to accompany himself on the piano.

Blas Vega reproduces the newspaper articles (*Chacón*) that reported the safety infractions in both Silverio's and El Burrero's cafés. Blas Vega details the relationship between Paco el Sevillano and the café in Málaga known variously as Café del Sevillano, Café de Bernardo, or Café de las Siete Revueltas (*Diccionario*). He tells us that Paco owned the café and passed it on to his son Bernardo.

Chapter Eighteen—Pope of the *Cante*

Chacón is thought to have gone to Málaga twice in the fall of 1887. Documentation is sparse. Blas Vega gives sketchy facts in his biography of the *cantaor*, including a brief description of the Café de las Siete Revueltas. I have supplemented that description with information from travelogues of the period. The guitarists of Málaga and their gatherings in the *ventorillos* of La Caleta come from the *Diccionario de Guitarristas*, by Domingo Prat (Romero y Fernández, Buenos Aires, 1934).

There is virtually no information available on the life of Trinidad Navarro Carrillo "La Trini" (born 1868), aside from her place of birth and death (Málaga), her growing reputation in the years around 1890, a few performance dates in the 1900s, a benefit for her in 1917, and her opening of a *venta* in La Caleta after her retirement from singing. There are a couple of anecdotes about her health problems in later life and one letter to Juan Breva asking for financial help. We also know that Chacón had a great influence on her singing, and that, in turn, Antonio became a devoted admirer of Trini's *cante*, sang many of her *coplas* later in life, and copied her style in some of his own *malagueñas*. We have no evidence that Chacón met Trini on his first trip to Málaga—their mutual influences came a bit later, probably in Madrid. But the nineteen-year-old Trini was certainly on her way to celebrity in the late 1880s, so it is plausible that Chacón would have known of her in 1887. The physical appearance of La Trini is taken from Fernando de Triana and from an excellent photograph of her as a young woman. Her personality and the style of her singing come from Fernando de Triana and Núñez de Prado, as well as from numerous recordings of her *malagueñas* by other artists.

The story of Chacón singing in the Café Universal in the afternoons, and the outrage in the press, comes from Blas Vega without documentation. He associated it with the second visit, while I chose to place it with the first visit for storytelling purposes.

There is no specific date available for Chacón's debut in the Café del

Burrero, but Blas Vega believes it was in the fall of 1887 and that Chacón alternated between the Burrero and Silverio's café through the next year.

Information about Concha la Peñaranda comes primarily from Fernando de Triana. Núñez de Prado dwells on her heroic need to live under the shame of the famous *copla* about her. Fernando tells of hearing that *copla* as a child (1870s).

África Vázquez is described by Fernando de Triana and Blas Vega (*Chacón*). Fernando attributes the letra, "*Viva Graná, que es mi tierra...*" to África, although it is always associated with Chacón, who sang it throughout his life. Did he learn it from her?

Silverio's need to sing in his café to bring in customers was described by Fernando de Triana. The story of General Sánchez Mira and other officials coming to listen to Silverio was told by Pepe de la Matrona (Ortiz Nuevo, p.201).

Oral legend tells us of the confrontation between Chacón and Juan Breva in the Café de Chinitas, although a precise date has never been established (1887-1890). Descriptions of the Café de Chinitas are taken from many sources, including paintings. The building is still there. When I visited the café it was a fabric store, but with a little imagination I could still see the original structure of the café.

The details of this meeting are taken from a long poem by Augusto Butler, the author of Javier Molina's memoirs (in Máximo Andaluz's *Romancero del Cante*, Editorial Proa, Bilbao, 1952; reproduced by Blas Vega in *Chacón*). In his poem, Butler assembled a *cuadro* of famous artists that would have been virtually impossible for various reasons (too young, too old, working in other places at the time, too many guitarists). He just threw in everybody famous. So I tried to include only those artists who realistically could have been there at that time.

The famous *copla* in which Juan Breva acknowledged Chacón's supremacy in the new *malagueña* may or may not have been sung by Breva himself—it may have been sung by others *about* the event.

The date of Chacón's return to Sevilla in early 1888 is an approximation. The story of his contract in Algeciras can be found in Blas Vega (*Chacón*, p.39). Pepa de Oro is described by Fernando de Triana (along with a photo) and Miguel Espín in his book on Latin American-influenced *cantes*.

The new Café del Burrero is well-described by numerous authors and has been depicted in drawings, paintings, and photographs. Many of the anecdotes come from Fernando de Triana. The connection of Paco el Sevillano with these anecdotes is purely fiction. El Mochuelo went on to become the most recorded flamenco singer of all time. His comment about where he came from is an actual quote from an interview in the magazine *Estampa* (by José Simón, 1928).

The confrontation between Chacón and Ramón el Ollero in the home of the marquis is entirely fiction, based on the generally accepted facts that Ramón did not sing in the cafés and competed with Chacón in private fiestas. Pepe de la Matrona said that the aristocracy in Sevilla accused Chacón of being pompous, of thinking he was a marquis (Ortiz Nuevo). The incident of the *martinetes* is an adaptation of a similar situation described by Matrona (Ortiz Nuevo, p.45). The comment about Chacón being able to divide a tone into four parts and the suggestion that he should study opera is taken from an actual incident that occurred later in his life, when he sang some *martinetes* for the opera singer Julián Gayarre.

The events involving Chacón and the closure of Silverio's café are largely fiction, but the earthquake and damage were real, as were the increasing governmental restrictions that made it all but impossible for Silverio to remain open. Blas Vega (*Silverio*) gives references for the events that followed.

In his memoirs, Javier Molina describes the performances in the Teatro Eslava, some of his conversation with Chacón, and his second trip through the pueblos with his brother, but he gives no dates for any of it. There is no evidence that Chacón heard about Silverio's death while in Jerez. In fact, there is no documentation of this period in Chacón's life, or his involvement in events surrounding the death and burial of his idol.

The facts of Silverio's death come from an interview with the *cantaor* Manuel Centeno (Blas Vega, *Silverio*, p.78), the death certificate, and two newspaper articles from June 1, 1889 reproduced by Blas Vega (*Silverio*, p.79). They are all in basic agreement about the date, time, and caused of death (heart attack). The specifics of the vigil and the burial are fiction, based on customs of the time. There is one discrepancy. The newspaper reports that Silverio was buried before five a.m. on the 30th. That would mean he died in the evening and was buried early the next morning. There would be no time for any of the customary burial procedures or any of the events related to us by oral history: the building of an extra large coffin, hiring a music company to lower the coffin from the balcony, the homage by Las Viejas Ricas, and all the normal events of a burial, including the gathering of friends reported by the newspaper. There is no explanation other than a possible error in the article. Perhaps Silverio was buried at five in the *afternoon* on the 30th.

All of Chacón's thoughts and actions during this time are fiction. There is no record of his activities during this period. We do know that he went to Madrid soon afterward.

Selected References

Ayuntamiento de Sevilla, *Silverio Franconetti: 100 Años de que Murió y Aun Vive,* Imprenta Escandón, Sevilla, 1989.

Azucena, La Gitana, *El Libro de las Adivinanzas,* Universidad de Cádiz, Cádiz, 1989 (originally published 1890).

Berjillos, Miguel, *Vida de Juan Breva,* Garvayo Gráfico, Málaga, 1976.

Blas Vega, José, *Los Cafés Cantantes de Madrid,* Ediciones Guillermo Blázquez, Madrid, 2006.

——————— *Silverio: Rey de los Cantaores,* Ayuntamiento de Córdoba, Córdoba, 1995.

——————— *Vida y Cante de Don Antonio Chacón,* Ayuntamiento de Córdoba, Córdoba, 1986.

——————— *Los Cafés Cantantes de Sevilla,* Editorial Cinterco, Madrid, c. 1985 (undated).

——————— *Conversaciones Flamencas con Aurelio de Cádiz,* Librería Valle, Madrid, 1978.

Blas Vega, José and Manuel Ríos Ruiz, *Maestros del Flamenco,* Editorial Planeta-De Agostini, S.A., Barcelona, 1988.

Blas Vega, José and Manuel Ríos Ruiz, *Diccionario Enciclopédico Ilustrado del Flamenco,* Creaciones Internacionales y Coediciones, S.A., Madrid, 1988.

Borrow, George, *The Zincali: An Account of the Gypsies of Spain,* E.P. Dutton & Co., New York, 1914 (originally published in 1841).

Butler, Augusto, *Javier Molina, Jerezano y Tocaor,* Editorial Jerez Industrial, Jerez de la Frontera, 1964.

Caballero, Angel Alvarez, *El Baile Flamenco,* Alianza Editorial, S.A., Madrid, 1998.

——————— *Historia del Cante Flamenco,* Alianza Editorial, Madrid, 1981.

Camacho Galindo, P., *Los Payos Tambien Cantan Flamenco,* Ediciones Demófilo, Madrid, 1977.

Cano, Domingo Manfredi, *Los Gitanos,* *Publicaciones Españolas*, Madrid, 1957.
Cano Manuel, *La Guitarra: Historia, Estudios, y Aportaciones al Arte Flamenco*, Universidad de Córdoba, Córdoba, 1986.
Carver, Norman F., *Iberian Villages*, Documan Press, Ltd., Kalamazoo, Michigan, 1981.
Clébert, Jean-Paul, *The Gypsies*, Penguin Books, Harmondsworth, England, 1967.
Colantes de Terán Delorme, Francisco, *Crónicas de la Feria (1847-1916)*, Biblioteca de Temas Sevillanos, Sevilla, 1981.
Cossío, José María de, and Antonio Díaz-Cañabete, *Los Toros*, Espasa Calpe, S.A.,Madrid, 1982.
Delgado, Antonio Limón, *La Artesanía Rural*, Editora Nacional, Madrid, 1982.
Delgado, Manuel Moreno, *Aurelio: Su Cante, Su Vida*, Escelicer, S.A., Cádiz, 1964.
García Chicón, Agustín, *El Estoicismo en la Malagueña y Otros Cantes*, Madrid, 1988.
Grande, Felix, *Memoria del Flamenco*, Espasa-Calpe, S.A., Madrid, 1979.
Isasi, Enrique de, *Con Una Copa de Jerez*, Hauser y Menet, Madrid, 1969.
Jenkins, Geraint, *Traditional Country Craftsmen*, Frederick A. Praeger, New York, 1965.
Jung, Cristof, *Nanas*, Flamenco Studio Mainz, Germany, 1976.
Lafuente, Rafael, *Los Gitanos, El Flamenco y Los Flamencos*, Editorial Barna, S.A., Barcelona, 1955.
Larrea, Arcadio, *El Flamenco en su Raiz*, Editora Nacional, Madrid, 1974.
Leblon, Bernard, *El Cante Flamenco: Entre las Músicas Gitanas y las Tradiciones Andaluzas*, Editorial Cinterco, Madrid, 1991.
López Moya, Diego, *Pastora Imperio, Su Vida, Sus Amores, Su Arte*, Tipografía Yagües, Madrid.
Luna, José Carlos de, *Gitanos de la Bética*, Universidad de Cádiz, Cádiz, 1989 (originally published 1951).
Machado y Álvarez, Antonio, *Cantes Flamencos*, Espasa-Calpe, Buenos Aires, 1947 (originally published 1887).
——————— *Colección de Cantes Flamencos*, Ediciones Demófilo, Madrid, 1975 (originally published 1881).
Marín, Rafael, *Método de Guitarra: Flamenco*, Sociedad de Autores Españoles, Madrid, 1902.
Más y Prat, Benito, *La Tierra de María Santísima*, Bienal de Arte Flamenco y Fundación Machado, Sevilla, 1988 (originally published, 1889).

Mena, José María de, *La Sevilla que se nos fué*, J. Rodríguez Castillejo, S.A., Sevilla, 1986.
Mercado, José, *La Seguidilla Gitana*, Taurus Ediciones, Madrid, 1982.
Molina, Ricardo, *Cante Flamenco: Antología*, Taurus Ediciones, Madrid, 1965.
―――――――― *Obra Flamenca*, Ediciones Demófilo, Madrid, 1977.
―――――――― *Cante Flamenco*, Taurus Ediciones, Madrid, 1981.
Molina, Ricardo and Antonio Mairena, *Mundo y Formas del Cante Flamenco*, Librería Al-Andaluz, Sevilla, 1979.
Montoto, Luis, *Los Corrales de Vecinos*, Biblioteca de Temas Sevillanos, Sevilla, 1981 (originally published in the magazine *El Folk-Lore Andaluz* in 1882-83).
Moreno, Juan Ballesteros, *Añoranzas Malagueñas: Pregones y Cantares*, Imp. Montes, S.A., Málaga, 1984.
Navarro, Pepe, *Muestrario de Malagueñeros y Malagueñas*, Gráficas Sorima, S.L., Málaga, 1974.
Núñez, Miguel Ropero, *El Léxico Caló en el Lenguaje del Cante Flamenco*, Universidad de Sevilla, Sevilla, 1978.
Núñez de Prado, *Cantaores Andaluces*, Biblioteca de La Cultura Andaluza, 1986 (originally published 1904).
Ortiz Nuevo, José Luis, *Setenta y siete Seguiriyas de la Muerte*, Hipérion, Madrid, 1988.
―――――――― *Pepe el de la Matrona: Recuerdos de un Cantaor Sevillano*, Ediciones Demófilo, Madrid, 1975.
―――――――― *Las Mil y Una Historias de Pericón de Cádiz*, Ediciones Demófilo, Madrid, 1975.
Ortiz de Villajos, Cándido G., *Gitanos de Granada (La Zambra)*, Editorial Andalucía, Granada, 1949.
Pabanó, F. M., *Historia y Costumbres de Los Gitanos*, Ediciones Giner, Madrid, 1980 (originally published 1914).
Pérez de Guzmán, Torcuato, *Los Gitanos Herreros de Sevilla*, Ayuntamiento de Sevilla, Sevilla, 1982.
Perry, Mary Elizabeth, *Crime and Society in Early Modern Seville*, University Press of New England, London, 1980.
Pineda Novo, Daniel, *Antonio Machado y Álvarez: Vida y Obra del Primer Flamencologo Español*, Editorial Cinterco, Madrid, 1991.
Plata, Juan de la, *La Tradición Flamenca de Jerez*, Cátedra de Flamencología, Jerez de la Frontera, 1987.
Plata, Juan de la, *Flamencos de Jerez*, Editorial Jerez Industrial, S.A., Jerez de la Frontera, 1961.

Pohren, D.E., *Lives and Legends of Flamenco*, Society of Spanish Studies, Madrid, 1964.
Quiñones, Fernando, *El Flamenco, vida y muerte*, Editorial Laia, Barcelona, 1981.
——————— *De Cádiz y Sus Cantes*, Colección Anteo, Barcelona, 1964.
Quintana, Bertha B., *Qué Gitano! Gypsies of Southern Spain*, Holt, Rinehart and Winston, Inc., New York, 1972.
Ramírez III, José, *Things About the Guitar*, Soneto Ediciones Músicales, Madrid, 1993.
Ramírez Heredia, Juan de Dios, *Nosotros los Gitanos*, Ediciones 29, Barcelona, 1972.
Regordán, Manuel Pérez, *El Bandolerismo Andaluz*, Arcos de la Frontera, 1987.
Rioja, Eusabio, *La Guitarra en la Historia*, Ediciones de la Posada, Córdoba, 1994.
Rioja, Eusebio, *Julián Arcas ó Los Albores de la Guitarra Flamenca*, Bienal de Arte Flamenco VI, Sevilla, 1990.
Rojo Guerrero, Gonzalo, *Cantaores Malagueños: Pinceladas Flamencas*, Benalmádena, 1987.
Romanillos, José L., *Antonio de Torres: Guitar Maker—His Life and Work*, Element Books Ltd., Great Britain, 1987.
Romate, Sánchez, *El Cante Flamenco: Guía Alfabética*, Jerez de la Frontera.
Ruiz, Manuel Ríos, *De Cantes y Cantaores de Jerez*, Editorial Cinterco, Madrid, 1989.
Sánchez Romero, José, *La Copla Andaluza*, Ecesa, Sevilla, 1962.
Sencourt, Robert, *The Spanish Crown: 1808-1931*, Charles Scribner's Sons, New York, 1932.
Sharpe, A.P., *The Story of the Spanish Guitar*, Clifford Essex Music Co. Ltd., London, 1963.
Sotomayor, Pedro M. Payán, *El Habla de Cádiz*, Fundación Municipal de Cultura, Cádiz, 1983.
Steingress, Gerhard, *Los Cafés Cantantes de Jerez*, Sevilla Flamenca, Sevilla, c. 1988 (undated).
Triana, Fernando de, *Arte y Artistas Flamencos*, Ediciones Demófilo, Córdoba, 1978 (originally published in 1935).
Ulecia, Alberto García, *Las Confesiones de Antonio Mairena*, Universidad de Sevilla, Sevilla, 1976.
Yoors, Jan, *The Gypsies of Spain*, Macmillan Publishing Co., Inc., New York, 1974.

REFERENCES

Young, John Russel, *Around the World with General Grant: 1877, 1878, 1879*, The American News Company, New York, 1879.

Wais, Francisco, *Historia de los Ferrocarriles Españoles, Vol. I & II*, Fundación de los Ferrocarriles Españoles, Madrid, 1968, 1974, 1987.

Glossary

This glossary contains only those words used frequently throughout the text. Words that are used a single time are defined within the text and not included here.

afillá: a raspy, hoarse voice in the style of El Fillo.
alante: in front; to perform solo.
alegrías: a festive flamenco style from the area around Cádiz.
alpargata: a canvas-topped, rope-soled slipper usually worn by the poor.
anda: literally "walk" but used as an exclamation to mean "Come on!"
ángel: similar to *gracia*.
arriero: muleteer.
atrás: behind; to sing for dancing.
bailaor: flamenco dancer.
baile: the dance.
barbaridad: barbarism; the exclamation *"Qué barbaridad!"* means "Good Lord!" or "Outrageous!"
bestis: beasts, animals (gypsy language).
bien: good, well, well-done.
buenas tardes: good afternoon.
busnó: gypsy word for non-gypsy; plural is *busné*.
café cantante: flamenco nightclub; tablao.
Cái: Cádiz.
calañés: old style of hat made of a velvet-like material and in two different shapes: a brimless, cylindrical cheese shape and a cone shape with different widths of brim.
caló: gypsy language; gypsy word for "gypsy."
calé: plural of *caló*.
canciones: popular songs.
cantaor: flamenco singer.

cante: flamenco song.
cante andaluz: the non-gypsy styles of flamenco song.
caña: a tall, cylindrical wine glass; an old song form predating the *soleares*.
caramba: a euphemism for *carajo*; also seen as *carambita* or *recaramba*.
carajo: originally the male sex organ, but used as a general curse word.
caray: euphemism for *carajo*.
casa de vecinos: a sort of apartment complex built around a central courtyard used communally for cooking, laundry, etc.
cejilla: a device clamped across the strings of the guitar to raise and lower the pitch.
céntimo: cent; 1/100th of a *peseta*.
chalán: gypsy livestack dealer.
chaval: young man.
chavo: young man.
chiquillo: boy.
compás: rhythm, specifically the counts and accents that define different flamenco styles.
copla: one of the poetic verses that make up the lyrics of a song.
corrida: bullfight.
cuadrilla: the bullfighter's team.
cuadro: a flamenco performing group that includes singers, dancers and guitarists.
cuarto: room.
Don: "Sir," a title given out of respect.
duro: five *pesetas*.
esparto: reeds used to weave chair seats.
falseta: guitar melody.
fandango: a popular song that emerged in Moorish Spain and evolved into distinct styles throughout the country.
feria: fair.
fonda: inn.
fragua: blacksmith forge.
gachó: non-gypsy; plural is *gaché* or *gachés*.
gitano (a): gypsy.
gracia: humor and personality in performance or personal style.
granaína: a style of *fandango* from Granada.
guitarra: guitar.
guitarrista: guitarist.
gusto: taste, pleasure; to be "*a gusto*" means "to be in a good mood."
hermano: brother.
herrero: blacksmith.

hombre: man; used as an exclamation, "Man!"
hostias: communion wafer; used as an expression.
joven: young man.
jozú: Jesus; used as an exclamation.
Jerezano: a person from Jerez.
letra: a verse of song; same as *copla*.
Lucentino: person from Lucena.
malagueña: a style of *fandango* from Málaga.
malo: bad.
manzanilla: a weak, sherry-like wine.
martinete: song of the gypsy blacksmiths; sung without guitar accompaniment.
matarife: one who does the killing in the slaughterhouse.
melisma: melodic runs on a single syllable of lyric.
mengues: demons.
mira: look; look here!
muy bien: very well; very well done.
niño: boy; child; baby.
ole: an expression of approval; in popular culture almost always heard as "olé" but in flamenco generally pronounced with emphasis on the "o"
oye: listen!
ozú: Jesus: used as an exclamation.
p'alante: same as *alante*; to perform solo.
palmas: handclapping.
p'atrás: same as *atrás*; to sing for dance.
peseta: basic unit of Spanish currency.
por: in the style of.
posada: inn.
pues: well.
real: twenty-five *céntimos*; one quarter of a *peseta*.
sabe?: you know?
salero: similar to *gracia*; spice and wit.
seguiriya: one of the basic gypsy styles of *cante*.
seguiriyero: singer of *seguiriyas*.
señor: Mister.
señorito: gentleman; patron of flamenco; often carries a negative connotation, i.e., that of a young man with money to throw around.
serranas: one of the older styles of Andalusian *cante*.
soleá, soleares: one of the basic gypsy *cantes*.
tango: one of the festive gypsy *cantes*.
temple: the singer's warm-up or tune-up, usually employing variations of *ay*.

tercio: one phrase of singing; may or may not coincide with a line of verse.
tío: uncle; used with a negative connotation as "guy."
tocaor: flamenco guitarist.
tocayo: person of the same name.
toque: flamenco guitar playing.
Undebé: gypsy word for God.
vamos, vámonos: let's go!
vara: gypsy walking stick.
vaya: go; used as an exclamation with various meanings, including "What a great—" or "Get out of here!" (You gotta be kidding!).
vendimia: grape harvest.
venga: come on!
venta: country inn or tavern.
zapatería: shoe shop.
zapatero: shoemaker.